The Bluestocking

Bye-Bye Baby
Ain't Goin' to Glory
The Last Gambit
The Liars' League
Dead Faces Laughing
Death of a Nymph
Murder in the Family
The Nice Murderers
One Man's Murder
He Who Digs a Grave
Sudden Death
A Week to Kill
A Time to Marry
The Hard Sell

The
Bluestocking

THE STORY OF THE FAMOUS

FORREST DIVORCE CASE

David Delman

ST. MARTIN'S PRESS NEW YORK

Design by Judith A. Stagnitto

Library of Congress Cataloging-in-Publication Data

Delman, David.
    The bluestocking / David Delman.
      p.   cm.
    ISBN 0-312-10432-4
    1. Trials (Divorce)—New York (N.Y.)—History—19th
century—Fiction.   2. Forrest, Catherine Norton Sinclair,
1817–1891—Fiction.   3. Women intellectuals—United
States—Fiction.   4. Forrest, Edwin, 1806–1872—Fiction.
5. Actors—United States—Fiction.   I. Title.
PS3554.E444B57   1994
813'.54—dc20   93-39584
                                                           CIP

First edition: February 1994

10 9 8 7 6 5 4 3 2 1

For Jacob Adam Delman

Special acknowledgments to Emilie Jacobson,
my agent, who kept me at it
until I got it right.
And Ruth Cavin, my editor, for sparking to
the idea so enthusiastically.

Foreword

*F*or readers of historical fiction, one of the issues is what's real and what isn't. So I thought this sampler might be welcome.

The Forrests were real. Actually, it's at least possible that Edwin Forrest, tragedian, was the best-known figure in the New York City of his time. And for thirty-eight days (December 20, 1851, to January 26, 1852), coverage of the war between the Forrests was glued to the front pages of eleven metropolitan dailies. Each charging the other with adultery, their suit and countersuit shocked, titillated, amused, and enraged a Victorian society as uncomfortable with divorce as ours is with long-term commitment. It put in the shade all other events, national and international, including the fall of the second French Republic.

The Forrest divorce case was then—and remains—the longest to be tried before the New York State Supreme Court.

I've made every effort to be faithful to the spirit of the trial. Central to this is the 183-page record contemporaneously produced by the anonymous Law Reporter for the *New York Herald*.

I discovered a copy of it years ago while browsing at an outdoor bookstall. Knowing nothing then of Edwin Forrest, I was nonetheless captivated. It seemed to me important, to contain messages, as if a note had been stuffed in a bottle and set afloat on some metaphoric sea. There is a picture of Catherine Forrest on the cover, a scratchy, indistinct pen-and-ink drawing, but I had the sense, even from that, of a remarkable woman. Two closely connected things happpened to me as I held that dog-eared paperback in my hands: my curiosity was sharply (and irrevocably) aroused, and I knew I had found congenial work for myself.

It follows that much of the novel's courtroom material is taken from actual testimony. Departures are usually for the sake of clarification, compression (their trial lasted thirty-eight days; mine only twenty-one, or to avoid boring technicalities).

Which brings me to the legal gentlemen, who were also real. Better, say larger than life. Charles O'Conor, counsel for Mrs. Forrest, loomed equally large in two later landmark cases. He defended Jefferson Davis after the Civil War and, in the mid-seventies, as a special prosecutor, helped bring down William Marcy "Boss" Tweed.

John Van Buren, counsel for Mr. Forrest, in addition to being the former attorney general for New York State, was the son of Martin Van Buren, eighth president of the United States.

With a minor exception here and there, all the witnesses were real. And of course the verdict was real.

In that connection, readers are advised to empanel themselves with the jury. I think they'll enjoy sifting the perjurious chaff from the honest wheat and comparing their own verdict with the one rendered. I did and found the process fascinating.

And finally the bizarre and bloody events of May 10, 1849, the Astor Place massacre, were all too horrifyingly real.

But this *is* a novel. And the above notwithstanding, I have allowed myself the customary novelistic prerogatives, as you will discover along the way.

"She's a bluestocking, an *advanced* woman.
Is that bad? I leave that for you to say
because I don't concern myself here with
moral judgments. The question is not
whether she's good or bad, the question is
whether she's strong or weak."

From the summation of John Van Buren,
counsel for Edwin Forrest,
FORREST V. FORREST.

The Bluestocking

On the Eve

*H*enry Stewart stood at the window of his apartment in the New York Hotel, watching November at work. It was only the ides, but in a foretaste of winter the temperature had swooped to freezing that morning, and now, puckishly, the wind was littering Broadway with flyaway hats and other insecurely attached items. He saw a lady's camisole go aloft at the Worth Street intersection and grinned. Heaven only knew the explanation for that.

And yet the late afternoon sun was working, too, though weakly. It glinted off the roof of the squat tenement that abutted the Broadway Theater, deepening the color, converting it to an unreal red, the red of a child's drawing.

Just below him, crossing from his side, the New York Hotel side, to the theater side, a pair of well-fed pigs comported themselves like the veterans of Broadway traffic they were. No panic, no undue haste. Done with the day's scavenging, they meandered home to tea. Traffic? What was traffic to any pig with a sense of history? A butcher's knife, now *that* meant something.

And in carriages, hacks, wagons, omnibuses, wheels of every

description, Broadway *humans* dervished more or less as always, refusing to be distracted by the vagaries of the weather. Studying them from three stories up, Henry imagined them fully engaged in their time-honored pursuits: hawking merchandise, buying merchandise, stealing merchandise. Delivering messages or street-corner sermons; making social calls or hay; bent on missions of mercy or skullduggery. Broadway. Jammed with its citizenry. Such a busy population. Henry watched, impressed as always by the New Yorker's single-minded devotion to his own agenda.

Checking his timepiece, he noted it was going on half after four. Peter Blaylock wasn't late yet, but Henry knew he would be. He always was. To Peter, time was subjective, a view that gave minutes and hours a certain elasticity. Well, it was his, Peter's birthday dinner that was being endangered, not Henry's.

Back to his studies. He smiled at the thought of how his father might react to that particular phrase.

"Snoop, snoop, snoop, that's what journalists do," he had said during their most recent debate concerning Henry's choice of profession. "Regardless of what they choose to call it."

Hands locked behind a spine as uncompromising as the rest of him, the Reverend Edward Stewart had paced his library. He was an inveterate pacer. Even pulpit-bound, he found it difficult to restrain himself when the subject truly stirred him. The more it did, the more he yearned to be peripatetic.

"Soldiering is active. Medicine is active. God's ministry is more active than you have ever credited, Henry, but journalism is not. It's the most passive of professions. Journalists are—"

"Parasites."

"In deference to my feeling for you, let us settle on 'outsiders.' Journalists are outsiders. They spend their lives recording the deeds of others. That's not what I wanted for you."

"I know."

"I wanted something . . . not necessarily for you to follow in my footsteps. Please believe that. If conviction is lacking, it's hypocrisy to pretend. You've said that to me, and I agree. But I wanted something for you . . . less frivolous."

"Journalism isn't always frivolous, Father."

"Oh, my boy, my boy."

"It can shed a light on nasty secrets. It can hold powerful people to account. Besides, it's all I'm good at."

"Humbug. Who says that? That horrible man who employs you? Bennett, that devil incarnate? You're barely thirty, still young enough to discover a hundred things you're good at. Mary was at work on you about it, I know she was."

"Mary wanted for me whatever I wanted for myself," Henry said stiffly.

His father had whirled to jab an accusing finger. "The trouble with you, sir, is you've been a widower too long. Time you gave over. The fact is, a man needs a good woman to point the way for him."

Which had caused Henry's mother to glance up from her book. "I'm a good woman," she had said to her husband. "I never noticed myself having that effect on you."

Now, as Henry watched, an old man came out to light the theater's gas lamps. As if in response, the crowd began to thin. An eye blink later, it had diminished to stragglers, to an omnibus here and there, to isolated clusters of pedestrians, to virtually nothing, as if a heavy rainstorm had caused everyone to flee. Amazing. Henry, after two years as a hotel resident, was still not quite used to the magical ebb and flow. The hot-corn girl, having just set up for business alongside the theater entrance, was now one of the few signs of life.

But that would not be the case for long. By six the crowd would begin to reshape itself. This time, instead of wagons and omnibuses, there would be barouches and broughams. The carriages would be handsomer, the foot traffic generally better dressed. Enter the theater crowd. And this with still an hour to wait for the doors to open and another half for the performance to commence.

Ruthie, the hot-corn girl, young, not twenty yet, with large dark eyes in a pale face, swung her arms up, wide, and across her narrow chest, battling the cold. Henry saw her mouth open and shut. She was rehearsing her lament. Henry couldn't hear her, but he knew the words by heart:

Hot corn! Hot corn! Here's your lily white corn.
All you that's got money, pity me that's got none.
Come buy my corn, and let me go home.

Piteous. And so effective. As a rule she was sold out before curtain rise. Even faster in bad weather. Henry, who had written a story on her for his newspaper, the *Herald,* knew she would kill rather than surrender her corner.

"*The Gladiator* tonight," announced the stand-up poster in front of the Broadway. "Acted by Mr. Edwin Forrest." Only that, and in a type size so discreet as to be almost shrinking. Still, what more was needed when it was a name with such pulling power: Edwin Forrest, America's leading tragedian?

Not so, the *Times* had protested that morning, the third in a series of disenchanted articles; merely our loudest. And went on to compare Forrest invidiously with his great rival William Macready, *England*'s leading tragedian: Forrest was a ranter, a raver, an unabashed scenery chewer; Macready a thespian angel, master of all things subtle and artful in the dramaturgical craft.

Enough to make Forrest choke on a breakfast kipper, Henry thought.

Be that as it may, the pittites, the people of the pits (as opposed to those of the boxes and private galleries), loved Forrest, were "enslaved by him" the *Times* had insisted, a shade mean-spiritedly, Henry thought. Well, love him or despise him, the fact was no one had ever been able to take Edwin Forrest lightly.

And these days Forrest was a name the public rose to more readily than it ever had—whether the name meant Edwin or, suddenly, unexpectedly, disturbingly, his wife, Catherine.

A carriage drew up before the theater entrance—as it did most evenings at this time—and the man himself alighted.

Ruthie, ready for him, curtseyed deeply.

Forrest bowed just as deeply. She parted with an ear or two, he with some money before disappearing into the theater. But Henry could see that he'd exited the scene smiling.

Yes, Forrest had the manner. Even those who least admired him had to grant him that if they were honest. He could be brutish, curmudgeonly, bullying, but when he wanted to charm he charmed. It had to do, Henry thought, with how remarkably unself-conscious the man was. Not standard for an actor, certainly, but an element nonetheless in that enigmatic persona of his. One seldom knew what to expect from Forrest; he—Henry was convinced—seldom knew what to expect from himself.

Henry recalled his own last meeting with Forrest as a case in point, about two and a half years ago now. It had been during the height of the excitement generated by the Macready-Forrest war, some six weeks after the Englishman's arrival here and his launching of what was surely the most benighted tour in theatrical history.

From the start there had been incidents. In Cincinnati someone had thrown a sheep's carcass on stage to punctuate a Macready soliloquy. In Philadelphia he had been pelted with vegetables and fruit. Clearly, the highly volatile, semiorganized group of ruffians calling themselves the Friends of Forrest wished to drive Macready back across the sea. Cohorts of them had been active in each of the five tour cities, including New York, where the trip had begun and was supposed to climax. Three performances of *Macbeth* had been scheduled; some wondered if they'd ever take place.

But Macready had his supporters too, of course. Less numerous in the United States than Forrest's, they were apt to be more affluent, more influential—able to muster up police, for instance, whenever they deemed it in the public interest.

Some saw class warfare in this alignment of partisans, others a burgeoning nativist movement, a thing to be valued rather than deplored. At any rate, to Henry, the world had seemed divided into ubiquitous feuding families: the Macreadys versus the Forrests, with each spoiling for a fight and common sense hiding in the corner.

He had considered himself a neutral, knowing well it was a condition Forrest refused to recognize. Forrest viewed neutrality as nonviable, like a language without reference points or a tree without roots. To Forrest, the middle ground did not exist. You were his or you were a traitor.

On a dismal, rainy day—early May, though chilly enough to be a full-fledged throwback to winter—Henry had jammed notepaper under his hat and gone calling. It was an interview he had sought for days—dutifully. He was not looking forward to it.

No servant; Forrest himself answered Henry's knock. But there was little welcome in that bleak expression. In the past the two men had got on tolerably: not friends, never that, but acquaintances who found each other's company pleasant enough as long as decent intervals between meetings were maintained. The actor, however, had not been pleased with the journalist's coverage of Macready vs. Forrest. "Weak-kneed," had been his term for several of Henry's reports, a description he had passed on to his longtime admirer James Gordon Bennett, the *Herald*'s publisher and Henry's employer. Bennett had sympathized but then replied, as he was famous for replying to irate public figures, friend or foe, "Reporters are not meant to be curbed, sir. I let mine go unleashed until they cost me money. After which I shoot them."

"Well, come in," Forrest said, stepping back from the door so that Henry could enter. "You have five minutes."

Forrest was an impressive figure, off as well as on the stage. Not as tall as Henry—a good three inches less than the latter's even six feet—he was much thicker through the chest, arms, and legs. "A tree of a man is Forrest" was a line from a piece of doggerel that had been popular last year. And he had once mocked Henry, though good-naturedly, Henry was willing to believe, by referring to him as "Stewart, the splinter of a man."

"I regard this, sir, as an intrusion," Forrest said.

Henry eyed him coolly. He knew better than to back off. Back off from a carnivore like Forrest and be gobbled up for breakfast. "Forgive me, sir, but you did say I could come."

"An intrusion nonetheless. Damn it, man, you press me at a time—"

"At a time, sir, when you are very much a public concern."

"I'm always a public concern. Should that strip me entirely of my prerogatives as a private man? What I owe the public is a performance. In order to supply it I must have my rest. Never mind, never mind. I've promised you five minutes, and I'll grant them. But first I must dose myself for this beastly headache. Be good enough to have a seat, sir."

He left the room—heavy, sulky steps, like Achilles seeking his tent.

Henry, who had been in Forrest's house before but not recently, glanced about him. From what he could see it was indeed the handsome house he remembered. Restraint and good taste, light colors rather than florid ones. Reflective of Mrs. Forrest as opposed to her lord and master, Henry would have bet a pretty penny. He was in the library, which was impressively book-lined. Serious titles, he acknowledged, particularly for a man who had already exchanged the schoolroom for the stage by the age of twelve. And he does read them, or so Bennett swore.

He caught his own tone. Ugh! Where was detachment, journalistic integrity, fair play? "Mind what you're about, boy," he told himself, much as Bennett would have, had he been near.

Forrest returned. His face was less pale, his eyes brighter. Ah, brandy, Henry realized, picking up a whiff.

"Speak," Forrest said. He slumped into the chair opposite Henry's. He crossed his legs, then uncrossed them to lean forward

like a wrestler offering a hold. "It's about that damned Englishman, of course."

"I'm afraid it is."

"Good God, a pair of actors engage in a petty squabble and no
one can think of anything else. What is my city coming to?"

But oh, how he liked it that way! Henry thought. For days his
city had made him its passion. In the Bowery saloons, the Upper-
Tenner salons, the coffeehouses, the oyster cellars, wherever
Gothamites gathered, nothing else mattered as much as what had
been just—so ingenuously—referred to as a petty actors' squabble.

And what, contrarily, he had also described as "A Second War
for Independence: American Actors for the American Stage."

As recently as the previous week, three newspapers, including
the *Herald,* had carried that message as an advertisement. Forrest
had paid them each a substantial sum for the service.

His hatred for the English actor was no doubt profound, but
Henry believed it was equaled by a counter-emotion, his deep
and abiding love for center stage.

Forrest said something inaudible. But then, as if discovering
unlooked-for merit in what he'd mumbled, he repeated it, now
with venomous clarity: "I say the man is a curse, a plague. What
right does he have to come here? He does it to insult me. Are
there not enough theaters in his own misbegotten country? Must
he popinjay it here where he's not wanted?"

Henry cleared his throat. "I take it then you see little hope of
a *rapprochement.*"

"Damn it, man, speak American."

"No chance of burying the hatchet?"

"Oh, yes, oh, yes indeed—in his skinny, superannuated neck.
When I visited his country in '46 he sneaked about to form cabals
against me. Within days after my arrival I had no friends. *He* did
that, Macready alone, damn his jealous, envious, treacherous
heart. And now he invades my country and expects to triumph
again. But he will not. I promise you, sir, he will not. He began
this warfare, just as his forebears did against our American boys.

But I'll finish it, by God, for it's an old Yankee custom, finishing things. Macready must be taught our customs. And the English do not learn easily, you know. They must be cuffed into it."

"Is it the Friends of Forrest who will do the cuffing?"

His face shut down, mouth thinning in a forbidding scowl. "The Friends of Forrest? I have many friends. Do you have a particular set in mind?"

"Yes, sir."

"Well?"

"I have the Friends of Forrest in mind who wear green uniforms, *Forrest* green, they call it, and cavalry jackboots. They stick knives in their belts and carry knobbed sticks. They parade before whatever theater Mr. Macready plays in and have caused a series of disturbances. Those are the Friends of Forrest I mean, sir."

"A peaceful parade is not a disturbance unless some overexcited reporter chooses to call it such. Besides, what does any of this have to do with me? Can I be held responsible for every—"

"A man named Ned Buntline leads them, sir, and I've heard he's paid by you."

"You've *heard?*" But he kept his voice soft, whispery almost. Henry, who had been in his audiences often, recognized it as technique, forerunner to an eruption.

"From sources that I trust," Henry said evenly.

Forrest glared, his eyes black and hot. Henry waited. But then, after all, there was no eruption. Instead, Forrest leaned back in his chair as if for better perspective. He smiled. "They say you don't frighten easily. I can see it's the truth."

"Thank you."

"But I can also see how much you've become my enemy."

"No, sir. I'm a journalist charged with a task. Nothing else."

Forrest got up and crossed the room to stare into the fireplace. When he had finished reading whatever there was in the book of dancing flames, he turned. "Mr. Buntline is his own man. He does as he wishes."

"Would it be possible, sir, to say to him that *you* wish the

Friends of Forrest to disband, that friendship for Forrest can be demonstrated best by quiet and sensible behavior?"

"No, sir, that is not possible. It's not my business to ascend the lecture platform. I'm an actor, not a politician or a preacher. Or a *journalist,* for that matter."

Henry started to speak but was cut off by Forrest's raised hand.

"Enough! I have been badgered sufficiently for one afternoon."

"Does Mrs. Forrest—"

"No more, I say!"

But there was no anger in his face. Instead, astonishingly, there was pain, naked pain. Henry was confused. Was it real? This was an actor, after all. It took him a moment to be convinced, but that didn't leave him any the less at sea. What was happening here?

Forrest had covered his head with his arms. "Leave me," he said, the words muffled. "Oh, please, please leave me."

Somewhat shaken himself, Henry did.

On the point of descending the stairs, however, he saw a short, wiry figure turning the corner of Twenty-first Street. The man approached quickly—small, bouncy steps with something like a hop at unpredictable intervals. It was an erratic walk and in part the explanation for his nickname: Buntline the Bedlamite. But only in part.

Henry waited for him. No Forrest green this day, but the cavalry jackboots were still in evidence, and he carried a furled umbrella like a weapon, occasionally stabbing the air with it as he marched.

No one in Henry's circle knew much about the early Buntline. He had burst on the New York scene two years ago, in his mid-thirties, claiming to be the former close associate of Buffalo Bill Cody, with whom he had had a heartbreaking falling out— painful details locked in the Buntline bosom. Immediately, he had placed himself at the disposal of Tammany Hall, proving his value soon thereafter. Whenever the Democrats wished to annoy their political enemies by converting a meeting to a shambles, they knew they could call on Buntline, a master at arranging the disruptive drunken brawl. As a further attribute, he had an extraordinarily showy temper. He could froth at the mouth and pop his eyes seemingly at will while cavorting, capering, and gesticulating wildly. This frightened some and, despite his lack of size, made him an effective bully. Other bullies, more physically prepossessing, appeared happy to serve under him.

Not long after his New York debut, Buntline had stormed the *Herald* office at the head of a squad of four to take issue with Henry about an article generally unflattering to Tammany nabobs.

Henry had ignored the four and thrown their leader down the stairs, tantrum and all.

Their meetings since had been without actual incident. Buntline invariably snarled but kept his distance.

On this day Henry discovered that he was glad to see Buntline. Forrest's unexpected breakdown had affected him strangely. He was still disoriented by it, jangled, in an odd way fragmented. Buntline, somehow, made him feel whole again.

"You can't go in there," he heard himself announcing. He hadn't meant to. It was certainly none of his business. But contrariness surged through his blood like a purgative.

Buntline stared at him.

"He's not feeling well," Henry said, "and doesn't wish to be disturbed."

"He'll see me."

"No, sir, he will not."

Sounds rumbled in Buntline's throat—incoherently, as if acid had eaten their meaning. Finally he became intelligible. "Out of my way, you," he said, climbing to within a step of Henry. "I have important news for him."

"Yes. And I can guess what it's about. But it will have to wait."

There was a moment of standoff. Then Buntline, suddenly furious, gathered himself to charge past Henry, who joyfully lost his own temper. He snatched Buntline's umbrella, poked him in the stomach with it, kept poking him until Buntline backed down the stairs, and went on poking him thereafter until his adversary, swearing and groaning, was in full retreat.

Fifty feet away, however, safely beyond the range of that devastating umbrella point, Buntline stopped. Legs pumping like pistons, he launched himself into a frantic jig, screaming, "Macready-lover! Arse-kissing, piss-drinking murderer! Son of a cruddy—"

He broke off when Henry took a step toward him and, still howling and cursing, abandoned the field.

Mood improved, Henry left the umbrella tipped against Forrest's door. As he descended the stairs for the second time, he was pleased to note the rain had stopped.

But one week later, outside the Astor Theater, a contingent spearheaded by the Friends of Forrest had confronted a group supporting Macready. A ridiculous battle, fought by ludicrous armies—except that when it was over twenty-two people lay dead. The Seventh Cavalry, there to keep peace but maddened by volley after volley of rocks and paving stones heaved at them by both sides, had fired indiscriminately into the crowd. From where he was crouched just beyond the theater entrance, Henry had been able to count four corpses, all women.

Henry left his post at the hotel window to pour himself a glass of claret, returning in time to identify Peter Blaylock while he was still a block short of Broadway. That wasn't difficult. Peter had a distinctively stiff-kneed gait, like a clothespin walking, and since he hated hats, his hair, even redder than Henry's, shone beacon-like in the dusk.

Henry shook his head to clear it of rifle fire and screams, and though he couldn't entirely, never would be able to, he grinned despite himself. Peter had two large bags swinging from his hands. Henry thought he could guess what was in them: oysters. Peter loved them to distraction.

As they played the two games of chess they had scheduled, Henry told Peter of the scenes he had been recalling while waiting for him. Peter made no comment. He played with total concentration. He did not like losing to Henry, and though he had a twenty-year history of doing so—they had known each other since they were ten—defeat was never allowed to affect the intensity of his next effort. Closely contested, these games too ended in victories for Henry.

"Damn you," Peter said when it was clear the black king must bow to the deadly cooperation between white knight and queen, "I hate discovered checks. They ought not to be allowed."

He grumbled a few minutes more and then, as he always did, recovered his equilibrium.

A truly sweet-natured man Henry told himself. Learn from him. A familiar injunction, delivered perfunctorily now since he was no longer optimistic about his ability to act on it.

"What was the question for Forrest to be?" Peter asked. "The one with Mrs. Forrest in it."

"I merely wanted to know how she felt about his harassment of Macready."

"Nothing more? That is, nothing . . . domestic?"

"I had no inkling then that there was anything domestic to ask about. . . . Delicious oysters, Peter," he said, consuming the last of the six dozen. "From Hambo's?"

"Where else?"

"May I ask you why?"

"Why?"

"Why, knowing you were being taken to a slap-up birthday dinner at Delmonico's, would you oyster your appetite to death?"

Peter, stretching legs even longer than Henry's toward the fireplace, said, *"Carpe diem,* Henry. How often must I explain that to you? There are five crossings between here and Delmonico's, correct?"

"I believe so, yes."

"At any one of them we could be hit by a runaway horse. Or carriage. Or brougham, for that matter."

"It happens."

"Indeed. So, seize the day, Henry. Which is to say, never put off the nearer pleasure for the sake of one to come. Would your heart break if we bypassed Delmonico's?"

"No."

"Good. I'll trot out for more oysters. And then perhaps one more game of chess, after which, on to the theater as planned?"

"Yes."

"To see . . . ?"

"The man himself." Henry pointed toward the window. "The Gladiator."

A packed house, but Henry's press credentials earned them good seats in one of the Broadway's upper galleries. They settled in comfortably. A most attractive theater, Henry always thought. Only four years old, its gold and white trim had lost little freshness; it was bright, cheerful, and at the moment uproariously noisy as 4,500 people, increasingly restive, waited for Forrest's entrance. He was their darling.

"The orchestra has now played 'Hail Columbia' three times," Peter said.

"And 'Yankee Doodle' twice. He's in the theater, you know. I saw him arrive. He wants this crowd at fever pitch."

"Ah, here's 'Yankee Doodle' again."

Midway into a third or fourth chorus, however, the orchestra abruptly broke off. The audience hushed too. All stared at the curtain, willing it to rise. It did not. Seconds passed. Then, just before the sounds of the first shuffling feet or hacking cough— that is, just at the point of maximum tension—Forrest emerged from the wings. Not in costume, in street clothes—cream-white silk shirt, uncravatted; dark striped trousers.

Unhurriedly, he moved to center stage before turning to face the audience, arms across his chest. Applause washed over him. Men stood on chairs; women waved programs, handkerchiefs, and fans. Canes thumped the floor bruisingly. And for ten tumultuous minutes Forrest did nothing to stop it.

Henry spoke into Peter's ear. "When he did *Macbeth* here last year, he let them go on for a full quarter hour. And mind you, they began before he was half through 'So fair and foul a day.'"

Peter grinned.

Finally, Forrest, smiling wanly, lifted a hand. Immediate silence resulted. His posture was relaxed, loose, informal. It was as if he had invited 4,500 guests into his house. He took a deep breath. When he spoke his voice was soft, but it carried. It carried amazingly, Henry thought.

"I look out at you and ask myself a question," Forrest said. "Why is this vast assemblage here tonight?" He paused for a row-by-row study, as if such a survey might furnish his answer. "Has it gathered simply to see a favorite actor in a favorite play? No, of course not. You have come—and oh, how I thank you for it—to express your sympathy for one who has been deeply injured. As you all know I have been these many months the best abused man in the United States—abused, villified, and desperately misrepresented. And why? You know why. Simply because I have behaved as every man in this audience would have under the same abominable circumstances; simply because I would not tamely submit to that most infamous of wrongs, the dishonor of my house. But you, my friends, see the injustice here and have risen to support my cause." All at once his body galvanized. He stood as erect as a man could, his hands fisted and rigid at his sides, his voice suddenly thunderous. "*My* cause, did I say? No, not mine alone, but yours too; the cause of every man in this hall, this community; the cause of every principled human being, the cause of every honest wife, the cause of all who cherish the ancient sacrament of marriage. *Our* cause, good friends. And I promise that next month when this deplorable trial begins, you will have a champion in the lists, a *gladiator* who will fight as hard for the purity of our homes, for the bedevilment of immorality, for the defense of God's commandments, as any warrior ever created by the mighty bard or any other poet."

He bowed deeply and swept from the stage. The audience erupted with love. The whole house seemed one monolithic mass of ecstasy.

Into the uproar Peter said, "Give him his due, Henry. He's a born showman. Admit it."

"Oh, yes. He understands his effects."

"I'll tell you, I would not like to be Catherine Forrest. Divorce for a woman is problematical enough, and this city won't be pleased with her. Divorce from *that* man . . . ? They'll want to stone her."

Henry sighed. He didn't think Peter exaggerated greatly.

The audience, exhausted by its display, was quieter now. People were settling back in their seats. There were even several among the pittites who, having remembered that they'd paid for a play, were now calling for it to begin.

Peter said, "Did I tell you? Silly's on the way home."

Henry, who'd been contemplating Catherine Forrest's future in the light of Peter's prophesy, looked at him blankly for a moment; then comprehension dawned: Silly, a nickname from their youth for Peter's little sister, Serena. He smiled. "Sweet Silly back from Paris at last. How very nice."

"It seems the child has notions."

"What sort?"

"Disturbing ones, the pater says."

But then finally the curtain did rise, and both men, passionate playgoers, turned their attention to the stage as Forrest, now in golden tunic and matching plumed helmet, strode martially onto it.

Hear Ye, Hear Ye

*H*enry jumped from the omnibus before it fully stopped and, half loping, half skidding over an ice-pocked twenty yards, completed his trip to the courtroom a solid hour before it would open to the public. Nevertheless, he had to push his way through a considerable gathering. Not all New York City's five hundred thousand were at war for the hundred available seats, but it seemed so. And he knew it would continue so throughout the trial, scandal being the ever-dependable commodity it was.

Not greatly to his surprise, he found Bennett already on the scene—and looking a trifle hangdog.

It had been Bennett's quite sensible decision the previous night that Henry, his managing editor and second in command, would supply their daily courtroom coverage while Bennett tended the home fires. Yet here he was.

"You needn't look at me that way, laddie. I didn't say I'd *never* set foot here."

"No, sir."

"I said I'd be making the occasional pertinent editorial comment. Well, how's a man to be pertinent if he don't ever see the lay of the land."

"I don't know, sir."

At bottom, Henry knew, Bennett trusted him to do the job, but he was nervous. Big stories always made him nervous. As usual he tried to hide this with bluster. Fixing Henry with the slow, cold, one-eyed squint so unnerving to his enemies, he went on to accuse him of a "desultory approach" to what he described as "the trial of the century." Henry pointed out that among the gentlemen of the press only the other Henry, Henry Raymond, founder of the embryonic *New York Times,* had managed to precede him, causing Bennett to grunt something Scottish and obscene.

And then they were engaged in a Bennett silence. Once these had terrified Henry. As an apprentice he had been launched into effusions and gaucheries by them. Later he had learned to endure them, thinking, however, that the world might end in a silence generated by James Gordon Bennett. These days he was proof against them. Bennett understood that, of course. Bennett, Henry knew, understood everything.

"I'll do you credit, sir," Henry said.

"Damn it, sir, see that you do."

When the squint refocused there was a quality to it that in another man Henry might have called warmth. In Bennett he merely thought of it as enigmatic.

"I remember well the day I hired you," Bennett said, "you a twenty-year-old rawbones with only a smattering of talent. Can you guess why I did?"

"Certainly."

"Ha! Not because you were all that prepossessing. Indeed not, sir. I see you in my office on the edge of a chair, a gangly, freckled person even skinnier than you are now, with that absurd red hair and no knowledge as to where to put those ham hands. Or your hat, for that matter. As I recall you placed it carefully athwart my inkwell, knocking it over. Ten years ago, that was."

"Eleven, sir."

"I hired you—"

"To amuse yourself at the expense of my father, knowing how it would infuriate him."

Bennett smiled.

Henry did not smile.

"He thunders at me from his pulpit. Regularly, informants tell me."

"He thinks you a pernicious influence on this city."

Bennett's smile widened. "Nor do you entirely disagree, but I know the craft, which is why you stay. And you'll do so until you convince yourself you know it better than I do."

Well, Henry thought, there was truth in that. It was equally true, however, that Bennett had worked some personal magic. Henry acknowledged—though never to the man himself—that he found things to admire in his employer's character. His directness, for instance; his lack of a dark, ill-natured side. And he was a fair man in a fight. He'd roar you into a funk if he could, but that aside he was straight up and down all the way. No stabs in the back from Bennett. Opinionated, irredeemably pigheaded at times, he was also dead honest. No one could say about him that he had ever sold his pen, a statement not applicable to the majority of newspaper owners in their city. Moreover, he was a born dissident. He loved pricking the balloons of the established, the self-enamored, and the self-righteous. To Henry, son of an eminently respectable clergyman who was as humorless as he was good-hearted, Bennett's irreverence was a source of secret (and guilty) pleasure.

His squint had passed to the head of his cane, and he sighed as his mood changed. "Stewart," he said, as if what he was about to impart was information freshly minted, which it was not. "I began this newspaper in a courtroom. Aye, I did, seventeen years ago; started with five hundred in dollars and a circulation not much larger. Helen Jewett, her name was. Pretty little whore until that bastard Robinson split her head open with an ax. I lived in this courtroom, Stewart, and the public loved me for it. Could not print the paper fast enough. Circulation went to fifteen thousand, and I was a made man. Never underestimate our city's appetite for gore."

Pointedly: "Are you planning to stay, sir?"

A tug to his claw-hammer coat and a squaring of his stovepiper. "Why would I be staying? I have a shop to mind, do I not?" And then, over his shoulder: "Look to your laurels, Raymond," he snarled at the *New York Times* man. Finally, on long legs that always seemed springier to Henry than they had a right to be at fifty-six, Bennett strode from the courtroom.

Trading lukewarm smiles with an amused Raymond, Henry took a seat next to him.

"The old warhorse can't let go," Raymond said.

"The old warhorse can still do better work than every other ink-stained wretch in this city, including whippersnappers like you."

Raymond, small, quick, black-bearded, and exactly Henry's age, made offensive noises, half chortling, half gagging. Henry liked Raymond but thought him overinterested in himself, which he knew paralleled the opinion Raymond had of him.

At about nine the notables and celebrities, all those with special passes, began filing into the courtroom, drawn like moths to the blaze of a big occasion. Among them Henry noted James Harper, well-known publisher; Boss Tweed, Tammany politico; various luminaries of the stage, such as young Edwin Booth and his brother, John; and a much better than fair sprinkling of Upper-Tenners (here an Astor, there a Rimmerhorn), venturing forth from their Waverly Place brownstones at an unaccustomed hour for the sake of titillation.

And inevitably Buntline—who spat when he caught Henry's eye. But it was an ambiguous sort of expectoration. It could be disclaimed or lied about should Henry choose to be affronted.

Eight other ink-stained wretches, representatives of most of the major dailies, were also in place by then, flanking Henry and Raymond.

But no sign yet of the principals: not the plaintiff, the defendant, or any of the legal gentlemen, though by now the courtroom was so densely packed—and the stairs and passages so thronged—that latecomers among Henry's colleagues were having trouble penetrating to the section reserved for them.

At last the clerk's voice: "Hear ye, hear ye, the Honorable Chief Justice of the Supreme Court of the State of New York."

Everyone rose.

And then, en masse oddly enough, appeared the stars: Mrs. Catherine Sinclair Forrest; Mr. Edwin Forrest; Mr. Charles O'Conor, counsel for Mrs. Forrest; John Van Buren, his opposite number; and a half step behind them Chief Justice Thomas Jackson Oakley.

For an instant, clustered that way, they seemed to Henry a group of shoulder-rubbing friends, but then vision cleared and he recognized the cluster for what it was, an accident of timing.

The younger of the two lawyers—forty and a shade—Van Buren bore himself like the president's son he was. And the candidate Henry had no doubt he expected to be, though old Marty, his father, was as bereft of political influence these days as the courtroom was of space. Van Buren was dark, strongly made.

O'Conor, five years older, was also taller and thinner: an aloof man. There was something haughty about him, at times chilly, though people liked him well enough. Even more of a walker than Henry, who saw him often, marching between his office in Wall Street and his home in Washington Heights, always in his superbly cut black broadcloth and a dramatic high hat. Unquestionably handsome, Henry thought. One of those beautiful Celtic faces. Long-jawed, blue-eyed, hair prematurely white.

And it was indeed a fine old judge—seventy and perhaps more—with eyes that could twinkle or freeze if need be. Small and spare, Chief Justice Oakley was Olympian as to reputation.

Bennett, who despised the legal fraternity with the gusto he otherwise reserved for the clergy, once had written of Oakley that "he is as staunch and honest as the tree his name recalls."

Catherine Forrest's hair was crow-wing black and parted in the center. She had a high, bold forehead and a direct, dark-eyed gaze. Her nose was prominent, slightly aquiline. The lips were full, the teeth faultless. She was tall, almost as tall as O'Conor, with a figure so youthful it was hard for Henry to think of her as having endured four miscarriages. Today, she was somberly dressed in gray bombazine, with a black silk bonnet and a black lace veil off her face. In her mid-thirties, Mrs. Forrest was certainly striking.

As was her husband, of course. He wore his customary black frock coat with velvet facings and Byronesque collar, so that none might fail to note the amount of snowy linen required to cover his mighty chest. Raymond, who liked him even less than Henry did, maintained that *The Gladiator* was his favorite play: the role large, the costume brief.

Separated by ten yards or so, two wide tables became enemy camps. Forrest and Van Buren occupied the one nearer Henry, while at the other Mrs. Forrest and O'Conor were joined by a small, very thin, very pale woman who from time to time reached out to grasp Mrs. Forrest's hand. It was a gesture meant to offer support, but it seemed to Henry that the donor was in greater need: Caroline Grinnell Willis, wife of N. P. Willis, New York's foremost magazinest and, though admittedly of less moment, Henry's longtime friend.

The Chief Justice leaned forward. In response the assemblage leaned toward him, but it was counsel he addressed—in that meticulous though slightly rasping voice that to Henry always seemed unwrapped for the occasion. "Gentlemen, only twenty-four jurors have answered to their names. I'll wait a bit longer to see if others come in, unless you're content to take a jury from the twenty-four."

After a brief discussion, counsel for both sides agreed to try, and the names of twelve jurors were drawn from the ballot.

CHIEF JUSTICE. Is there a wish to question?

VAN BUREN. As to prejudices, your honor.

CHIEF JUSTICE. Yes. Very well, then, proceed.

During the questioning, Mr. L. S. Batelle reported that he had often expressed opinions on the matter at hand. He was directed to stand down. Mr. W. E. Corey was excused on the same grounds.

Mr. Elias A. Day said he had followed the newspaper accounts closely and had expressed opinions. He also was excused.

Mr. Daniel Edsall felt bound to inform the court he had read the depositions when they appeared in the newspapers. Nevertheless he viewed himself as a friend to neither side and capable, therefore, of giving a verdict according to the evidence. The Chief Justice declared him eligible.

Three others were then called in lieu of those excused. Contrary to the general expectation neither lawyer made much of a fuss, and the jury was on the whole painlessly empaneled:

1. Stephen W. Meech, foreman
2. William Earl
3. Theodore DeWitt
4. Horace Beales
5. Daniel Edsall
6. Pelatiah P. Page
7. Meigs D. Benjamin
8. Thomas B. Harris
9. Calvin H. Merry
10. John E. Ernstputsch
11. Fred S. Schlessinger
12. John Caswell

It was during this process that a note was passed to Henry via an urchin who at once disappeared into the crowd. He unfolded it to read, "I had not thought to reckon you among my enemies."

Henry frowned. He was not Catherine Forrest's enemy, but

the thrust went home. Because he was not her ally either. He was instead that pallid thing, a neutral. He knew she had expected partisanship from him. Well, his preferences *were* with her, but it was true, too, there'd been little empirical evidence of that in his pretrial reporting. He imagined it hurt her and wished he could conceive a remedy. There was none. He could claim journalistic integrity to her forever, and she would construe it as . . . perhaps even cowardice. That thought sent the blood rushing.

When he looked up she was smiling tentatively. He kept his face expressionless. Her smile went winging, and she looked away. Now, he knew, they both felt misunderstood.

By the time O'Conor rose to open the case it was late enough in the day that Henry thought he might ask to adjourn. But he didn't. The room hushed. Henry glanced once more at Catherine Forrest. She seemed ready, alert but not anxious. Mrs. Willis showed anxiety for two. Her clenched fist was twenty feet from Henry; his wad of scribble paper was not whiter than her knuckles. In the meantime, Forrest's stare at O'Conor was meant to be lethal.

O'CONOR. Gentlemen of the jury, the action you're about to try is one which has attracted a great degree of attention. Nevertheless, you're called upon for a fair, impartial, and just inquiry. You're called upon to stamp the seal of your approval on what is true, and to stamp the seal of your repudiation on what is false.

O'Conor, Henry noted, had a trick of turning from the jury, selecting a point at the back of the room—a doorknob, a windowpane, a flyspeck—as if this placed him in communion with an authority higher even than Justice Oakley.

O'CONOR *(post-communion)*. Ostensibly, this suit is brought by Catherine Sinclair Forrest against Edwin Forrest for divorce, to relieve her from the bonds of matrimony. But in truth it's Edwin Forrest's action—his the first stone; his the first charge of adultery—hers merely the countercharge. Catherine Forrest is here only because he would have it so. Because he has brought her to such a point that she has no other recourse.

Now, gentlemen, it becomes my duty to acquaint you with some particulars of the life Mr. and Mrs. Forrest once led together. I shall endeavor to do it calmly, without distortion, without histrionics. As best I can, I shall let the facts speak for themselves.

Permit me to begin this way. In 1837 Mr. Forrest was by profession, as he now is, a tragedian, and as such had become as distinguished in this country as Mr. William C. Macready is in England. That famous name, gentlemen, is here introduced advisedly. I ask you to tuck it in a corner of your minds on the certain promise that I shall return to it.

In 1837, I say, the distinguished Mr. Forrest, during a visit to England, was introduced to Mr. John Sinclair, a singer and thus Mr. Forrest's colleague. Mr. Sinclair's family consisted of his wife and three daughters, including Catherine N. Sinclair, then nineteen years of age and a charming girl, as you can no doubt surmise. Lovely and vivacious. But also innocent and inexperienced.

Mr. Forrest laid siege. A dozen years older, a man of the world, romantic, famous, handsome . . . can you wonder that he carried the day? As the expression goes, he swept her off her feet. And within the year, he swept her out of England itself, away from home, family, and friends.

Married in 1837, by 1838 they were happily established in New York. Happily indeed. Mr. and Mrs. Forrest—we have his own word for it—lived together in as much bliss and in as great a state of harmony as any married couple could hope to achieve. A state that existed for twelve years, gentlemen.

By 1849 Mrs. Forrest's sister Margaret had become Mrs. Edgar Voorhies and was also domiciled in New York. On the fateful night of January nineteenth, Mrs. Forrest attended a party given by Mrs. Voorhies. For reasons we intend to speculate on in a moment, Mr. Forrest did not.

Mrs. Forrest returned home . . . let us acknowledge it . . . at a moderately late hour, just before midnight, to find Mr. Forrest waiting up for her. He demanded to know who had been at the party. Friends, said Mrs. Forrest, beginning to enumerate. He interrupted her violently, savagely. "No friends of mine," he shouted at her.

Mr. Forrest then discoursed on Mrs. Voorhies—Mrs. Forrest's sister, may I remind you—in language that took her breath away. When she could speak she came spiritedly to her sister's defense. She flatly contradicted him. She used a term she instantly regretted and subsequently apologized for, but one provoked, after all, by him.

To this, Mr. Forrest replied that as he would not suffer any man to say the same to him and live, he would not live with any woman who would use that word to him. Before Mrs. Forrest retired that night Mr. Forrest told her they must separate. *(brief communion)*

But then having come so precipitously to this decision, Mr. Forrest postponed the enabling of it. Why? Was he in hopes that Mrs. Forrest might rescue him by prostrating herself, by pleading with him to reconsider? If so, he reckoned without the inbred sense of honor that's as much a part of Catherine Forrest as are her flesh and bones.

She did not so abase herself. The establishment broke up. The furniture was removed to Mr. Forrest's country residence, and he placed his wife in a carriage and drove her to the house of his friend, Mr. Parke Godwin.

Ah, I see the mystification in your faces. Where, you are wondering, is the fire and the fury in all this? Where the evidence of hatred we have every right to expect from a husband so grievously sinned against that he must put aside his wife? Puzzling, is it not?

And tell me, gentlemen, what this is evidence of—that two or three days before the separation, Mr. Forrest gave his wife his own treasured, annotated *Hamlet* and wrote her name on the flyleaf; that in the carriage he presented her with a portrait of himself. Strange indeed to approach a separation in so affectionate a manner until one looks deeper, more analytically, into the stresses and strains that for some little time had been plaguing America's leading tragedian. Stresses and strains, I hasten to add, that had nothing to do with Mrs. Forrest.

In 1846, three years earlier, Mr. Forrest had returned from his second trip to England a soured and disappointed man. An angry man, his rancor directed at Mr. W. C. Macready, whom he accused of having headed a cabal to destroy his reputation as an actor. It was an open and shocking quarrel between them, a quarrel that intensified, that rose to a fever pitch in 1848 when Mr. Macready came here, invading, as it were, Mr. Forrest's homeland. It was a quarrel that excited the attention of every newspaper in the city and, thereafter, every citizen, splitting us into cohorts: Macready versus Forrest; or, as some have ventured to put it, England versus her colonies, a staging anew of our War for Independence.

Mr. Forrest, I take leave to say, was totally involved in the quarrel—nay holy war, gentlemen, might not be too strong a term. Its effect on him was overwhelming. Consumed with patriotic fervor, he was a man possessed, a man with no other view of himself than as a crusader and whose dedication to victory matched any fanatic's. A man, therefore, incapable of dealing with the ordinary, the domestic events of his life with detachment, with balance. Macready was Forrest's prism, distorting all he saw. And did it help in this context that Mrs. Forrest was English? No, gentlemen, I am afraid it did not. *(three seconds of communion)*

In December of 1849 Mr. Forrest wrote to Mrs. Forrest, from whom he had separated seven months previously. It was a letter containing certain accusations of gross misconduct. Mrs. Forrest's reply was such as might be expected from a virtuous, honorable, but obedient and submissive wife.

To no avail. Suddenly, Mr. Forrest had become implacable. Once again I see mystification in your faces. Why after all this time? Gentlemen, I do not have to tell you human motivation is a complex thing. Nor can I pretend to be in any way the alter ego of so distinguished a figure as Edwin Forrest. Yet I believe I can furnish an answer, two answers in fact, both having to do with the special nature of the man we are here considering.

The first is rooted in the situation already touched on, which is to say the Forrest-Macready war and the terrible, terrible climax thereof, the bloody tragedy we are all familiar with, that so horrified our city on May 10, 1849, when riot and rampage ran amuck in our streets. Twenty-two people met their fates that day. Twenty-two! Scores more wounded. Think about that, and now answer me this. Is it too far-fetched to theorize that Mr. Forrest may have felt a certain personal responsibility, even a sense of guilt, and that this so weighed on a sensitive mind that, like one of those Shakespearian figures he has so often portrayed—Hamlet, Lear, Macbeth—he was maddened, driven temporarily at least to utter irrationality? I think it is not far-fetched.

But I mentioned two reasons. *(five seconds of communion, followed by icy anger under tight control)* The other reason, gentlemen, is much more prosaic. It took awhile for Mr. Forrest to realize he must pay for his freedom, that if he was to put aside his wife, discard her as a used-up and hence valueless domestic item, it would cost him something. She wanted more than a pauper's pittance in settlement. Thank you.

And with that he abruptly concluded, sitting down in his seat so fast Henry heard an audible gasp from Mrs. Willis.

After a moment the Chief Justice, with a vigorous clearing of the throat, asked O'Conor if he wished to call his first witness.

O'Conor. Yes, sir.

Chief Justice *(to his clerk)*. Then you may proceed, Mr. Asher.

Clerk. Call the defendant, Edwin Forrest.

Studying Forrest as he approached the witness box, Henry wondered which he was—Hamlet? Lear? Macbeth? None of these, he decided. He was Brutus, self-contained, serene, noble.

O'Conor *(to the attack instantly)*. Did you know the actress Josephine Clifton?

Van Buren. Object.

CHIEF JUSTICE. Overruled.

VAN BUREN. Your honor—

CHIEF JUSTICE. Come, come, Mr. Van Buren. There can be no possible objection to the question as it now stands. Please continue, Mr. O'Conor.

O'CONOR. Shall I repeat the question, Mr. Forrest?

FORREST. It is not necessary. I knew her. She is not now living.

O'CONOR. How long ago did she die?

FORREST. I don't know.

O'CONOR. You do not?

FORREST. I'm not certain if it's a year or two years ago.

O'CONOR. In an actor, one might have predicted a better memory.

VAN BUREN. Object.

CHIEF JUSTICE. Sustained. Careful, Mr. O'Conor.

O'CONOR. Two years ago, Mr. Forrest? Can you not say it was two years ago you heard of her death?

FORREST. No.

O'CONOR. In the year 1848 did you go from the city of New York to the city of New Orleans for the purpose of performing in the Saint Charles Theater?

FORREST. I believe I did.

O'CONOR. Was it the spring of that year?

FORREST. It might have been.

O'CONOR. Did you, while you were in that city, hear of the death of Josephine Clifton?

FORREST. I believe I did.

O'CONOR. Then you *can* say—

FORREST *(over this)*. But I'm not certain. *(an exchange of counterfeit smiles)*

O'CONOR. Did you ever appear as an actor in the same places Miss Clifton appeared as actress?

FORREST. I did.

O'CONOR. Did you frequently travel with her on long journeys across the United States?

FORREST. I have traveled with her, but I'm not sure frequently is the precise term.

O'CONOR. Infrequently?

FORREST. Perhaps infrequently would not be precise either.

O'CONOR. Did you travel with Miss Clifton subsequent to your marriage?

FORREST. I suppose so.

O'CONOR. You merely suppose so?

FORREST. *(first real signs of irritation).* Of course I did. We performed together a good many years.

O'CONOR. Then the fact is you were being evasive.

VAN BUREN. Object.

FORREST *(over this).* The fact is I resent being badgered.

O'CONOR *(over this).* Mr. Forrest, subsequent to your marriage, did you ever have sexual intercourse with Miss Josephine Clifton?

VAN BUREN *(roaring).* Object! The question is obviously improper. Witness is not bound to answer it, nor has learned counsel any right to ask it.

O'CONOR. The question is perfectly permissible. I refer learned counsel to the Code. Section 157 states that while a witness may decline to answer any question implicating him in a felony, he is compelled to answer a question involving a misdemeanor. Adultery, sir, lapses to a misdemeanor after the passage of two years.

VAN BUREN. Irrelevant, sir, and well you know it. The central point here is that a husband cannot be a witness for or against his wife.

O'CONOR. Starkie on Evidence—

VAN BUREN. Starkie notwithstanding.

CHIEF JUSTICE. Gentlemen! *(Both subside.)* Mr. Van Buren, Mr. O'Conor is to be allowed to develop his point, after which I will rule. Mr. O'Conor, you have a case to cite?

O'CONOR. I have, your honor. I cite the ancient case of the English Lord Audley, who, for having perpetrated gross outrage on his wife, was indicted. Lady Audley was admitted as a witness against him. In due course Lord Audley was convicted, imprisoned, and, sir, if you'll forgive the expression, stretched. Thus we see that the law permits of exception, and though I find the witness's reluctance entirely understandable, he should be compelled nonetheless to answer the question.

VAN BUREN. The witness has no reluctance to answer. I alone object to his answering.

CHIEF JUSTICE. Gentlemen, your behavior is beginning to cause me concern. I have permitted considerable license to you out of a feeling that first days are inevitably first days, during which a certain amount of robustiousness is *de rigueur*. When one allows for this, experience has taught me, the effect is often beneficial. In my view, however, we teeter now on a thin edge. Do I make myself clear? Excellent. As for the issue before us, I've changed my mind. I will take it under advisement and dispose of it when, with cooler heads, we next convene. *(Pause. Admonitory looks, in sequence, for the empaneled twelve; for Henry and the other ink-stained wretches; for the groundlings; and, finally, for learned counsel, who stare back, not cowed, certainly, but alerted perhaps to a sterner set of circumstances.)* Very well, then, adjourned.

Catherine's Diary

I am furious today. Full of hate and venom, so much so that I can scarce sit still. 'Tis a general hate. Not even Edwin gets a disproportionate share. Oh, he gets a share but not the lion's. 'Tis men and their eternal beastliness that so enrages me.

The Hon. Charles O'Conor came to call this evening, and I was treated to one of his no-nonsense disquisitions. And yet, I swear, 'tis not O'Conor I hate, 'tis men, 'tis men.

"The suffering of women," he said, producing a piece of my conversation left over from an earlier tea, but on which he has been munching ever since, "is part of human history. Do you think a female movement can change that? We're all born to suffer and to bear it like decent people. And as for women, they have a source of happiness closed to men, the consciousness that their presence here on earth lifts the load of *our* suffering."

Insufferable man.

One way or the other I'm certainly having an impact on the Hon. Charles. Better say one way *and* another. Because 'tis evident there is ambiguity involved. I both attract and repel. Probably for the same old reasons in the same old ways: ho-hum, the body attracts; yawn-yawn, the mind repels. On the odd days, he loathes. On the even, he lusts. But that, too, has a certain complexity. The O'Conor lust comes mixed with antagonism. Latent perhaps but nonetheless real. One speculates that, at bottom, the Hon. Charles might really wish to pulverize poor me.

What is clear is that he has grown used to tyrannizing his women. One recognizes the type. He is breathtakingly handsome. In addition there is a rogue male quality to him that draws us like flies, more's the pity, and through the years our sex has spoiled him rotten. So much so, one senses that his whole being recoils at the very thought of female opposition.

Good. Let him recoil. I like it that he recoils. That's what I want from men these days—recoilings. The more the merrier.

"What a pretty speech, sir," say I. "Will you have another of these small cakes?"

"You disapprove my speech?"

"Merciful heaven, wouldn't that be unreasonable of me?"

"Perhaps. But then you see I consider that women have no business being reasonable."

With angelic restraint: "Do you regard us, then, as no more than oversized dolls?"

"I regard you as the dearest things in life, the only things which make it worth living."

And on it goes—with those riveting eyes. With that courtly manner. With that infuriating air of condescension.

Oh, how glad I was to see him go!

But when he had done so, Caroline—who always misses the point, God love her—turned to me, fan aquiver, and said, "I wonder that you dare dispute with him. He terrifies me."

"Well, he bores me," I said. Which is not quite true, of course.

Headachy. Ague lurks around the corner.

Will I be able to survive the day in court tomorrow? O'Conor plans to call me. I hate the thought of it. I hate all those people who'll be staring at me. I hate everything, in particular that little man, Meech, the juror, who eats me with his eyes.

I hate this house. I have lived here for two years now and hated every day of it. I hate the poverty it stands for.

I hate its red, rusty face and faded green shutters, of which the slats are limp and at variance with each other. I hate the Tenth Streetness of it. I hate it that it stands next to a grocer shop. The grocer shop has more gentility than my house.

My house indeed. The house in which I rent two shabby rooms. One of them has no view at all. (I think it fair to say an alley is no view at all.) The other, my *sitting room,* commands a row of tenements no less superannuated than the mansion that domiciles poor Catherine Forrest.

I chased Caroline home early.

By actual count the word "hate" appears a dozen times in this entry.

At the Rimmerhorns'

*T*he "rout" of the season, proclaimed so universally. Hearts quickened at the sight of a gold-bordered invitation to the Rimmerhorns'. Rout? In Henry's view, the perfect word for it, considering how much he wanted to run away.

What made perfectly sensible people participate in these barbarian rituals? What accounted for *him* preposterously disguised as the fiddle of the party, decked out in all the fatuous splendor of white weskit and dress coat, jowls sheathed by a stiff collar, and a silk cravat wrapped so high and intransigently that he could scarce turn his head?

Because it was clear people could choose not to go if they had character enough. "Let me *risk* curmudgeonhood," one could say to little Mrs. Annie Burton, who dragged him to these things in the interests of matchmaking.

They meant well, little Annie and large Robert—and Henry knew how insufficiently he would have managed without the Burtons during those first sharp months after Mary's death—but they refused to recognize him for what he was, a man women did not like. Which is to say young women, pretty women. Old women and little girls found him restful.

"Mary liked you," Annie was ever ready to point out.

"Mary was the exception that proved the rule."

Oh, what did any of it matter?

What need did he have of routs and balls and suchlike? He had only one need and that was for the strength to say . . . No!

Minutes moved leadenly.

Incarcerated in his gaudy clothing, Henry stood in sullen silence. He had decided that he dared not risk a vocal cord against the powerful braying of an orchestra three times as loud as was civilized. Brassy music, the glare of gas, the press of sweating bodies. Add to this his own reflexive attack on his own stupefied stomach—stunning it with barrages of oysters from the one hand and pâté from the other—and he was the very painting of a plea for rescue.

As if on cue a hand reached out to him. He clutched at it, allowing it to draw him elsewhere. He would have clutched the devil's hand, "elsewhere" clearly the crux. Elsewhere proved to be the library, an oasis tucked snugly under the eaves on the first floor rear and thus protected from the brunt of the din.

"There, you poor man, sit down," said the pretty girl, his rescuer.

An extremely pretty girl and yet no symptoms. No sudden clumsiness, no drying of the throat or embarrassingly noisy rumblings in the belly. Nor at that moment did it occur to him to wonder why (it did later), though he was instinctively careful in his response. "I'm obliged to you," he said.

"Could I have done less? So old a friend in peril? May I get you something? Brandy and soda?"

"Not necessary."

The mixture was prepared and brought to him anyway. "A doctor?"

Sensing that a leg was being pulled, he informed her coolly of his complete recovery. "Old friend, you said? We're acquainted?"

"Aren't you the Henry Stewart who lived at Seventy Green-wich Street?"

"I am."

"Whose playmate was my wicked brother Peter?"

At once the scales fell away, and the green eyes and bright hair became unalterably familiar. "Serena!"

"Dear Henry, six years and absolutely unchanged."

"You look . . ."

"Tell me."

"Much changed."

She laughed. "The soberest face in New York City, that's you, Henry Stewart. Annie Burton and I are agreed. Only Mary had the knack of lightening the gloom. How I hated her for it."

"Hated Mary?"

"Passionately. I was jealous. You'd been my beau since I was twelve—"

"Your beau?"

"And there she was, the interloper, casting a spell. She gave your face magic, Henry. Changed it, made it an all but handsome face, instead of the sober, wary one you show me now. Of course I hated her. And it did not help at all that she understood, that she was perfect to me. While you of course were blind as a bat to everything I was suffering." For a moment she was still. She touched his hand and then said softly, "I cried for you when Annie wrote me the dreadful news. For Mary, too. And for your baby. But mostly for you because I knew you best. I wrote you a thousand letters and kept tearing them up since none of them said what I wanted to say—and finally sent a stupid one out of desperation."

"Not at all stupid."

"It was. But then so is puerperal fever stupid. Anything is that kills so many mothers and babies. I think I shall become a doctor and wage a ferocious war against it. You needn't look at me that way, Henry Stewart. European women can be whatever they wish. Why not American women?"

"I wasn't aware European women, *en masse,* had achieved such—"

"Well, they have. You might ask my friend Mrs. Forrest if you need corroboration."

He kept silent.

"She *is* my friend, you know. My good friend. She thought she was yours, too."

He cleared his throat. "When did you get back to New York?"

"Tuesday. As a result of fatherly fiat. You seem surprised."

"It's not that. Peter told me you were coming. It's just that up to now, fatherly—"

"Yes. Well, the third time's the charm for fatherly fiat, let's say. Things do go by threes, you know. At any rate he came and jumbled me in with my easels and canvases, stating that in his view Paris was a good thing, by and large, but all good things must come to an end. And if you must know—not that I'm prepared to confess it to him—I think I'm glad to be home. I loved Paris. I always will, I suppose, but there came a day when I realized I wasn't born to be a painter. On that day I felt, somehow, as if Paris had turned its back on me. Does that make any sense to you?"

"No one I know says Paris is a good city to be disappointed in."

"Faithless Paris. But this New York of ours . . . so many changes, so brassy and crude, yet so exciting."

"Exciting? I find it pestilential. Hot and dirty in the summer. Cold and dirty in the winter. You've seen the streets. They're inexpressible, every crossing ankle-deep in wet filth. In the summer it's worse. Then the streets are like thin black pudding. It's no wonder cholera decimates us annually. Forgive me. I didn't mean to be so carried away, but we live in a pigsty and it grows worse all the time. Our politicians are corrupt and our citizenry lazy, so we do nothing about it but wallow."

"That at least is a constant," she said, smiling. "The way you lose your temper, I mean. It was always what redeemed you."

"Redeemed me?"

"From stuffiness. My father notwithstanding—"

"Ah, your father."

"He thinks you a wild-eyed radical, Bennett's henchman and a traitor to your class, but he's quite up the wrong tree, of course. It's not the radical in you that's objectionable. It's the stuffiness. And it shows in your work, you know."

"Does it indeed?"

"Does it indeed?" She mocked him. "There. Stuffiness. Do you deny it's made you beastly to Mrs. Forrest?"

"Beastly? Surely not."

"Beastly to her. Oh, in a cool, ever-so-subtle way. Why? Because she has a brain and chooses to use it? Because she has self-regard? Does that render her fit companion to the poor creatures in Mr. Barnum's museum?"

At this point, much distressed, Henry rose abruptly. As a result of which he nicked—no more than nicked—the foot of the small table next to him. His brandy and soda was dislodged, a third of it onto Serena.

"You probably did that on purpose."

In agony: "Oh, no, no."

"Henry, I was joking."

And while flailing away with his handkerchief—ineffectually, since he could not bring himself to touch her—he all but set fire to the house, catching a toppled lamp only at the last possible moment.

"Henry Stewart, come back here at once."

Wild horses would have been unequal to the task.

It was midnight now, five minutes past, and the whole of the New York Hotel was still. Three hundred rooms and everyone still, he thought, except for his wretched self. He lay in bed stiffly, sleeplessly, with nothing to distract him from the portrait of a bumbling, graceless clown.

Oh, God, the dark brownness of that stain, puddling in the pale blue lap!

"You should have sniffed chloroform tonight," he informed himself.

Peter Blaylock had once told him chloroform sniffers must be prepared for strange and sometimes terrible dreams in which the sensations of a fortnight were crowded into two seconds. He would have welcomed that. It would have been useful. He would have liked to crowd the sensations of the past evening into two seconds of excruciating pain and so exorcise them.

Except it would not work that way, he knew. He would probably underdose and so sit forlornly waiting for the omnibus that never comes. Or overdose and evanesce into the atmosphere, never more to be seen in familiar haunts.

But oh, how he disdained a woman without sense enough to be satisfied with what she was! If God had meant to create masculinized females He would not have given them bosoms so dazzlingly white and delectably round as to drive men wild with the longing in their hearts and the itching in their palms. Why did she have to grow up? Why was she not still the green-eyed child who had liked him?

Legal Gentlemen on Display

*I*t was near three before Henry fell asleep, yet he was sharply awake by six and surprisingly energized. He gave a final thought to Serena. It was, oddly enough, a grateful thought. He thanked her for nailing in place a definitive piece of evidence, an enabling piece. He understood now in the (so to speak) clear light of day, that she had been amusing herself with him, a cat toying with a ball of string. And so farewell routs, balls, skirmishes, and self-delusion. There! The decision was made. Never again would he allow himself to believe that her kind of woman could take him seriously. To women such as Serena he was merely a target, someone to sharpen skills on in preparation for more worthwhile prey. Annie Burton and her blandishments *must* be resisted. Dignity was at stake. Yes, and self-respect. He nodded, pleased with himself at having come to terms.

It had snowed during the night, at least four inches. Lighting the candles, he saw them reflected like dragon's eyes in the black windowpanes. The room was bitterly cold. He started the gas stove, exchanging the tingling of ear tips for the smarting of eyes.

No choice; it hurt to be that cold. But soon arctic became temperate, and he could get himself moving.

An hour later, bathed and dressed, he was rereading last night's *Herald* while breakfasting. Then, with time to spare, he ventured out for the half-hour journey to City Hall. No hacks. He hadn't really expected there would be. As every New Yorker knew, hacks, like police officers, were never around when wanted.

He did his patented lope-skid over slippery sidewalks until he happened on one of the sleigh caravans that had been substituting recently for the omnibus in snowy weather. These were not his favorite vehicles, but the alternative had become distinctly unpleasant. Boarding, he joined a hundred or so grim-faced passengers. Half—Henry among them—were without seats and so stood in wet straw, strap-hanging. All were exposed to the furious wind that threatened their hats and icified their feet—without quite numbing them, though, as Henry discovered each time his were stepped on. He lurched forward as the vehicle stopped. He tumbled backward as it started again. When he finally debarked it was to land in a snowdrift, knee-deep.

CHIEF JUSTICE. The law prevents husband and wife from being witnesses against each other. Yes, Mr. O'Conor, there have been exceptions, but these have been—as in the example you yourself cited—usually cases of violent behavior; cases, may I add, where there's no other evidence bearing on the issue. However, that's not what we deal with here. Here, Mr. O'Conor, you are, in effect, asking Mr. Forrest to give evidence in behalf of his wife, gaining her the verdict. No, sir, you cannot require that of him. I rule the question inadmissible.

O'CONOR. Mr. Asher, please note an exception.

CLERK. Noted.

CHIEF JUSTICE. Proceed.

O'CONOR. I have no further questions for this witness.

CHIEF JUSTICE. You may step down, sir.

Forrest did, making a business of the way he passed by O'Conor, as if the latter were leprous. O'Conor smiled. Henry wondered if he had really hoped to get his question answered. Perhaps he'd wanted no more than to put the dismal side of Edwin Forrest on display. In this he had probably been successful.

The clerk called Mrs. Catherine Sinclair Forrest.

Hurrying forward, O'Conor helped her to the stand, all solicitude. But it was clear she didn't need that. Her back was an arrow. Her quick glance swept the jury as if to say, The bond between us is to be tested now. Mr. Meech and Mr. Ernstputsch seemed particularly affected, Henry decided.

O'CONOR. It is Friday evening, Mrs. Forrest—the night of January 19, 1849. You have just returned from 40 Great Jones Street, where your sister gave a bon voyage party for her husband, who was about to embark for California. Do you remember that night?

MRS. FORREST *(softly)*. Of course.

O'CONOR *(a moment of communion)*. I know this is going to be a strain for you, and I deeply regret the necessity for placing you under it, but we both understand there's no choice. And I'm going to have to ask you to raise your voice just a bit.

MRS. FORREST. Forgive me. I *(impatient little shake of her head)*. I *will* speak up, Mr. O'Conor. You may depend on it.

O'CONOR. Thank you, ma'am. You recall that night?

MRS. FORREST. In detail, sir.

O'CONOR. Good. Now, since your husband gave you no opportunity to name any of the people on Mrs. Voorhies's guest list, pray will you identify some of them for us?

MRS. FORREST. Mr. and Mrs. Godwin. They came with Mrs. Godwin's father, Mr. Bryant—

O'CONOR. Mr. William Cullen Bryant, the poet and editor?

MRS. FORREST. Yes.

O'CONOR. Please continue.

MRS. FORREST. Mr. and Mrs. Stevens, Mr. and Mrs. N. P. Willis *(a smile at her faithful companion; tremulous smile in return)*, Mr. George Hill—

O'CONOR. Formerly mayor of Brooklyn?

Mrs. Forrest. Yes.

O'Conor. How many in all?

Mrs. Forrest. About twenty.

O'Conor. Including two clergymen, am I correct? The Reverend Samuel Parker and the Reverend Joel T. Teadley and their wives.

Mrs. Forrest. Yes.

O'Conor. Is there anyone whose identity you are hiding from us?

Mrs. Forrest. Sir?

O'Conor. I mean by that are you concealing from us the presence of an arch villain of some kind? A seducer, a corrupter, perhaps some low Bowery person? Anyone of that stripe?

Mrs. Forrest. I do not believe so.

O'Conor. You're quite certain? Not so much as one raffish specimen in the whole collection?

Mrs. Forrest. Raffish? Hardly, sir.

O'Conor. No, indeed not. A perfectly respectable gathering. One might almost say supremely respectable. Moreover, a gathering to which Mr. Forrest himself had been invited.

Mrs. Forrest. As had been my sister's habit. She would have been most eager to have Mr. Forrest in her house.

O'Conor. You came home around midnight?

Mrs. Forrest. Yes.

O'Conor. And you found him waiting for you. Was that unusual?

Mrs. Forrest. Yes. I saw a light on in the library, and I stopped to put it out. To my great surprise he was still at his desk.

O'Conor. And then what happened?

Mrs. Forrest. He stared at me as if I were an apparition. He ordered me to be seated. When I was, he instantly demanded of me why my *gracious* sister—

O'Conor. That was his intonation? He said "gracious" in that manner?

Mrs. Forrest. Yes.

O'CONOR. Sarcastically, aggressively.

MRS. FORREST. He wished to know why my *gracious* sister had chosen not to invite his friend . . . our friend . . . Mr. James Lawson to her party. I replied that Margaret's guest list was her concern and not mine. Nor was it his. I'm afraid my tone was sharper than it should have been.

O'CONOR. Mrs. Forrest, did you feel your sister to be under unjust attack?

MRS. FORREST. I did.

O'CONOR. And was that the reason for your sharpness of tone?

VAN BUREN. Object. He's leading his witness.

CHIEF JUSTICE. True but not unpardonably, Mr. Van Buren. Overruled.

O'CONOR. *Was* that the reason for your sharpness of tone?

MRS. FORREST. Yes.

O'CONOR. And was that the point at which Mr. Forrest suddenly leaped from his chair to hover over you?

MRS. FORREST. Yes.

O'CONOR. And begin a tirade that lasted . . . how long?

MRS. FORREST. Forty-five minutes, an hour. Perhaps longer. It seemed longer.

O'CONOR. And what was the substance of it?

MRS. FORREST. That she, Margaret, was a woman utterly without honor, without scruples or decency. And that on me she might soon act as a corrupting force.

O'CONOR. Mrs. Voorhies is a year younger than you, is she not?

MRS. FORREST. She is.

O'CONOR. What did you do during Mr. Forrest's tirade?

MRS. FORREST. I wept. And once or twice I screamed. And once or twice I said, "You lie, you lie."

O'CONOR. Nothing more?

MRS. FORREST. He gave me no chance to say more.

O'CONOR. Oh, yes, he did, Mrs. Forrest. Not that night, but the next day. In fact, he insisted, did he not?

MRS. FORREST *(softly)*. Yes.

O'CONOR *(admonitory)*. Mrs. Forrest . . .

MRS. FORREST. Your pardon, sir. *(vigorously now)* Yes, he did.

O'CONOR. Yes . . . he . . . did!

He whirled and made a sudden foray to his table, his supply base. Snatching a scrolled piece of paper from it, he brandished it like a saber, Henry thought, then waved it like a battle flag before recrossing the room—three enormous strides—and delivering it to Mrs. Forrest like sealed orders.

O'CONOR. The handwriting is yours?

MRS. FORREST. Yes.

O'CONOR *(taking it from her, turning it over to the clerk)*. Mark as an exhibit please, Mr. Asher. *(Five seconds of communion, after which he was thunderous)* Distraught . . . frightened . . . friendless . . . *wounded,* you wanted peace. You wanted at last an end to the horror, an end to the nightmare—

VAN BUREN. If it please the court, may we not have an end to the histrionics?

CHIEF JUSTICE. Mr. O'Conor, can you—

O'CONOR *(full gallop)*. He comes to you the next day and demands to know if you are willing to sign a document . . . nay, to copy a document he has fashioned and set your signature to. Is that not so?

MRS. FORREST. Yes.

O'CONOR. And were you?

MRS. FORREST. Yes.

O'CONOR. Why?

MRS. FORREST. Because . . . as you say . . . I wanted peace.

O'CONOR *(retrieving scroll from clerk, reading)*. "With the sincere and awful conviction that I stand in the presence of Almighty God, I call Him to witness and record the truth of what I now utter, and also that I utter it without mental reservation. I have never been unfaithful to the marriage bed. I have never at any time permitted any man to take a liberty with me that might not be warranted in the conduct of the purest wife. I have never permitted the caress or caresses, the embrace or embraces, of any other man than my lawful husband. All this, in the presence of Almighty God, I swear, and if it be not true, may peace, comfort, and happiness forsake my soul forever in the life to come. Signed, Catherine Sinclair Forrest, January 20, 1849.''

Silence gripped the courtroom. To O'Conor, it was a cherry cobbler of a silence, and Henry watched him savor it. In O'Conor's view, it was clear, the dismal side of Edwin Forrest was once more on display. Henry scanned the faces in the jury box—poker-playing faces. They knew they were being scanned. It had not taken them long to learn how to guard against it.

O'CONOR. Despite this, your husband failed to reverse his stand of the night before. His instructions remained intact, that a separation must take place. Did it happen the next day?

MRS. FORREST. No.

O'CONOR. The day after, then?

MRS. FORREST. No.

O'CONOR. Surely within the next two weeks?

MRS. FORREST. We did not separate until the first of May.

O'CONOR. But that's astonishing. From January nineteenth to May first is one hundred and one days. Is that possible? *(turning to Mr. Asher)* Have I miscalculated?

CLERK. No, sir.

O'CONOR. It must be he was out of the house during this period, so that, in fact, it *was* a separation. You stayed, ma'am, but he went. *(a shake of her head)* You *both* stayed? During that entire period both of you lived in the house on Twenty-second Street?

MRS. FORREST. Except for fourteen days, during which he went to Philadelphia to play a short engagement.

O'CONOR. So, for . . . bear with me, bear with me . . . for eighty-eight days after you were told by Mr. Forrest that you must separate, you remained together under the same roof?

MRS. FORREST. Yes.

O'CONOR. In the same chamber?

MRS. FORREST. Yes.

The courtroom held its collective breath. Would he ask it; wouldn't he? O'Conor waited, poised on the brink. At last he stepped back, shaking his head. Collectively, the courtroom sighed. In disappointment, Henry thought wryly.

O'CONOR. No. I say no. I say there are limits to the ordeal. Even in a case of this nature, a gentlewoman must be spared something.

VAN BUREN. Object. May I remind learned counsel that the ordeal, as he calls it, is occasioned by the plaintiff.

O'CONOR. Unwillingly.

CHIEF JUSTICE. Objection sustained. You made that point in your opening, Mr. O'Conor, and I expect you will make it again in your summation. In between, however, pray confine yourself to direct examination.

O'CONOR. Between the nineteenth day of January and the first day of May, Mrs. Forrest, did you husband treat you as an enemy?

MRS. FORREST. No, to the contrary.

O'CONOR. How to the contrary?

MRS. FORREST. For one thing he continued to employ me as his amanuensis; that is, as before, I answered much of his correspondence for him. In addition we drove in our carriage, just the two of us, to Fonthill on at least three occasions.

O'CONOR. Fonthill?

MRS. FORREST. The house that was then in the process of being built for us. Fonthill on the Hudson.

O'CONOR. During these trips was the word "divorce" ever mentioned?

MRS. FORREST. Never.

O'CONOR. What did you talk about?

MRS. FORREST. We talked very little.

O'CONOR. Why is that?

MRS. FORREST. I knew it was a difficult time for Edwin. It was during the height of his quarrel with Mr. Macready, and he was . . . preoccupied.

O'CONOR. Mrs. Forrest, two weeks after you separated you

wrote Mr. Forrest a letter, did you not, in which you outlined your financial needs?

MRS. FORREST. Yes.

O'CONOR. What did they amount to?

MRS. FORREST. The total of my anticipated household expenses came to $2,900, but I asked Edwin to agree to $3,000 annually. He said such a large amount was out of the question. He suggested $500 a year and one of his houses to live in, rent free. If I found that unsatisfactory, he suggested I move into a boardinghouse and learn to practice habits of stricter economy.

O'CONOR. Mrs. Forrest, do you have any idea how much your husband is worth?

MRS. FORREST. I do now.

O'CONOR. Because I undertook in your behalf an investigation of the matter, is that not so?

MRS. FORREST. Yes.

O'CONOR. But while you lived with your husband . . . ?

MRS. FORREST *(shrugs)*. Edwin is like most men in that respect. He keeps his worth between himself and his business agent. And from his wife, a secret.

VAN BUREN. Object.

MRS. FORREST. Forgive me. I didn't mean to say that.

CHIEF JUSTICE. No serious harm done, Mrs. Forrest. I'm sure Mr. Van Buren would agree. In the future, however . . .

MRS. FORREST. Yes. I must endeavor to answer only those questions put to me.

CHIEF JUSTICE. Quite correct. Continue, Mr. O'Conor.

O'CONOR. Your honor, I have here, in the form of a deposition from Mrs. Forrest, an analysis containing the fruits of the investigation just alluded to. I would like now to bring it to the attention of the court.

CHIEF JUSTICE. Proceed.

O'CONOR. Mrs. Catherine Sinclair Forrest states and avers as follows: That the said Edwin Forrest early in 1849 purchased certain premises called Fonthill in the county of Westchester for the purpose of making an elegant and costly residence for himself and family—the whole cost of said property then being about $50,000 but now worth much more.

The deponent further says that the said Edwin Forrest has the following additional property: four stores and lots of ground in Cincinnati, which originally cost $16,000 and are now worth much more; about fifty acres of land in Covington, Kentucky, which cost over $12,000 and are now worth at least $25,000; the house and premises at 284 Twenty-second Street in the city of New York, of the annual rental of $1,000; six houses in said city of New York, of the annual rental of at least $2,500; a house and three acres of land in New Rochelle, in the county of Westchester, which cost $6,000 and is now worth much more; and also a large amount of personal property consisting of goods, chattels, bonds, mortgages, treasury notes, and otherwise. These rise in value to many thousands of dollars, but the deponent cannot state the total with any certainty. And she further says, according to her best knowledge, information, and belief, that the said Edwin Forrest, if indebted at all, owes but some very trifling and inconsiderable sum and has a clear income exceeding $6,000 a year.

Having finished, O'Conor observed a full ten seconds of communion, turned to Mr. Meech, smiled, turned to Mrs. Forrest, nodded reassuringly, turned to Van Buren, bowed, and said, "Your witness, sir."

Not to be outdone, Van Buren shook his head as if at some particularly mordant piece of human comedy. He then rose. As he approached Mrs. Forrest, he stared at the floor. Had she perhaps lost a hair ribbon? He wished nothing more than to find it, return it to her, be of service. But Henry thought she was not in the least deluded.

VAN BUREN. Mrs. Forrest, would you ever have described your husband as a parsimonious man? I mean, before you separated from him.

MRS. FORREST. No.

VAN BUREN. Might you even have used the term "generous?"

MRS. FORREST. He often was, yes.

VAN BUREN. Then isn't it fair to say there may well be a principle involved?

MRS. FORREST. A principle?

VAN BUREN. In his insistence on a settlement amount that you regard as inadequate.

O'CONOR. Object. Why should *my* client be asked to rationalize *his* client's behavior?

CHIEF JUSTICE. Sustained.

VAN BUREN. Mrs. Forrest, we have heard you hint at Mr. Forrest's potential for violence. Did you not know this before you married him?

MRS. FORREST. Of course not.

VAN BUREN. Of course not. Mrs. Forrest, I put the case that you did not know it until the night of January 19, 1849, the night you turned his life around. And the reason you did not know it before is there was never any sign of it.

O'CONOR. Object!

VAN BUREN. And if there were signs of it subsequently, *you* were the cause of them.

O'CONOR. Object! Object!

VAN BUREN. Because that was the night on which he found a certain letter and knew beyond—

O'CONOR. Your honor, he must not be allowed to go on with this.

(Chief Justice Oakley has been wielding his gavel like a smithy, with neither legal gentleman paying heed.)

CHIEF JUSTICE *(a roar)*. Enough! Mr. Van Buren, Mr. O'Conor, pray let me call your attention to this implement. It is a gavel. You have seen its like before? Yes? Splendid. The next time I strike my desk with it, you will instantly lapse into corpselike silence. Both of you. And you will remain that way until I raise you from the dead. May I consider that a word to the wise? *(chastened nods from both)* The objection is sustained. Mr. Van Buren, you cannot cross-examine the witness on a matter that has not yet been put in evidence.

VAN BUREN. But that letter—

CHIEF JUSTICE. Is not in evidence. And will wait in the wings until you open your case. Come, sir, you know that as well as I do.

VAN BUREN *(sighing heavily for the benefit of the jury, then swinging about to face the witness)*. Like my learned friend, let me return with you to the night of January nineteenth. The quarrel has taken place, the decision has been made to separate. At what point did you plead with Mr. Forrest to remain silent as to the cause?

MRS. FORREST. I made no such plea.

VAN BUREN. It was Mr. Forrest's plea?

MRS. FORREST. It was Mr. Forrest's wish.

VAN BUREN. Do I understand you, madam? He quarreled with you bitterly, as bitterly as you so vividly described here a moment ago, excoriating you for . . . what did you say, forty-five minutes, an hour?

MRS. FORREST. Yes.

VAN BUREN. At the end of which period he suddenly ceased to thunder, turned meek as a lamb, and pleaded with you to tell no one what had caused the schism? Is that what you would have us believe?

MRS. FORREST. No.

VAN BUREN. Then enlighten us, pray.

MRS. FORREST. It was a week later that he said he wished the cause of our separation to be kept secret. He said it was no one's affair but ours. He said also he did not wish it known that any person lived after impeaching his veracity.

VAN BUREN. And that's why you separated? Because you impeached his veracity? You're asking us to believe that your marriage . . . that good, sturdy, near-idyllic marriage of yours . . . sundered because during one heated moment you impeached his veracity?

MRS. FORREST. I did not say it was rational, sir. Merely that it happened.

VAN BUREN. He made no other accusation?

MRS. FORREST. None. That is, none that night. Subsequently, of course—

VAN BUREN. *That* night, Mrs. Forrest. Not subsequently. *That* night the word "infidelity" was never mentioned between you? Not even once?

MRS. FORREST. It was not.

VAN BUREN. Nor the word "impure"?

MRS. FORREST. Never.

VAN BUREN. Nor the name Jamieson?

MRS. FORREST. No.

VAN BUREN. How odd. How very puzzling. Help me, Mrs. Forrest, for I am now at a loss to explain the document he made you sign the very next day.

MRS. FORREST. As was I, Mr. Van Buren, I do assure you.

VAN BUREN. When your husband asked you to cooperate in keeping the secret, did you agree?

MRS. FORREST. Yes.

VAN BUREN. Why? Surely the temptation must have been great to tell a few close friends—Mrs. Willis there, or your sister, for that matter—how deeply you were being wronged, how *irrationally* your husband was behaving. Or your parents, Mrs. Forrest, those anxious oldsters more than three thousand miles away. Tell me, madam, why let your parents endure the pain of wondering? No, pray let *me* answer for you, and you will tell me if I'm correct. When your husband asked you to keep the secret, you agreed because as a dutiful wife you had no choice.

MRS. FORREST. You are correct.

VAN BUREN. How noble.

O'CONOR. Object.

CHIEF JUSTICE. Tone, Mr. Van Buren.

VAN BUREN. Mrs. Forrest, I'm interested in the group that gathered in Mrs. Voorhies's house on the night of January nineteenth. A *supremely* respectable gathering, I believe it has been termed. *(Pause)* Have I somehow got that wrong? Shall I have the clerk read—

MRS. FORREST. That won't be necessary, sir. Yes, Mr. O'Conor used that term, and I'm prepared to subscribe to it.

VAN BUREN. You seemed a touch hesitant.

MRS. FORREST. Because—

VAN BUREN *(over this)*. You seemed a touch hesitant, ma'am, and I suggest it was because a piece of information has been withheld. Something pertaining to the group has not been made clear to the court and the members of the jury, isn't that true? I refer to the matter of how long it stayed intact. How long was that, Mrs. Forrest?

MRS. FORREST. I've already testified that I returned home at—

VAN BUREN. Oh, we know about that, the *witching* hour. We recall that vividly. What you did not say, however, is that both reverend gentlemen, their wives, and, as a matter of fact, the lion's share of that *supremely* respectable gathering was gone by ten o'clock.

MRS. FORREST. Was it ten?

VAN BUREN. I put that question to you, ma'am.

MRS. FORREST. If you say ten I suppose it was. I had no reason to be precise about the time.

VAN BUREN. May we settle on ten then?

MRS. FORREST. Of course.

VAN BUREN. Leaving behind a . . . oh, an iota less than a *supremely* respectable gathering. Might you be willing to acknowledge that?

O'CONOR. Object.

CHIEF JUSTICE. Sustained.

VAN BUREN. But learned counsel has made such a *point* of respectability, surely I have the right to joust with him on that?

CHIEF JUSTICE. That right you have. What you cannot do, sir, is demand testimony from the witness on matters transcending her competence. The difference between respectable and supremely respectable, real or imagined, requires expertise she does not lay claim to. Facts, sir. That is what we want.

Van Buren. Then facts you shall have, sir. Isn't it a fact, Mrs. Forrest, that you, your sister, and two or three of the men retired to the upstairs parlor shortly after ten o'clock?

Mrs. Forrest. Yes.

Van Buren. For what purpose, ma'am?

Mrs. Forrest. As I recall, because Mrs. Voorhies thought we might be more comfortable there.

Van Buren. Convivial, did you say?

O'Conor. Object.

Chief Justice. Sustained.

Van Buren. Can I have misunderstood, Mrs. Forrest? Didn't you retire there to drink brandy?

Mrs. Forrest. We retired there, sir, to be more comfortable. And so that my sister could play the piano for us.

Van Buren. And there was no drinking of brandy to cheer the departing Mr. Voorhies on his way?

Mrs. Forrest. I did not say that, sir.

Van Buren. So there was a toast or two?

Mrs. Forrest. Yes. Mr. Voorhies—

Van Buren. And Mr. Willis.

Mrs. Forrest. And Mr. Willis, too, yes.

Van Buren. And you, Mrs. Forrest. Surely you, too, drank your brother-in-law's health. Perhaps once, perhaps twice. . . .

Mrs. Forrest. No, sir.

Van Buren. Not even one glass?

Mrs. Forrest. No, sir.

Van Buren. Come now, ma'am. Suppose I were to tell you I have a witness prepared to swear—

Mrs. Forrest. Then you have a witness prepared to commit perjury. No brandy touched my lips that night.

Van Buren. No tobacco either? *(silence)* The court awaits your answer, ma'am. Weren't you offered and didn't you accept a *cigar* from one of the *gentlemen* present?

MRS. FORREST. I'm afraid that is the case.

VAN BUREN. And what have you to say about that, madam?

MRS. FORREST. No more than that it made me slightly ill. *(laughter)*

VAN BUREN *(over this)*. It's possible you're not alone in that. It's possible the sheer unseemliness—

O'CONOR. Object!

CHIEF JUSTICE. Where are you going with this, Mr. Van Buren?

VAN BUREN. She is a lady of advanced ideas, and—

O'CONOR. Object! Object! I do most heartily object. My learned counsel is addressing the jury, and he has no right to. He is neither opening nor closing and consequently must develop his case through testimony only.

CHIEF JUSTICE. Mr. O'Conor is obviously correct, Mr. Van Buren.

VAN BUREN *(showing just the edge of impatience)*. Then I have no further need of this witness.

O'CONOR *(back on his feet with alacrity)*. Mrs. Forrest, with your mind's eye scan for us Mrs. Voorhies's entire guest list. Will you say if there is one . . . just one . . . who you have reason to believe would have been, at that time, unwelcome by Mr. Forrest in his house?

MRS. FORREST. There is not.

O'CONOR. During the whole course of Mrs. Voorhies's party were you ever alone with any of the gentlemen on that list?

MRS. FORREST. I was not.

O'CONOR. Not for as little as five minutes?

MRS. FORREST. Not for as little as one.

O'Conor helped her off the stand. He smiled, he bowed. What he wished to be certain of, Henry thought, was that all present understood how very pleased with her he was.

The Tragedian at Home

*F*orrest did not like the young man's face. Not now, nor had he ever. Not from the day Bancroft had put him forward. He had told the theater manager so in no uncertain terms. There was something in that young man's face too clever, too knowing. Nor did Forrest like the way he spoke his lines—too familiarly. No, not that—too possessively. As if Iago had been born that very day, fathered by a young upstart named Thomas Mason. As if Edwin Forrest in the flesh were not two feet away, the same Forrest who had played Iago a thousand times, whose Iago, in fact, had been proclaimed as masterly and taken as a model by no less a thespian than Edmund Kean himself.

"Confound it," he said, breaking into the middle of "look-to-your wife," "you spoke that line in a bloody whisper."

"Sorry, Mr. Forrest," Mason said.

"In the third row they would not hear you with a bloody ear trumpet."

The young man's smile was bland. "Your pardon, sir, I thought I was being conspiratorial."

"Conspiratorial, my bloody arse!" He broke off. In the far

corner of the room Henrietta went on knitting placidly, but he knew his sister well enough to sense her growing displeasure. He forced himself to take a breath.

"Forgive me, my boy," he said. "Othello is not himself today."

Mason gave him charm for charm. "Not himself and still the greatest actor in the world," he said, with a deep, graceful bow.

Henrietta looked up. She resembled her brother closely, features so strong and blunt that it took awhile for most to discover the sweetness in her face. Some never did, and she remained for those merely the large, forbidding woman who guarded Forrest like the Golden Fleece.

She knew and understood this. For the most part, she had come to terms with it, though from time to time she bitterly regretted the impact plainness had had on her life. She felt she would have made a splendid wife and mother. Past fifty now, she had long since abandoned all hope in that direction.

Edwin was her child. Only a few years the older, she had always behaved more motherly than sisterly toward him, even when their mother had been alive. That was because his need had been great. And hers, too.

Watching her brother now, she rose from her rocker and then switched her glance to Mason, who had also been studying silent, lowering Edwin—with growing anxiety. Belatedly, it occurred to him that he might have put himself at risk.

"Edwin does seem tired to me, does he not to you, Thomas?" she asked.

"That ordeal in court," Mason murmured sympathetically.

"Yes. And I believe he has one of his headaches. Do you, Edwin?"

"A monster."

"Until tomorrow, then, Thomas?"

"Of course, dear lady." For Henrietta, the full blast of his boyish smile. But for Forrest, suddenly, a kiss on the hand—the kiss of fealty, given on bended knee—after which he swept out of the room.

"Sly little bastard," Forrest said between his teeth.

"It was an excellent reading, Edwin. The boy is clever."

"He reminds me of that snake Jamieson."

"He is not at all like Jamieson. He is merely a talented, ambitious young actor who hopes desperately for the part you have already promised him."

"He is insufferable, I tell you."

"Well, if he is, it's his talent that makes him so, and you of all people should recognize the breed."

He glared at her.

She went to him, kissed his brow. *"Is* it a monster of a headache, my Winnikins? Then off to bed with you, and in a few minutes I'll appear with compresses. Will you like that?"

He nodded.

"And shall I call Doctor Harris?"

"No." A growl. "He was Catherine's doctor, never mine. Don't want him near the place. He knows as much about medicine as that other bloody idiot."

"Which? I sometimes can't keep your bloody idiots separated."

By this time he was halfway up the stairs. He stopped, turned, shouted the name down to her. "Hawkes."

"Oh, yes," she said.

"Have you forgotten? He testifies tomorrow. Lies, lies, and bloody lies."

"I doubt he will do you much harm, Edwin."

But he had turned from her to continue his journey. "Lies, lies," she heard him say, intoning the words like an incantation— and in time with his progress. Henrietta smiled. It was so like the kind of thing he used to do as a boy. Chants. Nonsense rhymes. Racketing around the house to a rhythm of his own, often unaware he was doing it. "Edwin is not like other small boys," their mother had been wont to say, sometimes with alarm.

Waiting for Henrietta, Forrest tried to keep his mind a blank. He knew if he did not, Catherine would infiltrate, bringing up her own corps of hammerers in support of the tiny army already banging away at his temples. No good. In she came. Red mouth curved in a smile of spurious reassurance. Dark eyes pool-like with bogus sympathy. Lies, lies, and bloody lies . . . all of it. Cleopatra to the core. Bending over him now to . . . Henrietta!

"Oh, God," he said, "I thought it was—"

"Hush, hush."

"Did you see her today? Did you hear her?"

"Yes."

"That bitch pretending she's afraid of me. She's not afraid of the devil himself."

Henrietta changed compresses. "Is that feeling any better?"

"A mercy. Thank you. You are always good to me, my dearest. You and Mother; living saints, the both of you. The only two really good women I have ever known."

For a while she ministered to him in silence, a silence punctuated by his occasional heavy gasps of relief. Then, suddenly, he said, "Afraid of me? Why should she be afraid of me? Are you afraid of me?"

"No."

"Of course not."

"On the other hand, you have never been as angry with me as you are with Catherine."

He pushed her away and sat up, shocked. "You're defending her. By God, you are! I'll not have that woman defended in this house."

Gently but firmly, she placed her hands on his shoulders and forced him back down again. "You'll undo all my good work."

"She'll not be defended here. Is that understood?"

"It's not Catherine I'm defending, it's you. Edwin, don't look at me that way. You'll make me impatient. The point is that if you go on like this you'll end by doing yourself harm. You surely will. You must find a way to forget her a little."

"Forget her? Forget that—"

"A little, I said. A notch or two. For your own sake. Right now you're the way you were with Macready. Yes, you are. And you know what happened then, Edwin. You went to bed for a month with pneumonia. Edwin!"

"What?"

"Have you been listening to me?"

"Yes."

"No you have not been. Not a word."

"Where is Van Buren? I sent for him an hour ago. I want him here now. At once. Send my carriage for him."

"I most certainly will not. Mr. Van Buren is a busy man, and he has more than your affairs to think about. He'll get here when he can."

"Did you see the way he looked at her?"

"Who, Van Buren?"

"Meech, that pipsqueak foreman."

"Oh, Edwin."

"That bitch, that harlot. His eyes burn into her."

"Winnikins, dearest, you really will drive yourself insane."

He sat up again, staring at her. "I want her to die, Henrietta. Why won't she?"

She dipped the cloth into the water and dabbed at his left temple, then his right, then his wrists. He had slumped back into the pillows. After a moment his eyelids lowered.

Gently, she wet these too.

And at last he fell asleep.

Catherine's Diary

*E*arly to bed. Wide-eyed shortly after dawn. Myriad little games to trick myself. No avail. Myself is on to myself. This periodic wakefulness is a relatively new thing. Admit it, 'tis a post-separation thing. Before separation I slept heavily and late, except for those mornings when Forrest . . . for shame, Sister Katten.

Snowing again, but lightly now. New York is a cemetery. Of all its five hundred thousand, I am alone awake. Or perhaps Henry Stewart shares the night with me. He told me once that he was insomniacal. And Bennett too, he said. Heavens, what if Henry sleeps and Bennett is my partner.

A pox on you, Bennett. May some particularly noxious evil befall you. May a thousand demons and devils hover about you like gnats and prick you painfully with clever little pitchforks. And a similar doom for you too, Henry, my onetime friend. Well, perhaps a lesser doom. Not that you deserve any mitigation, Henry Judas Stewart. It's just that I persist in liking you, more's the pity.

Not beautiful, our Henry, with that carroty hair and those

large-knuckled farmer's hands and that ungainly length. No match, most would say, for the glorious Forrests or the redoubtable O'Conors of the world. And yet such nice eyes. Such a lovely, uncertain way of looking at one.

I recall the day we met during the Macready troubles. I thought then that he was irredeemably smitten with me, the dark and mysterious older woman of his secret dreams. But he has recovered, I see. Sooner or later all of them do.

Serena says the shyness results from the cholera that came so close to taking him when he was ten. They had closed those nice eyes. And then after all he lived. She says that till ten he was a hellion, after that much different.

With females, that is. With males he is from all reports as robustious as need be.

Perhaps with his eyes shut he saw Death, and it was a woman.

Edwin, most assuredly, would not be surprised to hear that.

O'Conor says court went tolerably well on Friday, that I impressed Mr. Meech mightily. I am less sanguine. Unlike Henry, Mr. Meech has odious eyes, fish eyes, hard to read. Also they pop open at unpredictable moments and make me want to giggle.

O'Conor's eyes are remarkable, I think. I have never seen eyes so changeable. Summer-sky blue when he suddenly announced today he would take no money for defending me. A duty, he said. And a privilege. Wrongs must be righted, or what are strength and power for? And stormy gray, those eyes, when I declined his invitation to a late supper in his rooms.

What a thrusting and a parrying there then ensued. But at last, like the seasoned campaigner he is, he bowed and beat a strategic retreat. But oh, the confidence the man exudes!

What will I do about O'Conor?

What do I *want* to do about O'Conor?

Will I do what I want about O'Conor?

Heaven knows.

On insomniacal nights this complaint-ridden diary does provide solace. It creates the illusion of order. That same hodgepodge of thoughts that serve to keep me awake I set down on paper, and by making more of them than they're worth, I erect a barrier against anxiety.

Cold out, snug in. Doughty little potbelly throws a sufficiency, evoking by contrast that bitter London winter of '37. Pater had all three stories full of furnaces and fireplaces burning at their zeniths, and yet the parlor thermometer would not budge beyond 38!

Bitter winter, did I say? Better say glorious, for it was the winter of Forrest, the winter of our content. My beautiful Edwin. Pater and I in St. James's theater. Enter Macbeth, and before the witches leave Sister Katten is hopelessly smitten. Entranced. Spellbound. Ah 'twas a fairytale of a year, during which no simpering milkmaid was ever more fatuously in love.

From the winter of our content to our triumphal sweep: the grand and gallant *United States* docks majestically in New York harbor. People transcendent, the whole pier one moving mass of humanity.

Not just a single one but a troika of formidable brass bands, blasting out "Hail Columbia" in endless and energetic variations. Everywhere, hand-painted signs with their Yankee Doodle messages: OUR COUNTRY FIRST AND FOREMOST; HATS OFF TO FORREST, THE AMERICAN CHAMPION; AMERICAN ACTORS FOR THE AMERICAN STAGE, and the like.

And then we are spotted: there's Forrest! And there he is indeed—at the gangplank with his arm around his Catherine. So obviously proud of me and wanting to show me off. And the indescribable roar that greets us, the thunderous applause, the thumping of canes on the wooden dock, the waving of hats and handkerchiefs, and the culmination in nine earsplitting hip-hip-hoorahs. After which he lifts me into the air, holds me high for all to see—his British beauty—kisses me fair on the mouth, and matches their welcome with a roar of his own: "We are home! We are home! God bless you all, we've come home."

How lovely.

And how different when the *Rochester* docked in September of

'46. Not that the crowd failed to jam the pier; it was there, as were the brass bands. Still, it *was* different. He made it different, Edwin himself. It was in his face, his bearing. As for his "British beauty," she could have submerged with the anchor and not been missed. "A soured and disappointed man," O'Conor said in his opening. There's truth in that.

Edwin has never stopped blaming Macready for what happened to him during that second British trip: his rude treatment by the London press, his difficulty getting bookings, and the poor houses that greeted him when he did.

Macready has never stopped denying collusion of any kind. Forrest was unpopular, he says, because Forrest was inept. Edwin is to be forgiven for not wishing to yield the point.

Digression: If I had not miscarried for the third time just the week before, might things have gone differently? Margaret says no. I'll always think yes. Edwin is the most mercurial of men. The effect of such news on such a temperament was bound to be profound. And shattering. Besides, if I had not been ill I would have been posted next to him in that fateful balcony box, a restraining influence. Margaret says that on Edwin Forrest, only chains are a restraining influence.

In one area, however, there is complete agreement. On a fateful March evening in Edinburgh's Theatre Royal, while Hamlet (Macready) was engaged in a piece of business that had to do, I gather, with a flaunted handkerchief and some fairly fancy footwork, he was hissed. From the upper-right boxes, a long, sustained *hissss,* like the sound of a steam engine: Edwin. Nor has he ever denied it. Who should know better than a fellow actor, Edwin said to assorted journalists, when a piece of business deserves to be hissed.

Macready was not amused. In fact, it's easy to isolate that now as the opening thrust in what became the Bloody War Between the Actors.

And, my stars, how excited we all were about it.

But now, a mere five years later, how many of us really care? Who besides the bereaved—and Edwin, of course—can even remember with any fidelity? Certainly not Sister Katten, whose lids at last are like barbells.

Trains and Boats

*A*nd now here was Christmas breathing hotly down Henry's neck. As usual he was unprepared. No one on his list had been shopped for. His mother would be disappointed in him but forgiving. His father would ascribe his shortcomings to Bennett's corrupting influence.

Every year, Henry vowed to do better. Every year, "better" turned out to be a wraith.

He studied the Chief Justice. How did his Christmas shopping stand? He seemed carefree. Well, he had minions to do his bidding.

Van Buren and O'Conor, too, had no doubt dispatched from their offices lesser legal lights to serve as surrogate Santas.

Raymond had confessed that his own surrogate was Mrs. Raymond.

For Bennett the problem did not exist. To Bennett, Scrooge was the stuff of heroes.

Suddenly, toward the rear of the courtroom, Henry saw a blaze of hair, signaling a familiar presence. Serena was approaching the Catherine Forrest table, where she was welcomed and made room for between the two ladies already there. Serena seemed not to see her "old friend." Or, wishing to protect her clothing, he thought sourly, she pretended not to and made a wide berth.

He decided that Serena was disgustingly efficient and had her Christmas shopping well in hand.

The clerk called Dr. John Hawkes.

Pale, very thin, Hawkes needed O'Conor's help to mount to the witness stand, where he was sworn and examined by Mr. O'Conor.

HAWKES. I am forty-three years of age. I am now on my way from Boston to Rochester and am spending the night in New York with a friend, Mr. Joseph Ransome, in the Fifth Avenue. I do not know Mrs. Forrest. I have seen both Mr. Forrest and Miss Josephine Clifton on the stage. Some three years ago I was traveling with my wife from New York to Rochester and stayed overnight at Utica. In the morning when we reboarded the railroad car, Mrs. Hawkes being unwell, I obtained for her the part of the car called the saloon. On entering we discovered that one of its two settees was occupied by a lady. My wife took possession of the other. Very soon after this the train started. About a half hour later Mr. Forrest entered the saloon and spoke to the lady. This was the first I had seen of him, but it was when I recognized him that I recognized her too, as Miss Josephine Clifton.

O'CONOR. Up to that time was Miss Clifton alone?

HAWKES. No.

O'CONOR. Who was with her?

HAWKES. A mulatto woman. At first I thought she was a servant. Later I decided she must have been something more.

O'CONOR. Yes. Well, we will get to that in a moment. During that trip where did you spend most of your time?

HAWKES. Some in the main car but with frequent visits to the saloon.

O'CONOR. To see your wife.

HAWKES. Yes.

O'CONOR. But you also saw Miss Clifton, didn't you?

HAWKES. Yes.

O'CONOR. How would you describe her condition?

HAWKES. She wasn't well. Often she seemed in considerable pain—groans, twistings of the body, contortions of the face.

O'CONOR. And did she remain so all the way to Rochester?

HAWKES. No she did not. She—

O'CONOR. In a moment, Dr. Hawkes. Did your wife stay in the saloon for the entire trip?

HAWKES. No, sir. We were both made to leave.

O'CONOR. *Made* to leave? By whom?

HAWKES. By Mr. Forrest.

O'CONOR. Couldn't you have refused him if you had so desired?

HAWKES. He was abrupt with us. Peremptory, sir. He *ordered* us to leave.

O'CONOR. And did he tell you how long you need stay away?

HAWKES. He said he would come and get us when it was permissible to return.

O'CONOR. Permissible?

HAWKES. He is a very large man, sir.

O'CONOR. Yes, he is. *(extended communion, during which Van Buren is clearly tempted to find his feet but resists)* And *did* Mr. Forrest tell you when it was permissible to return?

HAWKES. Yes.

O'CONOR. How long a period had elapsed by then?

HAWKES. About forty-five minutes.

O'CONOR. When your wife returned to the saloon, did you accompany her?

HAWKES. I did. And it was then I noticed the change in Miss Clifton.

O'CONOR. You may tell us about it now, doctor.

HAWKES. No more writhings or contortions. Nor did she complain of pain. She was much quieter, calmer.

O'CONOR. Did you see either Mr. Forrest or the mulatto woman give Miss Clifton anything?

HAWKES. He gave her a pill, or pills.

O'CONOR. Do you know what kind of pill?

HAWKES. Miss Clifton made no attempt to disguise its nature. She told us afterward that it was opium.

O'CONOR. Did Miss Clifton also tell you what was troubling her?

HAWKES. She said she was quite accustomed to those attacks. She said they were caused by her monthly flow.

O'CONOR. Is that a diagnosis with which you agree?

HAWKES. I do not.

O'CONOR. From all you saw of Miss Clifton's illness, did you form your own diagnosis, doctor?

HAWKES. Diagnosis? No. I formed an opinion.

O'CONOR. What was it?

VAN BUREN. Object. Surely, your honor, an opinion is not competent testimony.

O'CONOR. It is not an oyster-seller's opinion, it is a physician's.

CHIEF JUSTICE. Yes. A physician's opinion on a medical matter, Mr. Van Buren, and I see no reason, in point of law, why it should not be received.

VAN BUREN *(to the clerk)*. Exception, Mr. Asher.

O'CONOR. Dr. Hawkes, considering the symptoms you saw before you left the saloon, considering what you saw afterward, considering that when the train reached Rochester Miss Clifton was removed from it heavily wrapped on a warm September day, considering all that, will you tell the court what you told your wife that evening?

HAWKES. I told her I thought an abortion had taken place. *(gasps: too audible to sit well with the Chief Justice, who employs his gavel to restore order)*

O'CONOR. Your witness, Mr. Van Buren.

VAN BUREN. Dr. Hawkes, is it not at least possible Miss Clifton's discomfort was caused by . . . precisely what she said it was?

HAWKES. Possible, but not likely.

VAN BUREN. Would all medical opinion agree with yours, do you think?

HAWKES. Having two medical men agree is not an everyday occurrence. All medical opinion would be remarkable.

Laughter. Dr. Hawkes enjoyed it. Obviously, Henry thought, he was warming to his role.

VAN BUREN. Suppose I were to tell you I have depositions from four doctors practicing in this city, whose reputations are of the highest, who state it is both possible *and* likely.

HAWKES *(sobering)*. But they were not there, were they?

VAN BUREN. Tell me, sir, where did you get your medical education?

HAWKES. My medical education?

VAN BUREN. Indeed, sir.

HAWKES. I graduated from Fairville Western College of New York.

VAN BUREN. Would you repeat that, sir, a shade more slowly. For the benefit of the clerk, I mean. It may be an institution new to him. Fairville . . .

HAWKES. Fairville Western College of New York. In the winter of 1826 or '27.

VAN BUREN. What?

HAWKES. I said—

VAN BUREN. Oh, I heard what you said. I was momentarily taken aback because you seemed so imprecise about the year.

HAWKES. It was 1827.

VAN BUREN. And you began practicing . . . where?

HAWKES. Cherry Valley.

VAN BUREN. Forgive me. Did you say Cherry Valley?

HAWKES. Yes.

VAN BUREN. Cherry Valley, Mr. Asher. And Cherry Valley is where, Mr. Hawkes?

HAWKES. Dr. Hawkes.

VAN BUREN. Forgive me, sir. *Doctor* Hawkes.

HAWKES. Otsego County.

VAN BUREN. Will you spell that please, for Mr. Asher?

HAWKES. O-t-s-e-g-o.

VAN BUREN. Thank you, sir. You stayed there how long?

HAWKES. A year and a half, and from there I went to Newark.

VAN BUREN. Newark, New Jersey?

HAWKES. Newark in Wayne County, New York.

VAN BUREN. Oh, that Newark. You'll be careful to make the distinction, Mr. Asher?

O'CONOR. Object. I should like to know why learned counsel is experiencing this sudden need to colloquize with the court clerk.

VAN BUREN. Unfamiliar names, sir. Cherry Valley. Otsego County. Surely, in the interests of accuracy—

O'CONOR. Is learned counsel suggesting that a competent physician is to be found only in a metropolis?

VAN BUREN. Competent physicians are to be found everywhere. As are competent druggists.

CHIEF JUSTICE. Druggists? Did you say druggists, Mr. Van Buren?

VAN BUREN. I did, sir. And if I may be allowed to continue, you will soon see why.

CHIEF JUSTICE. Very well, then. But pray do move along a bit.

VAN BUREN. Mr. Hawkes, what made you leave Cherry Valley?

HAWKES. Doctor.

VAN BUREN. Pardon?

HAWKES. *Doctor* Hawkes. You referred to me as—

VAN BUREN. Yes, yes. *Doctor* Hawkes, why did you leave Cherry Valley?

HAWKES. An opportunity was offered to me.

VAN BUREN. An opportunity. Someone in Newark . . . that is, a physician in Newark asked you to share a practice with him? Something of that sort?

HAWKES *(hesitating)*. Well . . .

VAN BUREN. Not that kind of opportunity?

HAWKES. No.

VAN BUREN. Not quite, no.

HAWKES. It was an opportunity to go into the drug business.

VAN BUREN *(half turning to the Chief Justice)*. In other words, when you left Cherry Valley you also left the profession of medicine, is that correct?

HAWKES. Well, I'm back in it now.

VAN BUREN. Are you, sir? I'm certain we're all happy to hear that, but how long were you away from it?

HAWKES. How long?

VAN BUREN. A year or two? As long as that?

HAWKES. Fifteen years. But I'm back in it now, and if it were not for my own poor health I would have an excellent practice. An excellent practice, sir. As it is, I have all the patients I can readily manage.

VAN BUREN. *Fifteen* years. Bless me, that is a long time.

HAWKES. There are some things one never loses the knack for, sir.

VAN BUREN. I had heard that said about horseback riding, never about the practice of medicine. Well, be that as it may— when, pray, did you return to your medical way of life?

HAWKES. Two years ago.

VAN BUREN. But, according to your testimony, that famous train trip took place some three years ago, when you were in hiatus, so to speak. Which is to say, the court heard not a physician's opinion on a medical matter but an apothecary's. Isn't that so?

HAWKES. I suppose it is, if you wish to split hairs.

VAN BUREN. Split hairs, is it? *Were* you an apothecary at the time we are dealing with?

HAWKES. Well, if you—

VAN BUREN. A simple yes or no, sir.

HAWKES. Yes.

VAN BUREN. Why are you here today, Mr. Hawkes?

HAWKES. Doc—

VAN BUREN. Forgive me, forgive me, forgive me. *Doctor* Hawkes. Do you understand the thrust of my question, sir? I mean, it's evident your health is less than robust—

HAWKES. I suffer from—

VAN BUREN. And the trip from Rochester must have been difficult for you, yet here you are. Let me ask you something, sir. Would you describe yourself as a sensitive man?

HAWKES. My wife has often so described me.

VAN BUREN. Has she indeed? That being the case, you undoubtedly felt insulted by Mr. Forrest's behavior to you.

HAWKES. Of course I did. Would not you have?

VAN BUREN. Then I put it to you you are here *because* of that, because of a pact.

HAWKES. A pact?

VAN BUREN. A secret pact. I put it to you that three years ago you swore to yourself that Mr. Forrest's insult would not go unavenged. That though you couldn't knock him down physically—he being considerably the stronger—you would find some way to bring him down metaphorically.

O'CONOR. Object. It's tiresome of learned counsel to pretend he can read the witness's mind.

CHIEF JUSTICE. Sustained.

VAN BUREN. Do you like Mr. Forrest?

HAWKES. I have no opinion of him.

VAN BUREN. No good opinion of him.

O'CONOR. Object.

VAN BUREN. Your witness, sir.

O'CONOR. Why *are* you here, Dr. Hawkes? Let us have it in your own words rather than those learned counsel has chosen for you.

HAWKES. To do my duty, sir.

O'CONOR. Thank you, sir. You may step down.

As he did O'Conor hurried forward to help him, turning him over to the bailiff, who led him to the rear of the courtroom.

There his wife—shawl and muffler ready—waited to take him in charge, though she too was pale and thin with a faltering step. A pair of stricken Hawkes, Henry thought, wondering what they would say to each other about the day's events when they were back in their nest.

The clerk called William H. Doty. Red-haired, undersized, fifty, he was sworn and examined by Mr. O'Conor.

DOTY. I reside at 59 Grove Street in New York City. I am steward of the steamboat *Troy* and have been for two years past. Before that I was steward on the steamboat *Columbia,* that too between here and Troy. I know Mr. Edwin Forrest by sight. I knew Miss Josephine Clifton by sight in her lifetime.

O'CONOR. Did you ever see Miss Clifton and Mr. Forrest in a boat together?

DOTY. Yes. On the *Albany,* a night boat.

O'CONOR. Going where?

DOTY. *To* Albany.

O'CONOR. You saw them come on board together?

DOTY. I did.

O'CONOR. Describe their manner to each other.

DOTY. Arm in arm. Most friendly.

O'CONOR. And they remained friendly all the time they were on board, as far as you could see?

DOTY. Friendly enough to occupy the same stateroom.

O'CONOR. How do you know?

DOTY. I was traveling as a passenger that trip, and their stateroom adjoined mine.

O'CONOR. You could not be mistaken about that?

DOTY. No, sir. I recall, for instance, Miss Clifton speaking to me just before she retired. She spoke to me, and I spoke to her.

O'CONOR. What did you say?

DOTY. Something to the effect that she was looking well and that I hoped she would enjoy her trip.

VAN BUREN. And did she, then, wish you the same? And did she, then, ask after your wife and children?

O'CONOR. Your honor, please.

CHIEF JUSTICE. Restrain yourself, Mr. Van Buren.

DOTY. I regret to say I have no children, sir.

O'CONOR. Did you see Miss Clifton and Mr. Forrest in the morning?

DOTY. I did. In the corridor, on their way up on deck. Since they were going to Albany and I on to Troy, they received their debarking call earlier than I did, of course.

O'CONOR. In other words you were still in your stateroom after they left theirs, is that correct?

DOTY. That's correct. I saw them go by my open door.

O'CONOR. Did you look into their room after they left it?

DOTY. I took that liberty, yes. I regret to say, sir, I have always been insatiably curious. Mrs. Doty—

O'CONOR. Will you tell the court what you saw?

DOTY. I saw a bed made up on the floor.

O'CONOR. How on the floor?

DOTY. From mattresses. That is, they had taken the mattresses from the berths and put them together on the floor.

CHIEF JUSTICE. Mr. Doty, will you say again how you became certain Miss Clifton and Mr. Forrest occupied the stateroom adjoining yours? You did say, did you not, that you actually saw them in it?

DOTY. I did, your honor.

O'CONOR. Perhaps it would be good, Mr. Doty, if we backed up a bit and retraced our steps. It's critical that we give Judge Oakley and the jury as clear a picture of what happened as we can.

DOTY. That's the reason I'm here, sir.

O'CONOR. The year . . . was what?

DOTY. Eighteen forty-three.

O'CONOR. Six years *after* the marriage date of Mr. and Mrs. Forrest. Can you remember the month?

DOTY. No. But it was spring.

O'CONOR. April or May, then.

DOTY. Yes.

O'CONOR. Where were you when you first saw them approach the *Albany*?

DOTY. I was standing at the foot of Cortlandt Street, near the gangplank. Their carriage drew up and Miss Clifton and Mr. Forrest alighted, he carrying two carpetbags, which the *Albany*'s steward was just a shade slow in relieving him of, I must say. They then went on board. A short time later I encountered Miss Clifton alone, which was when we first conversed together. She asked me was I going to Saratoga, and I said not. Where was she going? I asked, and she answered, Albany for a two-week engagement. Shortly thereafter Mr. Forrest appeared, and they left together.

O'CONOR. Arm in arm.

DOTY. Yes, sir. A most friendly . . . one is tempted to say a most loving couple.

O'CONOR. When they left, you followed them?

DOTY. Yes, sir.

O'CONOR. Curiosity?

DOTY. I confess it, sir.

O'CONOR. Well, how was it satisfied this time?

DOTY. It was then I saw them go into their stateroom and discovered it was the one next to mine.

O'CONOR. Did you see anything else?

DOTY. From that point on, sir, it was more a matter of what I heard.

O'CONOR. What was that?

DOTY. I heard him kiss her.

O'CONOR. You heard him?

DOTY. It was a very loud, enthusiastic kiss. *(laughter)*

O'CONOR. You are certain it was a kiss?

DOTY. I scarcely know what else it could have been. *(laughter; gavel)*

O'CONOR. And then immediately after this bravura kiss, you heard the sound of a key being turned in the lock?

DOTY. I did.

VAN BUREN. Object. Leading the witness.

O'CONOR. Well, I shall lead no longer. He belongs to you, sir.

VAN BUREN. And eager am I to have him, sir. Mr. Doty, among the many things you are certain of concerning this Hudson River drama, you are certain, I suppose, that it took place?

O'CONOR. Object. Accusatory.

VAN BUREN. I meant no affront, your honor. I meant merely to suggest to the witness the possibility that he might have dreamed it all. There are those dreams, are there not, that become so vivid—

DOTY. I did not dream it, sir. It happened as I said it happened.

VAN BUREN. On the night boat *Albany*.

DOTY. Yes, sir.

VAN BUREN. Did you tell anyone about it?

DOTY. Anyone?

VAN BUREN. Anyone on the *Albany,* for instance.

DOTY. Not that I can recall.

VAN BUREN. You encountered the famous Miss Clifton, the even more famous Mr. Forrest, saw them illicitly in the next stateroom, heard them join in one of the most gustatory kisses in the history of osculation, and yet shared this mighty tale with absolutely no one? A paradigm of discretion you are, Mr. Doty.

DOTY. I think now I did tell it to one man.

VAN BUREN. What was his name?

DOTY. At this late date I can't recall his name, but I have seen him several times since. I understand him to be a merchant. From Charleston, I think.

VAN BUREN. From Charleston?

DOTY. Or New Orleans.

VAN BUREN. Very good, Mr. Doty. Not Boston or Philadelphia?

DOTY. No, sir.

VAN BUREN. Excellent. A merchant from Charleston or New Orleans should not be difficult to find by anyone who wished to verify your story. You have been most particularly helpful. Did you tell anyone else?

DOTY. Some stewards at the Merchants Exchange in Troy.

VAN BUREN. Names?

DOTY. One of them was named Davis.

VAN BUREN. From Charleston or New Orleans?

DOTY. Neither. He was from—

VAN BUREN.No matter. Anyone else?

DOTY. No.

VAN BUREN. No? Not even your wife?

DOTY. Well, aside from my wife.

VAN BUREN. Which is she from, Charleston or New Orleans?

O'CONOR. Object. Learned counsel's tone—

VAN BUREN. I withdraw the question. Let me see now if I have it straight. From April or May of 1843 to the present you have mentioned this piece of Hudson River folklore—

O'CONOR. Object.

CHIEF JUSTICE. Sustained. Find another word, Mr. Van Buren.

VAN BUREN. I'm not at all sure I can, sir.

CHIEF JUSTICE. Of course you can, sir. And I want it from you, one less inflammatory.

VAN BUREN. Incident?

CHIEF JUSTICE. That will do.

VAN BUREN. And yet incident implies—

O'CONOR. I make no objection to "alleged" in front of it, if it please my learned friend.

CHIEF JUSTICE. Try that, Mr. Van Buren.

VAN BUREN. Oh, very well. This *alleged* incident, Mr. Doty, has gone unmentioned by you since the spring of 1843?

DOTY. Aside from my wife, of course.

VAN BUREN. Of course.

DOTY. Until yesterday morning, yes, sir.

VAN BUREN. What happened yesterday morning?

DOTY. I was subpoenaed by Mr. O'Conor and forced to talk about it.

VAN BUREN. Forced?

DOTY. Isn't that the law?

VAN BUREN *(after a moment)*. Mr. Doty, do I detect a change in your demeanor over the past few minutes?

DOTY. Change, sir?

VAN BUREN. Have you before our very eyes become an *unwilling* witness?

DOTY. Well, I don't know about unwilling. I mean actually *unwilling*. It's just I don't really care to put my oar in another's craft, so to speak.

VAN BUREN. Did you tell that to Mr. O'Conor?

DOTY. No, sir.

VAN BUREN. Why not?

DOTY. Mr. O'Conor is not an easy man to sidetrack. *(laughter)*

VAN BUREN. But is it also true that you hoped to gain something by cooperating with him?

DOTY. I . . . a man temporarily down on his luck—

VAN BUREN. Answer the question. *Did* you think to gain something?

DOTY. I suppose I thought it not impossible. We all hear stories—

VAN BUREN. But now, as you listen to your own testimony, it has occurred to you that you might instead lose something. Lose a great deal, in fact. Isn't that true?

DOTY. I don't know what you mean.

VAN BUREN. Oh, I think you do, sir. You're not a fool. You know that people go to jail for perjury.

O'CONOR. I really must protest. It's as if he has this witness at the whipping post.

CHIEF JUSTICE. An apt description, Mr. Van Buren. And unseemly. Pray desist.

VAN BUREN. No further questions.

O'CONOR. *Have* you perjured yourself, Mr. Doty?

DOTY. No, sir. Of course not.

O'CONOR. Is there any part of your testimony you wish to recant?

DOTY. No, sir.

O'CONOR. Did you get anything from me in return for it?

DOTY. Fifty cents witness fee.

O'CONOR. Were there promises of more?

DOTY. No, sir.

O'CONOR. No further questions.

CHIEF JUSTICE. Further from you, Mr. Van Buren?

VAN BUREN. No, but he must not leave town.

DOTY. I shall be at 59 Grove Street until tomorrow evening.

VAN BUREN. Preparations may take a bit longer. I want to be certain to deal adequately with Mr. Doty. Can I call upon the court to compel him to stay?

CHIEF JUSTICE. Beyond tomorrow? I don't see how. You may cross-examine him now for as long as you like, but I do not see how you can compel a witness subpoenaed by the other side to remain at your pleasure.

VAN BUREN. Perhaps Mr. Doty will volunteer to stay?

DOTY. I would . . . I would indeed, sir, but I have an urgent appointment in Saratoga.

VAN BUREN. Perhaps learned counsel would—

O'CONOR *(shrugs)*. I have no further business with him.

VAN BUREN. Very well. Tomorrow it must be, then. Sleep well, Mr. Doty.

CHIEF JUSTICE. You may step down, sir. *(Doty exits briskly.)*

O'CONOR. Your honor, I had planned at this point to call Mrs. Caroline Ingersoll, but she is not in attendance. In fact, I have just received a note from her physician reporting her ill. Consequently, the plaintiff's case must rest for the present.

VAN BUREN *(leaping to his feet)*. Must it now? I think not, sir, or I move for instant acquittal on the charge of adultery.

CHIEF JUSTICE. Surely that is premature, sir.

VAN BUREN. At the very least, then, I insist on all the testimony for the plaintiff being in before we open.

CHIEF JUSTICE. Such insistence is not within your prerogative, Mr. Van Buren.

VAN BUREN. But your honor—

CHIEF JUSTICE. It is within the discretion of the court.

VAN BUREN. But the court must acknowledge that if new evidence is introduced after the defense commences we would be all at sea.

CHIEF JUSTICE. Then at sea you must be.

VAN BUREN. Is it not the responsibility of the court to protect me against being taken by surprise?

CHIEF JUSTICE. Is it learned counsel's responsibility to remind me of mine?

VAN BUREN. Forgive me, your honor, I meant no offense.

CHIEF JUSTICE. Well, then, none taken.

O'CONOR *(the voice of sweet reason)*. Perhaps if we were to adjourn, Mrs. Ingersoll would take advantage of the delay to recover.

CHIEF JUSTICE. Is there a likelihood of that?

O'CONOR. I haven't the foggiest, your honor. She's my witness, true, but she's not, as you may have gathered, a witness friendly to my cause.

CHIEF JUSTICE *(after due consideration)*. Let us adjourn and hope for the best.

Waiting for Mrs. Ingersoll

*W*hy, Henry wondered, could he not be as blithe about wickedness as Peter Blaylock?

After dinner and some flagons: "Henry, let's off to the Five Points. I need a whore."

Immediate attack of moral revulsion. Which, an instant later, was swarmed over by lust. Mary, Mary, he told himself, you kept me good.

Aloud, weakly. "I have no—"

Peter produced sausage-skin sheaths enough for two.

Henry was dragged off. And it had been as awful as he'd known it would be. Now, glancing out the window at the snow, which had replaced the rain and was again falling heavily, he tried to keep from wallowing in self-recrimination.

He needed distractions. He thought of his mother, then his father; it didn't work.

He thought of Mary. That made him uncomfortable.

He thought of Serena. Thinking of Serena was an effective counterirritant, but it left him confused and inexplicably angry.

He thought of Catherine Forrest.

He thought of the day they'd met. It was at the house on 22nd Street, an interview, his first on returning to work after Mary's death. In the midst of a series of commonplace questions on the theory of designing theatrical costumes, Henry had, to his horror, burst into tears. But she'd been undismayed. Her reactions had been instinctive and kind: tea and scones, then brandy and water until, in her view, his recovery was satisfactory.

"Grief," she'd said. "I know about grief and how treacherous it can be. It lurks like a bandit. And then when you least expect it to, it attacks."

He thought next of that strange street-corner meeting a few months later, not long before the open break between Forrest and Macready. A wintry night, much like this. Not late, but through an accident of fate or timing the street had been deserted except for him. He could recall the unsettling feeling of living in a dreamscape. All but silently, over Broadway cobblestones carpeted in snow, her carriage had pulled up behind him.

"Are you lost?" she had asked, rolling down the window.

He slowed his walk. "No, ma'am."

"Must I point out to you, sir, that this is influenza weather? Should you succumb, Mr. Bennett would be inconsolable. Are you on your way to the *Herald*?"

He told her that he was.

"Then we will carry you there. Join us."

That made him realize she was not alone. Her companion was a young man, Henry's age. Henry's height too, only much broader. He looked at first glance a bit like Edwin Forrest himself, but then Henry recognized George Jamieson, an actor in Forrest's company. He was less welcoming than Mrs. Forrest. In fact, as Henry prepared to climb into the carriage Jamieson climbed out and, feet spread, arms akimbo, stood there glaring at them. Them, equally. He was bareheaded. The wind whipped his blond hair and red scarf into a pair of bright horizontals.

Twenty yards later, and he was still planted.

"Picturesque," Henry said.

As she turned to look back he noted with interest that she blushed a little. She made a gesture of impatience that at last breathed life into the statue. Galvanized, Jamieson loped northward.

"He is beautiful," she said. "But a creature of limited understanding, I fear." She paused only long enough to load and lock and added, "I have regards for you, Mr. Stewart."

By now her skin tone was normal again, which is to say almost honey-colored. Remarkably un-English, Henry decided, wondering if it would be as smooth to the touch as it was to the eye. And having wondered that, wondered next if his thoughts were transparent—for certainly she was amused.

But all she said was, "Are you not interested in the identity of your admirer?"

"Admirer? Yes, certainly. Who is it?"

"A mutual friend. Serena Blaylock."

"Serena! You met her in Paris?"

"First there, some years ago. Her aunt brought her one night to see Edwin's *Hamlet*. Later she came backstage. We met again when she visited London and have been corresponding since. I find her a kindred spirit."

"Sweet Silly."

"Your pardon, sir?"

"A foolish nickname her brother gave her when she was a toddler."

"Well, she is scarcely that now, you know."

"Of course not."

For some reason she seemed uncharacteristically at a loss. And when she continued, Henry had the impression that what she meant was less than she put in words, though he was puzzled as to the more. "She has grown up," she said.

"Quite so," he said cheerfully. "She must be very much the young lady."

The effect of this was that he was regarded in that way females have when rendered speechless by a better than average example of male obtuseness.

"Even as a child her sketches showed great promise," he said, in an effort to redress whatever was wrong.

"Mr. Stewart—"

"Ma'am?"

"I very much fear you are abysmal with women."

He remained confused as to the evidence, but it was a conclusion he heartily concurred in. "I know that, ma'am," he said in all humility.

A few minutes later the carriage reached the *Herald*. Henry started to get out.

"Stay," she commanded.

He obeyed.

She studied him, then said, "Perhaps you are better with men."

"Do you want something of me, Mrs. Forrest?"

"Is it necessary that I want something?"

"No, but I think you do."

"Sympathy."

"Just that?"

"It's a great deal, sir. Without it there can be no such thing as friendship."

"I had not noticed that you lack for friends."

She leaned forward. "I am desperate for friends. My whole life is a search for friends."

Close up, her eyes were remarkable, he thought. They were large and slightly uptilted at the corners. Brown but with lighter flecks in them, as if they had been gold dusted. He clearly understood that her eyes were sources of power.

"I need you under my flag, Mr. Stewart."

"You have me."

"And does my husband?"

After a moment he said, "That is a flag of another color."

"No, no, no. I won't tolerate it. You must be as reliable for him as you are for me. Even more so."

"Why?"

"You know why. There's a time of trouble coming. You *know* there is. Already the city is choosing sides. And soon he'll need friends to stand by him, to protect him."

"Friends employed by influential newspapers," he said dryly.

She looked out the window. When she looked back she said, "I am a loyal wife behaving as one. If I seek favors, it is not in my own behalf. Your tone, Mr. Stewart, was uncalled for."

"Then I apologize."

"Do you?"

"Yes." Less stiffly: "Yes, of course I do. And if there should be trouble I promise to be fair to him."

She wrinkled her nose disdainfully. "Fair? What is that? All who know you would expect you to be fair. My objective was the occasional tactical tilt."

He smiled. "Well, perhaps I can promise even that."

"Then you may kiss my hand."

A duty he was performing when the carriage door was flung open: Jamieson, grinning, cocky, full of himself. He swept low in a courtier's bow and said, "I have news from Delmonico's. The maître d' waits lunch for us."

She said, "Did you run all the way?"

"I thought of you and flew, milady."

She laughed. Her face was bright, and as he and Jamieson changed places once again, Henry felt a small, senseless stab of jealousy.

A knock at the door snapped him out of his reverie. A *Herald* runner delivered a note from Bennett.

Seth Baker of the Courier *ambushed an hour ago. Both arms and a cheekbone broken. Assailants masked and sheeted, but none doubt 'twas that cowardly villain Buntline. Baker has been, as you know, insufficiently worshipful of Forrest. You have been at least as luke-warm lately. Though I name myself proudly a friend of Forrest (note lower case), I hate and despise fanatics. And fear them. And fear them, lad. I understand the spooney-headed pride you take in being thought heroic, but the wretch is dangerous. And of course he hates you. Value prudence and go carefully.*

Bennett was wrong. Henry had no view of himself as a hero, nor any wish to be mistaken for one. He did value prudence, but he valued honor too, which left him little choice when confronted by bullies. He did not enjoy the dilemma, but there it was. Crumpling the note, he tossed it in the fireplace.

Van Buren Opens

*T*here were six of them," Raymond said. "Hooded, of course, according to my source, who swears on his mother 'twas Buntline and his Friends of Forrest. Broke both Baker's legs and some ribs. For the next few days we should plan to leave the courtroom together."

Henry nodded. "Arms and a cheekbone, according to Bennett's source."

Raymond looked at him. "My source *is* Bennett's source. You didn't know?"

"I did, but didn't know you did."

After a moment they grinned at each other.

Mrs. Ingersoll continued unavailable. In her stead she sent her physician, who was not bad as an advocate either. He persuaded Judge Oakley that his patient's suffering was of such severity that ten days to two weeks would be required for recovery. That being so, Van Buren had no choice but to rise, face the jury, and open his case.

VAN BUREN. We—that is, the defendant and I—begin by having to find our way around a most monumental prejudice. Nay, it's true. I see in your faces that some of you find it objectionable that I should accuse you of prejudice, and still I say it's true. Not that I blame you. How can I blame anyone for what is inherent in mankind, which is to say, a sympathy for womankind. But the question is, Do we have here a situation that warrants such feelings? Do we have here, in other words, a situation consistent with womanly behavior, with womanly delicacy? That, gentlemen, is indeed the question, and I say we are a thousand miles from such a place.

Consider if you will Mrs. Forrest's charges against Josephine Clifton. So far as I know, so far as you know, that lady was virtuous. Testimony to the contrary comes from suspect sources. You have heard some; you will hear more and will have the opportunity yourselves to judge its shabby quality. Ah, but Miss Clifton cannot come into the courtroom and proclaim her innocence. How convenient for the plaintiff, how inviting. Because Miss Clifton is dead she cannot state that at such and such a time in such and such a city—whenever and wherever she is alleged to have permitted Edwin Forrest to know her carnally—she was instead in company of such and such a relative or friend. In other words, she cannot fight back. And I put it to you that therein lies the condition that makes her so appealing a target to Mrs. Forrest.

Moreover, I ask you to observe the plaintiff's singular self-control in this matter of her husband's alleged infidelity. Is it not indeed an act of stoicism to be struck in 1843 and cry out in 1851? Unless of course you believe with me that such a blow never took place, that Miss Clifton was nothing other than the world took her to be, Mr. Forrest's colleague, that any charge to the contrary is scurrilously false.

What is true, on the other hand—and central to the issue—is that while examining the contents of a bureau in their parlor, Mr. Forrest accidentally discovered a letter written to his wife, a fateful letter, a damning letter, the letter, in fact, that explains your presence here. It was from George Jamieson, a fellow actor, and it contained material damaging enough to satisfy any husband in this courtroom that he had been betrayed. You think not? Then pray let me read it to you.

O'Conor. No, sir, you may *not* read it to us. Your honor, how can learned counsel read that which has not been proved in evidence?

Chief Justice. Mr. Van Buren, Mr. O'Conor is correct.

Van Buren. Oh, no, sir. Fair is fair. I sat quiet while learned counsel opened his case. Why can he not do the same for me?

O'Conor. Such was my intention, sir. But you cannot . . . can never . . . read that letter . . . any letter . . . any document . . . anything at all until you have established its relevancy.

Van Buren. It was not my impression that Mrs. Forrest had ever denied receipt of said letter.

O'Conor. I repeat, that letter—whoever it belongs to, wherever it came from—has not established its relevancy. As to denials, Mrs. Forrest is not bound to deny anything until it is proved in evidence.

Chief Justice. Come, Mr. Van Buren. Surely you know he has the right of it. The letter cannot be read until it is proved. Have done with this now. Prove the letter in direct examination, and there will be no difficulty.

Van Buren. I must say I am taken aback, sir.

Chief Justice. In what way, sir?

Van Buren. You must admit, sir, it's not customary for counsel to be interfered with in his method of opening his case. Am I not permitted to tell the jury what I intend to prove?

Chief Justice. I have no objection to you stating—at large— what you intend to prove.

Van Buren. But—

Chief Justice. How can I possibly make it clearer to you, Mr. Van Buren? You will not be permitted to read that letter until it's proved in evidence.

Van Buren. Then I propose to state—*at large*—what is in it.

Chief Justice. Do so, if you choose, but carefully, sir. *(to the jury)* Gentlemen, at this point I think it useful to offer a piece of advice. The veteran juror pays as little attention as possible to openings. Why is that? Because experience shows that once an opening is past, counsel seldom lifts a finger to prove that which he has sworn to move mountains to prove. *(laughter)*

VAN BUREN. Your honor.

CHIEF JUSTICE. Yes?

A touch snappish. Something had been growing between Van Buren and the Chief Justice, Henry thought, that learned counsel would be wise not to nurture. At that moment Van Buren sensed it too and, making a powerful effort, mustered a smile.

VAN BUREN. All things considered, it might be sensible for me to shift to another area.

CHIEF JUSTICE. As you see fit, sir.

VAN BUREN *(to the jury)*. Gentlemen, let me simply put it this way. It is absurd to argue that Mr. Forrest separated from his wife because she was English, or because he was at odds with Mr. Macready, or even because she—horror of horrors—gave him the lie. None of that is to be taken seriously. Consider: just prior to the separation Mr. Forrest was in the prime of life, at the head of an honorable profession, and passionately in love with a woman he viewed as the very model of wifely virtue and decorum. Nothing on earth would have torn him from her except the absolute conviction that he had been dishonored. And that is what I shall prove here: that she betrayed him, that she turned his house into a scene of almost uninterrupted wassail, and that as a result of this he found himself a ruined man, his hopes blasted, his bliss destroyed. In short, had he become the kind of raving maniac my learned friend wishes to foist on you, it would not have been Mr. Macready to blame but Mr. Forrest's trusted lady. Thank you.

A buzzing in the courtroom, requiring vigorous thumps of the Chief Justice's gavel. Strong stuff, Henry thought.

The clerk called Dr. Richard Pennell.

Plump, bald, pink-cheeked, invincibly jolly-looking, in his mid-sixties, Dr. Pennell was sworn and examined by Mr. Van Buren.

PENNELL. I reside on the Fifth Avenue just above Twenty-first Street. I received my medical training at Harvard University. I was attached to the New York Dispensary from 1819 to 1831 and afterward to the New York Hospital. Miss Josephine Clifton was my patient from 1835 to the last time she was in this city.

VAN BUREN. So we can assume you knew her quite well.

PENNELL. Yes.

VAN BUREN. For the benefit of those members of the jury who were never fortunate enough to see Miss Clifton on the boards, will you describe her, Dr. Pennell?

PENNELL. She was a very large, athletic woman, perhaps as large a woman as I ever saw, but beautiful, of course.

VAN BUREN. For what reasons did you attend her generally?

PENNELL. For all medical reasons, but in particular for her monthly illness, which was always very difficult. She suffered intensely.

VAN BUREN. Who attended her besides yourself?

PENNELL. Over the years I consulted with Doctors Hosack, Manly, and Everts. We all concurred in the remedy.

VAN BUREN. Which was?

PENNELL. Leeches, warm baths, opiates, and so on . . . until the flowing of blood. With this came relief.

VAN BUREN. Dr. Pennell, suppose you see a lady in a railroad car in a recumbent position, suffering and complaining of great pain, writhing and so on, and suppose this lady, on being inquired of, states she suffers so every month and that she takes opiates for suffering. And then suppose, in a while, you see this lady much more tranquil in her behavior, do you infer from this that an abortion has taken place?

PENNELL. No, sir. I infer no more than that her flow has commenced.

VAN BUREN. Suppose there was—forgive me, sir—suppose there was a *lot* of blood in evidence, an *unusual* amount, would that necessarily—

PENNELL. Miss Clifton's flow was copious.

VAN BUREN. Thank you, sir. Your witness, Mr. O'Conor.

O'CONOR. Are you saying, sir, there could *not* have been an abortion?

PENNELL. In that hypothetical case of Mr. Van Buren's? I suppose there could have been.

O'CONOR. And if he had been describing Miss Clifton as opposed to a hypothetical person, would *that* make an abortion impossible?

PENNELL. Impossible? No, not impossible.

O'CONOR. Thank you, sir.

VAN BUREN. But knowing her medical history, abortion is not what *you* would have inferred, is it, Dr. Pennell?

PENNELL. No, sir.

VAN BUREN. Thank you, sir.

Dr. Pennell exited and in the process exchanged a convivial wink with Henry, who, as a child patient, had been dandled on his knee.

The clerk called Samuel H. Tupper, and Mr. Tupper was sworn and examined by Mr. Van Buren.

TUPPER. I am an agent to the Troy and New York Steamboat Company. I have been an agent for nineteen years, for different companies plying between New York City and Troy. I recollect the steamboat *Albany*.

VAN BUREN. I am speaking of April and May of 1843, Mr. Tupper. Can you tell me who commanded her then?

TUPPER. Captain Jenkins.

VAN BUREN. And where did she run?

TUPPER. From New York City to Albany.

VAN BUREN. Not to Troy?

TUPPER. No, sir.

VAN BUREN. Did you hear Mr. William Doty testify he was a passenger on that boat when she ran to Troy?

TUPPER. Sir, she ran from New York to Albany. She could not very well have carried passengers farther.

VAN BUREN. Why is that, Mr. Tupper?

TUPPER. Because she was a day boat.

VAN BUREN. A *day* boat. Surely not, sir. Mr. Doty *slept* on her. Miss Clifton and Mr. Forrest slept in the stateroom adjoining.

TUPPER. In May of 1843 she had no staterooms.

VAN BUREN. Tell the court, please, what makes you so certain.

TUPPER. Because it was in 1844—in January of '44, it was— that she had a hurricane deck and staterooms put in. Diller and Moore did it. Her first running as a night boat was in the spring of 1844.

VAN BUREN. Let me be sure I understand you, sir. Nary a stateroom until sometime in 1844?

TUPPER. No, sir.

VAN BUREN. Thank you, Mr. Tupper.

The witness was not cross-examined.

The clerk called S.V.R. Moore.

MOORE *(having been sworn and examined by Mr. Van Buren).* I reside in New York. I am a ship joiner, partner in the firm of Diller and Moore. In January of 1844, Diller and I were engaged for an alteration on the *Albany.*

VAN BUREN. What was the object?

MOORE. Our object was to get paid. *(laughter)*

VAN BUREN. What was the object of the alteration?

MOORE. It was to make a night boat of her.

VAN BUREN. Thank you, sir. No further questions.

The witness was not cross-examined.

The clerk recalled Mr. William H. Doty.

But Mr. Doty was not among them. Nor was there anyone in court who could provide information concerning his where- abouts. Much time was consumed listening to a succession of bailiffs describe their efforts to bring Doty to earth. Henry found himself stifling yawns. Finally, hope for Doty was officially aban- doned. Van Buren, however, did not seem unduly disturbed by this. He seemed to feel he had already got sufficient good out of him. O'Conor's expression was austere and unrevealing. A rap from Judge Oakley's gavel adjourned the court.

Funeral

*R*ain, rain—universal and relentless. Was there anything worse than a winter rain? Catherine Forrest, staring down at the wooden casket as dirt began to cover it, tried to forget about the rain. She tried to think about Millie. Bright-eyed Millie Kellogg, last victim of the Bloody War Between the Actors. Struck down by a stray militia bullet. Released at last from a pitiless coma and buried now in Fair Oak, at the outskirts of Harlem Township where she had been born. And where her eighty-year-old mother, a widow, still lived. Oh, God, enough! It was a senseless exercise. Millie and Death were impossible for her to bracket. Just stand and endure, she ordered herself.

Her mind drifted—to Edwin, to O'Conor, to a fireplace, to a hot toddy—and finally it was time to help Mrs. Kellogg back into the Willises' carriage, but as they were doing so she heard her name called. The Hon. Charles himself. Black-clad, but for him that was no change, of course. Positioned like some Stygian sentinel on a knoll just the other side of the waterlogged path. Here for what purpose? Relinquishing Mrs. Kellogg to Serena, she went to join him.

"You knew Millie well?" she asked.

"I knew her not at all. I followed you."

It occurred to Catherine that this was the kind of thing some men might say smilingly, proper accompaniment for a piece of gallantry. Not so O'Conor. Except at Edwin or Van Buren, he seldom smiled. And those smiles were meant to murder.

"You followed me for some specific purpose?"

He shrugged and kept silent. The rain that had for just those few minutes slowed to a drizzle picked up its pace, and he unfurled his umbrella. He moved closer, so she was more securely under its protection. "Are you ready to go home?" he asked.

"No."

"When you are, send them on and come home with me."

"No."

"Why not? I will provide tea and anything else you want. And nothing you do not. Do you believe me?"

"Yes."

"Then . . . ?"

She didn't answer. A glance toward the carriage showed her Mrs. Kellogg being held close by Serena, Serena's hand patting her shoulder. On the other side of Mrs. Kellogg was Caroline Willis. It seemed to Catherine that Serena was somehow managing to pat Caroline's shoulder too.

"Millie was once in Forrest's company," she said. "He dismissed her for not being up in her lines. They were in rehearsal for *Jack Cade,* and day after day she would fluff at the same point. It was driving Edwin mad. Finally, he could no longer stand it. Poor Millie. There was nothing wrong with her memory, you see—she was a quick, lively person—it was just that Edwin made her nervous. I don't know why I'm going on like this, but I can't seem to stop. Do you mind very much?"

"No."

"You have the appearance of someone who's good at listening. But then that's your art, isn't it?"

He kept silent.

"At any rate we were friends, Millie and I. She was a happy spirit. A joy. Not just for me, everyone."

"Except Forrest."

"Yes. That's what made her nervous, I mean that Edwin would never smile at her. Mr. O'Conor, I need your arm about me for just an instant. I seem to have gone a bit faint."

He offered it. To her great surprise her body was quivering.

"At times like this I understand it's best to weep," he said.

"I know."

"I understand it's helpful."

"Yes, but I have never been good at it."

And having said that she began to cry expeditiously indeed, while he folded her against him. In a minute or so she made herself stop and step away from him. "I'm quite recovered now, thank you." And then once again the sobbing and shuddering took command.

"Oh, God, it's just that Millie was on her way to my house when the noise and the excitement drew her, as it would of course, Millie being Millie. She had asked me to intercede with Edwin, and I told her I would, provided she could so master her lines that there'd be no longer any possibility of going up on them no matter what Edwin did. And I told her I'd work with her. We were scheduled to begin that morning, only I'd had an unexpected visitor, so I had to put her off until that night. If only I had not. If . . . if . . ."

"Who?"

She looked at him.

"Who was the unexpected visitor?"

"That's precisely the point. It was no one important."

"But who was it?"

She glanced about her and saw she was the last mourner left on the knoll. Just below, however, strung out along the quarter-mile path that led to the carriage stand, were perhaps fifty more. The rest—close to double that number—had by now disappeared into their carriages, many of which were already smartly under way.

"With decent weather," she said, "Millie might have set a cemetery record. That would have delighted her. I must go. They are waiting for me."

But he caught her hand. "You haven't answered."

"Merciful heaven, you sound exactly like Edwin," she said, pulling away from him. And as she hurried down the knoll she realized it was not the first time that particular thought had occurred to her.

She stepped into the carriage. Mrs. Kellogg was crying silently, Caroline noisily. Serena, dry-eyed, was continuing to comfort both. Catherine gave the driver orders to get under way.

Suddenly Mrs. Kellogg raised herself up to aim a finger at the window. "I blame that man for my child's death," she said. "A curse on you, Edwin Forrest."

She was pointing at O'Conor.

The Downstairs Guerillas

*H*enry, expecting to be joined by Bennett, arrived at Courtroom 3 to be met instead by a fifteen-year-old boy with skinny shanks and worldly eyes—the *Herald*'s star runner.

"The boss slipped on an ice patch. Busted up a leg."

"How badly?"

"He calls it a sprain, says Doc Palmer's an eejit, and he'll be walking good as new in a week. Doc give him crutches and says three weeks at least." He grew reflective. "I guess the doc's in a fair way to get fired."

"Don't be sassy. Does he want me?"

"Says to tell you on one leg and a somethin'-somethin' crutch he can put out a better paper than a whippersnapper like you. Meanin' no disrespect, sir."

Henry turned him, booted him gently in the rear, and pointed him *Herald*ward.

The clerk called Mrs. Christiana Underwood. Late fifties, short, with a prowlike chest, Christiana Underwood was sworn and examined by Mr. Van Buren.

MRS. UNDERWOOD. I live at 118 Sixteenth Street. I am married. My husband's name is Joseph Underwood. I am acquainted with Mr. and Mrs. Forrest. I was acquainted with Mrs. Forrest's family since I was eighteen. Her father was in the Argyleshire militia. He played some instrument in the band and also sang. I came here from England in '37 with my first husband, whose name was Thomas Bedford. Toward the latter part of '37, Mrs. Forrest called at my residence in Pearl Street and offered me a permanent engagement as her housekeeper.

VAN BUREN. This was the house on Twenty-second Street?

MRS. UNDERWOOD. Yes.

VAN BUREN. How did they strike you at the time, the Forrests—their demeanor to each other?

MRS. UNDERWOOD. They lived together at the time, very happy, very affectionate. All the servants thought so.

VAN BUREN. How many servants were there?

MRS. UNDERWOOD. Six. No, seven, including the Swiss boy for running errands. And when Mrs. Voorhies came to stay—Mrs. Forrest's sister Margaret, that is—there were her two. Mrs. V lived in Great John Street then.

VAN BUREN. Did Mrs. Voorhies come often?

MRS. UNDERWOOD. Only in Mr. Forrest's absence. The carriage that took Mr. Forrest away generally brought Mrs. V to the house. This was after . . .

VAN BUREN. Pray continue.

MRS. UNDERWOOD. *You* know.

VAN BUREN. Nevertheless, do continue.

MRS. UNDERWOOD. After Mrs. Voorhies had the baby. That was when Mr. Forrest became angry with her, after she had her baby. Out of wedlock, you see, sir. She came in one day, and when she took off her coat I thought she looked rather stout, and she said, "You are looking at me, aren't you?" And I said, "Yes, I am, because I think you are in the family way." And she said she was. And when Mr. Forrest found out he didn't want her in the house anymore, seeing as she wasn't married at the time, though later she was.

VAN BUREN. Besides Mrs. Voorhies, who else were Mrs. Forrest's steady visitors?

MRS. UNDERWOOD. Women? She never had many steady *women* visitors.

VAN BUREN. Men, then, if you please.

MRS. UNDERWOOD. Well, there was Mr. N. P. Willis, who I see there in the back of this room. Mr. Willis was in the habit of visiting.

VAN BUREN. Did Mrs. Forrest seem particularly fond—

O'CONOR. Object.

VAN BUREN. Oh, very well. Did Mrs. Forrest often speak of Mr. Willis?

MRS. UNDERWOOD. Yes, sir. She said he was very classic in his ideas. That's what she said, classic in his ideas, particularly about ladies' dresses. *(laughter)*

MRS. UNDERWOOD. I don't see what's so funny about that.

CHIEF JUSTICE. Nor do I. Ladies and gentlemen, I *will* have quiet in this courtroom.

MRS. UNDERWOOD. Classic in his ideas, is what she said. And she said that one evening when they were going to the opera, he arranged her ornaments and dress. And that while he was arranging these ornaments he kissed her shoulder. And she was very much terrified, she said, because Mr. Forrest was in the room. Like a giddy schoolgirl, that was how she spoke of Mr. Willis.

VAN BUREN. How often would you say Mr. Willis came to call?

MRS. UNDERWOOD. Once a week, sometimes twice, sometimes three times. And then later he came less.

VAN BUREN. How long were these visits? I mean of how long a duration might a typical visit be?

MRS. UNDERWOOD. I don't know. Sometimes he came in the day, sometimes at night. Once I returned from prayer meeting, and Mrs. Forrest met me in the hall, all flushed and flurried, and told me Mr. Willis was in the drawing room, and she wished him to leave without being seen. This was about ten o'clock at night. So I stood in the corridor to make sure nobody came from the kitchen while Mr. Willis was going out. But I don't know how long he'd been there that day.

VAN BUREN. What can you tell us of the visits of Mr. Willis's brother, Mr. Richard Willis?

MRS. UNDERWOOD. Mr. Richard Willis? Well, on one occasion he was in the house for three days during Mr. Forrest's absence.

VAN BUREN. Three? You did say three, Mrs. Underwood?

MRS. UNDERWOOD. Three whole days. Yes, he was, sir. How I came to know about it was this way. Mrs. Forrest and Mrs. Voorhies were going to a party at Mrs. Watson's, I believe, near the Fifth Avenue. I was in my own room, above the library, when I heard a great noise and laughing. So I came down to see what was the matter, and the servants were standing there laughing. I told them to go downstairs, and then I put out the gas in the library and went to bed. But the next morning when I saw Mrs. Forrest I asked her. She was writing, and I asked her, "Who was that man locked up in your bedroom for three days and three nights?" And she said, "My God, who says so?" And I said, "All the servants say so." She then told me to go down and say that Mr. N. P. Willis wanted Mr. Richard to go home to New Haven for Christmas, but that Mr. Richard didn't want to and had asked for a place to stay, and nothing more to it than that. And I do say this, that Mr. Richard Willis was not in the house to visit Mrs. Forrest but Mrs. Voorhies. At least in my opinion so it was.

VAN BUREN. The last night of Mr. Richard Willis's stay . . . that was the night they had a party?

MRS. UNDERWOOD. Yes, sir.

VAN BUREN. Tell us about that, please. First, who was there?

MRS. UNDERWOOD. Mrs. V, Mr. Richard Willis, and a Mr. Ibbertson.

VAN BUREN. How did they conduct themselves?

MRS. UNDERWOOD. They were singing and drinking wine. So there I was sound asleep in my own room when I was awakened by these loud carryings-on. 'Twas about six o'clock in the morning. I came downstairs as Mrs. Forrest was coming upstairs to get something, and I asked her what was the noise, and she said, "We have been sitting up all night amusing ourselves." And then she said the boy was gone for a carriage and that they were going home with Mrs. V so her husband wouldn't be angry with her for staying out all night.

VAN BUREN. Who else was among Mrs. Forrest's habitual visitors?

MRS. UNDERWOOD. Mr. George Jamieson was a habitual visitor, coming there often and going out with the ladies. But one day when he was there alone with Mrs. Forrest she tripped and hurt her ankle. She asked me to go to the druggist's for some liniment, and I did. When I returned, Jamieson was in the parlor getting ready to rub her foot. I said to him, "Sir, I can attend to that."

VAN BUREN. How was Mrs. Forrest positioned?

MRS. UNDERWOOD. She was lying on the sofa.

VAN BUREN. And Mr. Jamieson?

MRS. UNDERWOOD. Kneeling beside her.

VAN BUREN. Was his hand on her person?

MRS. UNDERWOOD. No.

VAN BUREN. But close enough to it so that you thought—

O'CONOR. Object. We have absolutely no interest in what this witness thought.

CHIEF JUSTICE. Sustained.

VAN BUREN. After you attended to Mrs. Forrest's ankle, what happened next?

MRS. UNDERWOOD. She asked for glasses and brandy and sent me about my business.

VAN BUREN. Mr. Jamieson remained with her in the room?

MRS. UNDERWOOD. He did.

VAN BUREN. Go on.

MRS. UNDERWOOD. Well, at about ten o'clock she rang the bell and desired me to tell the servants they might go to bed. She said I might, too. I said, "I had better wait up, as you'll not be able to walk the stairs." And she said, "No, no, the ankle's much better, and I'm quite certain I shall be able to manage."

VAN BUREN. So you went to bed.

MRS. UNDERWOOD. Yes, sir.

VAN BUREN. But not to sleep?

MRS. UNDERWOOD. Not till about midnight.

VAN BUREN. And Mr. Jamieson?

MRS. UNDERWOOD. The following morning Mrs. Forrest said to me, "That wretch"—or "That devil," I don't recollect which—"stayed all night." I asked her where he slept. "In the guest room," she said. I said, "But there was only a mattress and pillows but no pillow covers on that bed." She didn't answer. Instead she said she wanted him to get his breakfast before he went and asked me how she should manage that. And I said, "Well, he had better go out first, and then come back and ring the bell." And she said she would tell him to do that. Then I asked her where were the clean clothes that was delivered from the washer-woman and which I had laid on the guest-room bed. And she said she had put them away. Which was not so because when I went into the guest room there they were.

VAN BUREN. On the bed?

MRS. UNDERWOOD. Yes, sir.

VAN BUREN. Exactly as you had left them?

MRS. UNDERWOOD. Yes, sir.

VAN BUREN. In other words, as far as you could tell, that bed—which is to say, the bed in the guest room—had not been slept in.

MRS. UNDERWOOD. That's right, sir.

VAN BUREN. I see. May I infer from all this that here was another of those occasions when Mr. Forrest was away?

MRS. UNDERWOOD. He was in New Orleans.

VAN BUREN. What do you know of Mrs. Forrest being . . . *dressed* by a gentleman?

MRS. UNDERWOOD. That was Captain Granby Calcraft.

VAN BUREN. Will you tell us about that?

O'CONOR. She'll be delighted to.

VAN BUREN. Your honor, I must insist that my learned friend restrain himself. I understand the provocation. No one enjoys seeing his case shredded before his very eyes. But are we not taught to take the bitter with the sweet?

CHIEF JUSTICE. At any rate, we are taught to behave like gentlemen.

O'CONOR. Forgive me, sir.

VAN BUREN. Thank you, your honor. Mrs. Underwood, if you will. . . .

MRS. UNDERWOOD. Mrs. Forrest was going to a party at Mrs. Lynch's that Saturday evening, and she came down to where I was in the parlor working on the next week's marketing list. Wearing this exceedingly tight velvet dress, she was, which I always had difficulty fastening for her. Which even Mr. Forrest couldn't fasten that easy. And while I was trying to help her the bell rings, and it's Captain Calcraft steaming into the parlor before I could say "Well, now, sir," or anything else to slow him down. Which is when Mrs. Forrest says to me that she needs some things from Thompson and Weller's in Broadway and would I get them for her. So I went upstairs for my cloak, and when I came down again there she was all snugly buttoned up the back. "Oh, my!" I said. "How did you do it?" And she said Captain Calcraft was marvelous dextrous.

VAN BUREN. Was that the first time you ever saw the dextrous Captain Calcraft?

MRS. UNDERWOOD. No, sir. The first time I ever saw him, Mr. N. P. Willis brought him to a party at Mrs. Forrest's. Mr. Forrest was not home at that time either. Captain Calcraft came again next day in the forenoon and stayed till five o'clock. After that he came almost every day, and when he didn't come he sent his servant with notes and presents.

VAN BUREN. Presents?

MRS. UNDERWOOD. Usually it was bouquets and seegars.

CHIEF JUSTICE. What?

MRS. UNDERWOOD. Seegars. Ladies' seegars.

CHIEF JUSTICE. Are there such things?

MRS. UNDERWOOD. Oh, certain sure, your honor. Small white seegars tied with a blue ribbon.

VAN BUREN. And did Mrs. Forrest send presents to Captain Calcraft?

MRS. UNDERWOOD. Not presents, sir, but she did send notes. I took notes on two occasions from her to his house, number 9 Warren Street.

VAN BUREN. Was Mr. Forrest aware of these notes?

MRS. UNDERWOOD. Not as I know of, sir.

VAN BUREN. When Mr. Forrest was at home, did any of the gentlemen we have been discussing sit up late at night with Mrs. Forrest?

MRS. UNDERWOOD. No, sir.

VAN BUREN. What were the habits of the house when Mr. Forrest was at home?

MRS. UNDERWOOD. Generally, the servants went to bed at ten o'clock, and the house was perfectly quiet after that. I was never woke up at night by loud noises and laughing and carryings-on when he was home.

VAN BUREN. In other words it was an orderly, one might even say tranquil, house when he was at home.

O'CONOR. Object.

CHIEF JUSTICE. Mr. Van Buren, you are leading the witness.

VAN BUREN. Sorry. Mrs. Underwood, what was Mrs. Forrest's custom in regard to drinking wine?

MRS. UNDERWOOD. She drank generously.

O'CONOR. Object.

VAN BUREN. Could you be more specific?

MRS. UNDERWOOD. Two or three glasses of wine at dinner every day at least. And whenever she left the house in the morning to go visiting or shopping she always had an extra glass or two. She said for warmth.

VAN BUREN. For warmth?

MRS. UNDERWOOD. That's what she said, sir.

VAN BUREN. Mrs. Underwood, let us move now to the night of January 19, 1849. Do you perceive which night I am interested in?

MRS. UNDERWOOD. The night of the farewell party for Mr. Voorhies.

VAN BUREN. Correct. Tell us, please, what you know of it.

MRS. UNDERWOOD. Just that Mr. Forrest spent all of it at home waiting up for her. Walking about and sighing. Very wretched, sir.

VAN BUREN. Were you awake when Mrs. Forrest came home?

MRS. UNDERWOOD. No, sir. But the next morning when I went into her bedroom I saw she had been crying. I asked her what was the matter, and she said Mr. Forrest had something terrible in his head and she didn't know what it was. Then later when I was making the bed Mrs. Forrest came from the library into the bedroom and opened the bottom drawer of the bureau with her key. She let out a scream.

VAN BUREN. A scream, Mrs. Underwood?

MRS. UNDERWOOD. Like she was pierced.

VAN BUREN. Were there any words accompanying this?

MRS. UNDERWOOD. She said, "Oh, good God! Oh, Sister Katten, what a fool you are." Katten was a name her sister Margaret called her, you know, because when she was a child she couldn't say Catherine.

VAN BUREN. Pray continue.

MRS. UNDERWOOD. She said, "Forrest has opened my drawer and got all my letters." I asked her what letters, and she said, "My correspondence with my sister all the time I had been south." I said, "Oh, that isn't much consequence." And then she said, "And there was one foolish letter from Jamieson."

VAN BUREN. It was the letter from Jamieson she mentioned specifically?

MRS. UNDERWOOD. Yes, sir.

VAN BUREN. Go on.

MRS. UNDERWOOD. Well, I said, "It's not clever to keep old letters because you never know where the next pair of prying eyes is likely to come from." And she agreed that was so. She went upstairs and brought down a bundle of letters and spent an hour or so burning them.

VAN BUREN. Did she say anything else about the letter from Jamieson?

MRS. UNDERWOOD. Not that day, sir. But the following day she told me Mr. Forrest had seen Jamieson's letter and was determined on a separation.

VAN BUREN. Because of the letter?

O'CONOR. Object. Not competent.

CHIEF JUSTICE. Sustained.

VAN BUREN. Mrs. Forrest did say to you, did she not, that her husband had seen Jamieson's letter and that he therefore was determined on a separation?

O'CONOR. Object. Learned counsel is making his own context.

CHIEF JUSTICE. Yes, Mr. Van Buren. Mr. Forrest may very well have seen the letter. And he may well have insisted on a separation. And yet the two may have happened in contexts that have nothing to do with cause and effect. Do you take the point, sir?

Van Buren's mouth tightened. He did not, Henry thought, enjoy being instructed. O'Conor smiled. He enjoyed it mightily.

VAN BUREN. One final question, Mrs. Underwood. Did you ever notice anything in Mr. Forrest's deportment that might lead you to believe he was . . . shall we say irrational, unbalanced?

MRS. UNDERWOOD. Oh, no, sir. More than most . . . more than most, sir, he was a good-tempered man.

VAN BUREN. Your witness, sir.

O'CONOR (*five seconds of communion followed by a smile totally benign*). Mrs. Underwood, were you reasonably content in Mrs. Forrest's employ?

MRS. UNDERWOOD. Sometimes more, sometimes less.

O'CONOR. I set no standard higher than reasonably.

MRS. UNDERWOOD. Reasonably?

O'CONOR. Yes, ma'am.

MRS. UNDERWOOD. Reasonably, yes.

O'CONOR. Why did you leave her?

MRS. UNDERWOOD. To get married.

O'CONOR. When was that?

MRS. UNDERWOOD. On the twenty-fifth November, 1849.

O'CONOR. But up until that time you were at least reasonably content with Mrs. Forrest?

MRS. UNDERWOOD. Yes, sir.

O'CONOR. You and your nineteen-year-old son, who had also been reasonably content with Mrs. Forrest, though as far as I know he had no regular duties in her household. Am I wrong, Mrs. Underwood?

MRS. UNDERWOOD. He ran errands. Whenever she had an errand for him to run he would go willingly enough.

O'CONOR. I'm sure he would, I'm sure he would. *(six seconds of communion)* To whom did you first speak about Mrs. Forrest?

MRS. UNDERWOOD. Speak?

O'CONOR. Madam, you are here today on the witness stand testifying against that lady. Now that did not happen by magic. I mean to say that at some point you must have spoken to either Mr. Forrest or Mr. Van Buren or to someone who in turn spoke to one of them. Is that not so?

MRS. UNDERWOOD. Well . . .

O'CONOR. A simple yes or no will suffice.

MRS. UNDERWOOD *(a swift look toward counsel, which Van Buren ignored)*. Yes, sir.

O'CONOR. Who was it?

MRS. UNDERWOOD. Mr. James Lawson.

O'CONOR. Mr. Forrest's business agent?

MRS. UNDERWOOD. Yes, sir.

O'CONOR. Let me understand. After this lengthy and reasonably contented relationship with Mrs. Forrest, you one day sought out Mr. Lawson to tell him you had damaging—

MRS. UNDERWOOD. No, sir. 'Twasn't that way at all.

O'CONOR. Then what way was it?

MRS. UNDERWOOD. I went to Mr. Lawson on private business of my own.

O'CONOR. What private business?

VAN BUREN. Object. Surely Mrs. Underwood's private affairs are not relevant to the matter before us, your honor.

CHIEF JUSTICE. Well, let us wait and find out. You may answer the question, Mrs. Underwood.

MRS. UNDERWOOD. The fact is I went to ask Mr. Lawson's opinion about my son's boss. Underwood got him 'prenticed to a friend of his in the building trades, and in my opinion Jamie was being worked too hard. So I went to ask Mr. Lawson if that was *his* opinion.

O'CONOR. You were in the habit of going to Mr. Lawson in matters such as this?

MRS. UNDERWOOD. I went there once or twice before, yes, sir.

O'CONOR. Would it not be more precise to say that on those occasions it was money you asked for, rather than opinions? And that when you got it it was usually in return for something?

VAN BUREN. Object. If my learned friend knows what took place in Mr. Lawson's office let him explain how, since he was not there.

CHIEF JUSTICE. Objection sustained.

O'CONOR. *Did* you ever receive money from Mr. Lawson?

MRS. UNDERWOOD. He was kind enough to help me once or twice.

O'CONOR. And did you ever talk to him about Mrs. Forrest?

MRS. UNDERWOOD. About Mrs. Forrest, sir?

O'CONOR. About Mrs. Forrest, madam. That lady in whose service you were for so long reasonably content.

MRS. UNDERWOOD. Yes, sir, we did talk about Mrs. Forrest once or twice.

O'CONOR. And did the money you got from Mr. Lawson follow these occasions?

VAN BUREN. Object. He's implying—

O'CONOR. Never mind, withdraw the question. Mrs. Underwood, in what connection did Mrs. Forrest's name come up?

MRS. UNDERWOOD. Come up, sir?

O'CONOR. You seem to be having a great deal of difficulty understanding me. Shall I raise my voice?

MRS. UNDERWOOD. Oh, no, sir.

O'CONOR. Then what can I do to help?

MRS. UNDERWOOD. You can let me go home to Underwood. *(laughter, in which O'Conor joins willingly enough—until suddenly cutting it off)*

O'CONOR. Not just yet, madam. We have work to do, you and I. I have questions to ask, and you have them to answer. Simple questions and truthful answers.

VAN BUREN. Object. Your honor, his manner toward this witness is atrocious. He imputes to her motives—

O'CONOR. Impute? I impute nothing to her. I proclaim, sir, that this woman—

CHIEF JUSTICE *(Jovian)*. Mr. O'Conor! *(Not knowing he could thunder so, all are daunted by it.)* Contempt of court is not a charge I ever levy lightly. You, sir, are but one transgression away. Am I being understood?

O'CONOR. Yes, sir.

CHIEF JUSTICE. Civility, sir.

O'CONOR. Yes, sir.

CHIEF JUSTICE. I *will* have it in my courtroom.

O'CONOR. Certainly, sir.

And yet as Henry watched O'Conor through five seconds of communion, he thought him a shade less daunted than the rest: no flush to his cheeks, no flurry to his manner. Henry wouldn't have said O'Conor relished his reprimand, only that he may have accepted it as a fair exchange.

O'CONOR. Pray, Mrs. Underwood, return with me to Mr. Lawson's office and tell me in what manner Mrs. Forrest's name first came up in conversation with him.

MRS. UNDERWOOD. Well, I went to him to tell him I had to go to the pawn office—

O'CONOR. Not to ask his opinion concerning your son's slavemaster boss?

MRS. UNDERWOOD. We talked about one thing and then we talked about t'other.

O'CONOR. Go on about the pawn office, please.

MRS. UNDERWOOD. I said to him the reason for my dire straits was that people have not always been honest with me. I said to him if people acted upright and downright I should not have so much trouble. He asked me what I meant by that expression, and so that's how we got to talking about Mrs. Forrest.

O'CONOR. How? Because you said to Mr. Lawson that she was not honest?

MRS. UNDERWOOD. I said to him that she was very foolish.

O'CONOR. And what did Mr. Lawson say?

MRS. UNDERWOOD. What they all say, that he would as soon have suspected an angel from heaven as Mrs. Forrest.

O'CONOR. What else did Mr. Lawson say?

MRS. UNDERWOOD. Nothing.

O'CONOR. May I remind you, Mrs. Underwood, that you are under oath.

MRS. UNDERWOOD. Nothing that day, sir.

O'CONOR. *After* that day, Mrs. Underwood, did you at any time go before any examiner or officer and make a statement?

MRS. UNDERWOOD. Yes, sir. I went to Mr. Van Buren's house in Irving Place and someone took down what I said.

O'CONOR. At whose urging?

VAN BUREN. Object.

O'CONOR. Someone must have asked her to your house for that purpose. I do not see her saying, "Mr. Van Buren, may I—"

VAN BUREN. Asked, not urged.

CHIEF JUSTICE. A valid enough distinction. If you're still interested in an answer to that question, Mr. O'Conor, you'll restructure it.

O'CONOR. Mrs. Underwood, *did* someone urge you to visit Mr. Van Buren?

MRS. UNDERWOOD. Yes, sir. *(laughter, and a frown from Van Buren; Mrs. Underwood obviously on fire to get a certain something on the record)* Mr. Forrest called on me at my house. Yes, he did, sir.

O'CONOR. Mr. Forrest himself?

MRS. UNDERWOOD. I was that pleased and surprised.

O'CONOR. And flattered, too.

VAN BUREN. Object.

CHIEF JUSTICE. Sustained. Strike, Mr. Asher.

O'CONOR. What did Mr. Forrest say to you?

MRS. UNDERWOOD. First off, he apologized.

O'CONOR. He did? Truly?

MRS. UNDERWOOD. Oh, yes. Mr. Forrest is a proper gentleman. Always was, always will be. Not like some others I know who has the *appearance*. *(a sly, quick glance at O'Conor)*

O'CONOR. For what, specifically, did Mr. Forrest apologize?

MRS. UNDERWOOD. Why for not being of more help to me when the household come apart, of course. He said he was just too heartbroke to be thinking clearly.

O'CONOR. And after this handsome apology, the two of you talked at length about his troubles, isn't that right?

MRS. UNDERWOOD. Yes, sir.

O'CONOR. And no doubt you were a comfort to him.

MRS. UNDERWOOD. I like to think so, sir. He allowed as much.

O'CONOR. And it was at that time he asked you to go along to Mr. Van Buren's house in Irving Place?

MRS. UNDERWOOD. Yes, sir.

O'CONOR. Was it then or later you were paid?

VAN BUREN *(livid)*. Object!

O'CONOR *(speedily, before the Chief Justice's intercession)*. Question withdrawn. Mrs. Underwood, on what date did you sign that statement in Mr. Van Buren's house?

MRS. UNDERWOOD. I don't know, sir.

O'CONOR. Come now, madam. There were witnesses, and I do have a copy of the document. I merely want to put it in the record. February 28, 1850. Is not that correct?

MRS. UNDERWOOD. Yes, sir.

O'CONOR. By which date, it has been established, you were no longer living with Mrs. Forrest. However, your son was, was he not?

MRS. UNDERWOOD. Yes, sir.

O'CONOR. In other words, on departing the house of this wicked woman, you left your only son in her charge, as it were.

MRS. UNDERWOOD. He didn't want to come with me.

O'CONOR. You asked him to?

MRS. UNDERWOOD. No.

O'CONOR. Why not?

MRS. UNDERWOOD. Because I knew he wouldn't.

O'CONOR. The case being that he didn't find her nearly as wicked as you did?

MRS. UNDERWOOD. Jamie has his own way of seeing things. And when he makes up his mind black's white, white it'll stay till kingdom come.

O'CONOR. Mrs. Underwood, how do you know Mrs. Forrest drank wine at dinner? Did you dine with her?

MRS. UNDERWOOD. No, sir.

O'CONOR. You were never present at dinner?

MRS. UNDERWOOD. No, sir.

O'CONOR. Then how?

MRS. UNDERWOOD. I have seen the glasses and wine decanter on the table.

O'CONOR. But you never saw her drink any.

MRS. UNDERWOOD. No, sir.

O'CONOR. And yet you told this court that Mrs. Forrest took two or three glasses of wine at dinner every day. How could you know that?

MRS. UNDERWOOD. Cook must have told me.

O'CONOR. Or maybe it was Mrs. Forrest herself?

MRS. UNDERWOOD. Maybe it was.

O'CONOR. Or maybe you just made it up.

VAN BUREN. Object.

CHIEF JUSTICE. Sustained.

O'CONOR. Mrs. Underwood, can you describe for me the design of the interior of the house on Twenty-second Street?

MRS. UNDERWOOD. How it looks? You mean the rooms and all? I can.

O'CONOR. Pray do so.

MRS. UNDERWOOD. There is a dining room at the end of the hall. Upstairs there are four rooms and a bathroom. One of these rooms is a sewing room. It's in the rear. The next room toward the front—that's the main bedroom—takes up the whole of that side of the house, almost. The spare bedroom was in front and communicated with the hall. It did not communicate with her bedroom. There was also another spare bedroom, which was used as Mr. Forrest's dressing room.

O'CONOR. You have a remarkable eye for detail.

MRS. UNDERWOOD. Thank you, sir. I always did take notice. I mean ever since I was a bit of a girl.

O'CONOR. I am particularly interested in the drawing room.

MRS. UNDERWOOD. The drawing room?

O'CONOR. Yes, ma'am.

MRS. UNDERWOOD. Well, the drawing room was at the back of the house. It had four windows with blinds, which, as a general rule, were kept half open. There was no other mode of getting light into that room.

O'CONOR. How was it when company was there?

MRS. UNDERWOOD. Oh, there was never company in the drawing room.

O'CONOR. Never?

MRS. UNDERWOOD. No, sir, never.

O'CONOR. Then why did you tell this Court of a day when Mr. Willis was in the drawing room?

MRS. UNDERWOOD. Mercy, did I say that?

O'CONOR. Shall I have the clerk read your testimony to you?

MRS. UNDERWOOD. No, sir. If you say I said it, I must have said it. But I'm certain sure I was thinking of the library, because—

O'CONOR. You also implied that Mrs. Forrest was alone some time with him and that when you saw her she looked rather flushed and flurried. Did you mean to suggest improper behavior had taken place?

MRS. UNDERWOOD. No, except he most likely kissed her.

O'CONOR. Isn't that improper?

MRS. UNDERWOOD. There's some would think so.

O'CONOR. Don't *you* think it improper?

MRS. UNDERWOOD. Well, there's not all that much harm in a kiss. *(laughter)*

O'CONOR. Is there all that much harm in a kiss on a shoulder?

MRS. UNDERWOOD. That was pure giddiness on her part. Foolishness.

O'CONOR. Yes. And if it happened . . . *if* it happened . . . even more foolish to report it. One wonders why she told you. Do you have an explanation for that, Mrs. Underwood?

MRS. UNDERWOOD. She was always telling me things.

O'CONOR. That must be because she trusted you. *(six seconds of communion)* Well, now, you never actually saw Mrs. Forrest lift a glass at dinner. You never actually saw a seegar in her mouth. Did you ever actually see Mr. Willis take a liberty with her?

MRS. UNDERWOOD. I didn't actually, but—

O'CONOR. Yes or no, please.

MRS. UNDERWOOD. No.

O'CONOR. Good. Let us proceed to what you actually saw concerning Mr. *Richard* Willis. During the time he was supposed to have spent three nights in the Forrest house, did you ever actually see him there?

MRS. UNDERWOOD. The servants—

O'CONOR. Not the servants, Mrs. Underwood. Nor the green-grocer, nor the livery-stable man, nor the man in the moon. *You,* Mrs. Underwood. Did *you* see him there?

MRS. UNDERWOOD. I saw Jamie take his carpetbag to the stage next morning.

O'CONOR. What next morning?

MRS. UNDERWOOD. The next morning after . . . I don't follow you, sir.

O'CONOR. Well, let me put it this way. We readily concede that Mr. Richard Willis spent an occasional night at the Forrests'. He was, at the time, a family friend, and Connecticut, his home, is a long way off. Your contention is, however, that he once spent three nights running at the Forrests'. Isn't that what you are telling us?

MRS. UNDERWOOD. The servants—

O'CONOR. Madam, if I want information from the servants, I will put the servants on the witness stand. During the period he was alleged to have stayed three nights, did *you* see him on . . . let us say, *two* of those nights?

MRS. UNDERWOOD. No, but—

O'CONOR. Mrs. Underwood, isn't it true that much if not all of your testimony here today has been composed of what you never actually saw?

MRS. UNDERWOOD. That's not so. Besides, everybody—

O'CONOR. On the day you parted from Mrs. Forrest you had an argument with your son. Do you remember what it was about?

MRS. UNDERWOOD. An argument?

O'CONOR. I can call him to the stand and have him testify. He remembers, I assure you.

MRS. UNDERWOOD. It wasn't what you'd call an argument. A boy and his mother will sometimes disagree, but that's not the same as an out-and-out argument.

O'CONOR. You disagreed about Mrs. Forrest, is not that so?

MRS. UNDERWOOD. He's young. He don't know enough of the world to—

O'CONOR. Did he not say to you what I just suggested to be the case, that regardless of whether the man was Jamieson, Captain Calcraft, either of the Willises, or whoever, you never actually saw him take a liberty with Mrs. Forrest?

MRS. UNDERWOOD. I remember something like that.

O'CONOR. Can you tell me he was wrong?

MRS. UNDERWOOD. No, but—

O'CONOR. Your witness, Mr. Van Buren.

VAN BUREN. Though you may not have seen Mrs. Forrest drink wine at dinner, Mrs. Underwood, isn't it true that you have, nonetheless, seen her drink wine.

MRS. UNDERWOOD. Oh, yes, sir.

VAN BUREN. When?

MRS. UNDERWOOD. Generally in the early afternoon before she went out.

VAN BUREN. More than one glass?

MRS. UNDERWOOD. Yes, sir.

VAN BUREN. Often more than one glass?

MRS. UNDERWOOD. Yes, sir.

VAN BUREN. How often?

MRS. UNDERWOOD. On more occasions than I can count. She used to say sometimes she was cold and took the wine to warm her. Sherry, it was. *(pause)* Sometimes she would have cake with it. Sometimes we both would.

And then, for the first time, Mrs. Underwood looked directly at Catherine Forrest. It was a strange moment, almost as if, just for an instant, judge, jury, and the rest who constituted the company of the courtroom had faded away, leaving the women in limbo. And it seemed to Henry, curiously, that they were not enemies, that Mrs. Forrest almost smiled, that Mrs. Underwood's fingers made some small signal of sympathy. All in an eye blink. So fast, in fact, that afterward he couldn't be certain it had happened.

VAN BUREN. Mrs. Underwood, did Mr. Forrest or Mr. Lawson—or, for that matter, myself—did any of us offer to pay you for your testimony?

MRS. UNDERWOOD. You most certainly did not, sir. You gave me ten dollars for the butcher. And Mr. Forrest sent me an order for fifty dollars, but that was for the pawn office.

VAN BUREN. And that was all?

MRS. UNDERWOOD. That was all. Please may I go, sir?

VAN BUREN. Yes. You may step down.

Seldom, Henry would have wagered, had that plump form moved so swiftly. With only one last loving glance for Forrest, who churlishly chose to be busy with a note he was passing to Van Buren, she vanished to resume the story of her life. It was an autobiography composed of single-minded searching for the main chance. In all that vast Underwoodian structure, Henry supposed there was probably no more than a pea's weight of selflessness. "Yah!" he could hear her saying. "And will you, my pretty gentleman, look after me if I don't do it for myself?"

Well, and what had she left behind? Had she given Van Buren the help he clearly hoped for from her? How much of what she had testified to could be believed? Was she so deeply a Friend of Forrest, so fervent a partisan, that nothing she spoke was untainted? Henry thought O'Conor had shredded her on cross-examination. And yet: "Oh, Sister Katten, what a fool you are" lingered.

Did the burning of the letters take place as Mrs. Underwood claimed it had? *Was* the Jamieson letter as weighty a matter as Van Buren wanted the jury to think? Having put these questions to himself, Henry acknowledged how unsure he was of the answers. A long look at the jury persuaded him their condition was similar.

In the meantime the Chief Justice had adjourned his court—until Monday, a four-day holiday because he threw in Friday as his gift. And then with a broad wink, with a sly finger to the side of his nose, said, "Merry Christmas to all, and to all a good afternoon."

Appreciative laughter, particularly from Henry and the other ink-stained wretches, since most of them had spotted old Clem Moore, creator of Donner, Blitzen, et al., when he slipped in to join the standees in the back of the room.

Catherine's Diary

I suppose I may live through a worse Christmas Eve, but it's hard to imagine what form it might take. And yet this horror began quietly enough, even pleasantly.

All day I was cheered by a steady stream of visitors, culminating in the Willises. (A lavish and lovely bottle of scent from Caroline. She does have exquisite taste. From N.P. an inscribed copy of "my latest little collection.")

The Willises arrived just as Serena was gathering her things to leave. They begged her to stay for a Christmas Eve toddy. So she did. Toddy in hand, N.P. then treated us to readings from "my latest little collection"—at length; merciful heaven! After which he improvised a half-funny, half-bitter disquisition on Mrs. Underwood and the rest of the Downstairs Guerillas—his label for the battalion of servants Van Buren has enlisted in Edwin's behalf. (Oh, God, Mrs. Underwood was bad enough yesterday, but worse, we agreed, is still to come. Is it that they do not understand the meaning of betrayal? Or is it just that they define it in different terms?)

Of Mrs. Flowers, whom we expect on Monday, N.P. said,

"Flowers she may be, but I would not send her to a dying enemy."

Speaking of enemies, N.P. suddenly informed us that he and Van Buren have a certain history: classmates at Yale. "If I was not the first man in my year, then he was. But we were scarcely David and Jonathan."

"Rivals, my dearest, but not enemies," Caroline said, tremulous at the thought. "No one who knows you could be truly your enemy."

I looked—and N.P. looked—to see if there was irony in this. We should have known better. Irony, to Caroline, is a country beyond Africa. She would never visit there and thus was sincerity itself.

N.P. cleared his throat and said, dryly, "Well, we were at least friendly enemies." Glancing at Serena and inviting her to appreciate his way with a line. She seemed unmoved.

Poor N.P. He is looking rather unlike himself these days, the weight he has gained. Chubbiness doesn't suit his kind of handsomeness. At forty-six he is having to work harder at breaking hearts than in his famous heyday. He once explained his secret to me: "I have fair, wavy hair, a good, clear skin, and a sure grasp of what makes a particular furbelo fashionable. *Les petits soins,* Catherine, *ma chère.* The *little* cares. I address myself to them assiduously."

But Serena's heart seems safe from him.

And so in the midst of all this innocuous wassailing there comes a banging at the door and before anyone can go to it, it's flung open by the banger: Edwin, of course. Hulking there like some creature out of a Norse myth. Lowering at us, taking us all in, frightening us to death with that sense he generates of barely suppressed rage. "Get your coat," he growled at me.

"Edwin, please."

"Now!"

Serena, bless her, the one among us not cowed, moved in front of me, my shield. "She goes nowhere."

"Now, Catherine, or must I break all their heads, starting with his." A nod toward N.P., who, while not exactly *cowering* behind the Christmas tree was unconvincingly pretending to bedeck it with an ornament.

"Let it be," I whispered to Serena. "He won't hurt me, and it really is best to do as he says."

Her eyes glittered. "It is *not* best to—"

But my hand on her mouth stifled the rest of it. And since, at that moment, Caroline fainted, Serena was effectively sidetracked.

While Serena and N.P. went to help Caroline, I hurried to the closet for coat and hood. Edwin waited—fingers drumming on the door—while I dressed. He jerked me unceremoniously outside. He slammed the door. He dragged me down the walk and onto the street. The snow, which had begun just half an hour before, was now swirling furiously and showing every sign of sticking. It was cold. And slippery. And my lightweight drawing-room pumps were overmatched on all counts. Edwin of course took no notice.

For the next ten minutes he hauled me up and down the street, saying practically nothing. Assorted grunts and snarls. Once N.P.'s name came clear with something unprintable attached. Once George Jamieson's. And once O'Conor's. Up the street, down the street—about thirty paces either way—to the accompaniment of his tireless, tiresome cantata in G (G for guttural).

Until for the sixth time we were about to cross the plane of my door. Then he stopped me. His fingers gripped my arms tightly enough to force a cry from me. He bent his head so that his eyes were barely inches from mine. He said, "Why don't you die, Catherine?"

And I must tell you, diary, I was almost frightened enough to do exactly that. And then the door opened, Serena emerging sans anything at all in the way of outer garments. But in her hand a carving knife!

Hurrying down the walk with it. No question in my mind but that she would use it if he forced her to. Nor in Edwin's. He released me and backed away, an odd, shame-faced, small-boy's grin suddenly appearing.

By the time Serena reached us he had removed himself ten paces. She put one arm about my shoulders but the other arm, the knife arm, remained aloft and brandishing until it was clear that Edwin was slinking off.

She got me in the house. They all fussed over me and insisted on putting me to bed.

Caroline wanted to send for O'Conor—instinctive with her these days because he terrifies her, and so she thinks he is God.

But I said I wanted them all sworn to secrecy. I wanted none of what had happened to turn up in court.

"Why on earth not?" Serena demanded, green eyes at their most disapproving.

"I have no idea," I said. And didn't. And don't. Right now, having inscribed all this and made it fresh again, I could cheerfully strangle Edwin Forrest. But there were moments during our ludicrous up-and-down parade when I wanted to clutch that large and foolish head of his, hold it against my breast as in the old days, and say, "Hush, love. Let Katten make it better."

Oh, God, are not women absurd?

Serena's Idea

*H*enry sat in the family pew at St. Justin's listening to his father's sermon. Traditionally, the Reverend Dr. Stewart preached to children on Christmas Day, and since he loved children and was sensitive to them, his Christmas sermons were invariably entertaining.

Again and again this one made the children laugh. It made Henry laugh as well, a circumstance so pleasing to his mother that he felt a twinge of guilt. He sighed. Guilt was foolish. Henry knew how hard he tried to keep the family peace. By and large his father tried hard, too. But they came at everything from such divergent perspectives—politics, religion (Henry had turned agnostic in his teens), even the proper claret to bring up for this or that family occasion.

Still, over the years, father and son had become reasonably adept at managing their tricky patches. Except for Bennett. To the older Stewart, Bennett was the radical idea personified, a battering ram aimed at Property and Privilege, at the status quo itself. Bennett. Say the name, and Henry's father heard wooden carts clattering toward the guillotine. For Henry to be Bennett's right hand amounted to a betrayal so enormous that only his mother's vigilance prevented a permanent rupture.

And if *his* father was fixated on the subject, Serena's was even more so. It was that father who had taken a cane to Henry in City Hall Park the previous summer for merely printing the Blaylock name in the *Herald,* listing it there with infinite propriety, Henry had thought, among the fifty backers of the Academy concert season.

Well, all of that mattered surprisingly little today, he decided. He felt relaxed, replete with seasonal peace. Sermon over, the children raced for the back porch of the chapel and the giant tree erected there, hung with ribbons, lanterns, candy, and toys. Henry followed. He listened to the carols for a while, then whispered to his mother that he must be leaving.

She smiled at him. And because her smile, usually so full, was today a shade less than that, it seemed to him he saw signs of aging. She was sixty, tall and slender. Henry got his length from her, and both could eat apples off the head of the Reverend Stewart. (Henry grinned at the image.) She had also passed on her coloring, except that her hair was a darker red. It was in fact almost auburn, not unlike Serena's, he suddenly thought. In her youth she'd been a great beauty, everyone said. She had not passed any of that on to him.

Putting his arms around her, he hugged her hard, harder than he'd intended. As ever, she understood instantly.

"I'm only tired," she said. "Nothing to worry about, Henry dear, really. It's just all this Christmas. A good night's sleep, and I'll be myself again."

"See that you are."

"Will we have you with us for Sunday dinner?"

"Are you promising smoked oysters?"

"I will speak to Maria."

"Then I am yours."

"Good," she said and then seemed to hang fire for a moment. "Henry, we could have dinner guests. It's up to you."

"What is?"

She met his gaze directly. "The Blaylocks?"

"No, thank you."

Again she hesitated. "You know I've never been much for matchmaking. I've always felt that sort of thing to be an imposition of one's own tastes and standards where someone else's are obviously more to the point. You'll grant me that? Self-restraint, I mean."

"Of course."

"What I'm trying to say, I suppose, is that we all miss Mary a great deal, but I think it might be time. . . . Henry, Serena Blaylock is a most attractive young woman. Why don't you like her?"

"She doesn't like me."

"She seems to. Her interest seems—"

"Her interest, dear Mother, if interest there be, is in my scalp. And I have no interest in parting with that. Like all pretty young women she is nine-tenths huntress."

She smiled. "I was a pretty young woman once."

He kissed her cheek. "And probably as merciless as any." He checked his pocket watch. "I'm off," he said.

"Where to in such a hurry on Christmas Day?"

"My secret." He turned her and moved her gently toward the shelter of the chapel. "Inside with you now. If you catch cold Father will disinherit me, and then I never will be able to marry again." She went obediently.

The day had turned gold and blue. Last night's snow, not yet ready to transmogrify to slush, glistened in the sun, and though the wind was sharp, it was bracing rather than punishing. Delicious, he thought, while hurrying toward Brady's Daguerrean Gallery, which Peter Blaylock would be opening right about now in Henry's behalf. The "secret" was the photo of himself that his mother had finally grown tired of requesting. It would be a belated Christmas present, and he planned to surprise her with it after Sunday's dinner.

Peter Blaylock, six years older than his sister, sometimes fooled casual observers into thinking him her twin: the same green eyes, the same flamboyant hair, the same slenderness of build and erectness of carriage. But their smiles were different. Serena's could challenge or mock the way Peter's could, but his went further. In his there was something reckless, something essentially anarchic. But whether that was key to the man or only a boy's last stand, Henry could never be sure.

Twice, while still an undergraduate, Peter had dropped out of Columbia to tramp a path westward, the second time all the way to Oregon. Two years later, though close to the top of his law school class, he had announced to his father that he had fallen in love with the camera. Shutting Blackstone, he had opened the book of Mathew Brady, content to spend virtually every waking moment as one of the master's overworked and underpaid assistants. Predictably, Blaylock senior had exploded. From a practical standpoint, however, his father knew as well as the rest that Peter, mild of manner and as reassuring as a battlefield nurse, would do as he pleased.

Henry had paid a certain price for being close at hand when Peter did as he pleased: two suspensions from Columbia, the second a near expulsion, and a whole series of less dramatic punishments. But there had been rewards as well. In a good many important respects, Peter—adventurer, philosopher, sexual pacesetter—had been for Henry, and still was, an educational beacon.

"Inexcusably late," Peter said, shoving him into a chair.

"I—"

"Do not talk. Breathe as little as possible."

He then proceeded to immobilize Henry by slamming the back of his neck against a half collar of iron and clamping him there. Henry's hands, seeking comfortable resting places, went to his chest. Peter slapped them away. "When you breathe they'll move and blur the image."

"Oh, God."

Peter was unsympathetic. "Think of your mother. Besides, it could be worse. Brady stuffs sunken cheeks with cotton."

"I don't have sunken cheeks."

"But your ears are less flat against your head than they might be."

"Brady has an antidote for that?"

"Adhesive wax."

"Try," Henry said, "and what's left over will be fed to you for your supper."

Using mirrors, shades, and whatnots, Peter immersed himself in the complex game he played with light. Henry, unobtrusively as possible, studied his surroundings. Despite its undeniable clutter—cameras, curtains, tubes of oil colors, stacks of polishing cotton—the large workroom had a special quality to it. He could understand the pull it exerted on Peter. There was an aura, common to all places where mysteries were performed. Not that the room was devilish, which is to say grim or dark. There were skylights everywhere, and the sun's rays sliced in through them like a barrage of blazing arrows.

Henry was attacked by itches.

From under the camera's hood, Peter said, "Don't move, damn you," while removing the lens cap. "If you so much as blink you're a dead man."

Henry obeyed Peter's injunction to think of his mother—the sacrifices she was ever ready to make—and behaved admirably.

"Done, by God," Peter said at last.

"Bravo," said a voice from the room's threshold. Henry looked up: Serena. "Will it be a success?" she asked.

"Given the limitations of the subject," Peter said.

She sighed, then both Blaylocks glanced at Henry: twin grins.

"Snap me out of this thing," Henry said. "It feels like an Iron Maiden."

"Serena, help him. I have to do something magical with mercury vapor."

He hurried off to the darkroom while Serena bent over clamps and buckles. Henry smelled her perfume. It was something flowery, delicate; he was instantly lightheaded. She freed him.

He had to clear his voice. "Thank you," he said.

"You're in my debt twice over now. My memory of the Rimmerhorns is still vivid."

As was his, of course.

"Three's the charm, Henry. Be careful. Heaven alone knows what that might portend."

"How are you, Serena?"

"Splendid on this splendid day."

Which was the way she looked, he thought, abloom with health. Splendidly turned out, too: fur tippet, rich brown woolen coat open on beige brocade, matching bonnet, loosed and back on her head, so that masses of hair could come to glory. He tried not to stare.

"Are you here to be daguerrotyped?" he asked.

"No, I am not. I could say I'm here because Peter and I are driving out to see our Yonkers cousins, and that would be true. But not the whole truth. Because I'm also here to see you."

"To see me?"

"Henry, it's spooney-headed to respond to my sentences by repeating them."

"Forgive me."

"You're forgiven. You may now ask *why* I'm here to see you."

"Why?"

"To fix something up between us. If the weather holds—and I'm quite certain it will—we must go riding Sunday. I have a new habit you will like me in quite as much as you do in this."

She pirouetted and curtseyed low while Henry sputtered something having to do with a program so crammed with activity as to be absolutely beyond altering. Which she overrode.

"The paper is not issued on Sunday, nor is the courtroom open; consequently you're free as a bird. That being the case I'll arrive at your hotel at a quarter past nine. Be waiting. You needn't worry about alerting Gennario's to have horses prepared because I've already done so. Yes, Henry?"

"Nothing."

"Good. That's settled."

"Serena, I don't admire a woman who . . ."

"Go on."

"Nothing."

"Two nothings?"

"We're old friends. I have no wish to offend you."

"By saying what? Oh, let me say it for you. I can say it with more authority, having heard it so often. You don't admire a woman who speaks her mind. In fact, you're not at all certain a woman ought to have a mind, it being of so little practical value. Isn't that true?"

"No, it's not true."

"Of course it is. 'Be good, sweet maid, and let who will be clever.' I heard that first from my Aunt Emma. Then from a succession of governesses. And teachers. And from Papa. From Papa so many times I can describe for you with perfect accuracy the way his mouth forms each beloved syllable."

Peter materialized. Crossing to him, she took his arm.

"Nine-fifteen. Be prompt," she said to Henry. As he always did when Henry was discomfited, Peter grinned.

"I leave you the kingdom, lad," he said. "Tell Mr. Brady—" He broke off suddenly and bowed.

Turning, Henry saw Brady emerge from his office. But Brady was not looking at Peter. It was Serena he watched—judgmentally. He pursed his lips and rocked back and forth on his undersized patent leathers, while slapping little lilac gloves against a small bare palm. When the Blaylocks had gone he produced a thoughtful whistle.

"Do you know her well, Stewart?"

"Well enough."

"I shall have to daguerreotype her. When she came in I

thought her merely attractive. I now know her to be the most beautiful woman in New York. How do you explain such a transformation?"

"Easily. She's a witch."

At various times during Saturday night, Henry decided to flee or to be ill or to confront Serena staunchly and make her understand—in calm, measured, but impossible-to-ignore terms—that he resented her behavior toward him. Moreover, that he was not deluded by it. Let the huntress devote her redoubtable skill to the capture of some other scalp, one more calculated to spark envy in the trophy room.

He also decided, at intervals, that the whole thing was farce: she would not and had never meant to appear.

What with one decision or another he spent a largely sleepless night. But at thirteen minutes after nine the following morning (even bluer and more golden than the one preceding), when the knock came at the door and the houseboy told him of a young lady in a brougham, Henry dutifully went down, climbed in next to her, and sat sullenly silent during most of the twenty-minute ride to Gennario's.

Serena was silent too; not sullen, though. She was amused. Just before they arrived she tapped his cheek with a gloved finger. "Now enough of this. Look at me."

Her face was bright, her promised new habit green, her eyes a darker green.

"Yes," she said. "And the day is lovely, too."

At Gennario's their horses were brought to them, both mares, both still young enough to be spirited. Serena issued further commands. They were to take their mounts aboard the ferry to Hoboken and from there go forth along the Hudson cliffs.

Traffic was sparse: one or two carriages, a dray, a dozen or so dismounted riders. Inevitably, the ferryboat captain was smitten. When he dies, Henry thought, he will bequeath Serena his craft.

They debarked. A good hard ride, and suddenly Henry was enjoying himself. Every now and again—her hair flying, crop joyously awave—she glanced back at him as if to say, See how sweet life becomes for those who allow themselves to be guided by me?

Finally she signaled a rest. Henry pulled up next to her. Their path was about a hundred feet or so above the river, and when they looked down they could sight along the broad, silvery avenue it made leading to the Narrows. New York was vivid and distinct on the opposite shore, glittering like a heap of toys in the sunny distance. Toward Sandy Hook the water was studded with sails, and far up on the other side the river rolled away along shores that, even in a wintry time of bare trees and barren earth, looked warm and trouble-free in the sunshine.

"How wonderful it all is," Serena said. "No harsh words from you today about our city. Our city does itself proud."

They tethered the horses and made off along a little trail running perpendicular to the bridle path. It led, after twenty yards or so, to a wide flat rock, shaped curiously like the swayback of a horse. Serena mounted and patted a place next to her. For a while they were silent. Her eyes were on a gleaming sail as it hove into view around a bend in the river. His were on the line of her throat.

"Henry . . ."

"Yes?"

"Just Henry." But an instant later she said, "Henry, do I frighten you?"

"No." After a moment he added, "Though you are sometimes unsettling."

"That's because I'm more direct than the women you're used to, the Parisian in me. But you'd never believe I was wicked, would you?"

"Certainly not."

She turned to study him. "Then I think in this lovely place on this lovely day you should kiss me."

He thought it probable she could hear the pounding of his heart.

"Henry, has no woman ever asked you to kiss her before?"

"No respectable woman."

He wanted the words back, of course. They expressed the literal truth, but they were such clumsy words. They were the kind on which he had built a dismal reputation. Serena's expression remained intact, but he knew that had cost her something.

"You are not gallant," she said.

"I meant—"

"No, no. Pray, let's talk of something more . . . consequential."

"Serena—"

"Bennett. Let's talk of him. I despise him, you know," she said, hurrying past all attempts to interrupt. "I find him crude as well as arrogant. Often insufferable. Why do we view him so differently?"

Reluctantly, he yielded to her. "Not so differently," he said. "He *is* crude, arrogant, and often insufferable. But he's also the first man in his field. Before him there *was* no journalism. There was some pamphleteering, some political hackery, some long-winded sermonizing, but until Bennett there was nothing that made its mission the daily attempt to record our time: news. Cost what it will to get it."

"News. Of murders and robberies, every lurid detail of a divorce case. Is that what you mean by news? Taking a fine, sensitive woman like Catherine Forrest and throwing her to the wolves; how can you justify that? Do you know that crowds gather outside her house daily: gawkers, ghouls? When she ventures out—which is seldom—they follow wherever she goes. Still, she refuses to blame you for anything."

"Blame *me*?"

"She actually defends you. It's your master she blames. Bennett, 'The People's Watchdog.' "

"Like it or not, he's earned the title."

"Aren't women people? He's been horrible not only to Catherine but to a long list. He said, instead of delivering babies, Dr. Elizabeth Blackwell ought to stay home and let some man give her some."

"And yet every time there's a temperance meeting or a women's rights meeting, only the *Herald* reports it in depth. So there's something owed him."

"Oh, yes, he reports it. Atrociously. He said that of the eight hundred who attended the Women's Rights Convention in Hamilton last month, six hundred were overfed and undercorseted."

"He did not say that."

"He did. Catherine gave me the clipping to burn."

Henry's mouth was dry. "I said it."

She stared at him.

"At the time it struck me as . . ."

"Amusing?"

"As not far from the truth."

"Did it? And when next the New York State legislature convenes in all its majesty will you report to your readers that a goodly number of those august solons are disgustingly drunk, day in, day out, and that an almost equal number can only be stood upwind of, since the ritual of bathing—but why go on? We both know what's at work here."

"Serena . . ."

She rose, her face pale except for red splashes in each of her cheeks. She hurried down the path.

"Serena, wait."

She stopped. "A serious woman is anathema to you. A woman of flesh and blood, an honest woman who speaks her feelings. . . . 'Pon my soul, Henry Stewart, 'tis plain I have bitten off more than I can chew."

And she was gone again.

By the time he reached the place where they had left their horses only one of them remained. Unaided, she had somehow mounted hers and was away. Henry hurried to catch up and did, finally, just before they reached the ferry.

"Serena, please look at me. How can I talk to you if you won't look at me?"

She was stone.

Silence during the wait for the ferry.

Silence during the crossing.

At first this was pure agony for him, but soon his own surging anger leavened the effect. Very well, then, let her *have* her heart's desire. The confounded expedition had certainly not been his idea. *Let* it end absurdly.

The ferry made fast, she galloped off instantly. He followed at a more deliberate pace, across Washington Street, Greenwich Street, Hudson Street, into St. John's Park, and there the green habit and bright hair swept around a bend in the narrow path and were lost to him.

But he was denied the luxury of yearning after her. A twig cracked behind him, and before he turned he knew what he would find: a white-hooded company, mounted, coming toward him at a confident canter.

Henry swore at himself for criminal spooney-headedness. This was *their* park, their base of operations. Dawdling about in it had been nothing less than an open invitation.

From among the four Henry easily picked out Buntline—that poisonous little package—bouncing on his horse like some demented cavalry imp.

"Got you, Stewart." The voice was thin but rich in venom. "Gonna cut your dingus off and give it to Forrest for his Christmas tree."

Henry kept his own mouth shut, not wishing to provide encouragement.

They needed none. Without further ado they were on him, and though he twisted and turned furiously, giving them as difficult a target as possible, their heavy canes were doing brisk business. But not around the head. He judged from this that murder was more than they had in mind. Or less, he thought, as a savage thrust narrowly missed his privates.

It was then the Valkyrian onslaught descended.

"Beasts, cowards!"

Charging Buntline, and at such a pace it was clear she meant to ride him down. Nor was Buntline's escape route obvious. On first hearing her, he had made the mistake of swinging her way. Now it was too late—and the path too narrow—for him to swing back fast enough.

"Stop!" he screamed. "Bitch, you'll kill us both!"

The possibility had also occurred to Henry. He grabbed a cane from one of his mesmerized assailants. A solid whack across Buntline's shoulders, and the little villain was unhorsed. But an instant later Serena was too, her seat loosened as the animals collided. Still, with Buntline's body out of the way, the collision was less jarring than it might have been.

Or so Henry thought in that initial moment. When he reached her, however, and saw the cut on her forehead, the eye already discoloring, no discernable movement of her chest, he became terrified. He looked around for help. Buntline, mixing curses with groans, had remounted.

"Have the decency to find a carriage for us. The lady is—"

"Fuck her."

And rode after his cronies.

When Henry turned back to Serena he saw that a miracle had taken place. She was stirring. Her eyes had fluttered open. They focused on him.

"Three's the charm," she said and fainted again.

"These your horses, mister?"

A gap-toothed genie: George Dempsey, he turned out to be. Age ten, owner of a dog named Moses, desirous of one day joining Hook and Ladder Company Number Three, corner of Hudson and Christopher streets, which he had been approaching when he saw the pair of riderless horses, he told Henry without pausing for breath. But young George was far from all talk. Yes, he'd be pleased to find a hackney for them, and for two dollars he'd contract to return their horses to Gennario's. Gratefully, Henry gave him five.

In the cab Serena recovered consciousness and managed to say, *"J'ai une tête très grande,"* before shutting her eyes again.

Downstairs Guerillas II

*H*eadlines from the *Herald*:

Fire breaks out in Library of Congress.

Glorious post-Christmas news for the ladies: rich and useful gifts at marvelous prices.

Drive mounted to benefit suffering Hungarians.

Proceedings against three who helped slave name of Edward escape.

Fatal accident on Hudson River Railway: drunken laborer falls off train.

The Phrenological Cabinet (131 Nassau Street) invites the public to view its stock of skulls, casts of the most distinguished knaves who ever lived.

Dastardly attack on *Herald*'s managing editor (vivid account written by the newspaper's publisher).

Forrest trial resumes.

★   ★   ★

To Henry, the Chief Justice looked rosier for his Christmas holiday, trading small but learned jokes with counsel while waiting for
the clerk to get his list of witnesses in order.

The lawyers themselves appeared little changed—smiles for the
Chief Justice, wariness for each other. Forrest's scowl was as black
as ever. Mrs. Willis clutched Mrs. Forrest's hand with undimin-
ished intensity. That lady sat very still. Easy to feel she could be
lifted bodily from the courtroom and placed on the prow of a
ship.

Flanking her on the right was Miss Serena Blaylock. The
forehead cut and the bruise around her eye had yielded something
to healing and much to cosmetics. Did she have two eyes? Henry
could not have sworn to it, since she was resolute in keeping her
profile to him. Did she have a voice? Evidence, while slight,
indicated that she did.

"Serena, I would like to—"

Distantly: "Later. Please."

As he retreated he thought he saw sympathy in the brief glance
he got from Catherine Forrest.

The clerk called Robert Garvin.

Robert Garvin, thin, nervously quick, prematurely bald, was
sworn and examined by Mr. Van Buren.

GARVIN. I reside at 166 Hamilton Street. I came from Ireland
in June '43. I went to live with Mr. and Mrs. Edwin Forrest
shortly after I came here, employed as a waiter. I stayed at
Twenty-second Street until I was told by Mr. Forrest they was
breaking up housekeeping.

VAN BUREN. Do you know of a Captain Calcraft coming to
visit the house while Mr. Forrest was away?

GARVIN. Yes, sir.

VAN BUREN. Very good. I have in mind the library of that
house. State anything you can remember in reference to Captain
Calcraft and Mrs. Forrest being there together.

GARVIN. They was often there, sir. I went in once, and they
was keeping company.

VAN BUREN. Keeping company?

GARVIN. Sitting together, very close, on the sofa.

VAN BUREN. I see. And when you went in there did you bring anything with you?

GARVIN. I brought some whisky. Later I brought some wine.

VAN BUREN. Tell me, Mr. Garvin, as the day wore on did you notice a change in Mrs. Forrest's customary behavior?

GARVIN. I did, sir. When they came from the library to dinner they both seemed the worse for drink.

O'CONOR. Object. Is the witness, by his own mode of behavior, qualified to give an expert opinion? *(laughter)*

CHIEF JUSTICE *(first post-Christmas gavel rap).* I shall have to overrule you, Mr. O'Conor. It's my observation that in New York City in the year of our Lord eighteen hundred and fifty-one drunkenness occurs often enough as to require little expertise in order to be identified. You may proceed, Mr. Van Buren.

VAN BUREN. Thank you, your honor. Mr. Garvin, what led you to believe they were the worse for drink?

GARVIN. I consider Mrs. Forrest a nice carver generally, sir. But there was a chicken on the table, and she could scarcely strike it with her knife. That, and they was both having trouble with their speech. Slurring. And giggling a lot, you know.

VAN BUREN. Who else was at the dinner table?

GARVIN. Nobody. They were seated there at the head, just them.

VAN BUREN. So you served them their meal, and then what?

GARVIN. I left.

VAN BUREN. What about the gas?

GARVIN. That's right, I asked Mrs. Forrest should I light the gas, or rather I was going to light it as I usually did for dinner, but she said I needn't.

VAN BUREN. Does that mean the room was in darkness?

GARVIN. One candle. You could hardly see your hand in front of your face.

VAN BUREN. After you left the dining room where did you go?

GARVIN. To the kitchen. But later I returned to the dining room, thinking I might light the gas for them.

VAN BUREN. And did you?

GARVIN. No, sir.

VAN BUREN. Why not?

GARVIN. The door was fastened.

VAN BUREN. What did you do?

GARVIN. I lighted the gas in the hall. Then I entered the dining room by the pantry door.

VAN BUREN. And were they still there, Captain Calcraft and Mrs. Forrest?

GARVIN. Yes, sir.

VAN BUREN. Tell us what you saw, Mr. Garvin.

GARVIN. Mrs. Forrest was sitting on Captain Calcraft's knee with one arm on his shoulder and the other across his breast.

VAN BUREN. What was the condition of her dress?

GARVIN. Its bodice was unfastened. *(gasps from the spectators)*

VAN BUREN. What happened next?

GARVIN. Mrs. Forrest reproved me for not knocking at the door when entering. She said I was to be more careful in future. Then she told me I could go to bed, and she and Captain Calcraft went back to the library.

VAN BUREN. Do you have any idea how late Captain Calcraft stayed that night?

GARVIN. No, sir.

VAN BUREN. Now tell us, Mr. Garvin, if you were witness to any of the comings and goings of Mr. N. P. Willis.

GARVIN. Yes, sir. He was there frequently.

VAN BUREN. Accompanied by Mrs. Willis?

GARVIN. Sometimes, sometimes not.

VAN BUREN. When he came without Mrs. Willis, where did he and Mrs. Forrest customarily keep company?

O'CONOR. Object.

VAN BUREN. Visit.

GARVIN. Usually in the library, sir.

VAN BUREN. Did you ever see them there together?

GARVIN. Yes, sir.

VAN BUREN. Tell us, Mr. Garvin.

GARVIN. I was on the back piazza, watering some of the boxed flowers. All the blinds were down, except for one. I happened to be passing there and looked in, and there they were.

VAN BUREN. There they were . . . how?

GARVIN. On the sofa.

VAN BUREN. In what condition?

GARVIN. Lying on each other, is what I'd call it.

VAN BUREN. And how long would you say they remained that way?

GARVIN. About a half hour to an hour.

VAN BUREN. Did you happen to go into the room afterward?

GARVIN. Yes, sir. And I found some hairpins and an elastic garter.

VAN BUREN. Hairpins and a garter.

GARVIN. Hairpins and an elastic garter, sir. I showed them to Annie O'Brien, the cook. And they had not been there when I dusted up the room earlier in the day.

VAN BUREN. One last question, Mr. Garvin. How would you describe Mr. Forrest's deportment about the house? I mean by that, would you say he was a particularly irascible . . . a particularly bad-tempered man?

GARVIN. No, sir. Always gentlemanly.

VAN BUREN. Your witness, Mr. O'Conor.

O'CONOR (*obligatory five seconds of communion*). Robert, let me take you back to the night of the infamous dinner shared by Captain Calcraft and Mrs. Forrest. Are you with me?

GARVIN. Yes, sir.

O'CONOR. In reference to the condition of Mrs. Forrest's dress I believe you said, "Its bodice was unfastened." Is that correct?

GARVIN. Yes, sir.

O'CONOR. Robert, is the dining room in the Forrest house a smallish room?

GARVIN. Smallish? No, sir.

O'CONOR. How large, can you say?

GARVIN. No, sir.

O'CONOR. Well, I can. I measured it. Would it surprise you to learn that from the pantry entrance to the head of the table, point to point, the distance is no less than forty feet?

GARVIN. If you say so, sir.

O'CONOR. But isn't that interesting, Robert?

GARVIN. I don't follow you, sir.

O'CONOR. You said the room was in darkness, one candle only; you could hardly see your hand in front of your face. But forty feet away you could see the condition of Mrs. Forrest's dress?

GARVIN. Well, I could.

O'CONOR. Let's move to your equally interesting testimony concerning Mr. Willis. I see you on the piazza, Robert. There you are with your hose, watering those delightful boxed flowers. What time of day is it?

GARVIN. Between ten and noon, as I recollect.

O'CONOR. Between ten and noon. You are a marvel of precision, Robert. How many windows in the library?

GARVIN. Four.

O'CONOR. There are five. But never mind. Let us see if we can place the sofa correctly. Where is it? Next to the door as one enters the room?

GARVIN. No, sir.

O'CONOR. Then where?

GARVIN. Between the end of the fireplace and the side wall.

O'CONOR. Suppose I were to tell you you are wrong again. Suppose I were to say the sofa is actually on the same side of the house as the windows and thus impossible to see unless one poked one's head into the room. What would you say to that?

GARVIN. I'd say it may be there now, but it wasn't that way then. *(laughter)*

O'CONOR. Good point, Robert. Very well, then, you insist

that you had a full view of the sofa and its occupants. Is that correct?

GARVIN. I could see them plain.

O'CONOR. But they could not see you?

GARVIN. I . . .

VAN BUREN *(a shade belatedly)*. Object. Witness is required to testify only to what he himself knows, not—

O'CONOR. Good enough. Good enough, Robert. I accept that. Now how long did you say they remained . . . what was the expression you used? . . . lying on each other? Thirty minutes to an hour?

GARVIN. Yes.

O'CONOR. How do you know?

GARVIN. How do I know? I saw them.

O'CONOR. Through that window?

GARVIN. Yes.

O'CONOR. Then we have our answer, do we not?

GARVIN. What answer?

O'CONOR. They could *not* have seen you. Either that, or they are so debased, so far sunk in depravity it mattered to them not a whit that they were exhibitionists as well as adulterers. Am I making myself clear to you, Robert? I mean, there you were stationed in front of that window for thirty minutes to an hour, but they just—

GARVIN. I wasn't stationed.

O'CONOR. No?

GARVIN. I kept passing back and forth.

O'CONOR. Why?

GARVIN. In the course of doing my work, I had to keep passing back and forth.

O'CONOR. Back and forth, back and forth, back and forth, crisscrossing that one window?

GARVIN. Yes.

O'CONOR. How many times?

GARVIN. I can't recollect exactly.

O'CONOR. Exactly? Did I say anything about exactly? I would never say anything to you about exactly. Just guess, Robert. Six times? Three times? None?

GARVIN. Six times.

O'CONOR. You passed that window six times, and each time you passed they were still in that same position?

GARVIN. Yes.

O'CONOR. They never moved?

GARVIN. I didn't say they never moved. They—

O'CONOR. They did move?

GARVIN. Yes.

O'CONOR. A great deal?

GARVIN. No.

O'CONOR. Just enough to convince you they were alive.

GARVIN. Yes.

O'CONOR. But not enough to stop . . . what was that expression you used? . . . not enough to stop lying on each other?

GARVIN. No.

O'CONOR. And this lasted thirty minutes to an hour?

GARVIN. Yes.

O'CONOR. Most impressive. *(rowdy, braying laughter)*

VAN BUREN. Object. Let my learned friend keep his salacious—

O'CONOR. No more questions, your honor.

The clerk called Anna Flowers: middle twenties, a shade worn at the edges, but undeniably pretty. A few deep breaths were taken as bodies stirred and shifted about for improved perspectives. This was testimony all had been waiting for. Henry watched intently as, straight-backed and purposeful, she marched to the witness stand. The hubbub mounted, requiring the Chief Justice's gavel to quell it.

Mrs. Flowers was sworn and examined by Mr. Van Buren.

MRS. FLOWERS. I live in New Orleans. My husband's name is George W. Flowers. He is an inspector of pork and beef. My family at home is composed of three children and a niece of Mr. Flowers's. I am stopping at the Florence Hotel. In 1844 I went into service with Mr. and Mrs. Forrest as a chambermaid. This was in Twenty-second Street.

VAN BUREN. What gentlemen were in the habit of visiting the house while you were there?

MRS. FLOWERS. Mr. N. P. Willis, Captain Calcraft, and Mr. George Jamieson.

VAN BUREN. State, if you will, anything of a remarkable nature that you saw occurring between Mr. Willis and Mrs. Forrest.

O'CONOR. Object.

CHIEF JUSTICE. You will have to be more specific, Mr. Van Buren.

VAN BUREN. I should have thought by now the context was clear enough, your honor.

CHIEF JUSTICE. Nevertheless.

VAN BUREN. Mrs. Flowers, did you ever come upon Mr. Willis and Mrs. Forrest tête-à-tête?

MRS. FLOWERS. Pardon, sir?

VAN BUREN. Alone together.

MRS. FLOWERS. Yes, sir. Often.

VAN BUREN. Do you recollect Mr. Willis on one occasion calling on Mrs. Forrest before she was dressed?

MRS. FLOWERS. Yes, sir.

VAN BUREN. Tell us about that.

MRS. FLOWERS. It was seven-thirty in the morning. I know 'cause I was setting the breakfast table things, which I always done at seven-thirty. Mr. Forrest was away. When Mr. Willis came to the door I put him in the library. Then I told Mrs. Forrest he was here. She told me to leave her, that she would dress herself.

VAN BUREN. Did you see them together that day?

MRS. FLOWERS. No, sir.

VAN BUREN. Did you see Mr. Willis leave?

MRS. FLOWERS. Yes, sir. It was about four-thirty in the afternoon.

VAN BUREN. And do you remember another morning on which Mr. Willis came to call early?

MRS. FLOWERS. Yes, sir.

VAN BUREN. What happened?

MRS. FLOWERS. Mr. Forrest had come home unexpectedly the night before, and when I told this to Mr. Willis he turned right around and went away.

VAN BUREN. What else can you tell us about the behavior of Mr. Willis to Mrs. Forrest that took you rather by surprise?

MRS. FLOWERS. I saw them kissing once. I came into the drawing room, and there was Mr. Willis with his arm around her neck, and he was kissing her fit to be tied.

Laughter. Gavel. But O'Conor did not even lift his head. Catherine Forrest, too, remained unresponsive. Mrs. Willis, however, underwent a quiver or so until calmed by Serena, reaching over. A witch, a warrior, and now a nurse, Henry thought. Was there no end to her capabilities?

VAN BUREN. To your knowledge, did Captain Calcraft ever stay the night at the Forrest house?

MRS. FLOWERS. Yes, sir. She put him in the spare bedroom next to mine. About midnight I was awakened by the sound of laughing and talking in the corridor, and then Mrs. Forrest came into my room. She was in her nightclothes. She called my name. "Anna," she called, but I didn't answer.

VAN BUREN. Why not?

MRS. FLOWERS. I didn't want her to think I'd been listening. She used to accuse Robert Garvin of listening all the time, and I didn't want her to think the same of me.

VAN BUREN. So you said nothing.

MRS. FLOWERS. Yes.

VAN BUREN. And then what did she do?

MRS. FLOWERS. She went out again into the corridor.

VAN BUREN. And returned to her own room?

MRS. FLOWERS. That's what I thought at the time.

VAN BUREN. But it was not the case?

MRS. FLOWERS. No, sir.

VAN BUREN. How do you know?

MRS. FLOWERS. Well, I couldn't get back to sleep, so for a long time I just lay there tossing and turning. And then finally I got out of bed to go to the. . . . *(laughter)* Well, anyway, I took the lamp that was over the hearth and got out of bed. I went into the corridor. I saw the door to the spare bedroom open a crack, but at first I thought no one was there.

VAN BUREN. You were wrong?

MRS. FLOWERS. Yes, sir.

VAN BUREN. Who was there?

MRS. FLOWERS. They was. Mrs. Forrest and Captain Calcraft. I pushed open the door and saw them. I mean I saw this door open a crack, so without thinking I pushed it wide, and there they were. In bed. Both in the same bed.

VAN BUREN. How would you describe—

CHIEF JUSTICE. Mr. Van Buren, is it truly necessary to concern ourselves with particulars?

VAN BUREN. Does the court think not?

CHIEF JUSTICE. I do indeed think not.

VAN BUREN. Very well, then, Mrs. Flowers, just tell me what you said when you came upon them.

MRS. FLOWERS. I called Mrs. Forrest by name.

VAN BUREN. And did she answer?

MRS. FLOWERS. No, sir.

VAN BUREN. But she must have seen you.

MRS. FLOWERS. Oh, yes, sir. We was looking at each other, separated by no more than ten feet. I started to cry. And then I ran from the room.

VAN BUREN. You started to cry?

MRS. FLOWERS. This was seven years ago, sir. I was only fifteen.

VAN BUREN. Did Mrs. Forrest follow you?

MRS. FLOWERS. Yes, sir, but not right away. After about twenty minutes, maybe half an hour.

VAN BUREN. What did she say?

MRS. FLOWERS. Well, when I saw her I started to cry again, and she told me not to. She was still in her nightclothes, and she got into bed with me and hugged me and told me I mustn't cry. She told me she only went in there to see if there were sheets on the bed.

VAN BUREN. What was that?

MRS. FLOWERS. Sheets on the bed, sir.

VAN BUREN. And if there were none, presumably she meant to rectify that condition. The following morning, did you take a look at the spare room as you went by?

MRS. FLOWERS. Yes, sir. There was naught but a blanket. Two pillows without cases and a blanket.

VAN BUREN. Did you see Mrs. Forrest the following morning?

MRS. FLOWERS. Yes, sir. She came down very early. I was still setting the breakfast table when she came down to tell me to take Captain Calcraft a comb and brush and one of Mr. Forrest's shirts. I did so and then came back downstairs to the dining room.

VAN BUREN. She was still there?

MRS. FLOWERS. Oh, yes, sir. She was waiting for me.

VAN BUREN. What did she say to you?

MRS. FLOWERS. She said, "Anna, haven't I always treated you more as a friend than a servant?" And I said, "Yes, ma'am." And she said, "Friends don't tell tales on each other, do they?" And I said, "No, ma'am." And I never meant to. Even though when I left her employ all she give me was thirty dollars and some clothes for the baby.

VAN BUREN. How long after this . . . incident did you stay with the Forrests?

MRS. FLOWERS. Until the following April. That would be 1845. Until they left on their trip to England.

VAN BUREN. Between that time in the dining room and the time she left for England, did you ever mention that incident to Mrs. Forrest again?

MRS. FLOWERS. No, sir.

VAN BUREN. And after she returned?

MRS. FLOWERS. Just once, sir.

VAN BUREN. When and where was that?

MRS. FLOWERS. In the Saint Charles Hotel in New Orleans. That was in 1848. I was already married to Mr. Flowers by then and living in New Orleans, and Mr. Forrest was appearing in the theater there.

VAN BUREN. So when you learned that you went to see Mrs. Forrest.

MRS. FLOWERS. Yes, sir.

VAN BUREN. Any particular reason?

MRS. FLOWERS. Just for old time's sake. Just to say hello and give her my best regards.

VAN BUREN. But it did not turn out as pleasantly as you had hoped.

MRS. FLOWERS. No, sir. We had an argument. She said I'd made a great deal of talk about her in her absence. Which was not true at all, and it made all my good feelings about her go away. It made me very angry. So I told her then she was the cause of my ruin, and that in addition she'd broke her promise to me.

VAN BUREN. Which promise was that?

MRS. FLOWERS. Before she went away to England she told me she had told Miss Margaret—Mrs. Voorhies, I mean—to provide everything for me, and she hadn't done so. And as a consequence my baby was in want.

VAN BUREN. What did she say to that?

MRS. FLOWERS. She told me not to be so passionate, to lower my voice. She said the whole hotel could hear me. I said if my baby was in want it made no matter to me if the whole world heard. And then I told her I would go to see Mr. Forrest.

VAN BUREN. Mr. Forrest? Why?

MRS. FLOWERS. To ask him if he'd do something in behalf of my child.

VAN BUREN. What did she say to that?

MRS. FLOWERS. She said, "For God's sake, Anna, don't you do it. Haven't I always been your friend?" And she tried to hold me there, but I tore away from her and ran out of the hotel.

VAN BUREN. Why did she want to keep you from talking to Mr. Forrest?

O'CONOR. Object. Witness can testify only to—

VAN BUREN. Yes, yes. Did Mrs. Forrest *say* why she did not wish you to speak to Mr. Forrest?

MRS. FLOWERS. She said if you tell one thing he'll make you tell the whole.

VAN BUREN. Mrs. Flowers, do you have any harsh feelings toward Mrs. Forrest today?

MRS. FLOWERS. No, sir. All that was a long time ago, and life has turned out good for me. Me and mine is all right, so I harbor no grudges.

VAN BUREN. Would you tell the court why you are here today?

MRS. FLOWERS. Because Mr. Forrest asked me to come see justice done, and I couldn't refuse him.

VAN BUREN. One final question. Did Mr. Forrest ever give you reason to think him irrational or unbalanced?

MRS. FLOWERS. No, sir.

VAN BUREN. Bad-tempered?

MRS. FLOWERS. Never, sir. He was good as gold.

VAN BUREN. Thank you, Mrs. Flowers. Your witness, Mr. O'Conor.

But O'Conor seemed in no hurry to take her, and when he did finally rise, the Chief Justice motioned him down again, announcing that considerations having nothing to do with the trial itself made it sensible to curtail proceedings for the day. He did not explain what those considerations were, and Henry watched to see if counsel, too, would find it sensible. Van Buren did, beaming. O'Conor, poker-faced, refrained from argument.

Henry and Raymond found a hack to share. As it got under way, Raymond said, "I think you're growing fond of the lady."

Startled. "Which lady?"

"Mrs. Forrest, of course."

"I've always liked her."

"But I think rather more these days. Partisanship is creeping into your accounts."

"The match of yours, you mean."

Raymond smiled.

"Humbug," Henry said.

But that night, waiting for sleep, which took its customary circuitous route, Henry replayed the conversation. Raymond, he knew, prided himself on the quality of his insights. Consequently, Henry never acknowledged them. But was Raymond right? Had Henry lost objectivity? If so, he knew who had undermined him.

"Blast you, Serena Blaylock!" he shouted, shattering the New York Hotel's 2 A.M. silence. "There was never a day you were the equal of my Mary. Mary was . . . Mary would no more allow—"

But when he managed to conjure up that sweet beloved face, it arrived fuzzily and then fled as if panicked. Vivid was auburn hair instead of blond. Green eyes, not blue. Henry swore at himself.

Catherine's Diary

*S*erena crying in my arms. Only briefly, 'tis true, but oh, with what ferocity. Pulling away, she said, "I'm so ashamed. I keep doing that, bursting into tears like a ninny. My poor father's at wit's end, and what must *you* think of me?"

"What I think of you is well established. What I think of Henry Stewart is I would like to kick him."

"Yes. He deserves it."

"Why do we like him, Serena?" I asked, knowing it was wanted of me.

"You like him too?"

I nodded, and her face lighted with pleasure. When she realized this she snuffed out the blaze. But after a moment she said, "Have I told you how he saved my life?"

"No," I lied, knowing this, too, was wanted.

"A skating accident. I was behaving outrageously, desperate to be noticed by him. I went where I should not have, where he had expressly ordered me not to go."

"He should never have ordered. Not expressly. 'Twas ungallant."

"True. Though the ice *was* thin and the water deep."

"Did he jump in for you when the ice cracked?"

"And got me safe, after which he became so angry. You should have heard him roar."

"Did he kiss you in great relief before beginning to roar?"

"Yes."

"A mitigating circumstance."

"And he is the very soul of honesty. Peter says the most infuriating thing about Henry is his refusal to lie. Even to himself. Peter of course prefers to lie."

"Your brother is charming. All charmers lie."

"Henry isn't charming," she said.

"Agreed."

"And he's a dunce about women. But I think he can be taught. Do you think he can be?"

"All men can be, provided we're stern with them. What you must understand about men is that it's centuries since they've had to learn anything."

When she left a little while later it was with shoulders squared and expression set: Serena prepared for draconian measures. I don't envy you, Henry Stewart. At least not in the short term.

The migraine is better now. It has dwindled to a mild and manageable *thump-thump.* The summers I went on tour with Edwin—when I was not only his costume designer but his booking agent and his theater manager—I never had migraines. Edwin had them. I was too busy for them. Now I travel nowhere without laudanum.

O'Conor was superb with Robert. Battered the little rat into rat flinders. But Anna Flowers is a different sort of customer entirely. Anna is redoubtable. Shameless. Outrageous. I remember the day we caught her with Margaret's purse, caught her *in flagrante,* caught her without the possibility of a single saving lie. About sixteen she was then, I think. She wept, pleaded for forgiveness. Never again would she, et cetera, et cetera. If only she could be given a second chance. And when forgiveness was granted and the purse yielded up to Margaret, it was ten dollars lighter than it should have been.

"Oh, no, ma'am. There was never a tenner. If there'd been a tenner, wouldn't I have seen it?"

Wide-eyed, guileless, presenting us with logic irrefutable and stunned at the obstinacy of our resistance to it. And Margaret dissolved in giggles at the brass of her. And me too—knowing all the time I should be sending her packing.

And when I did not, Edwin said to me genially—he was always genial then—"Has it occurred to you, Catherine, that you might be too permissive with your servants?"

How ironic, in the light of current events.

But when I reported Edwin's comment to Margaret she said, "We treat servants here the way we treated them at home, the way our parents always treated them, as if they had 'hands, organs, dimensions.' Edwin treats them as furniture. And when he occasionally stubs his toe on one of them he will say Hang it or Confound it, but never, I am sorry. I need no lessons on how to treat servants from the likes of Edwin Forrest."

Well, the fact is when Edwin was away the days were often long and empty. And though I felt twinges of guilt about it now and again, I know I used servants to pass the time. Robert was funny. Underwood could keep us in stitches. And Anna was usually involved in something long-term, something nefarious or titillating, the exquisite turns of which Margaret and I would follow with undeniable eagerness.

At any rate, Anna Flowers will test the great O'Conor's mettle tomorrow. Pray he is not overconfident.

Let me at this point inscribe a note from the Hon. Charles which arrived this morning. And shall I press in this diary the perfect rose that accompanied it? Oh, I think not.

"Forgive me, dear lady, for deserting you during the Christmas season. Only business of the most extreme urgency could have drawn me from you. I wish you to know, however, that I thought of you a great deal. And that this rose is like you."

Cunning, is he not? O'Conor is contemporary man: pragmatic, sophisticated, self-preserving. The Hon. Charles will never bore a woman. He would not know how. He does not know how to love one either, but that will not stop hundreds of us from smashing ourselves against his smoothly lacquered surface.

A Moratorium

*C*oldest morning of the month, Henry decided, having exposed his nose to the room's chill. Reluctantly, he peeled back his blankets, then set about improving matters. Brisk set of exercises. Hot morning tea. Next he fired up water and, when the bathroom was steamy, stripped and immersed himself, thinking that were it not for *en suite* bathing he might grow tired of a hotel existence.

He soaked. In a moment or so he permitted the big toes of both feet to break the water line. While contemplating them he gave himself credit for having kept his mind free of Serena except for split seconds here and there. That, too, was in a sense warming, since it raised Henry in his own estimation. Acts of will implied strength of character.

"Hear me, Serena," he said aloud, though at a decibel level more circumspect than the previous night's. "I now banish you utterly from my brain."

Liking the sound of that, he declared an official moratorium, to take effect instantly. And to last—he sought a number—three days. Three days, yes, of banning the huntress. Three days of soldierly discipline, of behaving like a man. After that . . . well, let after that take care of itself. Lengthy journeys began with small steps. To Henry that seemed like wisdom. He stepped from the tub in a glow of optimism.

Clad in layers, he attacked the outdoors. The outdoors counterattacked. His bones felt brittle. But on this particular day he found a hack and clip-clopped to the courtroom smartly enough to howdy-do with the last char: she exiting, Henry entering. A jolly old Bowery bawd with the bright red nose of the confirmed toper. Bright red shawl, too, wrapped tight around the collar of a threadbare coat, the left pocket of which hung low (her trusty flask!). Scraggly gray hair. Watery blue eyes. And yet, clinging to her like the vestiges of a once heady perfume, an earthiness still potent enough to make Henry grin.

"Good morning, sorr."

"The same to you, ma'am."

And away she went but not without a last flattering look—Henry his usual smashing success with old bawds.

That person whose exile he had mandated had exiled herself from the courtroom, he noticed. Catherine Forrest caught him noticing.

O'CONOR *(after at least fifteen nerve-racking seconds of communion)*. Mrs. Flowers, when did you leave New Orleans?

MRS. FLOWERS. Seven weeks ago tomorrow.

O'CONOR. Having missed Christmas with your husband and family. And now it seems you will be apart from them over the New Year's holiday too. I must compliment you on your devotion to justice.

MRS. FLOWERS. Thank you, sir. But I can't take the credit. I hoped I would be finished and back by now. If I had known. . . .

O'CONOR. Of course. You've been in this city above six weeks, Mrs. Flowers?

MRS. FLOWERS. Yes, sir.

O'CONOR. Staying where?

MRS. FLOWERS. The first two weeks at the Mansion House. Since then at Florence's.

O'CONOR. And by what conveyance did you reach New York?

MRS. FLOWERS. Conveyance?

O'CONOR. By train? By stage?

MRS. FLOWERS. I came by ship, the steamship *Georgia*.

O'CONOR. And at whose direction did you come?

MRS. FLOWERS. No one's, sir.

O'CONOR. Pardon?

MRS. FLOWERS. Well, I mean it was Mr. Flowers who urged—

O'CONOR. I thought it was due to Mr. Forrest's urging that your passion was aroused.

MRS. FLOWERS. Yes, sir. But that was later. It was Mr. Flowers seeing the advertisement in the *New Orleans Picayune* that started it all. It said if I applied to the *Picayune* I would hear something to my advantage. *(smiles)* We thought I was going to get a fortune. *(laughter)*

O'CONOR. And did you?

MRS. FLOWERS. I got nothing at all.

O'CONOR. That *is* hard, Mrs. Flowers. You applied at the *Picayune* and got nothing at all from the gentleman who advertised?

MRS. FLOWERS. That's right.

O'CONOR. Who was that gentleman? Do you see him in this courtroom?

MRS. FLOWERS. Yes, sir.

O'CONOR. Well, then point him out to us. Yes, Mr. James Lawson, Mr. Forrest's business agent. You could not even get from him the price of a steamship ticket?

MRS. FLOWERS. I asked for nothing, and he gave me nothing.

O'CONOR. Who did pay for your passage?

MRS. FLOWERS. Mr. Flowers.

O'CONOR. But why? Ah, I see. He had learned the story from you and shared with you and Mr. Forrest that same passionate interest in justice.

MRS. FLOWERS. He said, "Anna, you have to go and tell the truth."

O'CONOR. Your husband is a remarkably selfless man.

MRS. FLOWERS. Thank you, sir. He is that.

O'CONOR *(three seconds of communion)*. But what reward did you expect when you arrived in New York?

MRS. FLOWERS. I'm just after telling you—

O'CONOR. Your pardon, Mrs. Flowers, you told me you received no reward while you were still in New Orleans, but surely you must have expected some little recompense when you got here.

MRS. FLOWERS. Not one cent. We are very well able to live without rewards.

O'CONOR. And would you have been very well able to live in New York these past six weeks at the Mansion House and at Florence's if Mr. Forrest had not paid your expenses?

MRS. FLOWERS. I would have been, yes.

O'CONOR. But the fact is he did pay your expenses.

MRS. FLOWERS. Yes, but I never asked him to.

O'CONOR. During this six-week period how often did you see Mr. Forrest?

MRS. FLOWERS. Once.

O'CONOR. Once. Are you quite certain?

MRS. FLOWERS. Twice. But the second time was but for five minutes.

O'CONOR. And you saw Mr. Lawson too? And Mr. Van Buren as well? Were they waiting for you at the pier with a brass band?

VAN BUREN. Object.

CHIEF JUSTICE. Sustained, Mr. O'Conor. You will please me if you ask the question—or questions—again, this time unattended by sarcasm.

O'Conor. Your pardon, sir. Mrs. Flowers, have you seen Mr. Lawson since you've been here?

Mrs. Flowers. Yes.

O'Conor. How often?

Mrs. Flowers. I'm not sure.

O'Conor. Six, ten, fifteen times? Which is closer?

Mrs. Flowers. Six times.

O'Conor. And Mr. Van Buren? Every day?

Mrs. Flowers. Not every day.

O'Conor. Sundays were your own?

Mrs. Flowers. Not just Sundays. Other days too.

O'Conor. What did all of you find to talk about?

Van Buren *(wearily)*. Object.

Chief Justice. Specificity, Mr. O'Conor.

O'Conor. You gave them your version of the facts in the case?

Mrs. Flowers. Yes, sir. That's what they wanted to know.

O'Conor. Day after day after day?

Mrs. Flowers. Yes, sir.

O'Conor. Why? Did they not believe you?

Mrs. Flowers. It wasn't that, sir.

O'Conor. Then what was it?

Mrs. Flowers. They wanted me well prepared.

O'Conor. Oh? Indeed? Well prepared? Rehearsed?

Mrs. Flowers. Prepared, sir. They said you would try and trick me.

Laughter again. And this time, Henry thought, O'Conor did not like it. Flowers grinned in triumph. O'Conor liked that even less.

O'Conor. I think you cope extremely well, Mrs. Flowers. I think you need have no fear of me.

Mrs. Flowers. Thank you, sir.

O'Conor. Shall we return to business?

Mrs. Flowers. I wait on you, sir.

O'Conor. You mentioned the Mansion House and Florence's

as places you have stayed during this six-week visit to New York, but there is I believe a place you have not mentioned.

MRS. FLOWERS. Do you mean the house on Mercer Street?

O'CONOR. Didn't you stay there?

MRS. FLOWERS. Not overnight.

O'CONOR. How long?

MRS. FLOWERS. I'm not sure.

O'CONOR. Mrs. Flowers, on the fifteenth of November, you arrived at that house at eleven o'clock in the morning, and you stayed until five o'clock in the evening. It's a boardinghouse run by a woman named Mrs. Wilson. You were conducted there by Mr. Lawson. Is each of those statements correct?

MRS. FLOWERS. If—

O'CONOR. Not if, Mrs. Flowers. Not but. Not why? Just yes or no.

VAN BUREN. Object. Learned counsel is browbeating—

O'CONOR. Tarnation! Is it browbeating to demand a simple yes or no concerning statements of plain fact? This witness thinks she can be clever with me, your honor. I resent that. I have a right . . . my client has a right . . . to responsive answers. She plays at whist with me.

VAN BUREN. Whist! 'Tis you who—

CHIEF JUSTICE. Enough. Silence, both of you. Gentlemen, you forget yourselves. Dignity. Decorum. I want them back at your disposal and on display in this courtroom. Instantly. Am I understood?

It was Van Buren's scowl that hung on, Henry thought.

CHIEF JUSTICE *(to Mrs. Flowers)*. If you attempt to duel with Mr. O'Conor you will get the worst of it, madam, I do assure you. Take the advice to heart. Yeas and nays are coin of the realm in this courtroom. Be so good as to circulate them whenever possible. Am I understood?

MRS. FLOWERS. Yes, sir.

CHIEF JUSTICE. Would you like the statements made by Mr. O'Conor read back to you?

MRS. FLOWERS. No, sir.

CHIEF JUSTICE. Are they true?

MRS. FLOWERS. Yes, sir.

CHIEF JUSTICE. You may proceed, Mr. O'Conor.

O'CONOR. Thank you, your honor. Mrs. Flowers, you spent six hours in the house on Mercer Street. Will you tell the court why.

MRS. FLOWERS. I went there in order to meet Mrs. Forrest.

O'CONOR. By arrangement with her?

MRS. FLOWERS. No, sir.

O'CONOR. By arrangement with whom?

MRS. FLOWERS. It was my own idea.

O'CONOR. But you were accompanied by Mr. Lawson, were you not?

MRS. FLOWERS. Yes.

O'CONOR. And didn't he stay with you the whole time?

MRS. FLOWERS. Yes.

O'CONOR. And didn't Mr. Forrest come to see you while you were there?

MRS. FLOWERS. He certainly did not.

O'CONOR. Not once?

MRS. FLOWERS. Not the shadow of him.

O'CONOR. It was not Mr. Forrest who dined with you?

MRS. FLOWERS. Mr. Lawson dined with me, not Mr. Forrest. It's a small house. If he'd been there I would have seen him. *(laughter, ignored by O'Conor)*

O'CONOR. If you wanted a meeting with Mrs. Forrest, why didn't you simply pay a call?

MRS. FLOWERS. Mr. Forrest didn't want me to.

O'CONOR. Why not?

MRS. FLOWERS. He said Mrs. Voorhies was with her. He didn't want me to be in her company.

O'CONOR. For fear she might corrupt you?

MRS. FLOWERS. I don't know, sir. He didn't go on about it.

O'Conor. Very well, madam, there you are in Mercer Street for the express purpose of inducing—

Van Buren. Object.

O'Conor. To what?

Van Buren. Inducing? Come now.

Chief Justice. Inducing is strong, Mr. O'Conor. You haven't established a basis.

O'Conor. Arranging?

Chief Justice. Acceptable. Please sit, Mr. Van Buren. This jumping up and down of yours . . . I find it more than a little disconcerting.

Van Buren. Your pardon, sir.

Chief Justice. Continue, Mr. O'Conor.

O'Conor. How did you expect to arrange this meeting with Mrs. Forrest? That is, what measures did you take?

Mrs. Flowers. I wrote two notes to her and sent them by a small boy. I sent the second when she did not answer the first.

O'Conor. Mr. Asher, will you furnish the exhibits to Mrs. Flowers so she can identify them. Are those your notes, Mrs. Flowers?

Mrs. Flowers. Yes.

O'Conor. With the court's permission I will now read them to the jury. Letter number one: "Dear Mrs. Forrest, I have just arrived from New Orleans, and I want to see you very much before I see anybody else. I am going to Brooklyn this morning, but I will be here until five this afternoon. Do please come and see me for I have so much to tell you. I don't want to be seen here until I see you. Call at 142 Mercer Street, Wilson's Hotel. Please send an answer by the bearer. Anna Dempsey Flowers. Directed to Mrs. Forrest, Sixteenth Street."

Letter number two: "Mrs. Forrest, you must excuse me for writing you so often but the reason is that I did not want anybody to see me. If you don't want to meet with me please send me word. The place is private and I am alone. Anna."

Clerk. Would you like copies made for the jury, sir?

O'CONOR. Yes. Thank you, Mr. Asher. *(five seconds of communion)* But you were not alone, Mrs. Flowers, were you?

MRS. FLOWERS. No.

O'CONOR. At the very least you had Mr. Lawson with you. And who knows how many others.

MRS. FLOWERS. No others. Just Mr. Lawson. For company, that was all.

O'CONOR. Is that the truth? Just Mr. Lawson? Just Mr. Lawson for company?

MRS. FLOWERS. I'm under oath, sir. How could it not be the truth?

O'CONOR. But when you're not under oath I take it you find it perfectly permissible to lie.

MRS. FLOWERS. I don't tell lies, sir.

O'CONOR. You told two to Mrs. Forrest. First, you told her you wanted to see her before you saw anybody else. And the truth there was you had already seen half the population of New York, including her husband, her enemy. And next you told her you were alone when in fact Mr. Lawson made you a twosome. Where was he to be positioned, incidentally? I mean in the event that Mrs. Forrest could have been lured to Mercer Street, was he then to dive under the bed, notebook at the ready, in order to—

VAN BUREN. Object.

CHIEF JUSTICE. Sustained.

O'CONOR. Why *did* you lie, Mrs. Flowers?

MRS. FLOWERS. I thought it for the best.

O'CONOR. For the best? How for the best?

MRS. FLOWERS. I thought if she came there I could say something that might be useful to her.

O'CONOR. Such as?

MRS. FLOWERS. I don't know . . . maybe something comforting in her time of trouble.

O'CONOR. Now that is kind of you, Mrs. Flowers. And here I was surmising that the best you had in mind was *your* best. But I was wrong, wasn't I?

MRS. FLOWERS. Yes, sir.

O'CONOR. And is it often the case that when you tell a lie it's for someone else's best?

MRS. FLOWERS. Yes, sir.

O'CONOR. Well, then, in that light shall we examine some of those other lies?

VAN BUREN. Object! Object!

CHIEF JUSTICE. Yes, of course. Now take care, Mr. O'Conor.

O'CONOR. Mrs. Flowers, before we leave the subject of Mercer Street, would you mind telling the court who paid the bill for your stay there?

MRS. FLOWERS. Mr. Lawson.

O'CONOR. Mr. Lawson, yes. Mr. Lawson for company *and* for paying the bills. *(five seconds of communion)* Mrs. Flowers, we heard talk yesterday of a baby in want, a baby in whose behalf you were ready to roar down walls if, by doing so, you could be assured of amelioration of that baby's pitiful condition. A little girl baby, is it? A little blue-eyed girl baby?

MRS. FLOWERS. Yes, sir.

O'CONOR. What color is her hair?

MRS. FLOWERS. Blond, sir. Like mine.

O'CONOR. Are you sure?

MRS. FLOWERS. Am I . . .

O'CONOR. You haven't seen her in two years!

MRS. FLOWERS *(recovering quickly after a perceptible flinch)*. She's with my mother.

O'CONOR. Your mother lives in this city?

MRS. FLOWERS. Yes.

O'CONOR. Well, let us talk further about this blue-eyed child of your heart. Am I correct—you have not seen her since you've been here?

VAN BUREN. Object. I've been patient, your honor, wanting to give the fullest possible fling to the other side, but I do not see where my learned friend is going with all this.

O'CONOR. To the core, to the hub, I do assure you, sir, as I think you know very well.

VAN BUREN. I know nothing of the kind.

CHIEF JUSTICE. Patience, Mr. Van Buren. A bit longer.

VAN BUREN. Do you say so, sir?

CHIEF JUSTICE. I think I must. Continue, Mr. O'Conor.

O'CONOR. Have you, Mrs. Flowers, seen your child in the six weeks you have been in this city?

MRS. FLOWERS. No.

O'CONOR. Why is that?

MRS. FLOWERS. Because my mother hates me.

O'CONOR. You left your child with someone who hates you?

MRS. FLOWERS. She doesn't hate the child, sir.

O'CONOR. Good point. Yes, excellent point. Why does your mother hate you?

MRS. FLOWERS. I don't know. She always has.

O'CONOR. For no cause?

MRS. FLOWERS. None that I know of.

O'CONOR. Hate. Such a strong word to use between mothers and daughters, but perhaps I can think of a reason why your mother might be seriously *annoyed* with you. Shall I try?

MRS. FLOWERS. Go ahead. I can't stop you.

O'CONOR. Isn't it true she didn't want you to testify against Mrs. Forrest?

MRS. FLOWERS. None of them did.

O'CONOR. Which none, Mrs. Flowers?

MRS. FLOWERS. My scaredy-cat brothers and sisters.

O'CONOR. How many are there?

MRS. FLOWERS. Six.

O'CONOR. And none of them wanted you to testify against Mrs. Forrest? Why is that?

MRS. FLOWERS. For one, they're scared of their shadows, scared the toffs'll say boo to them if they show any spunk. And for two, they was always against me.

O'CONOR. Could it not be they thought Mrs. Forrest was in the right?

MRS. FLOWERS. Right, wrong, down the middle . . . none of that has anything to do with it. They was always against me is all. Me on the one side, them on the other. Whatever it was I wanted to do, they was against it.

O'CONOR. Always?

MRS. FLOWERS. Always.

O'CONOR. But perhaps this disapproval became stauncher once your child was born out of wedlock?

VAN BUREN. Object.

O'CONOR. How can you, sir? You were the one who introduced the child to us . . . in direct examination. And here, all this time, the jury has been waiting patiently to learn where it came from.

VAN BUREN. Where it came from is not the issue. The point is you are getting ready to ask the witness to make a self-declaration of infamy, which she need not do.

O'CONOR. She *need* do it, sir, if the matter is relevant, which it certainly is.

CHIEF JUSTICE. Is it, Mr. O'Conor?

O'CONOR. I do assure you, sir.

CHIEF JUSTICE. Then I must overrule you, Mr. Van Buren, though I have no objection to any explanations or amplifications the witness might wish to put forward. You may continue, Mr. O'Conor.

O'CONOR. Your first child *was* born out of wedlock, Mrs. Flowers?

MRS. FLOWERS. Yes.

O'CONOR. Will you tell the court who the father is?

MRS. FLOWERS *(with intense bitterness)*. Captain Granby Calcraft. *(hubbub; raps of the gavel)*

O'CONOR. That very same Captain Calcraft you say you saw in bed with Mrs. Forrest?

MRS. FLOWERS. Yes.

O'CONOR. My heavens. And was it . . . my heavens . . . the very same night that he—

MRS. FLOWERS. It was not. It was three nights later. He—

O'CONOR. Patience, patience, we will get to that, I promise you. But let us for a few moments longer stay with Captain Calcraft and Mrs. Forrest, may we? That night . . . that fateful night . . . what time was it you went to bed?

MRS. FLOWERS. About eleven o'clock.

O'CONOR. And you were awakened around midnight?

MRS. FLOWERS. Yes.

O'CONOR. By the sound of loud voices and laughter?

MRS. FLOWERS. Yes.

O'CONOR. Doesn't that strike you as odd?

MRS. FLOWERS. Why should it?

O'CONOR. It strikes me that people who have the kind of naughtiness in mind you ascribe to Captain Calcraft and Mrs. Forrest tend to be more discreet. Loud talking and laughing, you say?

MRS. FLOWERS. And a little the worse for drinking, too, I think. *(laughter)*

O'CONOR. Ah, then that explains it. But why didn't you say so before?

MRS. FLOWERS. I wasn't asked.

O'CONOR. For shame, Mr. Van Buren. Such an opportunity missed.

CHIEF JUSTICE. Now, none of that, Mr. O'Conor. Just go on about your business.

O'CONOR. Let us review briefly, shall we, the events that led up to your shocking discovery. Mrs. Forrest enters your room. She calls your name. No answer from you. She goes out. Sometime later, you follow. You see the partly open door in the corridor. You push it open farther. You find them in bed together. You cry. Twenty minutes pass. She comes into your room. Now here is where it gets a bit hazy, by your leave. What *was* her explanation? Something to do with sheets on the bed? Or no sheets on the bed?

MRS. FLOWERS. She made no explanation.

O'CONOR. Still, she did say something about the lack of sheets, did she not?

MRS. FLOWERS. Yes.

O'CONOR. But why on earth would she? I mean, once having been seen by you in bed with Captain Calcraft, why on earth would it matter any longer what brought her to that pretty pass? Do you have thoughts on that, Mrs. Flowers?

MRS. FLOWERS. The drink—

O'CONOR. The drink, of course! When people are fuddled. . . . Ah, here's something that interests me. Your tears. Were they copious tears, Mrs. Flowers?

MRS. FLOWERS. I don't know what copious means.

O'CONOR. Did those tears stream down your innocent cheeks like rivers? Did you gasp first, then scream at this assault on the purity of your nature? What was the manner of your crying, Mrs. Flowers?

MRS. FLOWERS. I cried quietly.

O'CONOR. But loudly enough for her to hear you?

MRS. FLOWERS. Yes.

O'CONOR. And you cried, I suppose, partly out of a sense of betrayal . . . I mean that this was Mrs. Forrest, after all.

MRS. FLOWERS. Yes.

O'CONOR. And partly because you were a mere fifteen . . . and inexperienced?

MRS. FLOWERS. Yes.

O'CONOR. And yet, according to your own testimony, you had previously witnessed Mrs. Forrest making free with other men. Why should you have been so unprepared?

MRS. FLOWERS. This was different.

O'CONOR. True. And of course a young girl . . . fifteen . . . inexperienced . . . innocent . . . pure . . . yes, entirely understandable. That *is* the picture of yourself you wish to convey to this court, is it not? That *was* you at the time?

MRS. FLOWERS. Yes.

O'CONOR. Mrs. Flowers, have you ever been sentenced to the House of Refuge?

VAN BUREN. Object! I beg the court . . . will the court please inform the witness of her rights.

CHIEF JUSTICE. I will do so most gladly, Mr. Van Buren, but as a precursor I must have your view of them. And I warn you, sir, our views may be at issue.

VAN BUREN. Your honor, I will most happily submit to any rule of law, or any rule of decency put forward by you, but I would be unworthy of the sex I belong to and the position I occupy were I not to rise vigorously to Mrs. Flowers's defense. Sir, here is a woman hundreds of miles from her home, the mother of three children, the wife of a respectable husband, subjected to abuse and contumely. Clearly, the court should protect her. She is not on trial here, sir, and it is unfair, sir, that she be obliged to answer questions that will subject her to infamy and degradation. I therefore beg you . . . plead with you . . . for the sake of what the stronger sex universally owes the weaker . . . to inform her that she may decline to answer.

O'CONOR. Such gallantry is—

VAN BUREN. Will the court permit me to cite cases?

CHIEF JUSTICE. Of course.

VAN BUREN. Then I refer the court to *People Against Herrick* 13 Johnson, page 82. And also to cases from Wendell, which I will stipulate later, if the court so wishes.

CHIEF JUSTICE. Mr. O'Conor?

O'CONOR. *People Against Morgan,* your honor, and a hundred others in which the court has always ruled the witness is bound to answer unless the answer leads to self-incrimination.

CHIEF JUSTICE. Yes, Mr. Van Buren. There lies the essential point, I'm afraid. I'm aware of the cases you cite, and though they do seem to support you I find them heavily outweighed by opinion to the contrary. Incidentally, for your own edification, sir, I think one of those in Wendell is the result of a misprint, either that or the court reporter's inattention. I suggest you go back and look at it in that light. At any rate I don't believe it to be good law to suggest that a witness can avoid answering questions for any reason other than self-incrimination. Is self-incrimination involved, Mr. O'Conor?

O'CONOR. No, sir.

CHIEF JUSTICE. I gathered not. *(to Van Buren)* If it's the witness's early age we're concerned with here, the statute of limitations will sufficiently protect her. *(to O'Conor)* You may proceed.

VAN BUREN. Please note an exception, Mr. Asher.

O'CONOR. Mrs. Flowers, how old were you when you went to the House of Refuge?

MRS. FLOWERS. I don't remember.

O'CONOR. We can easily jog your memory by sending for the records, but just for now will you hazard a guess? Will you say whether you were older than twelve?

MRS. FLOWERS. No.

O'CONOR. You will not say?

MRS. FLOWERS. I was not older than twelve.

O'CONOR. Thank you. What were you sent there for?

MRS. FLOWERS. I don't remember.

O'CONOR. Was it for stealing a watch?

MRS. FLOWERS. I did not steal that watch. I was given it to hold by another servant in that house who ran away, and I was blamed. Dr. Rice abused me and brought charges against me without cause. I have been abused all my life. I never had justice done me.

O'CONOR. Are you finished, Mrs. Flowers? I don't wish to interrupt.

MRS. FLOWERS. Never once in all my life have I had justice done me.

O'CONOR. How long were you in the House of Refuge?

MRS. FLOWERS. I don't remember.

O'CONOR. A year? Two years?

CHIEF JUSTICE. Now I am becoming concerned, Mr. O'Conor. The matter of self-incrimination aside, it has been pointed out to you that Mrs. Flowers is *not* on trial here.

O'CONOR. But her credibility is, your honor. She has asked us to believe in Mr. Dickens's Little Nell, a creature so tender as to all but swoon away on encountering . . . what Mrs. Flowers alleges to have encountered. For the sake of my client I must demonstrate to the jury how much validity is in this portrait.

CHIEF JUSTICE. Have you not done that sufficiently?

O'CONOR *(after a moment)*. Well, perhaps I have.

CHIEF JUSTICE. Good. Pray continue with some other line.

O'CONOR *(five seconds of communion)*. I think we are ready now, Mrs. Flowers, for the story of you and Captain Calcraft.

CHIEF JUSTICE. Is that likely to be a long story, Mr. O'Conor?

O'CONOR. Longish.

CHIEF JUSTICE *(turning to the jury)*. Gentlemen, the circumstances which curtailed us yesterday continue in force. I say again they have nothing to do with our case and everything to do with nonessentials. I go from here to discuss them with my colleagues of the bench. My hope is for an early resolution to difficulties the nature of which I'm not at liberty to discuss. I dislike being mysterious, but I've been prevailed upon for silence a bit longer. At any rate the details would bore you mightily, I do assure you. So pray be forbearing. And patient. Stand adjourned until tomorrow morning.

Comic Interlude

*R*eleased from the courtroom early, Henry had gone to the *Herald* to write his story and stayed to help put the paper to bed. This was a task Bennett had relieved him of for the duration of the trial, but he'd found himself feeling deprived. He missed the work. He missed the minutiae, the mundane (often nagging) journalistic chores that fell to a managing editor and could drive him mad or fill him with grudging satisfaction when performed efficiently. He missed also the ink-stained camaraderie, the goatish joshing, that peculiar brand of comfort to be derived from masculine crudity.

The *Herald* bedded, he'd supped with Bennett, played chess with him, and been finally ejected by him shortly before midnight. Less plagued by loneliness than he'd been for days, he arrived home to discover he was waited for. A substantially built middle-aged man with massive forearms and a florid, bearded, scowling face leaped at him out of the hotel entrance: Peter Blaylock, senior.

"Sir, if you approach my daughter again I shall horsewhip you."

"You won't, sir."

Thundering. "Are you impertinent with me, sir?"

"For the sake of the affection we once felt for each other, pray understand me. I've suffered your cane on my person once. I warn you I won't do so again. Nor will I tolerate any other blow."

"You warn me?"

"But have no fear for your daughter, sir. Whatever her future plans are, they do not include me."

Grumble, gnash, grit, growl: "You're the devil, sir." And he marched off, puffing like a routed dragon.

The Cowper brothers, Henry's neighbors, who were amused at life and who liked to amuse others about it, and whose carriage had drawn up just after his, applauded.

He bowed to them.

They threw him invisible bouquets and silent kisses.

All highly comic, he tacitly agreed.

But later, a full half hour later, when he attempted to write a note to his mother, he snapped a quill and then kicked his wastebasket to flinders.

The "Consuelo" Letter

O'Conor appeared grim. Other days he'd had a smile to warm the jury like morning tea. Not this day. As for Annie, she was a bit red about the eye, Henry thought. Apprehensive tears? Or a touch of the flu? He voted for the latter. She was a true Bowery lass, Annie Flowers, street-toughened and hard to frighten.

Again the Exiled One was not there to bear witness.

O'CONOR. Mrs. Flowers, the connection between you and Captain Calcraft began, I believe you said, three days after the alleged connection between Captain Calcraft and Mrs. Forrest. Is that correct?

MRS. FLOWERS. I don't understand that word.

O'CONOR. Connection? *(Laughter: but O'Conor, though he caused it, does not rise to it.)*

MRS. FLOWERS. Alleged.

O'CONOR. It means that just because you say a thing happened does not mean it did.

VAN BUREN. Object.

O'CONOR. Oh, very well, then you explain it to her.

VAN BUREN. It is not the explanation I object to, it is the imputation.

O'CONOR. In the interest of time, I withdraw the imputation.

CHIEF JUSTICE. How refreshing—to see someone in this court-room serve that particular interest. Admirable, Mr. O'Conor. Pray proceed.

O'CONOR. Thank you, sir. Was Mrs. Forrest in the house when you and Captain Calcraft . . . connected?

MRS. FLOWERS. She was in Philadelphia with her husband.

O'CONOR. Who was in the house?

MRS. FLOWERS. Catherine, the other chambermaid, and James Underwood.

O'CONOR. Where was Mrs. Underwood?

MRS. FLOWERS. She went that time with Mrs. Forrest.

O'CONOR. Very well, then, here comes a knock at the door. It is Captain Calcraft. Who goes to answer it? You?

MRS. FLOWERS. Yes, sir.

O'CONOR. Why you?

MRS. FLOWERS. Because it was about half after ten at night, and the other two were asleep. I would have been, 'cept I had some darning to do. A heavy knock, it was. Enough to wake the dead, I promise you. And when I opened the door I could see what was the cause of it.

O'CONOR. What was?

MRS. FLOWERS. He'd a drop taken, as they say.

O'CONOR. How do you know?

MRS. FLOWERS. Well, sir, he just reached out and put his hand . . .

O'CONOR. Where?

MRS. FLOWERS. Where he shouldn't have. *(laughter)*

CHIEF JUSTICE. Your next question, Mr. O'Conor, need not be anatomical. I think the point has been made.

O'CONOR. He did not even ask for Mrs. Forrest?

MRS. FLOWERS. He did ask for her. When I told him where she was, he asked who else was in the house. When I told him that, he reached out with his hand.

O'CONOR. You of course pushed him away.

MRS. FLOWERS. Yes, sir. Pushed him hard.

O'CONOR. Very properly done. But I wonder why you didn't slam the door in his face.

MRS. FLOWERS. Not my place to do so.

O'CONOR. No?

MRS. FLOWERS. Oh, no, sir. Like he said himself, he was an honored guest in that house.

O'CONOR. He said that himself, did he?

MRS. FLOWERS. Yes, sir. He said, "You know Mrs. Forrest's house is always open to me." And then he said he wanted brandy and water and demanded that I get it.

O'CONOR. So you felt you had to.

MRS. FLOWERS. Yes, sir.

O'CONOR. Even though he had already made free with your . . . person?

MRS. FLOWERS. What choice did I have?

O'CONOR. Permit me to put that question to you, Mrs. Flowers.

MRS. FLOWERS. None, sir. Suppose he'd complained to my mistress. Why, then I'd have lost my place.

O'CONOR. Would you have?

MRS. FLOWERS. The thought was in my mind.

O'CONOR. Mrs. Forrest, who treated you unlike a servant, would have sent you packing for protecting your virtue? That was the thought in your mind?

MRS. FLOWERS. She might have. Mistresses will say one thing and then turn around and do you dirt, has been my experience.

O'CONOR. Yes. Well, let us return, shall we, to the tableau at the door. There's our shy, inexperienced fifteen-year-old . . . so virginal she can be moved to tears by you-know-what. And there's the marauding captain, having just made what amounts to forcible entry. He gets his brandy and water, I take it?

MRS. FLOWERS. Yes.

O'CONOR. And what else?

MRS. FLOWERS. Sir?

O'CONOR. What did he do next?

MRS. FLOWERS. He caught hold of me.

O'CONOR. And you ordered him to cease and desist, of course.

MRS. FLOWERS. I told him to let me alone, that Mrs. Forrest would be very angry with him. And he said Mrs. Forrest was never angry with him, that she thought a great deal of him. I said, I dare say she does, but if Mr. Forrest knew what was going on, *he* wouldn't think a great deal of you. And then he knocked me down.

O'CONOR. He hit you?

MRS. FLOWERS. He shoved me. And then he fell on top of me. Like an animal he was, tearing my bodice and pushing at my clothes. I tried to fight him off, but he was too strong for me.

O'CONOR. You cried out, no doubt.

MRS. FLOWERS. I hallooed and hallooed, but nobody came.

O'CONOR. So, finally, after all that fruitless hallooing, he had his way with you?

MRS. FLOWERS. Yes, sir.

O'CONOR. Rape, was it?

MRS. FLOWERS. Yes. Rape. Like an animal he was.

O'CONOR *(five seconds of communion)*. Mrs. Flowers, I am going to give you a chance to answer that question again. And please permit me to remind you that you are under oath. Well, then, was it rape?

MRS. FLOWERS. It's as amounts to the same thing. I mean he pushed me and shoved me and bothered me so I was too weak to resist any more. And then he took his pleasure of me.

O'CONOR. You had intercourse.

MRS. FLOWERS. Yes.

O'CONOR. How you must have hated him, Mrs. Flowers. You did hate him, did you not? There must have been murder in your heart. That villainous cad. That deflowerer. How you must have planned to revenge yourself on him. How long did he stay? *(silence)* Until after midnight?

MRS. FLOWERS. Yes.

O'CONOR. And what happened when he came to the door the following night? . . . Mrs. Flowers? Would you like me to repeat the question?

MRS. FLOWERS. I let him in.

O'CONOR. This poltroon, this scoundrel, this near-rapist . . . you opened the door and let him in? How is that possible? Wait, wait, I know. It was not your place to keep him out. He was, after all, an honored guest.

MRS. FLOWERS. Well, he was.

O'CONOR. And did he knock you down again?

MRS. FLOWERS. No.

O'CONOR. No? And yet you had intercourse again, did you not? *(She hesitates.)* Captain Calcraft is away from the city at the moment, but I do have his deposition. Is it necessary that I read it?

MRS. FLOWERS. Because he'd made a great many promises to me the night before.

O'CONOR. What kind of promises?

MRS. FLOWERS. Never you mind. That's as concerns me and nobody else.

O'CONOR. When Mrs. Forrest returned from Philadelphia, did you tell her what had happened?

MRS. FLOWERS. Yes.

O'CONOR. Right away?

MRS. FLOWERS. Yes.

O'CONOR. Mrs. Forrest says you did not tell her until she asked. And that she asked only when she noticed certain unmistakable signs.

MRS. FLOWERS. That's not so.

O'CONOR. Mrs. Forrest is lying?

MRS. FLOWERS. You can believe what you want, but I know what's true.

O'CONOR. Very well, let it be your way, but when you told Mrs. Forrest what did she say?

MRS. FLOWERS. She said, "Oh, Anna, it's too bad, a young girl like you. I will give him a good scolding." *(laughter)*

O'CONOR. Did you ever have intercourse with Captain Calcraft again?

MRS. FLOWERS. I did not. I told Mrs. Forrest I would not be in the same room with him. And whenever he came to the house I ran out of it.

O'CONOR. Did you ever have intercourse with Jamie Underwood?

MRS. FLOWERS. I did not.

O'CONOR. With Barnard McCabe?

MRS. FLOWERS. Oh, that is bad. Very bad, to say such a thing.

O'CONOR. Shall I read you a deposition from a witness who says she saw the two of you in bed?

MRS. FLOWERS. Read whatever you want, it's as makes no difference. I know who that is anyway. That's that Catherine Levins, who'd rather lie than breathe. She hates me. She'd be pleased to lie about me every day in the week.

O'CONOR. Another one who hates you. 'Tis a long list, Mrs. Flowers.

MRS. FLOWERS. I don't care.

O'CONOR. It includes your mother, your brothers and sisters, Mrs. Forrest, Captain Calcraft, I presume, and now Catherine Levins. Does anyone hold you in esteem?

VAN BUREN. Object. Absolutely outrageous, your honor.

CHIEF JUSTICE. Sustained. Strike, Mr. Asher. Mr. O'Conor, desist.

O'CONOR. Your child was born in May of 1845, is that correct, Mrs. Flowers?

MRS. FLOWERS. Yes.

O'CONOR. Did you ever charge this child upon Captain Calcraft by legal proceeding or affidavit?

MRS. FLOWERS. Yes. In some office in the Park here. I remember there was an officer named Hopkins or something like that.

O'CONOR. After making this charge, did you then hurry home to see Jamie Underwood and plead with him to swear he had never had anything to do with you?

MRS. FLOWERS. I did not.

O'CONOR. You are telling this Court then there is absolutely no possibility that Jamie Underwood and not Captain Calcraft is the the father of your child?

MRS. FLOWERS. Yes, I am.

O'CONOR. What happened to the charge you made against Captain Calcraft?

MRS. FLOWERS. It was withdrawn because he gave me money. But never enough. And I had to pay my own passage to New Orleans. And *she* gave me only twenty-five dollars. None of them ever did justice to me, and that's a fact whether you believe it or not.

O'CONOR *(five seconds of communion)*. No further questions, your honor.

Nor did Van Buren need her again, it seemed. Eyes smoldering, she left them. Not hurriedly, saucily. Chest up and out, hips swaying. Angry, certainly, but, as always, conscious of her power. Farewell, Anna Dempsey Flowers, Bowery tigress, Henry said to her silently. No better than you should be, but you've made your impact. And methinks the eighty or so males in the courtroom share a furtive reluctance to see the last of you.

CLERK. Call Dr. Roscoe McGowan.

VAN BUREN. Dr. McGowan is outside and refuses to enter, sir.

CHIEF JUSTICE. I'm not sure I understand.

VAN BUREN. He says he doesn't approve of divorce.

CHIEF JUSTICE. That's as may be, but has he been subpoenaed?

VAN BUREN. Yes, sir.

CHIEF JUSTICE. Cannot a bailiff be prevailed upon to persuade him?

VAN BUREN. He is a clergyman, sir, and I've been reluctant to use force. *(laughter)*

O'CONOR. Is this the witness whose testimony will prove that Mrs. Forrest once said, if a man is to be free his wife cannot be a slave?

VAN BUREN. Yes. And more.

O'CONOR. Your point being that Mrs. Forrest had . . . has . . . somewhat advanced views on the institution of marriage?

VAN BUREN. Precisely.

O'CONOR. Well, then, if it will expedite matters we will concede. You need not trouble the reluctant Dr. McGowan. *(laughter)*

VAN BUREN. Most handsome of you, sir.

O'CONOR *(faint emphasis)*. Nothing.

CLERK. Call W. R. Blake

Mr. W. R. Blake, tall, spindle-shanked, needle-nosed, bald of pate, but with flowing mustaches, being sworn and examined by Mr. Van Buren, deposed.

BLAKE. I reside at 80 Leonard Street. I am an actor. I know George W. Jamieson well and am acquainted with his handwriting.

VAN BUREN. Is this a sample of it?

BLAKE. Yes.

O'CONOR. I would like to know what the witness is being shown.

VAN BUREN. He is being shown what we are pleased to call the "Consuelo" letter.

O'CONOR. For what purpose?

VAN BUREN. Oh, come now, sir. You know very well what the purpose is. Who should know better? Were you not the one so clamorous that the defense must prove it in evidence before it can be read?

O'CONOR. Most assuredly. But is this gentleman a handwriting expert? Where is Mr. Jamieson himself?

VAN BUREN. Where indeed?

O'CONOR. Do I detect an imputation?

VAN BUREN. I assure you not, sir. It is just that you have asked where Mr. Jamieson is, and I, too, have wondered. As I have wondered about the whereabouts of Captain Calcraft, as well, and Mrs. Voorhies, for that matter.

O'CONOR. They are out of the country.

VAN BUREN. That much I know.

O'CONOR. Are you suggesting collusion? *(to the Chief Justice)* If he is—

CHIEF JUSTICE. If he is, you might consider blaming yourself, Mr. O'Conor, for engaging in this unseemly colloquy.

O'CONOR. Once again I beg forgiveness, sir.

CHIEF JUSTICE. Yes. Tell me, Mr. O'Conor, because I am not at all certain, were you making an objection to Mr. Van Buren's reading the letter?

O'CONOR *(five seconds of communion, then once again surprising everyone)*. No.

CHIEF JUSTICE. You were not?

O'CONOR. To be sure, I flirted with the notion, but that would have been mere legalism. I have no serious objection to the reading of Mr. Jamieson's effusion. It—

CHIEF JUSTICE. Enough. Mr. Van Buren, since there is now no objection, serious or otherwise, you may proceed to prove your letter in evidence.

VAN BUREN. The date is April 25, 1848. The point of origin the Hotel Claiborne, Cincinnati. *(reading)* "And now, sweetest Consuelo, our brief dream is over, and such a dream! Have we not known real bliss? Can slander's tongue or rumor's trumpet rend us asunder? No! A doubt of thee can no more find harbor in my brain than the opened rose could cease to be the hum-bird's harbor. And as my heart and soul are in your possession, examine them and you will find no text from which to discourse doubt of

me. Be happy, dearest. Write to me and tell me you are happy.
Think of the time when we shall meet again. Believe that I shall
do the utmost to be worthy of your love. And now, God bless
you, a thousand times my own, my heart's altar. I would say more,
but must stow away my shreds and tinsel patches. Oh! how
hideous they look after thinking of you." *(glancing up)* There is a
poem enclosed, which I will read as well:

> *"Adieu! adieu! and when thou art gone,*
> *My joy shall be made up alone*
> *Of calling back with fancy's charm,*
> *Those halcyon hours when in my arm*
>   *I clasped Consuelo!*

> *"Adieu! adieu! be thine each joy*
> *That earth can yield without alloy,*
> *Shall be the earnest, constant prayer*
> *Of him who in his heart shall wear*
>   *Sweet Consuelo.*

> *"Adieu! adieu! when next we meet,*
> *Will not all sadness then retreat,*
> *And yield the conquered time to bliss,*
> *And seal the triumph with a kiss:*
>   *Say Consuelo?"*

CHIEF JUSTICE. Can someone tell me who this Consuelo is?
VAN BUREN. The recipient of the letter was Mrs. Forrest.
CHIEF JUSTICE. Yes, yes, I surmised as much, but—
VAN BUREN. Consuelo is the heroine of an advanced novel by
George Sand.
CHIEF JUSTICE. George Sand. Isn't she that Frenchwoman of—
VAN BUREN. Advanced views. Extremely advanced views.
Even my learned friend must grant—
O'CONOR. Your learned friend will be pleased if words are not
placed in his mouth.
CHIEF JUSTICE. Enough, Mr. Van Buren. I suggest you address

yourself to Mr. Blake. He has shown remarkable patience and now deserves your fullest attention.

VAN BUREN. Indeed he does, sir. Mr. Blake, when did you last see Mr. Forrest?

BLAKE. I saw Mr. Forrest the winter before he separated from his wife. In December of '48 and January of '49.

VAN BUREN. Did you see him often then?

BLAKE. Yes. We were performing together. I played Iago to his Othello and King Claudius to his Hamlet.

VAN BUREN. May we assume, then, that you know him quite well?

BLAKE. Oh, yes.

VAN BUREN. What was his condition during this period?

O'CONOR. Object. What do you mean by "his condition"?

VAN BUREN. Your honor, it has been alleged that Mr. Forrest left his wife because she symbolized England to him, or because he hated Mr. Macready, or because she called him a name, or because he had taken leave of his senses. I wish to show he left his wife for quite another reason, and that this letter was central to that reason, and that when he found it, it shook him to his foundations.

CHIEF JUSTICE. How do you propose to proceed?

VAN BUREN. With testimony from such as Mr. Blake as to his state of mind during—

CHIEF JUSTICE. Really, Mr. Van Buren, you must know that such testimony is inadmissible, if for no other reason than because Mr. Forrest is an actor.

VAN BUREN. But is not an actor also a human being and subject to—

CHIEF JUSTICE. Objection sustained. Pray continue with some other line, Mr. Van Buren.

VAN BUREN. An exception please, Mr. Asher.

CLERK. Noted.

VAN BUREN. Mr. Blake, how long have you known Mr. Jamieson?

BLAKE. Two or three years, sir.

VAN BUREN. Closer to three than two?

BLAKE. Yes.

VAN BUREN. Well enough, then, to have been in his company on all sorts of occasions?

BLAKE. Oh, yes, sir.

VAN BUREN. What was the general character of Jamieson with regard to women?

O'CONOR. Object. My learned friend is attempting to construe evidence against Mr. Jamieson as evidence against Mrs. Forrest.

CHIEF JUSTICE. Sustained.

VAN BUREN (*suddenly surly*). Well, then, I have no further need of the witness.

CHIEF JUSTICE. Mr. O'Conor, do you wish to cross-examine?

O'CONOR. No, sir.

CHIEF JUSTICE. Please step down, Mr. Blake, and thank you. Mr. Van Buren?

VAN BUREN (*shreds of sulkiness clinging to him*). I had intended to call Mr. Edwin Forrest, who just now left the courtroom feeling ill. May I at least prevail on your honor for a recess?

CHIEF JUSTICE. Indeed you may, for somewhat longer than you might have expected. It's time now for me to clear up my minuscule mystery. Reluctantly, after some debate, my colleagues of the bench have informed me they can no longer grant the use of this chamber of their circuit court—and now we face transport to the Supreme Court General Term Room. But that must be prepared for us. Therefore, ladies and gentlemen, we are adjourned until ten o'clock Monday. And I say farewell to you in the hope that New Year's merrymaking will restore all our tempers.

New Year's Merrymaking

*A*s Henry stepped from the door of the hotel the wind sprang up to claw at his nose and ears. He shivered, sought a hack, futilely, and resigned himself to the twenty-minute walk required to reach the Burtons.

A brougham went briskly by. He recognized it—glossy black, striped with blue at the fenders and running board. Very sporting sort of coach. Eager young horses struck sparks from the cobblestones. It belonged to N. P. Willis, and Henry, breaking into a sprint, shouted his name. The brougham stopped—N.P.'s coach but N.P. not inside.

"My fate is to materialize in the nick and pluck you from the ravages of the weather," Catherine Forrest said as she arranged a blanket about his legs.

"Thank you, thank you," he said. "Good lord, 'tis cold out there."

"Cold as a *Herald* reporter's heart. No, I rescind that. You have been kinder to me lately. Has some intelligent woman had your instruction in hand?" Glancing at him blandly.

He did not answer.

"Well, I think it possible. Tell me where I'm to drop you, Henry. Unless of course you'd care to go with me, first to collect Mr. O'Conor and then on to the Willis's for a small party where you'd be most warmly welcomed."

"Would I be?"

"Ah, you mean Serena. The point is moot, as learned counsel might say, since she left yesterday for Boston to visit her aunt."

Henry gave her the Burton's address, and she in turn passed it on to the coachman. They drove in silence for a while. As always he was impressed by how comfortable she could make him feel. It was a talent. His mother had it too. He decided it was a talent cultivated women had in common.

"The Burtons. Do I know them?"

"No," he said and proceeded to tell her what splendid friends they were, how staunchly they had supported him at the time of Mary's death, how tireless a matchmaker Annie was in his behalf. He had not meant to say so much, particularly about the matchmaking. And once out it sent a weather-defying flush to his ears.

"You have the knack of getting people to talk to you," he said. "*You* should have been a reporter."

"A fate worse than death," she said, but lightly.

He turned to look at her. "Mrs. Forrest—"

"Catherine. Please. It's been awhile since I've thought of you as Mister Stewart."

"Catherine."

"Excellent. But I interrupted you."

"I merely wanted to say how well I think you're bearing up."

"You thought I might not bear up?"

"Anyone might not."

"Women are durable goods, Henry: soft surfaces, hard insides."

"Yes."

She caught something in his tone. "And hard to fathom?"

He smiled at her quickness.

"Well, men aren't easy either. And would you like to know

when we find you most mysterious? It's when you say you love us. It's then you're most prone to abuse us, lock us up, knock us about. Explain that to me. Never mind, I don't ask you to speak for your sex."

"Thank God."

"Henry, do you like women?"

"Very much."

"Do you think we have worth?"

"Of course."

"I think so too, I think *I* have worth. I even think I've a right to survive."

He hesitated, then plunged in. "I've wanted to ask you something."

"You or the *Herald*? If it's the *Herald* I won't answer. Or if I do I'll make no effort to tell the truth. Say which."

"The *Herald*."

"Despite being warned?"

"I don't think you lie easily."

"You're mistaken. It's about Edwin, isn't it? I know what it is, of course, but oh, very well, ask away."

"What would you have him do? I mean, if he truly believes you guilty . . . if he believes his honor to be at stake."

Her hand slapped against the side of the carriage—once, twice—hard. "Honor," she said bitterly. "A wife's infidelity stains a man's honor, but a husband's infidelity . . . ? Why, that's nothing at all, sir. A wink and a snicker amid the cigar smoke."

"The cases are different. I'm not as certain as I once was that they should be, but the fact is they are."

Leaning back against the cushion, she shut her eyes. "I know."

He looked at her.

She was silent then, long enough for him to think the discussion had ended. But when she opened her eyes again they were still angry. "And yet if honor's the issue, is it honorable in a man to reduce his wife to pauperism, to exile her as if twelve years of marriage had never happened? This is no tender city, Henry

Stewart. A pauper one day, degradation the next. You think not? Then tell me where we're to find safety. As governesses? By schoolteaching? Through sewing? I've seen them, those gentlewomen in reduced circumstances. Their existences are miserable. They cling to life out of habit and would *rush* toward death if the unknown were less frightening." She shook her head. "I've lost track. You asked a question. Well, never mind. I'm sure of this. I'll not cooperate in my own murder."

And he was confronted suddenly by the fighting spirit in her. She had known the odds from the start, knew them now perhaps even more grimly, but there was no surrender in her. Let them gather outside her house in double the number. Let them catcall themselves hoarse. She'd find a way to surmount them. He was convinced of it. Her gallantry moved him, and without volition his hand captured hers and squeezed.

Her smile blazed up. "Why, thank you, my friend."

The remainder of the trip was short. But when they arrived at the Burtons' she said, "What a fool Edwin Forrest is. He loves me. Yes, he does. Every day he comes into court, and I see him suffering from it. And if the jury gives him victory it'll be an empty one because he'll go on suffering. And for my part, no man will ever again mean so much to me. And yet he has willfully destroyed us."

Willfully? Implying the possibility of some other choice? Henry thought of Forrest and wondered if that man's nature was compatible with freedom of choice. And what about Catherine, for that matter? Which choices of hers could be described as free? Fewer than she was prepared to believe. Both were imprisoned by forces that only seemed accessible to interpretation and understanding. Perhaps that was true of everyone? The thought depressed him.

She leaned forward. "You stand at a crossroads, Henry Stewart. Take the wrong fork, and you share Edwin's fate. Take the other, and quite easily you could place yourself among the world's fortunate."

Fortunate, he thought, as he watched after her carriage. Yes, the way a hanged man is fortunate who is not also drawn and quartered. He stood there, the wind chewing at him, until his host came out and dragged him to safety.

At the Burtons', New Year's merrymaking proceeded sedately. The gathering was small, all old friends. They supped; played a bit of whist; dipped, from time to time, into the punch bowl; disported in a minor key. Henry fielded much talk of the Forrests, of course, and opinions differed as to which jurors were leaning which way.

Annie, eyes glittering, said, "That man is an ogre."

"Do you mean Forrest?" her husband asked.

"Yes, that *thespian*. And she . . . she is a heroine to endure so much so gallantly. Ah, if there were women on that jury!" She stamped a small foot in exasperation, while Henry and Robert Burton exchanged surprised glances. This was an Annie with a *side* to her.

Midnight. Kisses, handshakes, exchanges of warm wishes. Henry was hugged hard by Annie, who then began to cry. When he asked why, she called him a spooney-head and would not answer beyond that. But he knew she was thinking of Mary.

Peter came in just as the party was getting ready to break up, drew Henry to an out-of-the-way corner, and announced he was leaving Brady. No surprise. Henry had inferred as much from certain long silences, absent stares, and other signs available to those who knew the Blaylock language. And though he'd been trying to prepare himself he found he'd done so only in a limited sense. When? he asked. In a few days. Where? Peter shrugged, waving a hand vaguely westward. For a moment Henry was tempted to join him . . . wherever. Peter saw this in his face and grinned, knowing how inconsequential a flicker it really was.

They drank each other's health. But then Peter set his glass down, and—as if he were one of Brady's cameras—studied Henry intently enough to make him nervous.

"What is it?"

"Serena's in Boston with Aunt Emma," Peter said. "Do you know why?"

"Presumably there are fresh scalps to be gathered in Boston."

Silence.

"No, I don't know why. I confess that your sister is a mystery to me."

"Henry, a ten-year-old could solve the mystery of Serena."

"You're being absurd. Go to California. Here you do nothing but give me a headache."

Peter stood; then Henry did, too, and they clasped each other.

"Wish me well," Peter said.

"I do. Will we ever see each other again?"

"Of course."

That night once again Henry was insomniacal. He wondered if Bennett was. With a groan of self-detestation, he abandoned his riddled moratorium and wondered where Serena had done her New Year's merrymaking. And where was she now? Sound asleep, no doubt. No insomniac she.

Peter soon to be gone, Henry thought. He would be terribly, terribly missed.

What had he meant, a ten-year-old?

Catherine's Diary

*W*ould like to say something significant about poor 1851, which is *in extremis,* but can think of nothing. It dies in a twitching of icy rain.

A Call to Arms

*I*cy rain converted Broadway into cobble glass. Nevertheless, the Stewarts, *en masse,* made twenty-four New Year's Day calls. Tired at the outset, Henry, to his surprise, was less so when they finished. It was a custom falling into abeyance, New Year's Day calling—younger folk like the Burtons didn't any more—but Henry regretted that. Everyone was so welcoming. Ancient Mrs. Rimmerhorn still wanted to pat his head, comb his hair, tuck in his shirt, and say, "My how you've grown, Master Stewart." He knew she did.

Later he made a call on Bennett, whose wounded leg was not mending at the speed he'd predicted. Except for servants he was alone and sulking. He'd sent his ailing wife (la grippe, a prolonged bout) and young son south until spring, and Henry thought he might be missing them. It was hard to be sure. Bennett's habit was to rage at family sentiment, labeling it humbug. In disdain for consistency, he was fond of referring to the *Herald* work force as his family. Many in this work force, however, referred to themselves as bondsmen, a long-suffering group of 180 or so who daily climbed the dirtiest steps in the city to slave for old massa in his three-story plantation on the corner of Nassau and Bleecker streets.

Each New Year's Day (for the past four) Henry's ritual had been to appear before Bennett to ask for a salary increase. Success or failure did not flow from the merits of his case. Whim was the issue, a matter of Bennett's world outlook at the time. On this day it was bleak, and Henry went unrewarded.

Business out of the way, they played chess for the next few hours. Henry, the far better player, sought—and achieved—vengeful victories, as lopsided as he could make them. Paradoxically, Bennett's mood seemed improved by this.

Over cognac, Bennett informed Henry that O'Conor should never have let the "Consuelo" letter be proved in evidence, proclaiming it the turning point of the case. That plus the forthcoming Jamieson testimony, he said, would knock Mrs. Forrest to flinders.

"He came to dine with me last night—the tragedian, I mean—a dismal enough occasion. He looks ragged, worn down. The damnedest thing is he's still in love with that trollop. Aye, Stewart, that's what they are, every one of them."

"Every one of which, sir?"

"All those fancy ladies with advanced views . . . thinly disguised trollops, every one of them."

"Mr. Bennett—"

"No, no, you listen to me, lad. I'm right about this. All those bluestocking followers of that damned Frenchman Fourier. A damned frog. What does a damned frog know about this country? Utopian socialism, they calls it. I calls it humbug. And that's what it is, nought but humbug. And libidinousness, an excuse for forming happy little fucking societies. That's what they do, laddie. They live together and fuck each other's spouses. Aye, they may be able to fool that fathead Horace Greeley, but the *Herald*'s not the *Tribune* and never will be, and this old Scotsman's too clever for them by half. Did you know they've got maybe forty of them by now? Aye, forty. Phalanxes, they calls 'em. Fuckiaries, I calls 'em. Because what they do in them all day long is fuck, fuck, fuck."

It took Henry awhile to shift him to more congenial territory.

The trouble with the Superior Court General Term Room, Henry discovered on Monday morning, was its size—much smaller, a third less space for spectators. As the predictable result two fistfights broke out, one between a man and a woman, one disruptive enough to require police intervention. So that what with one thing and another it was not until after lunch that the trial resumed.

Minor surprise. Van Buren, who had promised Forrest, rang in a witness to precede him.

The clerk called Mrs. Elizabeth Demming.

Elizabeth Demming, angular, fussily dressed, in her fifties, being sworn and examined by Mr. Van Buren, deposed.

MRS. DEMMING. My husband's full name is Egbert Demming, and together we reside in Twenty-first Street in the house behind the house owned by Mr. Edwin Forrest. That house is on Twenty-second Street, but the two are actually on the same lot. His garden fence joins the rear of our house.

VAN BUREN. What night will we be concerned with, Mrs. Demming?

MRS. DEMMING. A night sometime in the fall of 1848. Though I would prefer being more precise, that is my best recollection.

VAN BUREN. Pray tell us what you saw.

MRS. DEMMING. It was between eleven and midnight, our usual bedtime. My husband and I were preparing to go upstairs when my sister Eleanor requested our presence at the library window. Through it we could see two people in Mr. Forrest's library, a gentleman and a lady, the gentleman with his arm around the lady's shoulders.

VAN BUREN. Tightly?

O'CONOR. Oh, tightly, to be sure.

VAN BUREN. Tightly, Mrs. Demming?

MRS. DEMMING. So it seemed to us.

VAN BUREN. Go on.

MRS. DEMMING. At first their backs were toward us, but then they turned and moved a step closer, toward the table, where there was a gas lamp. In the light of this we could see their faces clearly. We saw the gentleman kiss the lady.

VAN BUREN. Kiss her . . . warmly?

O'CONOR. Oh warmly, warmly.

CHIEF JUSTICE. Enough, Mr. O'Conor.

VAN BUREN. Warmly, Mrs. Demming?

MRS. DEMMING. So it seemed to us.

VAN BUREN. On the . . . forehead?

MRS. DEMMING. On the lips.

VAN BUREN. Mrs. Demming, who was the lady?

MRS. DEMMING. Mrs. Forrest.

VAN BUREN. Was the gentleman Mr. Forrest?

MRS. DEMMING. It could not have been. Mr. Forrest was on tour at the time.

VAN BUREN. Did you recognize the gentleman?

MRS. DEMMING. Oh, yes. He is quite well known.

VAN BUREN. Do you see him in this courtroom?

MRS. DEMMING. I do.

VAN BUREN. Pray say his name and point him out to us.

MRS. DEMMING *(finger extended)*. His name is N. P. Willis. *(hubbub, gavel)*

N.P. bore up tolerably well, Henry thought—if not with insouciance, at least without hysterics.

VAN BUREN *(to O'Conor)*. Your witness, sir.

O'CONOR *(minimum communion)*. How well do you know Mrs. Forrest, Mrs. Demming?

MRS. DEMMING. Not very well.

O'CONOR. Not nearly as well as you might if she had accepted any of the several dinner invitations you have extended, is that fair to say?

MRS. DEMMING. Perhaps.

O'CONOR. In the four years you've lived side by side, isn't it true you've spoken to her but once?

MRS. DEMMING. Yes.

O'CONOR. To complain about a cat that kept you up.

MRS. DEMMING. It kept us up all night.

O'CONOR. I see.

MRS. DEMMING. And my husband was ill at the time.

O'CONOR. Mrs. Demming, how well do you know Mr. Forrest?

MRS. DEMMING. Mr. Forrest?

O'CONOR. Yes, ma'am.

MRS. DEMMING. I have seen him perform.

O'CONOR. Often?

MRS. DEMMING. I suppose so.

O'CONOR. How often?

MRS. DEMMING. I'm not sure.

O'CONOR. More than . . . ten times?

MRS. DEMMING. Yes.

O'CONOR. More than twenty-five?

MRS. DEMMING. Yes.

O'CONOR. Isn't it your boast that you have seen him perform every major role in his repertoire?

MRS. DEMMING. I have never seen his Virginius.

O'CONOR. Failing that?

MRS. DEMMING. Yes.

VAN BUREN. Your honor, I am trying to be patient, but I cannot see where learned counsel is taking us with this. If it be proved conclusively that Mrs. Demming is passionate in her theatergoing, are we better off than we are now?

O'CONOR. How if she is passionate about Mr. Forrest?

CHIEF JUSTICE. Passionate, Mr. O'Conor?

O'CONOR. Too strong a word, your honor?

CHIEF JUSTICE. I leave that for you to decide, sir.

O'CONOR *(four seconds of communion)*. It might be instructive for us all to know she admires him warmly.

CHIEF JUSTICE. From afar?

O'CONOR. No more than that, sir.

CHIEF JUSTICE *(to Van Buren)*. I think he might be permitted to ascertain that. Yes, I think he must.

VAN BUREN. If you say so, sir.

CHIEF JUSTICE. Proceed, Mr. O'Conor.

O'CONOR. *Do* you, Mrs. Demming, admire Mr. Forrest warmly?

MRS. DEMMING. I do not know him, sir.

O'CONOR. As a tragedian, Mrs. Demming. It is fair to say, is it not, that you find Mr. Forrest's work to be of some distinction?

MRS. DEMMING *(a burst)*. I think he is the foremost tragedian of our time.

O'CONOR. Thank you, Mrs. Demming. I have no further questions.

She started to leave but stopped when Mr. Meech, foreman, suddenly erupted from amid his fellow jurors. His bald head was slightly shiny, his plump cheeks a shade more florid than was their wont, but his voice was stentorian.

MEECH. Question, please.

CHIEF JUSTICE. Proceed, Mr. Meech.

MEECH. On behalf of the jury, I put the question: How far is it from Mrs. Demming's house to Mr. Forrest's?

O'CONOR. It's exactly one hundred feet. And thank you very much, Mr. Meech, for presenting me with the opportunity to remedy my own neglect.

Meech, pleased, sat.

The clerk called Mr. Edwin Forrest.

Beautifully turned out today (Bennett notwithstanding), Forrest came forward: gold-headed cane, bottle-green coat, fawn-colored trousers, glistening boots, and enough snowy linen to make a modest Alp. One quick hot glance toward Catherine. She returned it steadily. It was Mrs. Willis who cringed.

VAN BUREN. On May 13, 1848, you opened at the National Theater in Cincinnati, is that correct, sir?

FORREST. Yes. *Othello.*

VAN BUREN. And Mrs. Forrest, was she with you on this trip?

FORREST. She was.

VAN BUREN. Was she then acquainted with Mr. George Jamieson?

FORREST. Yes.

VAN BUREN. He was in the company?

FORREST. Yes.

VAN BUREN. On the afternoon of the fourteenth, did you and Mrs. Forrest invite Mr. Jamieson to accompany you to a lecture on phrenology?

MEECH *(once again on his feet)*. "Phrenology, your honor?"

CHIEF JUSTICE. Ah, yes. As I understand it, 'tis a system by which character can be determined through studying the shape and protuberances of the skull. Does that get to the gist, Mr. Van Buren?

VAN BUREN. To the crux, your honor.

O'CONOR. To the bone, sir. *(some laughter, quelled good-temperedly by the Chief Justice.)*

CHIEF JUSTICE. Will that do, Mr. Meech?

MEECH. Oh, yes, sir. Very good, sir. Thank you, sir. *(and other obsequious sounds)*

VAN BUREN. Mr. Forrest, can you recall the hour scheduled for this lecture?

FORREST. Three o'clock.

VAN BUREN. You were to meet them in the lecture hall, is that correct?

FORREST. Yes. I went for a sitting to Mr. Ralph Jenson, a local portrait painter, and I was to go from there to the lecture hall. But Mr. Jensen was taken ill, so I returned to the hotel instead.

VAN BUREN. Yes. You returned to the hotel . . . early. *(pause)* I would like to continue now by reading Mr. Forrest's deposition submitted—

O'CONOR. Why read his deposition? The witness graces us with his presence. Can he not give his testimony in the ordinary way?

VAN BUREN. Would you prefer it?

O'CONOR. No, no, no. Do what you will.

VAN BUREN. I construe it as a time-saver, your honor.

CHIEF JUSTICE. Then by all means proceed.

VAN BUREN. Let the record show I am reading from the deposition of Edwin C. Forrest sworn before witnesses on February 5, 1851. As follows: "When I entered my private parlor in the City Hotel, I found Mrs. Forrest standing between the knees of Mr. Jamieson, who was sitting on the sofa, with his hands upon her person. I was amazed and confounded and asked what it meant. Mrs. Forrest replied, with considerable perturbation, that Mr. Jamieson had been pointing out phrenological developments. Being of an unsuspicious nature, and anxious to believe that it was nothing more than an act of imprudence on her part, I was for a time quieted by this explanation."

O'CONOR. What was it he said Jamieson was pointing out?

VAN BUREN. Her phrenological developments.

O'CONOR. Oh, those. *(laughter; gavel; admonishing look directed at O'Conor)*

VAN BUREN. And in the days succeeding you said nothing further to Mrs. Forrest concerning this incident?

FORREST. No.

VAN BUREN. How do you explain that?

FORREST. The deposition explains it, sir. I *am* of an unsuspicious nature. And I was *most* eager to believe that no more than an act of imprudence had taken place.

VAN BUREN. Very well, sir. Time passes. Eight months from the afternoon of May 14, 1848, to the night of January 19, 1849. During this period were your relations with Mrs. Forrest exactly as they had been before?

FORREST. Not quite.

VAN BUREN. How did they differ?

FORREST. Despite myself—that is, despite all efforts to the contrary—I was more on guard. I *did* watch her more carefully. Once I had had perfect confidence in her. It was true no longer.

VAN BUREN. And in watching her more carefully . . . ?

FORREST. Nothing. That is, nothing of a conclusive nature. Nothing that would be considered evidence in this courtroom. . . .

VAN BUREN. And yet—

O'CONOR. Object. If it cannot be considered evidence in this courtroom, then obviously there is nothing more to be said about it.

CHIEF JUSTICE. Sustained.

VAN BUREN. Tell the Court, Mr. Forrest, what was it that made you determined to separate from your wife? Was it her . . . Englishness?

FORREST. Certainly not.

VAN BUREN. Your emotional state at the time? I allude to the condition caused by your difficulties with Mr. Macready.

FORREST. That of course had nothing to do with it.

VAN BUREN. Then what?

FORREST. The letter was a gigantic blow.

VAN BUREN. The letter. The "Consuelo" letter, which you found in her bureau drawer the day of the quarrel. That is to say, the letter to Mrs. Forrest from George Jamieson.

FORREST. Yes. After reading it there was no longer any hope of her innocence.

VAN BUREN. And yet you waited until May 1 before actually separating. Why is that?

FORREST (*shrugging*). Because I was foolish.

VAN BUREN. In what way foolish?

FORREST. Foolishly, weakly . . . I could not bring myself to part from her. I take no pleasure in confessing that, sir, but I confess it.

VAN BUREN. What made you finally act?

FORREST. She had begun to tell it about that our separation was caused by—the point is, we had promised each other sacredly to say nothing to anyone about why we were separating.

VAN BUREN. And she broke that promise?

FORREST. She did.

VAN BUREN. Mr. Forrest, I know how reluctant you are to prolong this unhappy discussion, and yet there are things this Court must become privy to. You understand that, sir, do you not?

FORREST. I do.

VAN BUREN. Then I ask you, sir, what cause did Mrs. Forrest produce to explain the separation?

FORREST. Various causes. They changed with the wind, none of them redounding to my credit.

VAN BUREN. Among them, your troubles with Mr. Macready?

FORREST. Yes.

VAN BUREN. Or, that she had given you the lie, and you could not live with one who did?

FORREST. Yes.

VAN BUREN. Your personality in general?

FORREST. Yes.

VAN BUREN. In other words, that same motley assortment put forward by Mr. O'Conor in his opening address to the jury, is that not so?

FORREST. Yes.

VAN BUREN. But she never mentioned the real cause, did she?

O'CONOR. Object. Defendant can speak only to his view of the so-called real cause.

CHIEF JUSTICE. Sustained.

VAN BUREN. Well, then, speak to your view, Mr. Forrest. In your view what was the real cause?

FORREST. Her infidelity.

VAN BUREN. Your witness, sir.

O'CONOR *(without hesitation; without, in fact, bothering to rise).* Are you familiar with Madame Sand's book?

FORREST. Who is Madame Sand?

O'Conor. George Sand. The author of *Consuelo*.

Forrest. No, sir, I am not. I do not read French novels.

O'Conor. Then that no doubt explains it.

Chief Justice. Explains what, Mr. O'Conor? I confess I'm at a loss to follow you.

O'Conor. Why, sir, it explains why Mr. Forrest is unaware that the whole point of *Consuelo* is the heroine's determined, permit me to say indomitable, chastity.

Chief Justice. 'Pon my soul. Did you know this, Mr. Van Buren?

Van Buren. Yes, sir. However, I don't see its relevance, since that is certainly not the point of Mr. Jamieson's letter.

O'Conor. You may step down, Mr. Forrest. I've no further questions for you.

Van Buren seemed for a moment caught off balance by the brevity of O'Conor's cross-examination, Henry thought. But only for a moment. He rose with still another document in hand.

Van Buren. Your honor, I stand on the very precipice of closing my case. All that remains now is one final letter. A letter from Mrs. Forrest to Mr. Lawson, Mr. Forrest's business agent and friend. In fact, at the time this letter was written, June 11, 1848, Mr. Lawson considered himself, as you will see, a friend to both the Forrests. Your honor, I intend to show by this—

O'Conor. Your honor, I've no objection to the reading of the letter. I've long ago conceded what learned counsel wishes to show, that in certain areas Mrs. Forrest is a lady of advanced views. She makes no secret of it. In fact she insists on it. Moreover, I enjoy Mr. Van Buren's readings. He reads superbly. But let him confine himself to that. Let him reserve his comments for his summation.

Chief Justice. Yes, Mr. Van Buren. At this point you must let the letter speak for itself.

Van Buren. I'll be delighted to. As you will see, it was written in response to one of Mr. Lawson's. As follows:

"My dear sir: It's been a question with me for some days

whether I should reply to the letter I received from you in Pittsburgh or leave the matter you write about for future discussion, but as a chance for that seems somewhat remote I will for a few moments tax your well-known patience.

"You say, 'The *rights of women* is a notion I utterly abhor.' I don't quite understand that. You cannot mean women have no rights. The poorest and most abject things on earth have rights. Even female domestic animals have rights.

"Again you say: 'A man loves a woman as much for her very dependence on him as for her beauty and intelligence.' This astonished me. Do you truly value the love of a woman who clings to you only for support? In nursery days we used to call this 'puppy love' and value it minimally. The relative position of man and wife must be that of companions—not mastery on one side and dependence on the other.

"Again you say: 'Before blaming her husband for seeking after new fancies a wife should examine her own heart and see if she finds there some justification for him.' Here, my friend, I agree with you. And if, after self-examination, she finds the fault hers she should certainly amend it. But how if she finds the fault his?

"In any case a sensible woman who loves her husband in the true spirit of love, without selfishness, desires to see him happy. She would rather that he seek 'new fancies' than lead a life of self-denial and unrest, feeling each day the weight of his chains become more irksome. I am no admirer of despotism, no matter what form it takes.

"But that is aside from the issue, isn't it? The issue here is rights for women, which one day we shall have despite your abhorrence of them, my friend. One day an enlightened society—"

At this point there was a sudden disturbance in the back of the courtroom. Women—five, six, seven, a dozen, more—were standing and applauding. Henry saw Annie Burton, her small, slender body stiff as a martyr's, her gentle blue eyes aflame with militancy. A week ago she might not have been here. Even

Bennett had conceded that there'd been something of a shift in recent days. Among the female upper-tenners, Mrs. Forrest was in danger of becoming popular.

In the meantime Mrs. Willis had collapsed in Mrs. Forrest's arms and was sobbing uncontrollably. That lady—grave, composed—patted her back.

While the Chief Justice hammered with his gavel, Henry quickly turned to the jury to see what emotion held sway there. Foreman Meech looked outraged, but that, he thought, had its cause not as much in the letter as in the disturbance. (Clearly, Meech was one who liked an orderly flow.) Mr. DeWitt seemed amused, Mr. Schlessinger bemused—as if to say: Mr. Meech, I trust before long you will tell me what to make of all this. As for the rest, if they registered reaction, Henry had reached them too late for proper appraisal.

And yet he could not believe Van Buren had misjudged them. It was too bold a letter, too advanced for this jury to accept with equanimity. Only a jury sprinkled liberally with, say, N. P. Willises or, as Henry supposed must happen some day, a jury with women on it, could be expected to feel other than disquieted. The letter will hurt, he thought. Van Buren, equally pleased with the letter's satellite—still not quelled absolutely by the judge's gavel—smiled and waited patiently for silence to be restored, while O'Conor, expression phlegmatic, examined his boots.

CHIEF JUSTICE. Enough, I say! One minute more of this, and I'll order the courtroom cleared. *(silence at last)*

VAN BUREN. The letter does go on a bit, your honor, but not pertinently. The case for the defendant rests.

O'CONOR *(an eon of communion before approaching not the bench but the jury)*. Sirs, I too have letters. *(half turn toward the Chief Justice)* May I?

CHIEF JUSTICE. I'm not certain I follow you. There's material you wish to place in evidence?

O'CONOR. Five letters. All written by Mr. Forrest to Mrs.

Forrest—subsequent, that is, to the historic afternoon in Cincinnati after which Mr. Forrest says his view of his wife became jaundiced.

CHIEF JUSTICE. Are they short letters?

O'CONOR. Short indeed, sir, but extremely to the point.

CHIEF JUSTICE. Proceed.

O'CONOR *(reading)*. "Baltimore, Wednesday, November 15, 1848. My dear Kate: I am sitting at an open window in the Eutaw, and though it is cold the sky is a cloudless blue, just such a day as I yearn to have with you at Fonthill. The audiences continue to be very good, but please tell Lawson for me that I have no wish to prolong my tour at this time. I am tired. I wish to come to you as soon as possible. With all my love I am, my dear Kate, your own Edwin.

"Philadelphia, Saturday, November 25, 1848. My dear Kate: The costumes you made came yesterday, and I wore the Gladiator last night. I looked splendid in it. You would have been proud of me. At curtain I was called back out for nine cheers. They followed this with three groans for Macready. I hope you are well. My sister sends kindest greetings, and I send dearest love. Yours ever, Edwin.

"Philadelphia, Thursday, November 30, 1848: I am not so well, my dearest Kate, today as I have been for a few days past. I am suffering from severe headaches. I could endure these uncomplainingly but for the horror of going before the public in character—as a result of which the blood will be sent to my brain with tenfold force. Such is the *pleasure* of acting! I write this in great pain and in some haste. And in great longing to be with you. I will write tomorrow. Edwin.

"Philadelphia, Tuesday morning, December 5, 1848. My dearest, dearest Kate, you had better pay me a visit for a week or two. My suffering continues, and I need you. Come a week from today, the twelfth. Henrietta sends greetings. Your own, desperate Edwin.

"Philadelphia, Thursday, December 7, 1848. My dearest Kate:

I made an effort to write to you yesterday, but a pain which I had in my chest increased to such a degree I was forced to drop the pen and betake me to bed. My suffering continued until about the second act of *Richelieu,* when I found some abatement of the extreme agony. After the play I was rubbed with alcohol and finally recovered. I cannot trace this attack to any cause. Lawson—he arrived just before the opening curtain—blames Macready for it. He says I am too intense about Macready, and that I ought to try to forget him. But how can I? Does Lawson not understand how much more than a personal antipathy is involved? What do you think? Looking forward with eagerness to your visit, I am forever, my dearest Kate, your own Edwin."

Finished now, O'Conor crossed to the clerk and passed over his missives.

O'CONOR. Mark as exhibits, Mr. Asher, if you will. *(three seconds of communion, then a level stare for the jury) Jaundiced . . . ?*

But there was fire lacking in it. To Henry, O'Conor seemed like an overextended actor who senses rebellion in his audience but has exhausted the power that once would have settled its hash. On the other hand this was O'Conor the Great, Henry reminded himself. And playing possum was a famous game of his.

Van Buren, too, was on guard, Henry thought. He looked like a battle-wise fox, fully aware that overconfidence could rob him of the hen he'd just stolen.

CHIEF JUSTICE. Mr. O'Conor, do you have word as to the current condition of Mrs. Ingersoll?

O'CONOR. Her physician promises her when she is needed.

CHIEF JUSTICE. Good. But that will not be tomorrow. Yes, this oft-interrupted trial must suffer still another interruption. I've no choice in the matter. As a few of you know, I've been under some apprehension with regard to the safety of the floor in this room, which, I'm told, is supported by only two small pillars. The work crew to repair this cannot be assembled until tomorrow. By Friday morning, however, I'm assured all will be in readiness for us to resume—and then finish, I trust, with all dispatch. Make your plans accordingly and accept my apologies for whatever inconvenience is caused you by the law's delay. Ladies and gentlemen, we stand adjourned.

Catherine's Diary

*F*or the first time tonight O'Conor seemed less than rock-like. Or perhaps it was simple fatigue. He confessed to that and nothing else. I think, though, that he feels my overheated little letter lost us ground. Well, I would not be amazed if it did. But I'm in no mood for recanting. One day we will learn to treat sexual matters not as scabrous secrets but sensibly, sensibly, *sensibly,* as if we were all humans together.

At any rate O'Conor droops. In that regard, too, perhaps he is like Edwin. When Edwin came offstage to "nine cheers," full of himself because he'd performed well, he was voracious. He was . . . there was that night . . . in the dressing room! Merciful heaven, all the parquet circle could have wandered in. But self-doubt chills him, affects him like—whatever is the opposite of aphrodisiacal.

Vanderhoff joined us tonight for dinner, putting forward his proposal again. Shall I accept? His new theater won't open until April, and he makes it all seem so plausible. He's convinced, he says, that I have a natural talent for drawing room comedy and that I could appear to advantage in perennials such as *School for*

Scandal. He says he will study hard with me. Though at bottom an unvarnished opportunist, he is also an accomplished teacher. Edwin, who has hated him for years, acknowledges that much about him.

It's obvious Vanderhoff has in mind a two for one, so to speak—striking a blow at an ancient enemy and exploiting the box-office potential of a fallen lady.

How lightly I write that. How steadily the quill remains in my hand. How efficiently even pain can be managed when one grows practiced.

Well, the truth is we fallen ladies have few options. We must eat, clothe ourselves, keep a roof over our heads, live.

The faces in the jury box were not reassuring today.

I think I must tell Vanderhoff I count him my guardian angel and that he in turn may count on a name with which he can titillate his patronage.

There is a ferocious tingling at the back of my neck, needles up and down my left arm. No doubt a heart attack is building. Yes, I will be carried off sometime before dawn and thus end my troubles.

I feel . . . anxious tonight. Frightened.

An Upper-Tenner's Sort of House

*T*he clerk called Mrs. Caroline Ingersoll.

At last. Middle fifties, sufficiently respectable-looking, Henry thought, despite the suspect claret of her hair, Mrs. Caroline Ingersoll, being sworn and examined by Mr. O'Conor, deposed.

MRS. INGERSOLL. I reside at 4 Murray Street in this city. I have resided in this city some four years. When I first came to New York from Philadelphia in early 1847, I went to reside at 355 Greenwich Street. I lived there about a year. I moved from that house to 623 Houston Street and lived there about two years. I know Mr. Edwin Forrest, the defendant in this suit. I have known him since I lived in Greenwich Street.

O'CONOR. I am delighted to see you up and around, Mrs. Ingersoll. Have you quite recovered?

MRS. INGERSOLL. From what?

O'CONOR. From whatever it was that was ailing you.

MRS. INGERSOLL *(glaring)*. Busybodies was ailing me. That's all, nothing more. *(laughter: though clearly regarded as the major offender, O'Conor seems pleased to join in before the gavel restores decorum.)*

CHIEF JUSTICE. Mrs. Ingersoll, we are gathered here to do our duty according to the statutes of this city. Flippancy is out of place.

MRS. INGERSOLL. Sorry, your honor. I meant no disrespect.

O'CONOR. Mrs. Ingersoll, did Mr. Forrest ever visit you in your house on Greenwich Street?

MRS. INGERSOLL. He did.

O'CONOR. For the record, when would that have been?

MRS. INGERSOLL. When?

O'CONOR. In 1847? You have already deposed that you owned a house there then.

MRS. INGERSOLL. Eighteen forty-seven is correct.

O'CONOR. How often did he visit you? More than once?

MRS. INGERSOLL. Yes.

O'CONOR. Was he a regular visitor?

MRS. INGERSOLL. Depends on what you mean by regular.

O'CONOR. More than five times?

MRS. INGERSOLL. Yes.

O'CONOR. Ten?

MRS. INGERSOLL. Yes.

O'CONOR. Thank you, madam. When he came did he come alone?

MRS. INGERSOLL. Yes.

O'CONOR. For what purpose did he come?

MRS. INGERSOLL. For what purpose? Why, to engage a chamber.

O'CONOR. For how long?

MRS. INGERSOLL. Varied.

O'CONOR. Did he ever stay overnight?

MRS. INGERSOLL. I disremember.

O'CONOR. You have an unreliable memory, Mrs. Ingersoll?

MRS. INGERSOLL. A *treacherous* memory. Always have had.

O'CONOR. When he engaged a room . . . I mean chamber . . . was it customarily the same one?

MRS. INGERSOLL. Mostly.

O'CONOR. You kept it for him?

MRS. INGERSOLL. When possible.

O'CONOR. Describe it for us.

MRS. INGERSOLL. Describe it?

O'CONOR. Was there a bed in it?

MRS. INGERSOLL. Certain sure there was a bed in it. I said it was a chamber, didn't I? So there was a bed in it.

O'CONOR. Upstairs or downstairs?

MRS. INGERSOLL. Second story, a front chamber. And there was a small parlor adjoining, too.

O'CONOR *(three seconds of communion)*. For what purpose did Mr. Forrest engage this chamber?

MRS. INGERSOLL. He never said.

O'CONOR. Did you ever see him in his chamber?

MRS. INGERSOLL. No.

O'CONOR. You never conducted him to his chamber?

MRS. INGERSOLL. I never saw him any place except my parlor, which is the front room on the first story. What I did, I received him in the parlor and left him there.

O'CONOR. You left him there? Just . . . more or less . . . at his own devices?

MRS. INGERSOLL. He knew his way.

O'CONOR. So what you said to him was, "Good day, Mr. Forrest," and then faded into the woodwork, as the expression goes?

MRS. INGERSOLL. I retired sometimes through the folding doors and sometimes through the parlor doors. It was generally in the morning when Mr. Forrest came, and I had my household duties to perform. It was a large house, that house on Greenwich Street, and not an easy house to keep orderly.

O'CONOR. To keep orderly? No, ma'am, I am quite certain it was not. *(laughter)*

VAN BUREN. Object. Learned counsel is—

CHIEF JUSTICE. Yes, Mr. O'Conor, you are. Let us have no more of it, please.

O'CONOR. I take it then, Mrs. Ingersoll, that you never saw Mr. Forrest leave?

MRS. INGERSOLL. I told you, no.

O'CONOR. Then when did he pay for his chamber?

MRS. INGERSOLL. When next he came.

O'CONOR. Therefore you must have been fairly certain he would come again.

MRS. INGERSOLL. He told me he would.

O'CONOR. How much did you charge Mr. Forrest?

MRS. INGERSOLL. I disremember.

O'CONOR. How many chambers besides Mr. Forrest's did you have to let?

MRS. INGERSOLL. Four.

O'CONOR. Was each chamber provided with a bed?

MRS. INGERSOLL. I told you—

O'CONOR. Forgive me. Certain sure they each had a bed, or why else would they be chambers? How did you let them?

MRS. INGERSOLL. How?

O'CONOR. By the day? The week?

MRS. INGERSOLL. Yes.

O'CONOR. Which?

MRS. INGERSOLL. Both.

O'CONOR. By the hour? *(She hesitates.)* Speak up, please. By the hour?

MRS. INGERSOLL. I decline to answer.

O'CONOR. Your honor. I should like a response.

CHIEF JUSTICE. Why do you decline to answer, Mrs. Ingersoll?

MRS. INGERSOLL. I have important reasons.

CHIEF JUSTICE. May I ask what they are?

MRS. INGERSOLL. I can't tell you.

CHIEF JUSTICE. Mrs. Ingersoll, I cannot allow a witness to be her own judge as to whether reasons justify silence, do you understand me?

MRS. INGERSOLL. Yes.

CHIEF JUSTICE. Do you wish, then, to elaborate?

MRS. INGERSOLL. No, sir.

CHIEF JUSTICE. That being the case, I must order you to answer. Shall I have the question repeated?

MRS. INGERSOLL. Sometimes.

CHIEF JUSTICE. That is the answer to the question?

MRS. INGERSOLL. Yes.

O'CONOR. You sometimes rented by the hour?

MRS. INGERSOLL. On the occasion.

O'CONOR. And were those occasions shared by ladies and gentlemen?

MRS. INGERSOLL. Don't know what you mean.

O'CONOR. I mean were your chambers rented to gentlemen for the purpose of meeting ladies there?

MRS. INGERSOLL. No, they were not. They were rented to boarders. Both ladies and gentlemen.

O'CONOR. Boarders who, on the occasion, stayed only an hour?

MRS. INGERSOLL. Sometimes they stayed a day, sometimes a week, sometimes even a month. What business was it of mine how long they stayed? They stayed and they paid. Curiosity—

O'CONOR. Can you give me the names of some of the gentlemen who stayed a month?

MRS. INGERSOLL. No.

O'CONOR. Will that treacherous memory of yours permit you to give me the names of two—nay, a single gentleman—who stayed a week?

MRS. INGERSOLL. I disremember their names. They were gentlemen from other cities, transients. How would I know their names?

O'CONOR. Your ledgers?

MRS. INGERSOLL. I don't keep ledgers.

O'CONOR. Of course not. Those lady boarders, Mrs. Ingersoll, how long did they stay with you, generally?

MRS. INGERSOLL. Longer.

O'CONOR. Longer than what?

MRS. INGERSOLL. Generally two or three months. Sometimes longer.

O'CONOR. And generally how many were there at a time?

MRS. INGERSOLL. On the average, three lady boarders. There have been times where there was only one.

O'CONOR. And did they have husbands, these lady boarders?

MRS. INGERSOLL. Husbands?

O'CONOR. Is that a complicated question? I can see where it might be. *(laughter)*

CHIEF JUSTICE. Mrs. Ingersoll, I understand the difficulties of your position, but unless your responses to Mr. O'Conor's questions render you liable to criminal prosecution, we must have them. The parties at law here are entitled to them.

MRS. INGERSOLL. What was the question?

CHIEF JUSTICE. Mr. Asher?

CLERK. May I paraphrase, sir?

O'CONOR. Instead, permit me to rephrase, your honor.

CHIEF JUSTICE. Proceed.

O'CONOR. Did some of your ladies occasionally occupy the same chambers with some of your gentlemen? That is the question, Mrs. Ingersoll.

MRS. INGERSOLL. The answer is I don't know.

O'CONOR. It is remarkable how little interest you took in what was going on in your own house.

MRS. INGERSOLL. Remarkable it may be, but it's a fact. Curiosity—

O'CONOR. And later, in Houston Street, Mrs. Ingersoll, did Mr. Forrest ever visit you there?

MRS. INGERSOLL. Yes.

O'CONOR. Often?

MRS. INGERSOLL. I disremember.

O'CONOR. Four times a week?

MRS. INGERSOLL. No, that's nonsense. Never more than twice a week.

O'CONOR. Thank you, madam. You may have the witness, Mr. Van Buren.

VAN BUREN. No questions.

There was a mild hubbub as Mrs. Ingersoll stepped down and scooted away. Raps of the gavel restored silence. Restored, also, Henry thought, was the great O'Conor, who grinned hugely at Van Buren. The latter tried manfully to ignore him but finally could not.

VAN BUREN. What have you proved? An ill-run boarding-house. Nothing more, I warrant.

O'CONOR. Oh, something more than that, I think. And something more to come.

CHIEF JUSTICE *(a glare for each)*. Mr. Asher, may we have the next witness, please.

The clerk called William Appleyard.

Sixties, white-haired, russet-cheeked, broad-chested, and dramatically bow-legged, William Appleyard, being sworn and examined by Mr. O'Conor, deposed.

APPLEYARD. I am now an omnibus driver. During the latter part of 1847 and the forepart of 1848 I was a policeman attached to the fifth ward. I left off the seventh of May, 1848, I think.

O'CONOR. During that time did you become acquainted with the house on 355 Greenwich Street, that which was occupied by Caroline Ingersoll?

APPLEYARD. I disremember.

O'CONOR. You too? Mr. Appleyard, we have station book reports that—

APPLEYARD. Well, if you have the reports you have the reports. I just ain't posted up about them now. But if there are reports by me, I warrant those reports are correct.

O'CONOR. But you, at this moment, have no recollection of the house in question?

APPLEYARD. I recollect about a lot of houses.

CHIEF JUSTICE. Come, come, Mr. Appleyard, you make me

impatient. Mr. O'Conor has clearly stated it is a particular house he is interested in. The house at 355 Greenwich Street.

APPLEYARD. I have some slight recollection of it, your worship.

CHIEF JUSTICE. Honor.

APPLEYARD. Beg pardon, sir?

CHIEF JUSTICE. Your honor is sufficient.

APPLEYARD. Beg pardon, your honor.

O'CONOR. Were you ever in that house, Mr. Appleyard?

APPLEYARD. Greenwich Street, you say? Three fifty-five? Yes, I believe I was. Didn't know who owned it, but I believe I was in it once or twice in the line of duty.

O'CONOR. In the line of duty?

APPLEYARD. I mean when I was a policeman, but I ain't never been in it since. *(laughter)*

O'CONOR. By duty did you mean the duty policemen have to report suspected bawdy houses to their captains?

APPLEYARD. Yes.

O'CONOR. What caused you to visit 355 Greenwich Street in the first place?

APPLEYARD. Just to sight around. People said it was an upper-tenner's sort of house. You know, fancy.

O'CONOR. Well, when you sighted around, what did you see?

APPLEYARD. Nothing very bad.

O'CONOR. Nothing to indicate this was a house of a special nature?

APPLEYARD. If I did I more or less disremember.

O'CONOR *(five seconds of communion)*. Mr. Appleyard, is your wife in the courtroom today?

APPLEYARD *(reluctant)*. Yes.

O'CONOR *(to Chief Justice)*. May she be asked to leave?

VAN BUREN. Object. What possible harm—

O'CONOR. You know what harm. She is inhibiting my witness.

VAN BUREN. Absurd. The gentlemen of the press have recorded every word since this trial began. *(transfixing Appleyard with a meaningful stare)* The point is, she hears it today or she reads it tomorrow. *(Appleyard fidgeting, taking the point)*

CHIEF JUSTICE. Still, I believe Mr. O'Conor has the right of it. Mrs. Appleyard? Is Mrs. Appleyard in the courtroom? Mrs. Appleyard, will you . . . ?

She rose. Henry saw a mountain of a woman—swarthy, coal-black hair, the suspicion of a mustache. A moment earlier he had perceived Appleyard as robustious. Now the former policeman shrank before Henry's sympathetic eyes.

Not waiting for the Chief Justice to finish, Mrs. Appleyard made her way toward the aisle, tramping on innocent feet in the process. It was an act of savagery that went unprotested. None dared.

Gone. And though there'd been no backward glance for Appleyard, it was clear he still felt her presence.

O'CONOR *(emerging from behind Mr. Asher's table)*. Do you recognize these books?

APPLEYARD. Books? Them red cloth-bound ones?

O'CONOR. The ones I am waving at you, Mr. Appleyard.

APPLEYARD. Yes, sir.

O'CONOR. If they're familiar to you, pray identify them.

APPLEYARD. Them are station books.

O'CONOR. Station books. In which, intermingling with those of your colleagues, are various reports bearing your signature.

APPLEYARD. Well, if I made reports then I made reports, didn't I?

O'CONOR. And what was the essence of them as they applied to 355 Greenwich Street?

APPLEYARD. Essence, you say?

CHIEF JUSTICE. Appleyard, let's have an end to this. You understand the question, of course you do. Answer it, please.

APPLEYARD. Essence. Well, as I recall the essence . . . I mean from what I seen and heard from my own observation, I reported that particular house to be a house of a particular kind. I reported it to be a house of ill repute, a house of assignation.

O'CONOR. A bawdy house.

APPLEYARD. Yes.

O'CONOR. How many times?

APPLEYARD. How many times? Once or twice.

O'CONOR. Eight?

APPLEYARD. Eight if you say so, sir. *(laughter)*

O'CONOR. No further questions.

CHIEF JUSTICE. Do you wish to cross-examine, Mr. Van Buren?

VAN BUREN *(after a brief whispered conference with Forrest)*. We think not. We might have had a question or two for Mr. Appleyard, but none serious enough to postpone his reunion with Mrs. Appleyard. *(laughter)*

O'CONOR. Is the Reverend David Terry in court?

VAN BUREN. Not on this same point, I hope. *(laughter)*

CHIEF JUSTICE. Apparently, he is not. Is it important, Mr. O'Conor?

O'CONOR. He was one of those in attendance at Mrs. Voorhies's party. However, no, he is not essential at the moment. Mr. Asher, pray call Mr. Willis.

CLERK. Call Nathaniel Parker Willis.

N. P. Willis, being sworn and examined by Mr. O'Conor, desposed.

WILLIS. I am 46 years of age. I reside at 198 Fourth Avenue. I am one of the editors of the *Home Journal.*

O'CONOR. Do you know Mr. Edwin Forrest?

WILLIS. I do not.

O'CONOR *(smiling)*. But you did at one time?

WILLIS. Yes.

O'CONOR. Do you know Mrs. Forrest?

WILLIS. Yes.

O'CONOR. Did you ever take any liberty with Mrs. Forrest?

WILLIS. No.

O'CONOR. Did you ever kiss any part of her person?

WILLIS. No.

O'CONOR. Did you, either in the drawing room or in the

library of Mr. Forrest's house in Twenty-second Street, or any-where else, lie upon or against any part of Mrs. Forrest?

WILLIS. No.

O'CONOR. Did you ever hear any unchaste speech or witness any unchaste or immodest act of Mrs. Forrest?

WILLIS. No.

O'CONOR. Thank you, sir. *(five seconds of communion)* In what way did your personal acquaintance with the Forrests commence?

WILLIS. As a critic, I had been in the habit of writing about Mr. Forrest for some years, but I believe our acquaintance com-menced in 1835—by his leaving his card for me at my lodgings in London. Concerning Mrs. Forrest, I first saw her, a bride, in this city, in 1837. I went to call on her at the Astor House. After that I lived abroad for a while and do not remember seeing either of them until 1847.

O'CONOR. Explain the manner in which the acquaintanceship was resumed.

WILLIS. I was ill, seriously ill, with a brain fever. They came to my house to inquire after me. I did not meet them then, but when I recovered somewhat I was shown their cards.

O'CONOR. State how often you saw Mr. and Mrs. Forrest after your recovery.

WILLIS. Mr. Forrest's house was on the same side of the street with my lodgings, about a half mile between the two. In the process of recuperating I used to walk that distance. From time to time I would encounter either one or the other of them.

O'CONOR. Once a week then?

WILLIS. Once a fortnight is probably closer.

O'CONOR. A period that lasted about six months. After which you exchanged dinner invitations, is that correct?

WILLIS. They were to our house, we were to theirs, and on several occasions I remember going out with the Forrests to examine the progress being made at Fonthill.

O'CONOR. Both the Forrests?

WILLIS. He drove us in his carriage.

O'CONOR (*four seconds of communion*). When did you first learn that any such idea as your acting improperly with Mrs. Forrest was entertained by anyone?

WILLIS. In January of 1850.

O'CONOR. Eight months or so after Mr. Forrest decided they must separate. *How* did you learn it?

WILLIS. Through an anonymous letter sent my wife.

O'CONOR. She showed it to you?

WILLIS. Of course.

O'CONOR. I gather she did not take it seriously.

WILLIS. Certainly not.

O'CONOR. Do you have any idea who sent it?

VAN BUREN. Object. If it was anonymous . . . ?

O'CONOR. Perhaps the sender has confessed?

VAN BUREN. Has there been such a confession?

O'CONOR (*smiling, waiting a beat*). No.

CHIEF JUSTICE. Objection sustained.

O'CONOR. When did you cease being on good terms with Mr. Forrest?

WILLIS. A few days after Mrs. Willis received the letter.

O'CONOR. Still January of 1850?

WILLIS. Yes.

O'CONOR. In what manner did the rupture take place?

WILLIS. He stopped me in front of the Astor House and began a gross and indecent attack on his wife's character. I expressed my entire disbelief of the charges he was making against her and said I would require proofs other than his assertions, and that until we had those proofs Mrs. Willis and I would treat her as the friend we had always known. He went on for some ten or fifteen minutes with this coarse and disgusting abuse and then left me, telling me he should hold me responsible for any meddling with his domestic affairs.

O'CONOR. But on that occasion he did not strike you.

WILLIS. He reserved that for a later meeting.

O'CONOR. On the evening of June sixteenth in Washington Square.

WILLIS. Yes.

O'CONOR. Tell us about it, please.

WILLIS. He knocked me down from behind, placed his foot on my neck, and proceeded to beat me with my own cane, shouting at the top of his voice that I was the seducer of Catherine Forrest.

O'CONOR. The seducer of Catherine Forrest. Was that the precise phrase?

WILLIS. Yes.

O'CONOR. Had you ever encountered that phrase before?

WILLIS. Yes. In the anonymous letter to my wife.

O'CONOR *(five seconds of communion)*. What would you estimate as the difference between your weight and Mr. Forrest's?

VAN BUREN. Object. If there is relevance in that comparison the jury can determine it for itself since both men are present in the courtroom.

CHIEF JUSTICE. Sustained.

O'CONOR. Mr. Willis, pray tell the court how you finally managed to get free of your assailant.

WILLIS. The police arrived.

O'CONOR. Is there anything you would like to add to the account you have just furnished us?

WILLIS. His friend Lawson was with him. Lawson said to me, just as the police arrived, "Lucky for you they got here. He would have cut your heart out."

O'CONOR. Your witness, Mr. Van Buren.

Grim-faced, Van Buren approached N.P., but the latter seemed undaunted. Henry sought in vain for a flash of recognition. Classmates they may have been, but Yale was long ago and, according to N.P., dislike had been mutual.

VAN BUREN. But you *have* been alone with Mrs. Forrest, have you not?

WILLIS. I think I may have been.

VAN BUREN. You think? A parade of witnesses has so testified. Was every one of them lying? *(no answer)* Did you hear the question?

WILLIS. I did not realize it was a serious question.

VAN BUREN. Mr. Willis, this is a courtroom, not some upper-tenner salon. We do not play games here, sir.

WILLIS. If it was a serious question, then the answer is—no, they were not all lying; that is, not constantly. I probably have been alone with Mrs. Forrest from time to time. Nor do I apologize for it.

VAN BUREN. You think it perfectly proper for a man to be closeted for hours on end with someone else's spouse?

WILLIS. Hours on end is your term, sir.

VAN BUREN. Then there is a point at which it becomes improper?

WILLIS. Of course.

VAN BUREN. How long is required?

WILLIS. I know of no firm measurement.

VAN BUREN. An hour? After that would they be beyond the bounds of propriety?

WILLIS. I really could not say.

VAN BUREN. Come now, Mr. Willis. We depend on you. Are you not this city's final arbiter in matters of this sort?

WILLIS. You flatter me, sir.

VAN BUREN. Oh I think not, sir. Or perhaps it was your brother who assumed the platform at the New York Lyceum a few months back to deliver an address on . . . not politics, not philosophy, not literature . . . no, not any of those . . . and certainly not religion. . . . Can you help me, Mr. Willis?

WILLIS. Fashion.

VAN BUREN. Fashion?

WILLIS. A more complex subject than you seem willing to credit it as being.

VAN BUREN. Do you say so, sir?

O'CONOR. Your honor, where is he going with this?

CHIEF JUSTICE. Yes, Mr. Van Buren, where?

VAN BUREN. I merely wanted to establish Mr. Willis's credentials, his sphere of influence as it were, but if learned counsel objects, why, no matter. Back then to the original line. Mr. Willis, *were* you ever alone with Mrs. Forrest for longer than an hour?

WILLIS. I suppose so.

VAN BUREN. Yea or nay, please.

WILLIS. Yes.

VAN BUREN. But you regard this as perfectly proper?

WILLIS. We are friends.

VAN BUREN. Do friends—that is, in your description—do friends think it proper to express affection for one another by touching?

WILLIS. Why not?

VAN BUREN. May I regard that as an affirmative?

WILLIS. Yes.

VAN BUREN. Touching each other how?

WILLIS. How?

VAN BUREN. Would you prefer where?

O'CONOR. By where, does learned counsel mean which room of a house? Your honor—

VAN BUREN. On her person, Mr. Willis. Might you, properly, touch your friend Mrs. Forrest's hand, for instance?

WILLIS. Of course.

VAN BUREN. Her cheek?

WILLIS. Possibly.

VAN BUREN. Her . . . mouth?

WILLIS. Probably not.

VAN BUREN. 'Pon my soul, I think I'm getting the hang of it. And what is permissible with one's hand would be similarly acceptable for one's . . . lips? Pray, is that correct, sir?

WILLIS. Generally.

VAN BUREN. Oh, I *mean* generally. No *more* than generally, sir. So generally, then, friends are permitted to salute each other with a kiss on the cheek?

WILLIS. Yes.

VAN BUREN. Good. Let us see where the omnibus has stopped now, shall we? You and Mrs. Forrest have been friends for . . . is six years a fair estimate?

WILLIS. Yes.

VAN BUREN. Six years. And in all that time you have never so much as kissed Mrs. Forrest's cheek? Do I have that right, sir? *(N.P. hesitant)* Would you like me to have Mr. Asher read your testimony, sir?

WILLIS. That will not be necessary.

VAN BUREN. Then may I have my answer?

WILLIS. I meant improperly.

VAN BUREN. But you *have* kissed her?

WILLIS. Yes.

VAN BUREN. You testified that you had not, but you had? Were you lying?

O'CONOR. Object.

CHIEF JUSTICE. Sustained. Strike, Mr. Asher.

VAN BUREN. I see, I see. When you said no, it was because you meant you had not kissed Mrs. Forrest in an improper way?

WILLIS. Yes.

VAN BUREN. Perhaps what you really meant was not in a public place?

O'CONOR. Object. Witness has already stated what he meant.

CHIEF JUSTICE. Sustained.

VAN BUREN. Mr. Willis, when did you first learn of the Forrest's separation?

WILLIS. In the early part of May, 1849.

VAN BUREN. Who told you?

WILLIS. Mrs. Forrest.

VAN BUREN. Did she tell you why?

WILLIS. She told no one why.

VAN BUREN. How do you know?

WILLIS. How do I know? I heard her so testify.

VAN BUREN. And that is sufficient?

WILLIS. Of course.

VAN BUREN. Such trust you have in the lady?

WILLIS. As do all her friends.

VAN BUREN. All? Or perhaps just those among you who know her . . . intimately.

O'CONOR. Object. That is outrageous.

CHIEF JUSTICE. Yes. Go carefully, Mr. Van Buren.

VAN BUREN. Mr. Willis, in the issue of July '49 you wrote in the *Home Journal* that central to the Forrest rupture was the bitterness caused between them by the Macready affair.

WILLIS. Did I?

VAN BUREN. You have forgotten that too? Shall I produce the article?

WILLIS. No. I remember it now.

VAN BUREN. I submit you could only have got that from Mrs. Forrest.

WILLIS. Absurd.

VAN BUREN. She is famous for having held that view.

WILLIS. If so, she never expressed it to me, though many of those close to her did.

VAN BUREN. Many? Name me but one.

WILLIS. Mrs. Voorhies comes to mind.

VAN BUREN. It was she you got it from?

WILLIS. Probably.

VAN BUREN. I would like you to be certain.

WILLIS. Then consider me certain.

VAN BUREN. You seemed rather less than that a heartbeat ago.

WILLIS. Well, I am certain now.

VAN BUREN. Of course you are. And how convenient it is that Mrs. Voorhies is three thousand miles away.

O'CONOR. Object.

VAN BUREN *(fiercely)*. I grow weary, your honor, of constantly bumping up against the same everlasting obstacle. Mrs. Voorhies is inaccessible to me. Mr. Jamieson is inaccessible to me. Captain Calcraft is inaccessible to me. Even Mr. Richard Willis is inaccessible to me. It is an exodus to rival the Old Testament's. One can see them all in the same ark—

CHIEF JUSTICE. Enough. Mr. Van Buren, this is unseemly. Members of the bar should not behave this way, sir. No, sir, they should not.

VAN BUREN *(after a breath)*. My apologies. I am afraid I rather lost my temper. My deepest apologies, sir.

CHIEF JUSTICE. Quite, quite. Now pray address yourself to Mr. Willis.

VAN BUREN *(another breath)*. This article you wrote, sir. Was it perhaps the reason Mr. Forrest attacked you?

WILLIS. Hardly. I wrote it after he attacked me.

VAN BUREN. For vengeance's sake, in other words?

WILLIS. Once again, sir, those are your "other words."

VAN BUREN. Then why did you write that article?

WILLIS. To set the record straight. It had come to my attention that Mr. Forrest was becoming a veritable headquarters for scurrilous information.

VAN BUREN. That you had seduced his wife? That you were meddling incorrigibly in his affairs? Information such as that?

WILLIS. Lies such as that, yes.

Explosion: Forrest surged to his feet and shouted incoherently. Instantly, Van Buren was at his side to both soothe and restrain. N.P. paled. Braver than Henry would have predicted, however, he held his ground while Forrest struggled to get at him. Two bailiffs and Mr. Asher, the court clerk, now joined Van Buren, who, maintaining his grip, kept whispering sweetly to his volcanic client—while the Chief Justice gaveled furiously. Finally, after an almost five-minute eruption, Mount Forrest simmered and was capped; order was restored. The Chief Justice, eyes locked with Forrest's, spent another minute on reprimands and warnings and then instructed Van Buren to proceed without further delay.

VAN BUREN *(still breathing a degree beyond normal)*. Mr. Willis, are you a member of the Church?

O'CONOR. Object.

CHIEF JUSTICE. Sustained. What this trial scarcely needs is an additional conduit for irrelevant matter.

VAN BUREN. Again and again Mr. O'Conor has, in divers ways, attempted to impugn the credibility of the defendant's witnesses. Isn't turnabout fair play?

CHIEF JUSTICE. Mr. Van Buren, the question has been declared irrelevant, and I don't choose to discuss it further with you. If you wish to take an exception, pray inform Mr. Asher.

VAN BUREN *(after a moment)*. No, thank you, your honor. *(turning to his table, conferring briefly with Forrest, lifting a document, returning to the bench)* Your honor, Mr. Willis spoke just now of setting the record straight. Mr. Forrest instructs me that he's eager to do the same, and since he's been accused here of a blackguardly attack, he would like to put in evidence this brief announcement which he furnished the *Herald* for publication on the twenty-fifth of June, 1850. Do I have your permission, sir?

CHIEF JUSTICE. Proceed.

VAN BUREN *(reading)*. "To all those who give credence to reports that I, Edwin Forrest, struck Mr. N. P. Willis from behind, I say unequivocally these are humbug. I approached him frontally. I knocked him down. I held him by his coat collar with one hand and beat him not with his cane but with a gutta-percha whip, which I had brought with me for the purpose. Mr. Willis knows why I beat him. Soon the remainder of this city will know it too. Signed, E. Forrest." *(pause)* I am finished with this witness.

CHIEF JUSTICE. Mr. O'Conor, do you wish to redirect?

O'CONOR. Yes, your honor. *(to N.P.)* I know you have already testified to this, but I would like it said once again. Have you, sir, in any way, under any circumstances, taken a liberty with the person of Mrs. Forrest?

WILLIS. No, sir.

O'CONOR. No further questions, your honor.

CHIEF JUSTICE. You may step down.

Adjourned.

On Impulse

*F*rom the library window of 62 Boylston Street, Henry had a charming view of the Boston Common. Much activity there, a bustling, pleasant kind of activity. People moving briskly toward other people who would be glad to see them, he decided. There was a cheerful, optimistic aspect to it all.

His own mood was growing less optimistic by the minute.

Letting his breath out heavily, he recalled the impulse (ill-considered, he knew now) that had brought him to this pass. Don't *think,* he had ordered himself. For once in your life, just *do.*

Last-minute items jammed into a carpetbag. The usual slip-slide-stumble down sleet-swept Broadway until at last gold was struck: the hack required to convey him to the wharf by 5 P.M., in time to board the packet boat *Massachusetts.*

A half hour later she had steamed out of the harbor, carrying Henry and a hundred others.

At nine, after some aimless deckside meandering, some idle deckside conversation, and copious cups of coffee, he had taken to his berth—a slab less than ten feet wide, the *Massachusetts* being built for speed rather than comfort.

Intermittent reading and dozing for a while. Having finally fallen solidly into sleep at around two, he'd been awakened three hours later by a combined chorus of foghorns and raucous snorers. Another hour passed before he could nod off again.

Topside at seven just as the *Massachusetts* zipped past Newport.

Providence by eight. By train to Boston, reaching the depot at half past ten, a respectable seventeen and a half hours after leaving New York. The omens were good, he had foolishly told himself.

From the depot to Tremont House, his hotel. From there to 62 Boylston Street, the handsome red-brick structure belonging to Aunt Emma Dorrance. The view from its library window *was* charming, but Henry had already spent twenty minutes admiring it.

"I'm sorry to have kept you waiting," Serena said, suddenly materializing. "On the other hand, I didn't expect you."

Henry was unable to take her in at a single glance. He never was. At times he saw her eyes first, at times her hair. It was the impact that was constant, which explained now why seconds passed before he noticed the copy of yesterday's *Herald* clenched in her hand as if she had just finished choking it. Though the headline over Bennett's editorial was mostly obscured, Henry knew it read A TRUMPET CALL TO LIBIDINOUSNESS.

"You seem well," he said. "Are you having a good visit?"

"Henry, please don't talk to me that way."

"What way?"

"You sound like either of our fathers."

He stiffened. "Whoever I am, I'm not Bennett."

They studied each other, but it was as if through cataracts. Was it possible there was something like hurt in her face? He couldn't be sure. And if he had been he wouldn't have known what to do about it. His own hurt was like a whirlpool, sucking into it whatever sensitivity might have been at his disposal. He felt discouraged and dull, pointless.

"I shouldn't have come," he said.

"Then why did you?"

"It was a mistake."

"Lord, but you try my patience, Henry Stewart. No one else is as skillful at it. True, you cannot help what you are. It's just that what you are infuriates me. When I think of Elizabeth Blackwell forbidden the medical school of Harvard. And Lucy Stone the pulpit. And Amelia Bloomer followed everywhere by ignorant, foul-mouthed louts vilifying her because the sight of a woman in a sensible costume terrifies them. When I think any of that, I must tell you I feel homicidal."

"You were thinking some of that in connection with me?"

She shook the newspaper. "Catherine Forrest's beautiful letter, her brave and beautiful letter, described as a—how dare he?" Once more the newspaper was shaken. "A trumpet call to justice is what it is. If I'd been in that courtroom—"

"Serena, look at me. Truly, I am not Bennett. He is thirty years older. He has white hair. He has one eye. He squints. Do you understand? There's no reason to mistake us for each other."

"But you work for him."

"Yes."

"And you admire him."

"In many ways, yes, but—"

"I've heard your lecture, Henry, and have no need to hear it again. Why can't I make *you* understand? What is at issue here is not the history of journalism but the future of women!"

He turned once more to examine the Common. A little boy was chasing a giggling little girl. They were about nine or ten, enjoying themselves. Henry sent a brain wave the boy's way: Quit now before it's too late. When he turned back he could see that some of the anger had drained from Serena. The newspaper was no longer brandishable. She had let it drop, and limply it was spread out on the floor. There was a drawing of Catherine Forrest on one of the inside pages. Henry examined it, and though it was upside down he noticed that Stevens, their artist, had got her hair wrong. Parted too far to the left. He made a mental note to speak to him about it.

"I've been invited to do something important," Serena said, though with less verve than the words might have justified.

"May I ask what it is?"

"Certainly. Did you ever meet Margaret Fuller?"

"In New York. Right after she went to work for Greeley's *Tribune.*"

"Did you like her?"

Henry toyed with the idea of lying, but truth-telling was too old a habit. "Not a great deal, no."

"Oh, God, does it never disturb you to be so predictable?"

"Yes."

She shut her eyes. When she opened them again she continued with the same odd variance between tone and message. "I admired her tremendously. To her and Madame Sand and Catherine Forrest I owe the positions I take in a great many fundamental areas."

"I know."

"And, in a manner of speaking, I will be following in her footsteps. Ten years ago she instituted a program of Conversations, subscribed to by the ladies of this city. It was a great success. Had she not been lost at sea, she'd have been asked for a sequel by my Aunt Emma, among others."

"Your Aunt Emma has suggested you in Miss Fuller's stead?"

"The circular has already been written and delivered to the printers. And by next Thursday it will be mailed. You find the idea ludicrous?"

"No."

"Then why are you smiling?"

"I wasn't smiling at you."

"At whom then?"

"At myself. At how absurd I am. Seventeen hours of traveling to discover what I knew perfectly well before I left home."

"And what is that?"

"I was meant to remain a bachelor. Good day, Serena."

When he was some half a dozen paces down Boylston Street he heard the door pulled open violently.

"Henry!"

He stopped.

"There's something I want you never to forget."

He waited.

"That I find you hateful."

He bowed. The door slammed shut. Leadenly, he resumed his progress. A curse on pretty women. They delight your eyes and break your heart.

Bone weary on his return to the New York Hotel Sunday afternoon, Henry went directly to bed. He dozed fitfully and woke up staring after four dream-ridden hours.

Florence's Oyster House struck him as his only short-term solution. There he could eat and drink himself into insensibility. He found N. P. Willis at a table in a dark corner of the room. It was clear he'd been in position for a while. Henry joined him.

"A ripe pair of scoundrels they are," N.P. said a half hour later, his first words. He spoke with no sign of slur, which was no small accomplishment, Henry decided. "Van Buren and Forrest, I mean. By God, they belong together. Would you like to know the simple truth of the matter, the why, as it were, of this filthy divorce case? Pray let me delineate. He could no longer face her intellectual superiority. I tell you there's no more to it than that. While she lived in his house he was forced into daily confrontation with it, and he found this intolerable. That being the case, he enlisted the kitchen and the brothel against her to filthify her name so he could kick her out like a mistress paid up to parting."

"Another brandy, N.P.?"

"No, thank you, Henry. You know I drink only champagne."

"Then have another oyster."

"I sent him a challenge."

"Forrest?"

"No, no, of course not. Van Buren. I told him I bitterly resented his ungentlemanly conduct toward me on the witness stand—"

"Duels are against—"

"—and suggested we meet in Charleston, or any other convenient point in the southern states."

"You heard from him?"

"Instantly."

"Oh, God. He'll fight you?"

"He will not. He referred to my note as a 'silly and scurrilous communication' and refused categorically to give me satisfaction. I had no choice but to write him again, saying he was a coward and fit companion for that roster of blackguards who compose his client list. Henry, your face has turned white."

"I know."

"Where are you going?"

"To be sick."

And he was, horribly.

Catherine's Diary

*L*etter from Margaret this morning. Both parents doing well, she says. Father mending beautifully, she says. How certain Margaret was, the day she left, that she would arrive in England to find him dead. But I knew better. Can't kill tough old oaks that easily. The Sinclairs have always been fighters. Hah! Up the Sinclairs!

Margaret at the Drury Lane for Macready's farewell, speaking of tough old oaks. Applause tumultuous, she says. Everyone weeping. And he in turn both funny and fond.

Why did Edwin hate him so? Does he still? Why does anyone hate anyone? What causes hate? Did I ever hate anyone? I used to say I hated Miss Brierly, the governess who cut off Margaret's braids. But did I really? Enough to kill? Of course not.

And having written this, I suddenly remembered that Miss Brierly's fame rests only partially on her skill as a Delilah. How odd that I should forget her prowess as a jailer. She scissored Margaret's braids, and I went for her. She overpowered me, hauled me into one of the corridor closets, hauled Margaret away. And left the door locked. (Parents junketing on their annual West

Country tour.) What were we, nine and ten? Yes. I can still hear
Margaret screaming as she was dragged off, then the screams
fading, then nothing.

July. And cruelly hot. But it was not the heat that mattered as
much as that "nothing." It went on for hours. Margaret said later
it was only two. I did not believe her. I still can't. A storage closet.
Hardly enough room to stand. Dark and thickly silent. Two
hours? To me it seemed a life. A third hour and perhaps I would
have gone mad. I take it back. I did and do hate Miss Brierly
enough to kill.

Does Edwin hate me enough to kill? It seems so. But why?
Because he thinks I was unfaithful to him? Is that reason enough
to snuff out a life? Oh, I know it has been. On that basis men and
women have been snuffing each other out for centuries. But why,
why? It has to do with our sense of perishability, does it not? I
mean that we are all so terrifyingly finite. It makes so many of us
self-lovers. And self-lovers are, often as not, everyone else–haters.

Macready is a diary-keeper, too. He once said to me, A lonely
man keeps a dismal diary.

Glorious Forrest

*T*here was no falloff in numbers, Henry discovered on Monday morning, passion for scandal outpacing concern for life and limb. Predictably, however, seat scarcity had turned the mob's mood surly. Henry's mood matched. As he fought his way to the press section, a scaled-down version of Mrs. Appleyard tramped on his instep. She got his elbow in her cushioned midriff.

The "ripe pair of scoundrels" were at their customary table. O'Conor, Catherine—looking slightly drawn—and Mrs. Willis, looking spectral (at the approach of her ordeal), were at theirs. No sign of N.P. anywhere. Playing truant for the sake of his head and stomach, Henry decided, and groaned at the condition of his own.

The second Margaret Fuller was evidently still in Boston.

The clerk called Cornelia Grinnell Willis. The lady started, hand to her throat. Catherine stroked her comfortingly, then said something to O'Conor.

O'Conor. May I ask the court's indulgence? A brief recess, your honor, so that Mrs. Willis can get a breath of fresh air before commencing the examination.

CHIEF JUSTICE. Will fifteen minutes be sufficient, Mrs. Willis?

MRS. WILLIS. Oh, yes, Judge Oakley.

CHIEF JUSTICE. Very well, stand adjourned until then.

Something about this displeased Van Buren, Henry noted. Scowling, he whispered to Forrest, who scowlingly replied. But they remained at their table, as did O'Conor at his. The ladies exited together. At the press table the prevailing question was, Did O'Conor mean to end that day? Opinion was divided. Raymond led the ayes and offered to cover bets. Some takers; Henry refrained, already leery of the risk incurred in betting against *The New York Times*.

The ladies returned. Fresh air seemed to have done good work. Either that, Henry thought, or a bracing speech from Catherine had put color in the witness's cheeks. Her back was straighter, her step steadier; gone the weeping Willis.

CLERK (*again*). Call Cornelia Grinnell Willis.

MRS. WILLIS (*sworn and examined by Mr. O'Conor*). I am the wife of Mr. Nathaniel Parker Willis. I first became acquainted with Mr. Forrest when he called on New Year's Day, 1847. I first became acquainted with Mrs. Forrest about four weeks later. Together with her sister, Mrs. Voorhies, they called on me at the New York Hotel, where we were living then."

O'CONOR. Thereafter, fairly steady visiting back and forth?

MRS. WILLIS. Yes.

O'CONOR. You came to them for dinner, they came to you for tea, that kind of thing?

MRS. WILLIS. Yes.

O'CONOR. Did this visiting include both the Forrests?

MRS. WILLIS. Oh, yes. Except when he was on tour, of course. When he was at home we saw him often.

O'CONOR. Late in the year 1848 you became quite ill, did you not?

MRS. WILLIS. It was after the birth of my child.

O'CONOR. How long a period did this illness last?

MRS. WILLIS. Five months. For three months I was unable to leave my room.

O'CONOR. Did you have a nurse with you?

MRS. WILLIS. Part of the time. The rest of the time I was attended only by the ordinary servants.

O'CONOR. Did Mrs. Forrest pay you attention during your illness?

MRS. WILLIS. She paid me great attention. She performed a series of errands and commissions for me that I simply could not have done without.

O'CONOR. Thank you, Mrs. Willis. I have only a few more questions for you, and then soon you will be free to go.

MRS. WILLIS. That is quite all right, sir. Truly, I am feeling quite well now.

O'CONOR. Mrs. Willis, during your period of friendly intercourse with Mrs. Forrest, have you ever seen her in any degree affected by liquor?

MRS. WILLIS. Never, sir.

O'CONOR. Did you ever hear any unchaste or immodest expressions from her?

MRS. WILLIS. Never.

O'CONOR. Did you ever notice any immodest act on her part . . . that she was too free with gentlemen?

MRS. WILLIS. No, sir, certainly not.

O'CONOR (*five seconds of communion*). Too free with your husband?

MRS. WILLIS. Never, never, never!

O'CONOR. Your witness, Mr. Van Buren.

VAN BUREN. Mrs. Willis, obviously you are very fond of Mrs. Forrest.

MRS. WILLIS. Yes.

VAN BUREN. Yes. We have all seen the evidence of that. Day after day you have been at her side in this courtroom, underscoring a friendship of rather remarkable intensity. One wonders how it all began.

Mrs. Willis. How?

Van Buren. What were the sources of this friendship. The great attention she showed you during your illness of 1848, was that one of them?

Mrs. Willis. Of course.

Van Buren. Of course. Completely understandable that you would have feelings of gratitude toward her because of it. And she has an even greater call on you than that . . . there's an even larger debt to repay, isn't there?

Mrs. Willis. She saved my baby's life, she and Mrs. Voorhies. The child's temperature—

Van Buren. So that what could be more natural under the circumstances than for you to rally round?

Mrs. Willis. I'm not sure what you mean.

Van Buren. No more than I suggested a moment ago, that you feel deeply in Mrs. Forrest's debt, isn't that true?

Mrs. Willis. Yes.

Van Buren. You would do almost anything to help her, would you not?

Mrs. Willis *(passionately)*. She deserves it!

Van Buren. Might you even . . . *say* anything to help her? Never mind, never mind. Forgive me, Mrs. Willis. Having clearly overstepped the bounds of propriety, I can only cease and desist. I withdraw the question. *(half turn to the jury, plus a significant pause; then, as if to himself)* But perhaps the point is made anyway. Your witness, sir. *(killing glances exchanged by counsel)*

O'Conor. You may step down, ma'am.

Smilingly, he went to her aid, but it seemed to Henry that Van Buren's trap had been skillfully set and a certain amount of fizzle had been the result. Having mounted the stand a potentially powerful character witness, Mrs. Willis descended as someone who, to pay off a debt, might have gilded the lily. Nor was this lost on the lady herself. She was weepy again. Catherine performed the obligatory shoulder-stroking.

Clerk. Call John W. Forney.

O'CONOR. Your honor, Mr. Forney is not in court, and I now have serious doubts as to my ability to produce him. All my subpoenas have proved fruitless. However, late last year I was able to get from him a deposition, which I would like at this time to place in the record.

CHIEF JUSTICE. Do so.

O'CONOR *(reading)*. "John W. Forney, of the city of Philadelphia, occupation, editor of *The Pennsylvanian,* a daily newspaper; being duly and publicly sworn doth depose as follows: 'I do know Edwin Forrest, who is by profession a tragedian. I have known him about fifteen years. I have been during all that time on the most intimate, confidential, and friendly terms with him, and am so still.

" 'I have looked at the document now exhibited to me and acknowledge it as a copy of a letter written by me to George Roberts of the *Boston Times.* I believe it to be a true copy. The said Edwin Forrest was not present when I wrote said letter. It was sent off without being shown to him, though I told him I had written it directly after having done so. The said Edwin Forrest and myself spoke of writing such a letter, but he did not see it before it was sent. Nevertheless, I wrote the letter by his authority. It was sent, in confidence, to a person whose discretion I foolishly had confidence in for the purpose of vindicating a valued friend. That is all I have to say. Jno. W. Forney.' Examination taken, reduced to writing, and by the witness subscribed and sworn to, this twenty-second day of December, 1851, before me, Oswald Thompson, President Judge of the Court of Common Pleas, of the city and county of Philadelphia."

CLERK. Exhibit marked.

O'CONOR. I would now like to put into the record the letter referred to in Mr. Forney's deposition.

VAN BUREN. Object. Hearsay material and obviously inadmissible.

O'CONOR. Hearsay? What is hearsay? The fact that there is a letter?

VAN BUREN. No, sir. That a letter passed between Forney and Roberts is incontestable. But that any suggestion concerning it came from Mr. Forrest is certainly contestable.

CHIEF JUSTICE. I think we must have the letter, Mr. Van Buren. The question of how it came to be written can concern us later. Objection overruled.

O'CONOR *(reading)*. "January twenty-fifth, 1850. Dear Roberts. Our friend Forrest is now here, and is about to apply for a divorce from his wife. He has had, for eighteen months, the proofs of her infidelity, but has chosen to keep them quiet, and would have done so still, but for her folly in censuring him for leaving her. The facts are these. Eighteen months ago, while playing in Cincinnati, he caught Mrs. F in a very equivocal position with a young man in his own parlor—not in actual connection but near it. She protested innocence, and he let it pass by—loving her as he did most profoundly. They journeyed on to New Orleans, and so home to New York.

"After they reached home and had been there for some time, he found, one evening, on his wife's table, a *billet doux* in the handwriting of, though not signed by, this young man, in which she was alluded to in terms the most amorous and unmistakable. The language referred to her 'white arms, that wound about his neck,' to the 'blissful hours they had spent together,' and the letter had been kept as a memento until it was quite well worn. Upon this evidence, with other confirmatory proofs, he intends applying for a divorce. And you are now in a position to serve him in a manner he will never forget.

"The person who wrote to Mrs. F, and in whose company she was detected, is George Jamieson, now playing in your city. If you don't know him you can, as the editor of a leading daily paper, soon make his acquaintance. What Forrest needs is to obtain in some way an admission from Jamieson. I named you to Forrest as a safe, steady, and intelligent friend, and he will remember you always if you act for him in this most vital matter.

"He suggests you might institute intimate relations with J, and then induce him, either in your presence or in company, to admit—as a thing to be proud of—his connection with Mrs. F. J is fond of a glass and, in a convivial mood, might well become communicative. No harm will come to him. He is game too small for Forrest, and any admission he may make is important only as aiding an injured man in getting relief from a hateful bond.

"Can you manage this thing, my friend? It will require skill and caution and, if successful, will warmly endear you to Forrest. He is nearly crazy at the idea of being placed in his present position, but he will spend half he is worth to be released from it. This matter must be kept secret. Excuse me for troubling you in regard to it. My ardent attachment to glorious Forrest must be my excuse. Won't you help to relieve him? Please write as soon after receipt as you can find opportunity to look about you. With kind regards, I am, dear Roberts, yours, very truly, Jno. W. Forney."

Having crossed to the clerk to hand him the letter, O'Conor then, slowly, eyes downcast like a penitent's, made his way to a point that cunningly divided the distance between the jury and the Chief Justice.

O'CONOR *(eight seconds of communion)*. The plaintiff has no more to say. *(buzz-buzz-buzz, gavel-gavel-gavel)*

CHIEF JUSTICE. Adjourned until nine-thirty tomorrow morning.

Raymond, jostling Henry on the way to the hansoms: "The man is an outrage."

Taken aback. "O'Conor?"

"Forrest, Forrest, damn his eyes."

But that evening Bennett said, "Did it ever occur to you, lad, that Forney might have just gone off half cocked? I mean . . . aye, Forrest may have issued a call for help, but 'tis no more than a pipsqueak penny-a-liner's word for the rest of it."

"Then why didn't Van Buren put Forrest on the stand to disavow the bloody letter?"

"Ah, laddie, how could he have? Forrest, gentleman that he is, would never go back on a friend, pipsqueak though he be. Think, sir, how could he put himself in a position where he had to publicly shift blame from his own mighty shoulders to the pigmy shoulders of the pipsqueak Forney?"

Bennett, impatient with his crutches, seemed even ornerier than usual that evening. Henry was informed that Bennett wanted him to take the Washington office in charge. For how long? he asked. Indefinitely. For a year, Henry offered. For two, came the rejoinder. For more salary? Bennett squinted: how much more? Henry hesitated, then named a figure and was told he'd been smoking opium. We'll talk again when the crutches are gone, Henry said. But, things being as they were, he was not averse to a change of scene, and later he wondered if the canny Scot scoundrel had sensed that.

The Gentlemen at Their Port

*T*hey had agreed about the port, agreed about the cigars. Henry and his father then skimmed over a range of Columbia College topics carefully selected to keep the mercury from rising. There was a trusteeship coming open. His father wanted it for him. Henry said he thought he was too young. His father thought not, and they idled away some afterdinner time counting committee votes for and against.

The front doorbell rang. A servant went to answer and appeared a moment later with an unexpected caller. Startled, Henry rose to greet Serena's father. His own father—on the most spurious of pretexts—instantly disappeared, in this way suggesting to Henry that their caller was not universally unexpected.

"A glass of port, sir?"

In the senior Blaylock's face all the curves were downward. But he nodded temperately enough.

Pouring. "Pray take a chair and tell me if you have news of Peter."

"Only that he's got as far as Chicago. A short note: two lines, hurriedly written. Peter, I fear, will not prove a satisfactory correspondent."

"I fear you are correct."

Mr. Blaylock sipped. Henry sipped. Mr. Blaylock's fingers drummed. Henry's tongue made inane clicking noises behind his teeth until he realized what he was doing and made himself stop.

"I saw—"

"Serena," her father said. "I know you did. That's what I wish to speak to you about. She is, I mean."

Stiffly. "You need have no further concern on that score, sir."

"Concern?"

"Any hopes I may have had I now know are without substance."

"Oh, hush up, boy."

Propelling himself from his chair, he stalked across the room to stare intently at a street on which stood nothing more extraordinary than his own carriage. He turned to face Henry.

"I don't know what to make of this, any of this. What does it have to do with hardware? Or good French wine? What, I ask you, does it have to do with any kind of honest shipping? How can I be expected to cope?"

"You have my sympathy, sir."

"Sympathy! I want no sympathy from a whippersnapper like you."

"Then what is it you do want?"

The anger seeped from him. "I . . . don't know."

Silence again. Mr. Blaylock's eyebrows were white ledges. From under them he regarded Henry morosely and yet, also, hopefully. "Henry, why does she cry? She came home from the Dorrances, from Boston, and I heard her in her room. For almost an hour. Serena crying, who fell out of trees and, yes, off horses without . . . and she won't say a word to me."

Henry drained his port.

"Young man, I demand an explanation."

"From me?"

"Do not dally with me, sir. Before he left, Peter said enough to indicate I might come to you for one, and here I am."

Henry refilled both glasses and carried Mr. Blaylock's to him. "Pray believe me, sir, I'm as at sea as you are."

"Do you *wish* to marry her?"

"Would you permit it?"

"Of course I would. Child of my oldest friend. Almost a son to me during all the years of your growing up. Why on earth would I not?"

"At our last meeting—"

"Humbug! You know me better than that, Henry. I blow hot, I blow cold. But I love the people I love, though 'tis true I may abuse them from time to time. Besides, one day soon you'll return to your senses."

"And what, sir?"

"Leave that rascal. And come to work for me."

"I won't, sir."

"Then damn your ungrateful eyes."

Silence once more.

At length a sigh from Mr. Blaylock's depths. "It seems possible Serena's tears have to do with you. I ask you plain now, is it so?"

"I cannot believe that it is."

"Is it one of those awful things where she wants you but you, for some inexplicable reason, don't want her?"

"She does not want me, sir."

"Peter—"

"Is sometimes wrong."

Mr. Blaylock gulped down his port—without having tasted it, Henry knew—and resumed pacing. He stopped, refilled, pointed his finger. "Go to see her, sir."

"No, sir."

"Why in God's name not?"

"Because it's useless. Because I won't ever again allow her, or any other woman for that matter, to play me for a fool."

"Must I drag you there?"

"You can try. You won't be able to."

"Look at me, sir. I outweigh you by forty pounds, and I'm eager to put every one of them at my daughter's service."

Henry sat, crossed his arms on his chest, and waited.

Mr. Blaylock stared, muttered something scabrous, hurled his goblet at the fireplace where it shattered, and exited—a trace unsteadily.

After a while Henry rang for a servant. Then, not waiting for her, he took the anvil brush and pan and began, absently, to poke at the scattered shards. The servant arrived. She offered to bandage the cut on his finger. He refused. She brought him his coat and hat. He shrugged into the former, jammed the latter low on his forehead, and made his own unsteady exit.

Van Buren Sums Up

*T*he morning began with some legal shilly-shallying having to do with the precise size of the Forrest estate. No one took it seriously, no one really cared, and yet it went on interminably.

Forrest had been early in attendance, grave of expression but restless, fingers incessantly at his cravat.

Catherine and Mrs. Willis arrived later. They were accompanied by their friend, now back from Boston, who looked as if she had never shed a tear in her life.

Henry exchanged nods with N.P.

The morning wore away. Lunch. Half past one, and at last Van Buren seemed ready. He rose. As soon as he did, however, so did a dozen or so ladies from among the spectators and marched out in a body. Van Buren allowed himself a slight smile, then waited for quiet. It settled on the room, complete and charged.

Van Buren. Gentlemen of the jury, there's no argument between opposing counsel as to which are the major areas of inquiry. The first is whether the defendant, Edwin Forrest, has committed adultery. The second—and I mention them in the order in which I propose pursuing them—concerns the plaintiff. Has Mrs. Forrest committed the adultery maintained against her?

As it happens, there are also two parts to the plaintiff's case. Part one, of course, can and should be dismissed out of hand. It's a vulgar and transparent tissue of lies. Who points the finger at Josephine Clifton and Edwin Forrest? Why, William Doty does. Which William Doty? The very same who saw Miss Clifton and Mr. Forrest in a stateroom on an Albany night boat the year before it became a night boat and consequently a year before such staterooms existed.

Who else? Why, here we have Dr. Hawkes. *Doctor* Hawkes. Easily confused with *Apothecary* Hawkes. Is there a man in this jury box who will take his testimony seriously?

No, my good friends. Mr. Forrest has nothing to fear from *that* brace of finger-pointers. Humbug is what they've offered, and humbug I know you have perceived it to be. And more of it to come, I regret to say, as we move now to consider part two of the plaintiff's desperate accusation.

Plaintiff swears Mrs. Ingersoll kept bawdy houses. Mrs. Ingersoll swears she kept boardinghouses. Who's telling the truth? Well, the fact is plaintiff has given us no witness to say he or she ever saw on Mrs. Ingersoll's premises a single improper act or heard an improper remark. That is the *fact,* my friends, and I ask you please to keep it firmly fixed in your minds. After all his twisting and turning, all his mighty efforts, learned counsel could produce no testimony directly to this point. At length, wearily, he could only impute, not prove. And if he could not prove, then the law says you cannot condemn. *(pause, his glance seeking the roof-beams, a trajectory made famous by his opponent)*

Now I must reiterate the warning I issued on the day I opened this case. My friends, I ask you again to divest yourselves, as nearly as you can, of certain understandable, even commendable, prejudices. Do you remember, on opening day, the anxiety I expressed on finding myself engaged in controversy with a woman? I stated to you that the universal feeling—certainly of all civilized men—is in favor of the female portion of creation. I don't complain of this. It's just and proper that it be so.

But gentlemen, in this specific case we deal with a woman who needs not one jot of special concern. Is she dependent, for instance? Certainly not financially. Day after day she has demonstrated the means to procure the attendance of witnesses from every part of this state and from several others, when she deemed it necessary. So, too, in the matter of counsel. She has the means to supply herself with an attorney whose acuteness and energy are exceeded by none who practice . . . perhaps none who have ever practiced at the bar. Is she in need of friends? Hardly. They are plentiful and powerful.

And now I ask you to consider one more way in which she is not like her sisters. She's a bluestocking, an *advanced* woman. Is that bad? I leave that for you to say because I don't concern myself here with moral judgments. The question is not whether she's good or bad, the question is whether she's strong or weak. An advanced woman, my friends, is a woman bold enough to voluntarily abandon the protection of society. She says to you, I need you not; I am self-sufficient. *I* say to you, Take her at her word.

Catherine Forrest stakes no claim on your gentler feelings. Moreover—and we must bring ourselves to acknowledge it— she's a woman utterly without truth. A woman who'll say whatever she construes to be advantageous at any given moment. You've heard her insist that her husband had no suspicions concerning her purity before January 1849. Yet how can that be true when a full eight months earlier, in a hotel room in Cincinnati, he discovered her deep in the embrace of George Jamieson.

You have heard her say it was because she gave Forrest the lie that they separated. She'd have you believe that a marriage solid as a rock for twelve years broke apart because in a heated moment she spoke ill-considered words to her husband. Gentlemen of the jury, would that be unforgivable in your house? Cause for anger, yes. Supreme irritation, most assuredly. But cause for an act as drastic as separation? I think not.

You have heard her say it was Forrest, not she, who pleaded for the pact of silence once the separation became inevitable. *He* says *she* pleaded for secrecy—to hide from the world her faithlessness. And because he had no wish to crush her, only to separate from her, he allowed himself to be persuaded.

Ah, but that was a mistake. He knows it now. He probably knew it then but she is *such* a persuasive woman, so intelligent, so charming and attractive, that mistakes of that kind are almost unavoidable. Gentlemen, pray be warned. Pray be on your guard. Don't make the same mistake Edwin Forrest did. Because we come now to consider the yea or nay of the charge of adultery as it applies to Catherine Sinclair Forrest, and, I beg of you, consider it with your intellects. Discipline your hearts.

And if you remain detached, dispassionate, how can you find her other than guilty? Mrs. Underwood's testimony alone is enough to overwhelm her. Irrevocably, it sullies, besmirches, defaces beyond recognition that portrait of purity my learned friend has been at such pains to paint. But Mrs. Underwood's testimony stands far from alone. There is Mrs. Demming's at its shoulder. Add to that the passionate entwining Robert Garvin saw, again with Mr. Willis as partner. Add to that what Anna Flowers saw, now with Captain Calcraft as Mr. Willis's proxy. The evidence mounts. Like the debts of a bankrupt, each bill of particulars adds its crushing weight. And what you are left with finally is a bluestocking, an adventuress, an amoral seeker after forbidden experience, a dabbler in iniquity, a woman to whom her vows are no more meaningful than if she had come here from some venal villa of decadent Rome.

Learned counsel will tell you the testimony of Anna Flowers is unreliable because she spent time in the House of Refuge, that Mrs. Underwood is ungrateful, that Garvin is vindictive, that Mrs. Demming is . . . I don't know . . . myopic perhaps, but none of that will get him by the enormous obstacle that looms in his path when he tries to discredit *all* of this testimony. The ominous totality of it. The sheer cumulative effect of it. No, my friends, Mrs. Underwood does not stand alone. She is supported again and again. Are they all perjurors? Gentlemen, you cannot believe that.

Nor can you believe in anything but the damning fact of Jamieson's letter, the "Consuelo" letter. It's there. It won't go away, much as learned counsel may wish it to. You recall how desperately he fought to keep it from being read. Who can blame him? Who can listen to its ardent phrases and not know it for precisely what it is: "And now, sweetest Consuelo, our brief dream is over, and such a dream! Have we not known real bliss? Have we not experienced the truth that ecstasy is not a fiction?"

Gentlemen, when you come to declarations of love . . . when you come to avowals of ecstasy . . . when you come to clasping people in your arms and sealing meetings by a kiss . . . you come to what, with ordinary mortals, is regarded as evidence of adultery.

Can I be accused of overstating? Truly, I don't see how. Yet alter the circumstances slightly, and I for one would have been ready with a gentler view. Suppose, for instance, she had acted differently on receipt of the letter. Suppose she had taken it immediately to her husband, saying, I have had this from an unwelcome source, from a cad who threatens our domestic bliss. Here. Pray deal with it. That, I eagerly concede, would have been the act of a virtuous woman. But she *kept* the letter. In fact, she hid it, and when she discovered its loss, you have heard how she cried, "Oh, Sister Katten, what a fool you are!" Dismay. Anxiety. All the tawdry trappings of unmistakable guilt. And *this*, gentlemen, was the cause of their separation, not some trumped-up nonsense about lies or Macreadys or whatever. *This*, gentlemen, was the soul-shattering piece of evidence that Edwin Forrest had in his possession that fateful night of January 19, which brought about their bitter quarrel.

I'm almost done now. I think I have dealt adequately with the major aspects of this case. If I have not, then an innocent man will suffer for my shortcomings, and I say to him—if thus it should proceed—I will regret it almost as bitterly as you, Edwin Forrest.

Gentlemen of the jury, Mr. Forrest adored his wife. His life revolved around this woman for whom conjugal fidelity is akin to despotism. Whenever his profession forced him to be away he looked forward to his return with the greatest eagerness. As a tragedian he had built for himself a reputation unequaled in this country, unrivaled and undisputed. He believed he had a help-mate whose abilities and accomplishments in her own sphere matched his. He had a home which, in gratitude, had been made to her fancy, erected to meet her views. He said to me once, "I was a poor boy. I struggled until I reached the acme of profes-sional fame. And now that I'm on the topmost rung I find it all dust in my mouth. My God! What a thing it is to have one's happiness entirely dependent on a faithless woman." Gentlemen, I pray you bear in mind the evidence in this case. Solely the evidence. Only the evidence. And if you do that you will de-cide justly and rightly, and I will be content with your verdict. Thank you.

Hubbub. Excitement. Foot-stamping, catcalling, huzzahing.

Henry glanced across the room at Catherine. Calmly, she chafed one of Mrs. Willis's hands while Serena attended the other.

Catherine appeared serene. But Serena, though brisk of move-ment as ever, seemed worried, he thought.

Raymond, too: "He's struck her hard, the cad."

That evening, however, Bennett said, "O'Conor will throw dust in their eyes, Mr. Stewart, mark my words, and she'll sashay out to drive some other poor fool to distraction."

How the sands keep shifting, Henry thought.

Settling . . . Out of Court

*C*atherine's first thought was that O'Conor's rooms were a cry against self-indulgence. And then she thought the spareness had the effect of calling attention to itself. A kind of showy simplicity, she decided, smiling inwardly, because it so squared with her view of the man. Minimal furniture, the occasional (impeccably chosen) painting, a few beautifully made rugs thrown here and there—each object tacitly insisting on its innate superiority.

Fireplaces were omnipresent, all somewhat larger than ordinary. Two dominated his library, as if keeping the cold at bay was a symbolic concern to the Hon. Charles as well as a physical one. Both fireplaces were ablaze. Books, in floor-to-ceiling cases, covered three of the four walls.

Having ushered her into the room, he now took her coat and things. "You're chilled, dear lady. I shall bring you some brandy at once. Sit, make yourself comfortable."

He indicated a brocaded settee (in sober gray), one of a pair, near the larger of the large fireplaces. She sank into it. He left her, reappearing a moment later with a tray on which the centerpiece was a dish of oysters. Two brandy snifters flanked it. She reached for hers.

"You have no servant?" she asked innocently.

He arranged himself on the matching settee. Face devoid of any particular expression, he said, "I've dismissed him for the night."

She allowed him to note a brief smile before turning away. For a while they sipped in silence, studying campaign strategies in the flames. She felt his gaze shift.

"Your gown is charming. Velvet suits you."

"Thank you."

"The red . . . it deepens all your colors. Moreover, you have exquisite shoulders. But I suppose you've been told that *ad nauseam*."

"Never *ad nauseam*."

Another pause. His gaze remained fixed on her, and she had the sense of gathering forces.

"As I left the courtroom today," she said, "I heard a man inform his friend that Van Buren had nailed the trollop in her coffin."

"He was wrong as well as vulgar."

"I thought Van Buren was formidable."

"He was."

"And yet the verdict will be mine?"

He gestured impatiently, with a shapely but surprisingly small hand, and then employed it in stroking his smoking jacket, which was black, of course, but with a white silk cravat to set it off. "Do you object to this informality?"

She looked at him full. "It was hardly unexpected. We both know why I'm here."

"Do we?"

"To pay my fee."

She thought he blinked, as if just flicked by the thrust as it went by. But his tone gave away nothing.

"You're here, dear lady, because there's no reason for you not to be. Neither of us are conventional people. Both of us, long ago, each in our way, made the decision not to be bound by rules that seem pointless to us. Isn't that so?"

She kept silent.

"And you're here," he said, "because it's my hope we can be friends."

"Friends."

"Indeed."

"Do I take it, then, you've no interest in becoming my lover?"

He stood. "May I attend to your glass?"

"You may attend to my curiosity."

"Madam, I've no interest in going where I'm not wanted." And bending to her quickly, he lifted her chin so that their faces were only inches apart. "Dear lady, there *is* no fee."

She kept silent.

"Do you believe me?"

She made him release her. "Not in the least."

He studied her, then shook his head, the weary gesture of a man not dealt with as he deserves to be. After a moment he took her glass and retraced his steps with it.

While waiting for his return she became aware suddenly that nerve ends were prickling, that her heart was beating noticeably fast. It was a high-stakes game she played with him, a serious game. Phantom chips, but oh, how winning mattered!

When he returned he resumed his seat without speaking. Nor did he look at her. He had positioned himself, however, so that it was easy for her to look at him. She knew she was to understand that she had hurt him.

"The oysters are superb," he said. "And I have gone to much trouble to get them. You will oblige by not leaving them untasted."

She obliged. "Delicious."

He turned to her. "What we do tonight and what I do tomorrow are as separate as the poles. Surely you believe that. It's my craft, dear lady, my profession. Surely you believe in my loyalty to my profession?"

"I believe in your loyalty to your appetites."

It startled him. In doing so it elicited the closest thing to a real smile she had ever had from him. "You are a remarkable woman," he said.

Her gaze on his was unwavering.

"If I were at all inclined toward romantic love I might well write my poems to you," he said.

"How honored I am." She got up and gave him her glass. "Where would you like me to undress? Here or in the bedroom?"

He stared at her. "I don't understand. Am I poaching on someone else's ground?"

"No."

"Then please explain. I'm in no mood for female mystery."

"There's nothing to explain. Nor is there any mystery. I await your instructions, sir."

Lifting the poker, he thrust it at the fire a shade more vigorously than was needed, she thought. Seconds passed.

"Sir?"

"Oh, the bedroom, by all means the bedroom," he said and waved a languid hand in that direction.

She went. She shut the door behind her and found a chair just as her knees grew weak. A straight-backed chair, of course. There was only one other in the room. They were placed on either side of his bed. But the bed was not the narrow, cheerless affair the chairs predicted. It was large and comfortable-looking and covered with a dark red spread. And next to it was a table, on which was set out a decanter of sherry and two glasses. She poured and drank a little. She thought of the austerity of the Hon. Charles, and how it never seemed to stretch far enough to achieve actual discomfort. Warmed by the glow of the fireplaces (two in this room also), she sat and sipped and allowed the hammering of her heart to quiet. And she did not undress.

It was a quarter hour later that she heard the apartment door shut behind him. She got up. She put her glass on the tray and returned to the library where she found his note:

Called away unexpectedly. The oysters are delicious. Please do finish them. In half an hour a hack will come by to take you home.

Gentlemanly. Ah, but she smelled the rage in it. She hugged herself. She had beaten him. Beaten him for a ghost army of vanquished females whose degradation had been meat and drink to him and whose silent accolades rang in *her* ears like music. She danced to it.

Finally, she had to stop. She sat down, tired, breathless. And in that state certain wolfish outlines became clear to her. She had outdanced euphoria. She sighed. A great victory, but she could be made to pay for it easily enough. Would she be? She thought it possible that he, O'Conor, didn't know, wouldn't until he stood at the crossroads—and then might do something generous and later detest himself for it, or detestable for revenge's sweet sake. Or . . . the range was limitless, she supposed.

She turned her attention to the oysters. They *were* delicious. She *did* finish them.

Hah! Up the Sinclairs!

O'Conor's Turn

O'Conor rose, bowed to Catherine and the two ladies of her honor guard. Mrs. Willis dithered a little. Serena took Catherine's hand. Catherine, gaze level, smiled at O'Conor, who smiled back as if at a partner in an enterprise of great moment. To Henry, both seemed confident. He wondered if they were.

Turning to Judge Oakley, O'Conor bowed again. By the time he faced the jury, however, his expression had changed. He was angry now and wanted all to perceive this. Eyes fierce, hands clawed over invisible daggers, he'd become a Celtic war chief.

O'CONOR. Gentlemen of the jury, at last we draw to a close. Nothing remains for me but to present those final few arguments that strike me as absolutely requisite. I shall endeavor to do so calmly. That may be difficult, for there are passages in this case calculated to test more sanguine natures than my own. But I'm resolved on good manners, on gentlemanly deportment. *(the briefest of communions)*

You've been told that there are in this case two distinct questions—first, whether Edwin Forrest is guilty of adultery. Second, whether Mrs. Forrest is. The first was passed over by counsel on the other side with prudent speed. Nor will I dawdle with it either, for I promise you it won't take long to nail the charge in place.

Did Edwin Forrest commit adultery with Josephine Clifton? He says no. Let him. I have a richer vein to mine.

I have Mrs. Ingersoll. Mrs. Ingersoll and her . . . boarding-houses. Boardinghouses, indeed. The kind of boardinghouse for which she cannot recall the name of a single boarder. And in which from October 1846 to May 1851—some four and a half years, mind you—Mr. Forrest was a frequent visitor. What was his business there? Judiciously, he maintains silence. Mrs. Ingersoll is tomblike. But do we need their voices? Your honor, may I refer you to the opinion of Sir William Scott in *Loudon versus Loudon*? It's possible, he says, that a man may go once into a house of ill fame to collect a debt. Or perhaps he may be misled there in some way. These things happen. But when a man goes repeatedly to a house of ill fame he does not go there to say his paternoster.

Truly, that's sufficient, is it not? Is there really a necessity to dwell longer on these sordid matters? Can anyone doubt that the plaintiff has proved her case, that Edwin Forrest, during all the years when she was his dearest Catherine, when his life revolved around her, when being parted from her however briefly caused him bitter unhappiness . . . during all those years, I say, can it be doubted that Edwin Forrest was an inveterate whoremonger? *(hubbub; gavel; three seconds of communion)*

We come now to Part Two of this case's structure, the question of Catherine Forrest's infidelity. Gentlemen, will it surprise you to hear that not even her husband believes her guilty? He did not doubt his wife's purity in 1846, did not doubt it in 1848, and does not doubt it today. I see surprise in some of your faces, and I, for one, am not surprised to see it there. For a natural question occurs. If he believes her innocent, what motive can he have for wishing to destroy so excellent a wife?

Well, gentlemen, the law does not oblige me to answer that.

Mr. Forrest's behavior is the issue here, not his motive. Oh, it's easy enough to speculate. Was there a new attachment waiting in the wings? That would constitute a motive. Or was his mind so unhinged by his troubles with Macready, so soured against foreigners, the English in particular, that Catherine Sinclair Forrest became transmuted from beloved wife to hated scapegoat? I have, I know, suggested that to you previously, and if I repeat it now, it's still no more than one among several possibilities. And that's the point, is it not? It simply doesn't matter why Edwin Forrest's behavior followed a certain pattern. Sufficeth that it did. And it's the pattern that must be our business. Pray let's examine it.

In his deposition of May, 1848 Mr. Forrest stated that having returned suddenly and unexpectedly to his room in Cincinnati, he found Mr. Jamieson in such immodest proximity to the person of his wife, that he was impressed with the belief that there was something improper between them. He charged her with the evidence of her guilt, she denied it, and for some time he was satisfied.

Satisfied? Indeed he must have been. On the following morning, as scheduled, Mr. and Mrs. Forrest got ready to bid adieu to Cincinnati, and who came to their room to say farewell? Why that self-same Mr. Jamieson.

Continuing now with the saga as Mr. Forrest would have it: On January 20, 1849, this upright, decent, self-respecting pillar of the community goes rummaging through his wife's bureau until he finds the celebrated "Consuelo" letter. The sight of it carries to his mind such instant and absolute conviction of his wife's guilt that he parts with her . . . three and a half months later. Gentlemen, gentlemen, is this outrage?

And how was it between them on May first, the day the separation finally took place? You recall his fury then, do you not? Why, he gave her his Shakespeare, followed with his portrait.

No, my friends, Edwin Forrest had no belief whatsoever in his wife's guilt. But he did, for reasons we can only guess at, wish to put her aside. And if she'd been content—that is, if she'd agreed to be victimized—there would have been no charges brought against her, and we would not be in this courtroom today.

Well, let us look into that. Let's take a minute to see how, in his warmhearted view, a wife of twelve years was to be provided for once the separation was agreed upon. Why, while *he* was to be lord of Fonthill, *she* was to be boarded among strangers and doled out a weekly pittance for clothes and incidentals. To his great surprise she rejected his proposal.

Precisely what was it she rejected? Various sums were suggested by him. The first munificent amount was $500 a year plus a house to live in worth $375 a year. But this project, too, came to naught.

Grudgingly, then, inch by inch, he was forced to boost his offers until, gasping with exertion, the amount reached $1,500. She, in the meantime, stood firm at $3,000 as the amount necessary to assure even a semblance of her former condition, and why on earth should she accept less? Thus stands the gulf between them even now. He could not budge her. This lady who, if she were guilty, ought to have been trembling with either gratitude or fear, showed neither, only a sturdy insistence that regard be paid to her rights as a wife.

It's time now, I think, to examine the opposition's trumped-up charges, which is to say Mrs. Forrest's alleged connection with George Jamieson, N. P. Willis, and Captain Granby Calcraft. We have of course already touched on the trumpery as it affects Jamieson. For what allegedly took place in Cincinnati in May of 1848, you have first the defendant's word. Gainsaying it, you have the plaintiff's fierce denial. To help you navigate between them, you have as a guide the affectionate, nay *tender* course of their lives between May of '48 and January of '49, and I don't doubt you will find your way.

As for that famous oft-dragged-out letter, it is, as my learned friend maintains, irrefutable. It was most assuredly written. It was certainly sent, and we acknowledge that it was received. But addressed to whom? To a sort of divinity, if you will. It has no

individuality, no name, no signature by which it could be identified as the homage of a particular gentleman. It might have been
copied from some book, and in all probability it was. The "Consuelo" letter is the way they refer to it, sneeringly—as if there
were something heinous in that description. Pray, for just a
moment, let's consider the nature of this Consuelo they have
attempted to besmirch.

She's the heroine of a modern French novel, a heroine charac-
terized by the highest degree of amiability and chastity. Yes,
chastity, as any of those on the other side might have discovered
easily from a reading of the book. Except of course they were not
interested in such a discovery.

Having noted this, pertinent though it be, I say to you that I've
run a risk. Yes, I fear I have, inasmuch as you will now undoubtedly reward this epistolary effusion with much more attention
than it deserves. Probably learned counsel is right; probably Mrs.
Forrest should have given the letter to her husband or, at the very
least, burned it. But she didn't. Instead she tossed it casually into
one of her bureau drawers because it simply never occurred to her
that it might be worth a second thought.

I call your attention now to the evidence bearing on Mr. N.
P. Willis. Let us begin with Mr. Garvin's testimony. This is the
tale in which Garvin, that indefatigable gardener, peered through
the window and discovered Mrs. Forrest and Mr. Willis carnally
entwined on the sofa. He could make this discovery because the
shades, usually drawn against the heat, had been inexplicably
lifted. And the sofa, usually against the west wall where it's all but
invisible from most garden vantage points, had been moved to the
east wall. By whom had all this been done? By Mrs. Forrest and
Mr. Willis, of course, in order to place themselves in full view for
the purpose of being testified against.

Along those same lines please recall Mrs. Egbert Demming at
her window. Something draws her attention to the house of Mrs.
Forrest. In the library of that house are Mrs. Forrest and Mr.
Willis. Because there is a light behind them, Mrs. Demming can

see that Mr. Willis has one hand at Mrs. Forrest's waist, the other on her shoulder. Indeed she can, gentlemen—at a distance above thirty yards through the darkness of the night, through the glass of her own window and the glass of Mrs. Forrest's, hawk-eyed Mrs. Demming is able to make a flawless identification. Unlikely? Do you think so? Well, perhaps Mrs. Demming, too, was fearful of her story's credibility, so she had them walk around to the other side of the table, stand there for a moment with the gas directly over their heads, after which they departed the room, I suppose for bed.

Gentlemen, some dissection, by your leave. Mr. Willis, a married man, calls on Mrs. Forrest with licentiousness in mind. He goes into the library with her, remains until around midnight, and then says, "My dear, let us to bed. But first, let us to the window and have a hug so our neighbors may see us."

They go to the window and perform this embrace. By and by he says, "My dear, our backs have been to the window. The ceremony is not perfect until we have performed all the requisites necessary to be identified. Don't you remember when something like this was done by us before, we moved the sofa into that corner and raised the shades so that when Robert Garvin or any of the servants came by they would have a perfect view? We ain't the kind of people who lower shades and do these things in private. Thus, let's turn around and show our faces. But no, they cannot see our faces for the light is on the other side; therefore we must walk round the table where the light is better, so the thing may be perfectly accomplished. And *then* we will go to bed." I ask you, gentlemen, is there not something surprising in all this? Is this what you and I have come to regard as predictable human behavior?

We arrive now at the third name on the list, Captain Calcraft. I have decided not to discuss the imputations against him because I think a more powerful refutation is to be achieved another way. Those imputations come to us primarily through the testimony of a remarkable young woman who has traveled a considerable distance to do us this service. I mean the testimony of Anna Flowers. My friends, can the slightest reliance be placed on anything she says? You know what brought her here. It was not, as she proclaims, love of justice. Clearly, it was love for the dollar. The newspaper advertisement promised she would hear "something to her advantage," and to Anna Flowers that phrase is poetry. When money is the object it's hard to imagine anything at which she would balk. Certainly it would not be perjury.

During cross-examination I called your attention to intrinsic falsehoods in her testimony. Now I want to call your attention to the most important area affecting the credit and credibility of Mrs. Anna Flowers. I mean the villainous transaction that took place on or about the fifteenth of June, 1850, in which Mr. Forrest and his agent, Mr. Lawson, joined Mrs. Flowers as participants. That was the day given over to the attempt to lure Mrs. Forrest into a trap. What was the precise nature of this trap? I cannot tell you. I confess I've not been able to find out. From certain dark corners of my mind come guesses, but I won't burden you with them. Instead I'll confine myself to the visible configurations.

The site was the famous house on Mercer Street. Mrs. Flowers, on the advice of her henchmen, rented a bedroom there. She then wrote not one but two notes to Mrs. Forrest, both composed of arrant falsehoods. What was their object? As I say, I don't know, but does anyone ever *idly* go through such a process of lying and deception? Isn't the stench of plotting unavoidable? And yet it's been suggested that Mrs. Forrest *should* have gone to the house in Mercer Street. If she had she would have learned something of great benefit to her cause. Pray, what things of benefit could she have learned from her enemy? Things of evil, things of falsity, but no things of benefit. It was a trap, purely and simply. And Anna Flowers's participation in the scheming stamps her for what she is—a liar and a cheat. She is not to be believed in what she says about Mrs. Forrest. She is not to be believed in what she says about Captain Calcraft. *Falsus in uno, falsus in omnibus*—false in one, false in all—is a maxim of the law. Applied here, it leaves Anna Flowers utterly without credibility.

Anna Flowers, Dame Underwood, Robert Garvin, Mrs. Demming: what a lackluster crew of witnesses. Fie on them, banish them to that place reserved for those who gossip, backbite, and perjure—to a hall of the pernicious.

Gentlemen, I have almost reached the end. I shall do no more than make a final observation or two. The facts establish most clearly that Mrs. Forrest has at all times conducted herself chastely, modestly, and uprightly, that she has been guilty of no censurable impurity, that she has committed no act to which you could attach a label worse than incautious.

Moreover, I think the facts establish, beyond the shadow of a doubt, that Mr. Forrest is as guilty as his wife is innocent. All that's required now is for you to relieve the lady of the one thing about her she feels to be stigmatized—her surname, which she'll be at liberty to abandon when you render the verdict law and justice require. Mr. Forrest's real estate is set down by himself at $150,000, and his personal property is estimated at $4,000 a year, plus the handsome revenue he derives from the practice of his profession. On behalf of Mrs. Forrest I ask no more than she has always asked, no more than would have kept us out of this courtroom, no more than is needed to allow her to live in approximately the style she's used to: $3,000 a year. It is indeed a modest request. In fact, in my view it's a pittance, but I speak for a client who, in this, refuses to be guided. Gentlemen, I thank you.

He sat, and Judge Oakley at once announced a ten-minute recess before delivering his charge to the jury.

"A triumph," Raymond said, beaming. "Mark my word, they won't be able to resist him." As certain of his position, Henry noted, as he had been after Van Buren's summation, though the positions were diametrically opposed.

Henry focused on the jury. Did Meech reflect Raymond's enthusiasm? Were Page, DeWitt, and Edsall similarly enthralled?

As always those were difficult faces to read, faces guarded like prerogatives, jealously: locked smiles, shut expressions.

He shifted to Catherine. As he did she happened to turn his way. She smiled for a moment before her glance passed over to meet Meech's. It was a brief meeting, as if a longer connection would have been too intrusive to be tolerated by her. Mrs. Willis leaned over to whisper, drew an absent nod in response. It seemed to Henry that Catherine looked as people do when they've begun to care less about something they once cared a great deal about. Probably that was nonsense, Henry told himself. Probably what he was seeing was no more than an energy low point, the predictable emotional sag of trial's end.

When Serena hugged her Catherine brightened, became animated.

And then Forrest stole the scene from her. Suddenly enraged by something Van Buren had said to him, he swung his cane. The *whap* of it on the edge of a chair caused a universal swiveling in his direction. "Let them roast in hell!" he said, a snarl.

He had the room's entire attention.

He glared all down.

Henry's glance joined the mass retreat, and he was glad of the Chief Justice's return.

CHIEF JUSTICE. Very briefly now, let me submit the case. Gentlemen, it's not one which depends upon a minute examination of the testimony. Instead, it rests almost exclusively on the credibility of the witnesses. If you should, for instance, believe the testimony of Doty, the proofs are undoubtedly against Mr. Forrest. If the testimony of Anna Flowers is to be relied on, the proofs are against Mrs. Forrest. If you believe them both, then both the Forrests are guilty, and I will discuss that possibility with you in a moment. It being, therefore, a question of credibility, all the court feels called upon to do is to list certain rules of evidence, which, incidentally, are not much more than plain common sense.

These number three: first, the probability of the fact testified to; second, the general character of the witness testifying; and, third, the presence or absence of contradictions. Let me elaborate just a little. Evidence surrounded by improbable circumstances should always require strong proof; the more improbable the circumstances, the stronger the proof.

Concerning contradictions in testimony, I must needs inform you they are not always as damning as counsel makes them out to be. Sometimes they are caused by simple lapses in memory or by an altered view of things. Sometimes they're not contradictions at all, merely made to appear as such by overzealous advocates. And then sometimes of course they provide excellent indications that a witness is lying. As in so many other sensitive areas you will have to make the determinations. Be on your guard.

Gentlemen, this case has its share of peculiar aspects. In ordinary trials, for instance, with respect to divorce, there's but one side of the question to be looked at—either the husband proceeds against the wife or the wife against the husband, and there's only a single circumstance for inquiry. Here, however, each party charges the other with adultery. Now the legal effect of this is that if on the evidence you find both parties guilty, the law will leave them where it finds them. That is to say, neither party will be entitled to a verdict against the other, since the law never grants divorces to guilty people.

Finally I wish to make a point about notoriety. Around this case there has been created a feeling which is, I fear, most dangerous to the orderly flow of justice. The press, I am sorry to say, has in great degree contributed. The consequence has been that in every tavern or barroom or oyster cellar or barbershop—every place, in short, where newspapers circulate—the Forrests have been daily tried. People have taken sides and freely expressed their opinions, so that it would be singular indeed if you, the members of the jury, who have been obliged to live in this goldfish bowl, were not affected by it. Well, you will somehow have to rise above it all. Because it's your clear and present duty to do so. Gentlemen, the case is now yours.

In the wake of this there was a curious, heavy silence—of aftermath, of deflation. None seemed eager to look at his neighbor. It was as if, Henry thought, they all felt prurient. Stripped of quasi-legal function, they were now exposed and shamed as nothing more than a collection of Peeping Toms.

The jury left hurriedly, eager to put this atmosphere behind. Meech, the shepherd, shut the heavy oak door after his flock, but not without a quick final glance at Catherine. Her glance was elsewhere.

Six hours later there was still no verdict.

No verdict, but one nerve-racking false alarm.

At ten minutes to eleven, Meech sent word that he wished for a reconvening. The Chief Justice sent word he was ready to receive them. At five minutes past eleven the jury members filed in, and Mr. Asher called the roll. Forrest and Van Buren were in court. Not so Catherine. No sign of Catherine—or any of her friends—since Judge Oakley's charge to the jury.

CLERK. Gentlemen, have you agreed?

MEECH. We have not. May it please your honor, there's confusion as to whether frequent visits to a house of ill fame is to be seen as sufficient proof of adultery.

CHIEF JUSTICE. The panel must be sole judge of that. If you're satisfied that the house is of a particular description, and if you're satisfied that Mr. Forrest visited there, it's for you to draw the inference. That's all I can say. The matter is of fact, not of law, Mr. Meech. Do you take the point?

MEECH. Yes, sir.

Again the jury retired, but a few minutes later a second message was received. On perusal, the Chief Justice reported to counsel that the jury had informed him agreement was not imminent. He then ordered adjournment until ten the following morning.

An Unexpected Visitor

*A*nd so the matter rested.

Unlike Henry. At around 1 A.M., Henry, restless, had abandoned his attempt to arrange the New York Hotel's night music into a lullaby. He'd got out of bed, found a robe, stoked his fireplace, positioned the new Longfellow collection on a footstool near his reading chair, and was now in his kitchen, at the table, chin pillowed on his arms, watching his teakettle. While waiting for it to whistle, he addressed himself to Catherine Forrest.

Well, lady, are you guilty?

Raymond swears you're not and that the sequestered dozen will reward your innocence.

Bennett says they'll smite you regardless. Forrest is of their kind, he says. They understand him. They know why he's compelled to punish you, and in his shoes they'd do the same. Guilty or innocent, he says, they'll stone the bluestocking.

And as for me, your friend?

Forgive me, lady, but amid all the perjury I found truth here and there. Van Buren was right. Marital fidelity is low on your list. Despotism was the word you used in your famous letter to Lawson. And despotism is a thing against which you would always kick. I can see you yielding up your life for a lover or a sister or Forrest himself, more's the pity, or a cause—so long as it's not chastity. You're too hungry for experience. Too much the magnet for sensual men. Too much left alone by that narcissist you married. Too little occupied.

There. It's out. And now I add that from the bottom of my heart I hope for Raymond to be right and Bennett wrong. Fare you well, Catherine Forrest, bluestocking. In my view you're worth the aggregate of those who are arranging your future. . . .

A sharp knock at his door woke him. Longfellow fell from his lap. Two A.M. Who the devil . . . ?

Another knock, this time accompanied by a voice calling his name and ordering him to open up at once. And ending the mystery. Belting his robe more securely around him, he let in Serena.

She swept by him. "Shut the curtains, Henry. Unless you wish some prying Mrs. Demming to have a field day. Or night. Or morning. Whatever."

He shut the door, and the curtains, and retrieved from the floor the cloak she had dropped there. He hung it in his foyer closet.

"I find myself terribly nervous, do you believe that, Henry? Well, I am. In Paris of course I wouldn't be. In Paris they view these things sensibly; ask Catherine. There a lady is at perfect liberty to call upon whom she chooses."

"At two in the morning?"

"*Whenever* she chooses. Are you shocked?"

"No."

"Not shocked?"

"Merely irritated, I think. Your father—"

"Yes, yes, but you can sermonize about that another time. Now there's only a half hour or so before my driver returns from the fool's errand on which I've sent him, and I wish to discuss more important things."

His glance was wary. "What things?"

She sent her own glance on an imspection tour. "You do yourself quite nicely here. And you're much more orderly than I had been led to believe was typical of young bachelors. Peter says you have a rage for order."

"Peter enjoys his jokes at my expense."

"N.P. tells me you leave for Washington tomorrow."

"Tomorrow? No."

"When then?"

"I don't know. Not tomorrow."

She studied him. "Henry, am I the first lady to appear here?"

"Yes."

"The first female?"

He kept silent.

She smiled and said, "Were any of them offered a glass of sherry?"

He muttered something about lateness and unseemliness but went to the decanter on the sideboard.

"How many have there been?"

"Dozens," he said, giving her a glass.

"You're not joining me?"

He fixed his expression at maximum grimness. "What is it you want here, Serena?"

Her own expression changed. The teasing fled, and he knew that what replaced it had been lurking just beneath the surface and was close enough to panic to trigger in him the rise of something similar.

"Please don't be ungenerous," she said, hands clasped—a gesture that was both prayerful and involuntary, he thought.

"I don't understand."

"This is difficult for me. You must be kind. If you're not I'll leave instantly, and you'll never know what brought me here. The choice is yours."

Let her go, an inner voice wailed. And for an instant he believed he could. But then, while he looked at her, the opportunity was lost. How utterly unfair, he thought, for a woman to be so lovely. It struck at a man's philosophy. Profundities became absurdities. Intellect turned to gruel, and a man found himself leaning forward so the ring for his nose could be more easily accommodated.

"Say something to me, Henry."

The best he could do was repeat: "What is it you want here?" Sandwiched in a groan.

"You know, you know."

"How can I? When I came to Boston—"

"Don't speak to me of Boston. In Boston I behaved badly. But you brought it on yourself. All that morning I had been thinking ill of you, and the more I thought the angrier I became. And of course the more ridiculous I felt for having pursued you so brazenly."

"But there in Boston I was pursuing you."

"Oh, don't be a goose, Henry. I was not prepared to be pursued. At least not quite so soon. It flustered me. Because I was no more than halfway between being furious with you and beginning to miss you—and then suddenly I was having to contend with you. Stamping around, looking foolish, saying spooney things, and acting in general as if everything were my fault."

He went to the fireplace to warm hands that had gone cold.

"Henry . . ."

Turning to her, he saw that her eyes had begun to fill. She looked as he had never expected to see her look—frightened.

"If you wish me to leave . . ."

And then, for once in his life, Henry Stewart could give himself credit for behaving sensibly where ladies were concerned. He didn't speak. Instead he launched himself at her. He kissed her. And having done so, he repeated the act. He moved her to the sofa, sat down with her, and kissed her repeatedly. Kisses so fast, so hungry, that at last they attenuated into one monster of a kiss that ended by flinging them to opposite sides of the sofa. There they remained—tense, quivery, afraid to touch.

But after a while their fingers crept to a rendezvous.

"It's remarkable," Serena said.

"What is?"

"Henry, your eyes are red as paint. I mean, this . . . sexual business. I mean the feelings a man and a woman can unleash in each other. They quite leave one shaken."

"Yes."

"Henry . . ."

"What?"

"I must go."

"I know."

"But pray, for just an instant, place your hand . . . yes, there. Merciful heaven!"

He sat at his desk, his mind a maelstrom. On impulse he reached for his quill. If he set something down it might reduce the jumble. In the past such an exercise had helped. He wrote quickly:

I'm a man older than his years, people say; a man who values quiet. Serena does not promise quiet. She promises to make a revolution of me. Now as I sit here watching my shadow's candlelit mating dance, I confess to pinpricks of dismay. But in the main?

In the main I feel linked to the poets.

She is so beautiful. And there is character in her face. Sweetness and humor, too. And there's the way she brushes her hair back when the wind catches it. There's the way she walks, long strides that often as not finish with impatient kicks at her skirt. When she says my name—

He put down the quill but then, a moment later, lifted it again.

"I like all men who plunge," Bennett once said to me.

Catherine's Diary

*W*hen I thanked him for having been brilliant, O'Conor bent over my hand and said, "I would have done the same for Anna Flowers, dear lady."

He left the courtroom, acknowledging applause with graceful nods and lordly gestures. I watched his exit, a tall, handsome, cold-eyed man who's not quite through with me, I shouldn't wonder.

Serena said, "That man hates you."

"All of us," I said.

And I think that's true. I think there's a category of men inimical to our category of women. I don't feel comfortable about that. I don't enjoy it that for some I am an immediate *bête noir*. Actually, the experience frightens me. My instinct, at such times, is to placate, to disarm, to make a point of my femaleness. In other words, to behave like a coward.

Serena is not like that. Nor is Margaret. Resolved: Be more like them. Bravery is, if nothing else, prettier than cowardice. Even one's hair, I do believe, is more lustrous when one is being brave.

Oddly enough, Edwin is not in that category of men born to

hate us. With Edwin the problem is his need to be worshiped. He was raised in a house where that was his steady diet. His mother and sisters fed him on worship from the time he was a baby. He became addicted.

But what if there had been babies for us? One baby out of all those who died. One baby to live, to soak up my energies, to make me feel purposeful. One living baby for me to feed at my breast, to caress, to shape, to watch grow. Would it have made a difference? Oh, God, how could it not have? I mean to Edwin, too. One tiny living baby out of so many taken from us. Why was that too much to ask?

And even now weeping comes hard to me. A first, promising sob, and just when I think it a prelude to something satisfactorily large, it dwindles.

N.P. is lugubrious. Caroline prattled all through dinner, but N.P. chewed his mustache. He says I missed chances, berates me for not making more of Meech. (I would have, but I kept forgetting.) The man was besotted with me, N.P. says. Meech's last look was all besottment, N.P. says, while Catherine Forrest stared through him as if he were curtain gauze.

The truth is my mind had gone wandering. If Meech sent a swain's look my way, I unfortunately did not see it. There was a secret ceremony going on at the moment. I was saying goodbye to a part of my life. A twelve-year segment, gone. Edwin, gone. Houses, servants, friends, gone. And I, too, will be gone—soon. And that's what it was, diary. While Meech was sending a last-ditch lover's look my way, I was making my silent valedictory. Because it was in that moment, suddenly, I knew how alien I am to everything here. I must leave. I will leave. Verdict yea or nay, I'll be gone from here in six months. That much I'll give them. They have made me hate it here. But try as they may, they will not make me hate myself.

The Verdict

*F*irst. Has or has not the Defendant, Edwin Forrest, since his marriage with the Plaintiff, Catherine Sinclair Forrest, committed adultery as in this complaint charged?

Answer: HE HAS.

Second. Has or has not the said Plaintiff, Catherine Sinclair Forrest, committed adultery, as alleged against her in the answer in this action?

Answer: SHE HAS NOT.

Third. What amount of alimony ought to be allowed annually to said Plaintiff?

Answer: THREE THOUSAND DOLLARS.

The members of the jury say they find for the Plaintiff on the whole issue in the pleadings. *(Signed)* Stephen W. Meech, Foreman.

Upon application of Mr. Van Buren, a poll was ordered. When each man answered that the above was his verdict, it was recorded as the unanimous voice of the jury.

Afterword

O'Conor was lionized. Numerous dinners were given in his honor, including a lavish one by his colleagues of the New York bar. In addition, thirty ladies (from upper-tendom) presented him with a magnificent silver trophy to commemorate his championship of a cause they regarded as theirs by extension. (No male money was accepted to defray the cost.) His career flourished.

Van Buren, on the other hand, lost face. And lost as well, some speculate, whatever slim chance he might have had to follow his father to the presidency of the United States. To be sure, he continued to practice affluently and to wield power in Democratic Party politics. Still, some of the shine was rubbed from a luminous legal career, and it is O'Conor who has the landmark cases in his biography.

Until the day Forrest died, he wore the verdict like a hair shirt. *A great wrong has been done,* he wrote in *his* journal. *To prevent a repetition of it the offenders should be scourged, and what scourging is so effective as to keep their names a mockery and a scorn forever in the mouths of men.*

The names referred to, of course, were O'Conor's and Catherine's.

Shortly after the trial ended, Forrest began a run at New York's Broadway Theater remarkable for its duration and its vitriol. It stretched to sixty-nine consecutive packed houses, a record-breaking statistic for the time. During this, between the acts, he hammered audiences with passionate and lengthy castigations of the above offenders.

Five times he appealed the verdict, never successfully. Finally, in 1868, sixteen years after the original judgment, he surrendered to the inevitable, and Catherine was awarded a less than princely $68,000 worth of back alimony. Of this, O'Conor claimed $38,850.71, considerably more than the nothing he had publicly announced would be his fee.

Catherine, too, took to the boards at trial's end. In desperate need of money, she accepted an offer of tutelage from George Vanderhoff, a veteran English actor. A crash course indeed, for the very next month she opened in Philadelphia's Chestnut Street Theater (opposite Vanderhoff) as Lady Teazle in *The School for Scandal*.

She, like Forrest, was a box-office sensation. And if not actually the darling of the critics, she scored with most and was panned by none.

Soon after, she moved to San Francisco and became, for a while, a first-rate theater manager, in which role she employed Edwin Booth, Forrest's successor as America's foremost tragedian.

She died in New York on June 9, 1891, almost twenty years after her former husband. Neither ever married again.

Concerning some of the other notables among the dramatis personae: Henry Raymond, after launching *The New York Times* (in 1849) and seeing it nicely along the path to power and glory, died, still a relatively young man, at forty-nine.

James Gordon Bennett bequeathed the *Herald* to James Gordon Bennett, Jr., under whose stewardship it flourished for a good many years. In 1924, however, Bennett's *Herald* and Horace

Greeley's *Tribune* merged, a combining that, while it lasted, must have caused both founders annual unrest on All Hallow's Eve.

During his lifetime, N. P. Willis remained a best-selling writer, but fifty years later his books were all out of print and his name largely forgotten. He did some praiseworthy work as a Washington correspondent during the Civil War and died two years after its end, on his birthday. Charles Dana, editor of the *New York Sun,* James Russell Lowell, editor of the *Atlantic Monthly,* and Henry Wadsworth Longfellow were among the pallbearers.

As for Mr. and Mrs. Henry Stewart, who can doubt they lived happily ever after.